BY THE SAME AUTHOR

Prose
Brotherly Love
In the Time of Greenbloom

Poetry
The Frog Prince and Other Poems
28 Poems

GABRIEL FIELDING

Eight Days

HUTCHINSON OF LONDON

HUTCHINSON & CO. (*Publishers*) **LTD**
178-202 Great Portland Street, London, W.1

London Melbourne Sydney
Auckland Bombay Toronto
Johannesburg New York

★

First Published 1958

*This book has been set in Times New Roman type.
It has been printed in Great Britain by Tonbridge
Printers Ltd., in Tonbridge, Kent, on Antique Wove
paper and bound by Taylor Garnett Evans & Co., Ltd.,
in Watford, Herts*

TO
Jonathan Milne Barnsley

I came to Carthage, where there was, as it were,
a frying-pan full of flagitious loves, which
crackled about me on every side.

> St. Augustine: *The Confessions:*
> Book 3, Chap. 1.
> Translation of Sir Tobie Mathew, Kt.

Do not the senses have their delights, and is the
spirit then to forgo its own joys?

Give me a loving man and he will know what
I am talking about, give me one who is full of
desiring, show me a man thirsting and sighing
for the fountains of his heavenly fatherland,
give me such a man and he will understand
what I am going to say.

> St. Augustine: *The Homily for Pentecost.*

Sequence

Sunday

THE third day he awoke in some confusion after a dream about the Prison.

He had crossed the sunk lawn during 'Exercise' to enter the reception cells. The men were there behind him as he waited for the sound of keys on the far side; and he knew that he was watched as he waited to be let in. Many of them were watching him as they went round in their thick boots, talking: the blacks with the blacks, the little men with the little, the large and heavy with the large and heavy; all of them strolling in a humour that was not good nor bad but only watchful and cussed.

He kicked at the door again and heard it echo hollow beneath the cliff of wall. Intolerably slow: they should fix a bell. He hated this waiting.

''Orse-doctor!' came the shout and he did not turn. And then again, from a man further along the chain circling the stony beds of dahlias and chrysanthemums, 'Horse-doctor!'

It was taken up; but not by too many; only, he guessed, by the recently disgruntled, those who had won no concessions from him on sick parades. He turned and faced them and, instantly, none of them was looking in his direction. He watched the door again, heard the swing of keys, and knew it was about to open. He took his stethoscope out of his pocket and waited there in the sunlight.

'Horse-doctor! 'Orse-doctor! Horse-doctor!' came the bitten shouts. He swallowed for the thousandth time the desire to retort and thought instead how simple it would be if they were horses.

The sunlight was strong. It forced him to open his eyes and as he did so the dream faded, leaving only the recollection through which the present returned to him. He saw the high ceiling, the bars of sunlight from the venetian blinds spaced across the thin coverlet of his bed. There was smoke in the room and down below, in the yard, Aminah was singing.

He got out of bed and moving over to the window canted the slats of the blind so that he could see her where she stood there washing for Mademoiselle, washing and singing very softly, the falsetto notes as sharp as the smoke from her tamarisk-wood fire. He saw the flat brown feet like new shoes, the flexed arms and the black tongue of hair licking the seven coins round her neck as it swung to her movements.

'Naiēe-aiēē-nyah,' she sang as he stood there unseen observing her strangeness, innocence, knowingness.

She paused, a thin golden lizard quite motionless; and he pulled the cord which raised the blind. It went up with a clatter and below him she shrieked piercingly, a sound as sharp as an Arab knife.

'Aminah!' he called, leaning pyjama-jacketed out of the window. 'Good morning! Aminah.'

She covered her face with her wet hands for a moment and stared back up at him above their finger-tips: she sliced at the air between them viciously and then, in her white skirt, she ran back into the darkness of the wash-house.

There was no one about at all. It was ten o'clock perhaps, perhaps nine. Apart from the dream, he had slept heavily. He scanned the steps leading up behind the wash-yard wall to the Church of St. Francis on the fringe of the French Section. The steps were quite empty, not even an Arab to be seen. Through a gap in the red tiles of the wash-house roof he saw the smoke from Aminah's fire rising thinly in the bright sunshine.

He leaned out further and apologised. He could see the bottom of her skirt and the feet beneath it, quite distinctly: the place was not deep enough for her to get right out of his sight.

'No Prison this morning, Aminah!' he said. 'Come out, I want to talk to you, I did not mean to frighten you; but I dreamed about the Prison—that I was back there——'

She made no reply. He heard the rapidity of her rubbing on the wash-board, saw her skirt swaying above her ankles as she punished one of Mademoiselle's pillow-slips.

'Salaam oo allei koum!' he called out and waited for her to return his greeting.

'Oo allei koum salaam!' she muttered back at him without pausing in her work.

Contented, he turned back into his room and began to shave. The guide book was reliable.

'If an Arab does not return this greeting, the traveller is advised to be very cautious in all future dealings with him. The Arabs are a profoundly religious people, and the phrase, meaning in effect, "Peace be with you all" is invariably returned unless—etc. etc.'

Dressed, he went slowly down the dark stairs, handed his keys to Salem, half asleep behind his thin white beard at the reception desk, and went round to the front of the hotel to the bar for his rolls and coffee.

'Good morning, Mademoiselle Lucie,' he said as he took his seat at the dusty counter. 'How is your war?'

'*Comment?*'

'*La guerre,*' he attempted in his awful French. '*La guerre des Français et des Arabes. Ça va bien aujour d'hui?*'

Mademoiselle smiled very prettily : '*Je ne suis pas interessée dans les guerres. Your coffee, Monsieur!*'

'*Merci.* But surely wars affect business, don't they? I mean a war as close as this one, just over the border?'

'*C'est une guerre de deux sous,*' she said harshly, '*et d'inconvenience seulement.*'

'In what way an inconvenience, Mademoiselle?'

'*Ca tracasse les servants.* If it goes on too long it will—*le tourisme sera foutu.* There will be another *assassinat.*'

'Another murder? When was the last?'

'Six mon's.' She gave him a look and then she said, 'an Englishman.'

'Was he a spy?'

'Je ne sais pas, mais je crois que c'était un vaurien.'

'What about Americans?'

'Pas d'Americains—not yet.'

'Tk tk! Too bad!'

She was very nearly pretty when she laughed, all the lines moved to the most becoming places: 'Americans are rich, too rich to kill. Here they do not kill beggars or *milliardaires,* only *la classe movenne.'*

'I shall have to be careful.' He liked her because she was so efficient, thirtyish, a little gallant. 'Aren't you nervous sleeping here alone with all these Arabs working for you?'

'Moi? No, no, I was born here. *Mes parents ont fondé l'Hotel de la Gare.* Now they are dead.' She shrugged.

'And why don't you get married?'

'Comment?' with her head on one side.

'You heard very well, Mademoiselle.'

'Per-haps.'

'It's because you don't want a man taking all the money while you do the work?'

'I do not like men, *je n'aime pas les hommes,'* she said without stiffening, so that he was inclined to believe her.

'Last night,' he persisted.

'Ah that was business,' she interrupted. *'Hier soir c'etait du "business."* '

'Very chic business,' he said from his café filtre. 'A Spaniard, a smart Arab, a Frenchman, all young—and you with your hair like this, lipstick on, and little pearls round your neck, ooh la la!'

She laughed politely as she said, 'Now go, *allez allez Monsieur! J'ai beaucoup a faire.* Will you be taking your dinner here tonight?'

'No not tonight, I'm bored, *ennuyé.* I don't think I like the Zone.'

'No?' very politely.

'It's too quiet. I expected it to be very dangerous but I'm beginning to think my own country may be more so, though greyer.'

'All I know about England is that they have air-ing cupboards for drying the clothes they put on. *C'est vrai n'est ce pas?*'

He was suddenly irritable. 'But you are not interested, Mademoiselle. You don't care whether I'm bored or not.' He got off the stool, took a stale croissant from the dish beside his glass, and remembering Mass, replaced it and prepared to leave.

'Vous-êtes marié, Monsieur?'

'My wife is dead,' he was moving away. 'She died six months ago.'

He was in the archway, half-way between the darkness of her bar and the light of the sea battering in through the palms beyond the glass of the entrance.

'Et votre chambre?' she called biting her pencil.

'I don't know. I'll take my pyjamas but leave my case. I'm going to Shibam but I'll be back sometime, I've got another eight days——'·

'Eight days. *Huit jours?'*

'Yes,' he pushed open the wide glass into the first of the morning heat; the bell of the Church of St. Francis jumped in softly from the hill.

'You have children, *Monsieur le Docteur?'*

'No,' he shouted over his shoulder, 'none. I have no children, Mademoiselle Lucie.'   .

And he made his way up the long flat steps to the white church standing high above the harbour. He would be per-haps five minutes late; but it was forgivable because the sermon would probably be long and incomprehensible. He had drunk only coffee that morning; by the time the moment came the statutory hour would have elapsed and provided it were not a high Mass, he would be able to receive Holy Com-munion after the *Domine non sum dignus.*

He wanted his Communion very much indeed because he was hungry. He wanted only to know that he had it inside him: an incorporated fact which nothing could displace so that afterwards he could resume decisively this first holiday since his confirmation and since M's death.

On the left-hand side at the top of the steps there was a gravelled courtyard beyond a white arch. He crossed it quickly and went into the loud interior of the church, immediately disappointed to find that it was a school service in which instruction was mixed with singing. The whole of the centre of the nave was occupied by polished-haired little boys, the adults, mostly Spaniards too, crowded into the dark side-aisles.

He managed to get fairly near the front and kneeled with a group of other men behind a row of large women in black whose rosaries were clacking through their scented hands.

The singing master, who seemed to have eyes in the back of his head, stood on the chancel steps and synchronised the singing with the pace of the celebrant's prayers. Harshly as ravens the children sang out their hymns, their voices thrown out of their hundreds of thrown-back heads, their eyes wandering, restless as his thoughts, to their leader, the roof, the High Altar and back to their books.

He found himself remembering his conversation with Mademoiselle Lucie and wishing she had been the sort of person in whom he might have confided. It would have been helpful to have discussed his restlessness with her.

Mary's death and his subsequent conversion had left him wondering what his life had amounted to. Years of attending to criminals, the butt-ends of violence. Was that why he had come to the Zone? He supposed so. He had wanted to get as near to real violence as possible. And at this point he admitted it was not just danger, but salacity too.

Now with her body dead, gone and buried, her spirit so remote, the temptation had whipped at him fiercely; all the sharper for his knowledge of its implications. He knew that he was deliberately seeking an occasion of sin, but argued that such a journey would be a retreat too, a testing ground of what had happened to him and was even now happening as he kneeled, incredulous of his long incredulity, before the central sacrament of his faith.

An elderly Franciscan, yellow, brown and white, came forward to preach the sermon. His words streamed at the children as they sat there fiddling; tiny movements, jokes, inattentiveness as minute as the restlessness of standing corn.

But to Chance, trying at first to follow and then giving up, odd-seeming Englishisms fell out of the language: *concupisensia, mortalidad, apostolicita.*

He attempted some synonyms: 'desire' for 'concupiscence,' 'death' for 'mortality,' but he could find no equivalent for 'apostolicity,' unless it were 'grace,' the doctrine of which was in any case beyond him. He built the words up as he waited for the old man to stop shouting at the little boys who had it all to come. The last elusive word he had picked out or invented held him as he remembered a legend about confirmation. Someone had once told him that there was a 'rustle of apostolic feathers' after the laying on of hands, the convert becoming briefly an evangelist despite himself, an attracter of persons and events, a maker of circumstance. After so much resistance, intellectual, emotional and aesthetic, he had found the concept attractive; the idea of a sudden supernatural endowment no longer merely vulgar or laughable, but possible and glorious.

And thus far, he realised, with eight days remaining, he had discovered only increasing boredom with himself and with everything about him. The Zone had proved to be quieter, less libidinous and more pacific than the confines of Soho; less significant than the prison-round.

Tomorrow he would cross the border on his French visa and get nearer to the actual fighting. Here on the edge of a tideless sea and an unseen desert there was nothing to hold him. All the women were veiled and hostile, while socially he had discovered no sharpness. The Europeans seemed to be as busy amongst themselves as hoteliers after a tourist-glut, while the Americans he had hoped to find had remained hidden, presumably culture-swopping in clubs and villas too expensive or private for him to enter.

He returned to the present as the sanctus bell rang; by an effort of will he was given the grace of a dull prayer. The Mass moved on to its climax; as the consecration approached, heralded by its peremptory flurry of bells, he was lost for the time, ardent and momentarily at peace.

Later, in the Rue d'Espagnole, he paused beneath the palm trees on his way to the Harbour.

Mussulmen, Berbers and their wives were coming in from the hills riding donkeys. Whiter than sea-birds, the women wore great hats with straw ropes and bobbles round the crowns. Under their burnooses some of them carried babies on their backs so that they seemed to be in the penultimate stage of grotesque pregnancies. Under the palms they rode in a fierce silence broken only by the horny clopper of the donkey's hooves as they passed along to the tethering posts at the foot of the Street of Goldsmiths.

Chance looked beyond them, across the railway line curving round the white margin of the Bay, across the sand itself, to the solid plane of the blue sea and a far coast beyond it. Ahead of him the Old Town blocked the horizon of the hill; dwellings, domes, minarets and mosques tumbling glacier-white to the quays where funnels and masts stood like reflections in the heat. He heard no footsteps behind him as he moved on towards the bus station; and he jumped nervily when he felt the close grip of his arm, and sprang round to face the man who was smiling at him.

'Marcovicz!' The skin of the cripple's face was as soft as ever; beneath it the great swathes of neck muscle, like trunks of ivy round bones, were as he remembered them; and the grip of the hand into which he placed his own, so well, so fatally remembered.

'My God! You gave me a fright.'

The eyes, yellow as a lion's, searched his face as they had so often done, with such affectionate care, with so much of suffering reasonableness in their regard that he should never have forgotten them, should always have remembered the long smile before speech, the characteristic more individual than the curled hair, the live muscles and the bruisable skin.

They stood there under the palms, not a shadow waving, not a mast moving, even the distant Arabs on the sand apparently stopped in their journeys. For a moment they smiled into one another's faces, their hands gripped, their lips parted and their heads quite still.

'How are you, Doctor Chance?' came the slow sweet question as the questioner began to pump his hand slowly up and down. 'I can't tell you how many times I've wondered how is Doctor Chance. I've often thought about you, I've prayed for you. Remember?'

'Yes, Marcovicz.'

'Oh it does me good to hear you say that name again. I knew I would you know; when I went on to the Loch I said to myself, 'There is one man who believes in me, one man who stood up against them all and upheld my dignity as a human being, and that man is Doctor Chance!' He paused. 'It meant a lot to me.' They smiled again. 'Do you believe me?'

Chance withdrew his hand gently, 'I'm sure you did, Marcovicz.'

'And years later, just as I said, we meet again. Life is strange, isn't it, Doctor Chance?'

'It is.'

They fell into step and began to walk along under the palms; the older man springing along on his artificial foot, gaily, beside the younger man's more meditative gait.

'You haven't changed,' he went on. 'The moment I saw that

head—you have a tired way of holding it—I used to tell you
of it in the rounds, didn't I——'

'Yes, I believe you did.'

'Of course I did! Why I remember as though it were yesterday coming up to you as you walked into the hospital one
morning and saying, 'You're worried, Doctor Chance. Oh,
Doctor Chance, you're a worried man this morning! And do
you remember what you said?'

'No.'

'You said, "You're quite right, Marcovicz." And believe me
I'd have given half of my remission to see you smile that
morning.'

'You're very good.'

'You were good to me, Doctor. When I most needed faith
in myself you gave it me. There wasn't much you could do,
but you did it. Over and over again you'd say, "Marcovicz, I
do not think you are mad. I do not at present hold your
sanity in question." '

'Did I say that?'

'You did, Doctor Chance.'

'I must have been paranoid myself,' said Chance dryly,
walking on. Behind him the older man halted, his smile gone;
then he scuttled to catch the speaker up. He smote him on the
back, laughing and jumping, almost dancing on the air and
shadows.

'Oh ho-ho,' he capered. 'Still the same. For a moment you
had me. I'd forgotten, Marcovicz had forgotten, that you used
to catch him like that; and that reminds me of something
else; you used to say, "Marcovicz, you are a very vain man."
Remember?'

'Yes.'

'Ah-ha! You remember that! The argument we had before
I was extradited and transferred back to the nick at Hamburg
at the end of the War, you remember that too?'

'I think so.'

'I do. I've never forgotten it. Not a word of it. You surprised me that day. You're a very brave man. You took

a risk in saying what you said to me that day, didn't you?'

'Perhaps I did.'

' "Perhaps I did," he says. You know you did. Why I might have——' he broke off, smiling up at Chance who was half a head taller. 'You know what I was like then. I've no need to remind you, have I?'

'No.'

'But come,' said Marcovicz, 'isn't that me all over? Tiring you out, thinking only of myself, talking at you all the time and in the sunshine when you're supposed to be resting, having a holiday!'

Chance smiled. 'I'm used to it.'

'And I haven't even asked you yet what you're doing here or where you're going or how long you're staying. I suppose you're wondering what *I'm* doing here. I'll bet, Doctor Chance, you've already said to yourself fifty times, "Now what is Marcovicz doing here in the rich man's playground, sunning himself in the South, when he can't have been out of the nick more than six months." You've said that, haven't you, Doctor Chance?'

'Well——'

'Of course you have. I knew it. Oh! isn't it a lovely world to be free in. *Free,* Doctor Chance! Do you know what that word means to a man who has spent nearly all of his life behind walls? To find himself out in the sun again, by the sea he never spoke of? Have you ever asked yourself what a man dreams of in prison? What are his nightmares? Have you?'

'I suppose I must have wondered.'

They were outside the Bus Station. Fallen tickets lay still in the absence of any wind, the door yawned dark by an empty seat: across the concrete, buses were being piled high with Arab luggage. They sat down together.

'I'll tell you. A man's nightmares in prison are dreams of fair women, of great spaces, flowers, fine food and leisure. *These* are his nightmares. When he wakes from these dreams he wakes weeping. I told you that before and you laughed at me didn't you? You said, "Marcovicz, you are a dishonest man. Why must you lie to yourself?" '

'Did I?'

'You did. I was angry. I was hurt, I admit it.'

'Was I wrong?'

'No, you weren't wrong. But you were hard. You were very hard on me in those days. You laughed at me. You wouldn't let me turn my nightmares into dreams.'

Chance sighed.

'But you mustn't be sorry. You mustn't apologise, it's all over. Why, it's finished. We're both free. We can share a cigarette without dodging a "Screw," we can talk as man to man, eat together at the same table. We can go anywhere we like together. We could get on a bus and sit side by side and drink from the same bottle, couldn't we?'

'We could.'

'Oh,' said Marcovicz, putting his arm round him briefly, 'it's good to see you again, to know you again. Where are you thinking of going? Have you got money? Let me buy the tickets. Name our destination and Marcovicz will pay.'

'I was thinking of going to Shibam.'

'Shibam?'

'Yes. Why, don't you like Shibam?'

'It's a crap-hole, Doctor Chance. There's nothing to see there. But of course if that's where you want to go I'll get the tickets. No, put your money away. I've dreamed of this, of the day when I'd be able to say to my friend, "Doctor Chance, put your money away. Today, I, Marcovicz, will pay." ' He stood there a little hunched, his powerful shoulders framing the pale upward-glancing smile, then his body straightened with the customary jerk as though all his decisions were, in a sense, physical.

'I'll be back in a minute. Don't you move from that seat until I'm back. I've more to tell you, much more.' He leaned forward suddenly. 'But perhaps I'm being presumptuous? You don't want to spend an hour of your holiday with a man

who's committed half the crimes on the German calendar—
and been found out! Why, already you must be regretting
that you ever came here. I can see it in your face, Doctor
Chance. You are saying to yourself, "Whatever possessed me,
God, to come here to this of all places for my well-earned
rest, when the first man I must meet and be forced to do with,
is Marcovicz!' You must forgive me. I'll go—immediately. I
won't even try to show my gratitude or pay off any one of my
debts for fear of being misunderstood, scorned, despised.' He
laid a wide hand on the other's forearm, 'I'll tell you what I'll
do. I'll slap my gratitude in its white face and I'll say "Lie
down! What right have *you* to be grateful? You may think
you have paid but you haven't. You are Cain, they wouldn't
stretch you because you couldn't kill; but that doesn't mean
they want you." I'll say, "Marcovicz, you were always work,
never pleasure," and I'll go.'

He stood there, tense, in front of the man on the seat who
had stretched his arm along the back of it as he considered.

Chance did not look up at him as he waited; he seemed
only to be watching Marcovicz's feet, watching the right,
natural foot tense and relax inside its open sandal as he
awaited his reply.

'Get the tickets, Marcovicz,' he said suddenly.

'Oh that's the man!' Marcovicz patted his back again
quickly. 'That's my Doctor Chance. I was testing you that's all.'

Chance smiled at him, but said nothing.

And he sat there waiting, watching the Arabs round their
buses. Their voices reached him now, their high heckle, and
the drivers and conductors shouting amidst the squawking of
chickens and the banging of luggage.

In a moment Marcovicz was back, waving the tickets above
his head.

'Got them!' he shouted. 'And an hour to fill in, and plenty
to show you. Come on, don't let's waste a minute of our time
together.'

But Chance sat on, very relaxed.

'What do you want to show me?' he asked.

'Not "what," Doctor Chance, but "who." It's not a thing, it's a woman; and, apart from that, I'm going to give you coffee. You like coffee, don't you? Why I used to bring it to you every morning when you got me that little job in the Prison Gymnasium!'

'Is it far?'

'Just across the sand, there, over in front of the Miramar. A walk'll do you good.'

'Very well.'

Chance got up and together they crossed the concrete, clambered the low wall beside the railway line and made their way beside a line of bolted and padlocked bathing huts to the sand.

The older man moved across it talking continuously, springing on ahead and then returning to Chance who walked more circumspectly, only half listening to his companion's flow of speech.

Ahead of them, the sand was scored over with the naked footprints of the Arabs; single lines running off in all directions as though flocks of man-sized birds had wandered there during the night; never two together, the lines crossing, veering, joining, and parting singly; always singly.

Over against the sea, further along the apron of the Bay, right over eastwards below the empty Villa Hutton, there were perhaps six solitary figures; brown shapes with hands clasped behind them and heads forward under their cowls as they slouched, not aimlessly, on their tortuous journeyings over the sand.

'. . . And I ask you,' Marcovicz was saying, 'do they expect a man to remain continent for ten years? To lock him away with his desires and find anything resembling a man at the end of it?'

Chance said nothing. He walked on, his hands behind him, unconsciously imitating the posture of the distant Arabs.

'You were right to despise me,' went on the cripple, 'but I'm going to prove to you that it was force of circumstance. You even sympathised with me because you said that you

yourself were a passionate man. And oh friend! do you think
I didn't know it?' In his excitement he sprang at him gripping
both his arms; his close-curled head coming between Chance's
eyes and the prospect of the sea. 'I'm asking you; do you
think I didn't know?'

'You knew what, Marcovicz?'

'That you were taken, Doctor Chance, by women. That you
loved them, yearned for them, needed them. There were men
like you in the Loch, in every *gäfängnis* I was ever sent to,
whether in Germany, or even the one in Scotland where
we came to know each other. I know more about prisoners
than you, I know more about them because I've seen them
from the other side. When a new man comes in, *we* don't
need to read the charge-sheet. We see it written over the
man's body, in the way he moves, talks, stands. Why! when
I've been out I've walked into a restaurant and I've watched
them all guzzling in there and I've said for each one,
"Embezzler! Perjurer! Larceny boy! Con-man! Sexer!" I've
gone right through the calendar like that. I've even stood in
the dock and as the Judge pronounced sentence I've said to
myself, "And you, Brother, you up there! You have Carnal
Knowledge shouting so loud out of your eyes it's a wonder
you don't deafen yourself." ' Marcovicz laughed, 'Am I right?
Don't you go for women like some men go for gold, mobs,
power, death?'

Chance halted, looking down at his feet meditatively.

'Yes,' he said, and then, before the other could respond,
added, 'Perhaps I should say not that I do; but that *I would*.'

Marcovicz dropped his arm.

'Ah, you would,' he said. 'But you haven't. That's the
difference. That's what you're saying isn't it? You are remind-
ing me as you reminded me before that we were separated
not by our natures but only by our actions.'

'By our beliefs, Marcovicz.'

'Our beliefs, that's right, I remember.' He turned and began
to walk on ahead, Chance following him. The spring came
back into his step as he talked again with rising jubilance.

'That came into our last argument. I remember you saying, "Marcovicz, what I like about you is that you're a real sinner, like me. You seem to crouch there under the sky—protesting against great circumstance," I think you said. "You sin as your people sinned in the Desert, not against their conception of Society, but against God Himself." That's what you said, isn't it? Am I right?'

They had halted some little distance in front of a wooden building thrown up between the perimeter of the bay and the railway line. A notice spanned the roof:

RENDEZVOUS DE LA PLAGE
Café, Restaurant, Baignade

and behind it, separated only by the Rue d'Espagnole and its palms, loomed the closed façades of the luxury hotels of the French section.

Marcovicz's excitement was now supreme. He paced the soft sand backwards and forwards in front of his companion, shaking his head as he talked and giving swift glances at the café and the sky as though at any moment the one were about to explode into the other.

'We are all used, Doctor Chance,' he said. 'I may be only a Jew, a convict, a man who couldn't kill when he set out to kill; but after fifty years of life I'm trusted again. Can you know what that means to a man who has not even his nationality to believe in, a man rejected by his fellows, by all nations?'

Chance stood there patiently. His eyes took in the blistered blue paint of the Rendezvous, the sand piled against its foundations, the ipomea withered on the surrounding trellis, its brown blooms rustling in the wind from the sea.

'But you're tired,' said Marcovicz, halting in front of him and peering anxiously up into his face. 'You know my history already.'

'Some of it, only some of it,' said the other, 'and it doesn't really matter, you know, not really. In a way the past would only be important if we weren't free to change the future.'

'Doctor Chance! I never saw my father and mother die. If my life had been different and I, Marcovicz, wanted to cover their graves with my tears I could not find the ground they were in. Listen to me! Listen to a man who must tell you that all Germany is his graveyard, who must grind his thumb on the map of Europe and say, "That is the burial ground of *my* people!" And then tell me that my past is not important. But don't think I blame you. A man who does not blame himself can blame no one else but God.'

He paused, his eyes beautiful in themselves, fixed on the Doctor's face who for his part held their gaze for a moment and then a little impatiently broke loose and without replying moved on towards the café.

Marcovicz hurried after him and caught his arm. 'Have you nothing to say to me, then?'

'What have we come here for? What were you going to show me?'

'It can wait,' said the other aggrieved. 'Don't you see that until I know you understand me, it will have no meaning for you?'

'I don't understand anyone I'm afraid; and in any case, Marcovicz, it's getting late; and if we're to have coffee and catch the bus——'

'But you must understand *me*,' Marcovicz shouted. '*Me!* Doctor Chance. I want you to meet someone: a woman, beautiful, a woman who—but it's no good if you won't listen, if you didn't hear what I said about the persecutions of my people.'

'What people?'

'Why, the Jews. What I was telling you about all Germany being my graveyard——'

'I did hear you.'

'Then why don't you——?'

'Because you were enjoying yourself.'

The older man stood there in front of him very greedily; he frowned, he licked his lips, his yellow eyes narrowed then opened wide and suddenly he started to laugh: great cries sailed out of his open mouth so suddenly that he seemed himself to be as startled by their sound as was his listener.

'Oh ho ho,' he shouted. 'What a man you are. You don't believe me, do you? I was dramatising, wasn't I? You said to yourself, "All this stuff about the Jews. What does Marcovicz care for Jews except when they're rich and alive? That's what you said to yourself, isn't it?'

'I did,' said Chance.

'You admit it! And you're nearly right. If you'd said'—he was serious again—'if you'd said——'

'If I'd said what?'

'If you'd said, "What do the Jews care for Jews," you'd have been even more right, wouldn't you?'

'Perhaps I would.'

'Of course you would. You're a wise man! You know that none of our persecution could ever have happened down the ages if all the Jews had cared for Jews. That's our tragedy, that our scorn starts full in our own faces while the rest of the world only gets the side of it. I'll tell you what we are, Doctor Chance: we are God's favourite jesters and you do well to laugh at us.'

'But I don't laugh at you.'

'Don't you? Well I do. Believe me, I laugh and I shall go on laughing until I die laughing.'

They were silent for a moment, not looking at one another; the doctor balanced a little uneasily before his companion almost as though he depended for physical support on the increasing wind from the sea, the grey-haired man newly still, a little dejected, his gaze directed at the sand.

Chance spoke:

'This woman——' he began.

'I was going to tell you about her,' said the other dully. 'I wanted you to know before you met her; but it doesn't seem important any longer.'

'It probably isn't,' said Chance watching him intently.

'You wouldn't believe a word I said,' went on Marcovicz. 'You would say, "Hypocrite, he thinks he has a mission, work to do; but I know his record and he's not to be trusted." ' He tuned away, 'It's no good!'

'No it isn't,' Chance said suddenly, 'because you're still behaving like a prisoner.'

'A prisoner?'

'It doesn't seem to have occurred to you that if *you* are free, then I am too. I no longer have to listen to you tactfully or dissuade you from action or threats.'

'But you helped me, you stood out for me——'

'I was paid to help you and in any case an ordered prison's a matter of policy.'

'Policy?' repeated the other, astonished.

'Don't interrupt me, Marcovicz. Nobody is free, least of all a prison official. You hold hundreds of us for our lifetime behind your bars. For months as your prisoner I had to suffer your posturings and self-justification, your absurd interest in yourself and your crimes. But now I'm as free to avoid you as you once were to bore me.'

'You may be right—I begin to see——' began Marcovicz.

But Chance interrupted him, asking, 'Now what is this girl's name?'

'Magdalena.'

'Is she English?'

'Magdalena's a Belgian, Doctor Chance. Innocent. A woman not a girl and yet a girl duped into womanhood, tricked into coming here to make money the easy way by a manner of a swine, by a low-down fat cheek-wobbling ponce from Sydney, Australia——'

Chance looked up. 'A white slaver?'

'No, not a white slaver. That's what the screws and the staff would call it; but we call it "sexing," that's all.'

Chance smiled. 'And where do you come in to all this?'

Marcovicz smiled, his lips drew back over his irregular teeth and he raised his head higher as he gazed at the doctor and beyond him.

'Ah!' he said, 'I *know*. There's nothing I don't know when it comes to The Game and by what some would call coinci-

dence but which I don't, I happened to be here in this very
part of the world before Magdalena ever arrived.'

'I see.'

'I could tell you more. All about our plans, Magdalena's
and mine, of the plans of George Fraser, and of how they're
going to go—unrewarded.' He threw back his head and repeated the word, 'Unrewarded! That's good, isn't it? He
waits and he plans. He's worked out the price he's going to
get from the richest men in the Zone, one at a time to begin
with, for the first year or so; and then two men. Later, at a
reduced rate, three or four men until the perishable goods
have perished and he's only able to make three or four
hundred per cent. on his little investment in Magdalena.'

'And what does your friend think about this? After all, if
she came here to make money and this man Fraser paid her
fare, then . . .'

'Listen,' said Marcovicz, 'I have bought Magdalena a
monkey, a little striped marmoset with a face like a High
Court Judge; and do you know what his name is? Do you
know what she calls him?'

'I think I could guess.'

Pivoting on his plastic foot inside its smooth sandal, Marcovicz spun in a vortex of the silver sand.

'And he's with her all the time, night and day, watching
over her, her goings out and her comings in. And he bites!
Fraser bites everyone and anything but me and Magdalena!'
He paused. 'Don't you think that's good? Who but I would
have thought of it: of a little monkey called Fraser?'

Chance smiled again. 'Yes, it's good, Marcovicz; it's very
amusing.'

'But don't let us waste any more time now,' said the other,
his good spirits entirely restored. 'Why, we have the whole
day together, we're going to Shibam, remember? We can talk
on the bus. I'll tell you everything then, you shall know all
my secrets and share in them.'

'Thank you, Marcovicz.'

By the door Marcovicz paused. 'You're laughing at me

again. But I can stand laughter from my friends; and, don't forget that I understand you. I read you. I know that you'll not laugh once you've met Magdalena.'

He opened the door eagerly and followed by Chance moved into the bar of the Rendezvous de la Plage. It was a dark room. Small tables encircled by rings of chairs ran down the left-hand side beneath windows blinded for the winter. On the other side the wall was spanned for half its length by a bar on which was an Espresso coffee machine, empty glass cake-boxes and clear cones of piled tumblers. Two doors, one behind the centre of the bar and the other in the empty section of the inner wall, gave access to the living quarters.

A man, the proprietor, stood behind the Espresso machine and watched Marcovicz with no pleasure as he bounded down the length of the room talking rapidly in a strange mixture of bad French, English and German whose meaning Chance was only half able to follow. Very soon a woman in dusty black, yellow-faced and sour, joined the proprietor and stood there beside him putting in quick words as she listened to the conversation.

Her eyes flickered over Chance waiting beside the open door to the beach and returned heavily to Marcovicz as he sought the means of introduction.

'Mon veritable compagnon, Monsieur le Docteur, que j'ai connu pendant beaucoup d'années en Angleterre. I want mon ami to meet Mademoiselle.'

'Mademoiselle?' questioned the woman sharply.

Slapping a handful of French notes on to the top of the bar Marcovicz beckoned to Chance.

'Un café, deux cafés filtres, Madame Pernet! No, trois, un pour Magdalena. Et vin, vino tinto, the best you've got, le plus mieux, 1947.' He spoke an aside to Chance: ' '47, I'll never forget that summer in East Lothian, picking *himmbern* in that fool of a governor's garden.' And then in his normal voice: 'They don't understand do they that this is a famous meeting? C'est mon ami le Docteur, un specialiste neuropathique de Londres, who has come here to fix Magdalena's headaches,' and he rattled on at them, neutralising their apathy and countering their suspicions only with difficulty and slowly.

Chance, watching Monsieur Pernet produce a bottle and glasses while his wife with equal reluctance filled the containers for the coffee and set them on the cups, was amused by Marcovicz's unease. The false implications of his words as far as he understood them held him outside the group; and therefore he stayed by the open door and allowed Marcovicz to see, whenever his support was solicited, that he was giving the conversation only a part of his attention. For his eyes continually strayed to the vista of the beach where the Arabs walked so solitarily and slowly across the planes of the sand. At this moment, one of them, he noticed, had halted like a pointer against the blue face of the sea; centrally and quite motionless as the hands of a clock stopped at midday.

'It's very dark in here this morning,' Marcovicz was saying, 'darker than a prison, isn't it, Doctor Chance? We want brightness. Plus de lumière, s'il vous plaît, Monsieur Pernet! *Kann ich mehr licht haben?* We'll pay for all we use.' Swiftly, without changing his bantering tone or the light of his expression, he continued to Chance alone, 'They're mean bastards, watching the goods for Fraser until I can move her. Suspicious, too, hein! Madame Pernet? Judging a man not by his good intention but only by the size of his wad. Merci, Monsieur! moi and mon ami le Docteur, we will take the cups to the table. One of these nights,' he whispered, 'I personally will put a match and a little drop of paraffin to this shack and by the morning there'll be roast pig for breakfast—*geröstet schweine fleisch*. Eh! Monsieur, Madame! Have a drink with us? *Lass uns ein haben!* Anything you fancy, while I go and tell Magdalena we're here.'

'Elle n'est pas ici. Magdalena se promène dans la ville,' said the proprietor as Marcovicz moved towards the closed door in the wall.

Marcovicz smiled at him.

'Elle n'est pas tout à fait dans son assiette,' the man elaborated urgently, his eyes on his wife. 'Do not—derange, she is—sick.'

'Sick? So are we all. That's just why I've brought the Doctor. Elle à son malaise habituel sans doute. Monsieur Chance est un specialiste de Londres.' His fingers were on the handle of the door.

The woman moved up swiftly to the near end of the bar and leaned over it, her yellow eyes suddenly small with venom.

'Monsieur Fraser!' she hissed, 'Monsieur Fraser! C'est interdit—pas des étrangers, Marcovicz!'

'Monsieur mon ami n'est pas étranger,' replied the other without moving. 'Monsieur Fraser soi-même à commandé,' he turned casually to Chance. 'Tell them you've been called in, Doctor Chance; for *my* sake! Help me to make my dream a reality and save her, save a beautiful girl as you helped to save me.'

'From what, Marcovicz?'

'From Fraser, Doctor Chance. These money-grubbers wouldn't understand because they've never been convicted; but Magdalena is beautiful, a believer. She has a Rosary, she goes to Mass. She plays the Game only for the money, gets the money only for her family. And she is sick! Magdalena is sick. You ask her. Come on, Doctor Chance, in a few months I'll need no help from anyone; but if you help me now you'll be saving more than one life.'

As he spoke, the door in front of him opened and a girl stood there nursing a marmoset against the pink jumper she wore with a sharply waisted coat and skirt.

'Bien entendu!' she said unsmiling. 'We heard your voices, Fraser and I, *he* was excited, he wanted to see what you were all doing.'

Marcovicz seized her hand. His vitality surged up afresh as he kissed it in the palm and on the back of the wrist, while the monkey squeaked and whistled from its vantage point in the crook of her arm.

C

'What did I tell you? Isn't she beautiful? Come over and sit down, Magdalena. Lights! Monsieur Pernet. Music, le radio! Switch on the wireless! Now sit next to each other. Magdalena, this is Doctor Chance, an old friend of mine from England; you must have heard me mention him; the man who cured me of my nerve-trouble years ago when all my investments went wrong.'

The girl, dark-haired, very fresh and innocent-looking, glanced blankly at Chance still without smiling and then ruffled the marmoset's head.

'But you're looking pale, Magdalena. It's that headache again, you must drink your coffee while it's hot and then we'll have wine, while you tell Doctor Chance about your sleeplessness. He'll write you a prescription and reassure you as he reassured me years and years ago when the shares came tumbling down and I found myself on the pavement faced with starting the long climb all over again.'

He swallowed his coffee at a gulp and putting his elbows on the table and his chin on his hands gazed upwards at them; his eyes moist and smiling, his head swaying slowly from side to side and his voice suddenly thick with nostalgia, he went on more floridly than ever:

'Oh what a moment this is. How I've dreamed of it! My two best friends face to face, sharing wine, smiling and united. Don't ever let anyone tell you again that dreams never come true, that what's done is done and can never be mended. It's false!' He leapt suddenly to his feet and his expression changed. His lips drew together, the smile vanished and wide fists grew white at his sides. 'False, I say. No man is condemned by his past to lovelessness. It stoops down, love stoops down suddenly and rescues a man; it picks him up bodily from the slime which is not of his own making but into which, like a child, he has fallen because he trusted himself to the heights. Isn't that so, Doctor Chance? Magdalena?'

'You talk very fast, Jacob. I fear I do not always know what you are saying.'

The girl's eyes questioned Chance coolly as Marcovicz returned to his chair.

'Of course,' he said. 'There I go again, talking about myself when what I want is to hear *you* talk. Tell the Doctor about your sickness Magdalena. He knows everything: all about that corseted baboon Fraser, all about your home and the Convent. Just let him know your symptoms and you'll be able to go out again in the evenings, out with me, with him, dancing at the Safari, drinking at the President, dining at the Scheherazade. I'll leave you, I'll go across to the Espagnole and buy cigarettes for the journey. I didn't tell you, did I? The Doctor is taking me to Shibam for lunch. But first we decided to come and see you because I've told him about the wonder of our meeting; immediately he wants to meet you too, to help you to overcome your lack of self-confidence, so that once again you may trust in the great Architect, the Creator, Jehovah himself and regain your faith in men.'

Standing up he seized Chance's hand. He placed it in the girl's and with both of his own squeezed them forcefully, pumping them gently up and down as though he wished to weld them indissolubly together.

The girl winced, a little cry escaped her, and the marmoset somersaulted on to the table, bit Chance on the wrist and then returned to its perch in the crook of her elbow.

'*Verflucht!* Iodine!' shouted Marcovicz. 'Bandages! I'll get those too. Don't worry, Doctor Chance, you'll get no infection. I'll be back in five minutes. Start on the wine, confide in one another. Withhold nothing.'

He fled down the silent room, jumped over the threshold on to the sand, waved once, and was gone.

Chance looked down at his wrist and then with his other hand sought for and produced a handkerchief. Wordlessly, the girl took it from him, up-ended the bottle of wine and applied the soaked section to the wound.

'Thank you.'

'*C'est rien!* The wine is alcoholic and that is an antiseptic, yes?'

'Yes.'

'I am very sorry. Fraser is *très méchant*. He thought you had hurt me.'

'Yes,' Chance repeated. He noticed that they were alone. The door behind the bar was open; it looked like an ear he thought suddenly, and was as soundless as an ear.

'You are very quiet, Monsieur Chance.'

'I'm afraid so. To tell you the truth our friend is a little noisy, it always takes me a few minutes to get used to him; really, to recover from him I suppose?'

She smiled.

'He misunderstands me most persistently,' Chance went on. 'Because my work requires me to be a listener, he imagines I'm even weaker than I look.'

'You do not look weak,' she said with professional appraisal. 'To me you seem like very many western men who have grown thin or fat waiting for something which has already passed them.'

'You are wrong.'

'How is that?'

'It would take too long to explain, Mademoiselle.'

'Then why have you chosen to come to the Zone *en vacances*. It has a certain reputation.'

He was amused. 'Let's say that you were very nearly right, that *I* hope to find something here which I have recently overtaken.'

There was silence and then she said, 'I am sure that we have something to say to one another.'

'Have we?'

'*Are* you a doctor, Monsieur Chance?'

'I am.'

'You are a Catholic also?'

'Yes—a recent convert, Mademoiselle.'

'You must forgive me for asking but I do not ever, to begin with, believe anything that I am told by anyone, least of all by Jacob; though there is no harm in him.'

'No?'

'None. He is a kind man; a good man. I find his offer tempting. I do not of course believe *entièrement* his financial stories though I do believe that somewhere he has money and that one day he will get it.'

'Have you known him long?'

'A few weeks only; but in my profession, as you will know, Doctor Chance, a few weeks can be a lifetime where knowledge of a man is concerned.'

Chance tied the knot of the handkerchief a little tighter, pulling at it with the fingers of his left hand and his teeth.

'In your profession, Mademoiselle? You are——?'

'Non,' she interrupted, 'not a fille de joie, not a prostitute; they do not travel. I am a—concubine—I think you would call it. That is to say it is my pleasure to make one man very happy for a time—for a price.'

'Yes I see.'

'I seek men who, though not old, are not young and no longer free. They have to be *sympathique,* not quite disillusioned, do you understand? And in reasonably good health. They also have to be rich——'

'They must be a little difficult to find I should imagine.'

'They are, Doctor Chance; that is why I have to have a man like Mr. Fraser, who is what I suppose you would call my agent. He arranged for me to come here and very soon, when he has made suitable engagements for me, I shall leave this place—I do not like it, it is not at all what I am used to—and then I shall work throughout the off-season and the season and this time next year I shall return home to Antwerp to rest.'

Chance poured out a glass of wine and drank from it, the girl watching him unmoving save for the rhythmical play of her fingers caressing the head of the marmoset.

'You are happy, Mademoiselle?'

'I do not expect to be happy,' she said desultorily. 'Do you?'

'No, I suppose not.' Chance was hesitant. 'What I meant was, do you find your life satisfying?'

'Very. If I had married—and I thought of it once I can

assure you, and would have married had anyone rich enough ever proposed to me—*if* I had married I might have made one man happy for a time, for a few years until he grew bored and left me for someone younger or—different. As it is, I've already made six men happy although I am not yet twenty-five years old. I hope before I am ten years older to give to many other men one more glimpse of what they have lost and there's no reason that I can see why I should not be (I think you would say) rewarded, is there?'

'None,' said Chance. 'I was only wondering how you—I mean, Mademoiselle, you yourself are a Catholic too, aren't you?'

'But yes,' she said with surprise. 'I have a very great devotion to Mary Magdalene, my name-Saint. I pray regularly for her intercessions for my clients, Catholics, Mohammedans and Protestants alike. Since most of them will die before me, I hope too that they will repay me for my prayers by praying for me.'

'Oh.' Chance emptied his glass.

'You are troubled. You do not understand me?' She sounded a little sharp and Chance looked across at her.

'No, I'm afraid I don't. I only know that it is wrong.'

'You do?'

'Yes.'

Her gaze fell to his hands.

She sighed. 'You are very obviously a convert,' she said. 'They are always so scrupulous.'

Chance was silent. He watched her sudden concern for the marmoset, the way she tried to soothe it not too obtrusively. He fiddled with his bandaged wrist and said suddenly:

'About Marcovicz——'

'Jacob?'

'Yes, Jacob. I know a certain amount about him, parts of his life story.'

'But of course, he was a patient of yours so he will have confided in you. Or am I mistaken?'

'No, no, you are quite right. In a sense he was a patient

of mine for a short time in Scotland, during the War. In a way he was something of an international problem after his escape from Germany.'

'I know that he was a very brave man, that he escaped from a concentration camp and made his way to England.'

Chance smiled briefly. 'I see. He told you that, did he?'

'They confiscated his business in Germany, all his estates, and he vowed to fight against them with the British. He spent the whole war with the Commandos, and now he is bringing a case, through the International court for the restoration of his property. It is true, is it not?'

'In a sense, Mademoiselle. He *is* a German citizen. He did nothing if not serve in Scotland throughout most of the War, returning to his German home soon afterwards. But that is not the point. What you must know about him is very personal and extremely important—to *you*.'

Her impatience was obvious. 'Surely even in Britain such things are never told by doctors.'

'There is no time to argue about it, Mademoiselle.'

Getting up, tucking at the marmoset and talking sharply she said:

'Jacob has behaved very kindly to me. He is a safeguard. I do not lightly trust myself to strangers, not even to Mr. Fraser who is after all only a business associate. If ever it should be necessary I am very sure that Jacob would act for me swiftly. For this reason I do not wish to have a relationship poisoned—that is the word—by someone I have known for a very much shorter time than I have known Mr. Marcovicz.'

'If you would let me explain, Mademoiselle. You are confused. You may be in very great danger. You see, where women are concerned, I happen to know that Marcovicz is——'

Behind him Marcovicz greeted them. His shadow thrown by the bright sunlight fell before him on the linoleum, and in a moment he was there between them, dropping packets of cigarettes, matches, bandages and a bottle of iodine on the table.

'So you are talking about me? Marcovicz is——? Marcovicz isn't——? What is Marcovicz? Go on, tell me, Doctor Chance. What am I? What were you going to say? I like to hear people talking about me; if I had a fairy godmother and she gave me one wish it would be to sit still for a week, a month or a year and hear relayed to me all the things that have ever been said about me behind my back from the time of my infancy until this moment when I hear someone saying, "Marcovicz *is*——" Ah! that is the question; he is *what*?'

Chance reached for an open packet of cigarettes.

'He was saying, Jacob, that you were worried about me, about my health.'

'Good, good. That shows you what a mind I have. How suspicious I am; how I always think the worst; yet, as it turns out, you were only discussing Magda's health. Tell me, has he listened to all your symptoms and prescribed for you? Has he explained to you how you can make the return to normality, to life with one man, one good man and true? Has he cured you as he helped to cure me? Has he?'

'He has told me that I am confused, Jacob. He has said, I think, that my confusion about one thing is confusing me about others; that I may be in danger.'

'In danger?'

'Yes.'

Marcovicz's head fell in the posture of humility but his eyes, the restlessness of his glance jerked to and fro from one to the other of the faces which confronted him.

'Of what? From whom?'

'Ah!' she said. You would not understand because you do not share our religion. We have a way of talking beyond what we say; sometimes we can only guess what is meant when a thing is said.'

Chance intervened, 'I'm afraid, Marcovicz, we didn't have sufficient time for me to make myself clear even to myself.'

The German's smile was slow and sweet; a wilful banishment of ignoble suspicion. The hand was extended with a firm grip of forgiveness, apology and longanimity, then withdrawn again as though its owner felt himself suddenly presumptuous.

'Then you must meet again. Tomorrow, no tonight. That's my weakness, I like things to happen immediately; if they are slow I seize them, I take events by the neck and I force them to my service. You shall meet Magda at the Botticelli this evening. You shall dine together.' He turned to the girl, 'He shall hear your story, all of it at his leisure and then he'll be able to help us both.'

There was a pause, perhaps a social moment, like those adults experience with children, a desire to correct excesses.

With some diffidence Chance laughed as he said, 'At the moment I feel quite incapable of helping anyone.'

But the other swept on, anticipating the embarrassment, leaping his hurdle to attain the goal from which he would not be diverted.

'Now don't talk like that, Doctor Chance. I know you must be tired, why I remarked on it this morning earlier, and I know that you are laughing at me, but I also know that by this evening you'll be feeling different; you'll be refreshed, won't he, Magda?'

Chance moved away, literally backing one step out of it as he cut in :

'I'm sorry, Marcovicz, but I think if you don't mind that I shall go to Shibam by myself.'

The German sat down. Watching him as he looked up at them, far beyond them, Chance saw the smile of slow and unpleasant sweetness spread across the oddly feminine contour of the cheeks.

The girl moved nearer to him, 'If anything I have said has offended you I beg of you not to punish Jacob for it. He has very few friends and it is perfectly true that he often speaks of you. He never thought he would ever see you again and therefore I know how much this has meant to him. I would

be pleased to do as Jacob suggests, to meet you anywhere in
the Town this evening for dinner?'

Chance was not looking at her. He stood beside his chair
watching the marmoset as it sat perfectly still in the crook of
her black sleeve blinking with great rapidity, its grey forehead knitted above the tiny shining eyes which returned his
gaze without any comprehension whatsoever.

'I beg your pardon, Mademoiselle. What were you saying?'

'Oh it was nothing,' she replied wearily. 'Nothing at all. But
you did say I interested you. I only wanted you to know that
your interest is returned.'

'I apologise. I'm afraid I am sometimes a little forgetful.'

Marcovicz looked up with a heavy, swimming, glance. 'She
was asking you not to take offence. Magda is anxious, very
anxious, to meet you again this evening.'

'Oh yes I remember. The trouble is that I slept too heavily
last night. I had a series of dreams which confused me, and
meeting you this morning was a shock.'

The other picked up the wine bottle and refilled the three
glasses eagerly.

'It's all arranged then? You meet tonight at The Botticelli,
nowhere else, at eight o'clock—without me. I shall be busy.'

'The Botticelli, Jacob? Do you think it is wise?'

'Of course it's not wise.' Marcovicz bobbed over to her and
slid an arm gently round her waist. 'Force the issue, Magda!
Confuse them! Bewilder them. Kick up the sand until they
cough and struggle and choke; and when they recover let
them run to *me* and ask for my help.'

He picked up the things from the table and started to stuff
them back into his pockets as the girl came forward to say
good-bye to Chance who ignored her, shaking her hand without conviction, being about, apparently, to pat the marmoset
when he remembered the danger in time, then smiled and
with no word walked quickly out of the Rendezvous de la
Plage on to the wide beach towards the sea.

A few moments later the Jew lolloped after him to catch
him up; reaching him half-way between the shore and the

tide-line, turned him leftwards towards the bus station lying between the Harbour and the waterfront of the Old Town.

The Rapide for Shibam was a very small bus and as hot as an oven on wheels. Off-white fabric covered the backs of the seats and partially screened the small windows against the dead heat of the twelve o'clock sun. The air within the bouncing restricted space was pungent with brilliantine and exhaust fumes; every seat was occupied.

In the back of the bus where Chance and Marcovicz sat, six Arabs in blue double-breasted suits and dull red fez reclined in pairs reading Arabic newspapers; as many women, self-segregated and silent, occupied the front seats. In blue burnouses with starched head-dresses and embroidered yashmaks, they sat severely upright, all that was visible of their features: the even brows, round black eyes and sharply cut lids, as uniform as their dress and as reposeful as their hands and feet, shod, as Chance observed, in the delicate footwear of wealth.

The wide avenues of the French section of the town were quickly superseded by longer visions of the crowded streets of the Moorish quarter. Outlying European cemeteries and salmon-tiled Spanish churches gave place to isolated blocks of flats. The road narrowed, whitened, and in a few minutes the bus drew up behind several others at the Frontier Post marking the limit of the International Zone.

The road was full of poorer Arabs and country produce. Live chickens tied by the legs in bundles of six flapped in the roadside dust, plaited baskets of flower bulbs, custard apples and peppers lay on the brown verges and, everywhere, sheeted women stood awaiting the return of their husbands from the Customs shed.

Chance wandered moodily among them smoking obsessively and leaving all the practical arrangements to Marcovicz.

Quite soon, since the Rapide had been given preference, they were given permission to pass beneath the black-and-white barrier and return to their seats. In a silence which the

interruption had heightened rather than diminished, the driver
started his engine and the bus resumed its journey on the
Spanish side of the border.

The brown-baked hills flanking the coastal plain drew
nearer. The arid seasonal marshes in which some species
of white bird stood heat-bound in the withered rushes, the
fragile Arab encampments and bent trees gave place to a thin
scree and a landscape of sun-flayed serra. Valley succeeded
hill, hill rose from valley and the road rose higher and higher
into a hinterland of rounded crests and sluggish cloud.

Within the bus no one spoke. Marcovicz let his cropped
head roll against the top of the seat, his lower lip and his
chin drawn a little downwards by the gross relaxation of his
neck muscles. Chance crouched forward, obtuse and irritable,
his eyes half-seeing through the small dusty section of the
window, while before and behind, the Arabs sat stiffly with
their eyes directed straight ahead of them.

The surface of the road improved a little, the bus increased
its pace and the valleys grew wider. In a short time, without
the intervention of any village, Shibam appeared suddenly: a
white city like coarse china flung into a hollow of hills there
to rest beside a dark and dirty lake overhung by a mountain
rising into heavy cloud.

The Rapide skirted the water on which no boat sailed or
rested, turned down a steep slope beneath telegraph wires and
lamp standards into a grey concrete terminus at the foot of
the rising foundations of the City. Amid the shouts of drivers
and the noise of engines, as silently as they had assembled
and travelled, the passengers collected their light luggage,
descended the steps to the stained concrete and dispersed
separately through different exits.

Outside, small boys touting for hotels or tours of the carpet
factory, shoe-shiners and pimps, besieged Chance until he was
joined by Marcovicz when, as suddenly as they had come,
they disappeared back into the buildings.

Chance took the lead, with the Jew, who was a pace or two
behind him, walking quickly but with an unvaried pace: the

dancing motion, the sudden springs and leaps of his usual gait absent. Chance too walked faster than was his habit and his head turned less frequently. Once, before they entered the hotel, he paused and looked upwards at the cloud-mass; but otherwise, perhaps intentionally, he gave no clue to his companion as to what he might have been thinking or feeling. In the hallway, ignoring the two porters, he halted and without looking directly at Marcovicz said:

'We'll eat here, if you don't mind.'

'Here? All this way to eat in a bloody pub?'

'I'm not feeling too well, Marcovicz. I don't particularly care where we eat so long as we eat soon.'

The older man relaxed his vigilance just perceptibly.

'Oh your stomach! How could I have forgotten? I was wondering why you were so quiet. If you'll forgive me; I don't think it's like you. I kept thinking "He's upset! Something has upset him; and on this of all days too." I thought—but let me get you something to eat immediately: some goat's milk, a plate of rice?'

'Thank you. I'd be grateful if you'd just go and order the food; something light for me; fish say or some boiled, not fried, rice. I'll join you in a few moments. I want to wash.'

'Of course I will, Doctor Chance.' He drew nearer. 'But what a shame when I wanted you only to be happy, to rejoice, to discuss everything with me frankly and openly as you always used to in the prison. I've been thinking about that argument of ours, the last one, remember? You go and wash and by the time you're back I'll have food on the table and wine.'

'No wine for me thank you, not at the moment.'

'No? Ah well! I'll order it, you might feel like it later.'

They parted and Chance washed sombrely. He scarcely noticed any of the details of his surroundings and was very absent-minded. He had hoped to find a machine in the cloak-room similar to those in English hotels where for the price of sixpence aspirins, laxatives and, specifically, indigestion pills could be extracted from a little steel drawer. He spent quite and jugs. As he got to his feet, white and silent, and started to run, he saw the doctor only ten yards from the Medina gateway, running fast; and springing forward into the roadway, rushed after him.

Within the maze Chance turned right and then left. He fled over the cobbles, threaded his way past the Arabs whose glances were never quite at him, doubled behind a cooking stall where yellow fish sizzled in olive oil and backed swiftly into a narrow passage: an inlet into a main duct of the Medina.

Behind him someone shouted, a word beginning with the cough of the Arab aspirate; but he ignored it and ran up some narrow steps into a snail-shell cul-de-sac terminating in an archway. He hesitated and saw behind him Marcovicz, smiling and dexterous, beginning the ascent of the steps.

'Go back!' he shouted, 'Go back, Marcovicz!' before he dived into the darkness where the living quarters met over his head and the senile in their rags lay drowsing on the dry stones.

There were six doorways: he chose the third on the left and swung it to behind him as he went on up a spiral of stairs to a room under the flat roof. A woman, young and unveiled, her mouth open, screamed as he crossed the floor and made for the unglazed window where foot-long tuba-shaped flowers hung downwards against the bleached sky.

He was through it in a moment, carried swiftly down the flexible branches to the main stem of the datura as though by a parachute. He dropped on to a short stone terrace and lay still only twelve feet above one of the narrow streets of the quarter.

In the opposite wall, a Mosque towered white against the sun. He heard the clatter of the wooden sandals as those leaving dropped them on the cobbles before stepping back into them; saw, through the doorway, old men cross-legged on the tiled floor absented in their prayers, and beneath him, the silent passing of the people who moved on as some time searching the walls for such a machine before he realised the unlikelihood of there being one, even before it occurred to him that in any case he had no English money with him. Apart from the recurrent empty disorder of his stomach which when pronounced always made it difficult for him to recollect himself, he was dismayed by the thickening consequences of his encounter with Marcovicz and disposed to resent his weakness in having allowed them to involve him so finally.

The memory of the interview in the café, the long arid bus ride, his dyspepsia, all combined to renew his sense of detachment from the events which pressed upon him and whose results he knew he could not now avoid.

Returning to the restaurant he ate slowly and abstemiously, only half listening to his companion's preliminary remarks. He waited until the worst of his physical discomforts had subsided before giving his full attention to the underlying meaning of the other's words.

Marcovicz ate rapidly and without discrimination. He filled and refilled his glass from the wine bottle, crunched up whole shells and their contained fish, peppers, chillies, gherkins and flesh fragments in his Spanish rice and talked violently. He ate as a man eats before a journey or a battle but without any self-preoccupation. Throughout the meal he kept his eyes fixed on the younger man's head and face, never allowing his gaze to fall to the level of the table, the plates and the glasses.

Fragments of rice, wine-stains, a few thin shells and a debris of bread-slices accumulated round his plate. His face grew pale and on his neck the dusky veins stood out like worms.

'And you sat there, Doctor Chance, like a Quaker visitor in the Prison Hospital—no, the surgery it was—because if you remember, I had caught you there, planned it for three days in advance to get you alone because official interviews I do not like. Take the judge off his throne, I say! The prisoner from the dock and the doctor from behind his desk and show me a man. I can deal with a man, I'm not afraid of a man but I can't deal with an official. I dislike officials because they are not men, they are only one side of a man; and the day I got the gun I'd had smuggled into the Hamburg nick and stuck it up against the grey belly of that German screw, the *gäfängniswärter*, with buttons mark you, and pulled the trigger three times I was not putting an end to a man, I was simply liberating an official, releasing something. Aha, you smile at that, don't you?'

'No, Marcovicz.'

'But you do! And I know what you're thinking. You're thinking what you thought that day, the day I've been talking about, when I caught you with your sleeves rolled up in the hospital. You remember that, don't you, what you said to me?'

'I think so.'

He smiled. 'You think so? *I* remember it very well.'

'Has it worried you?'

'Not worried, Doctor Chance, not worried. It's come back to me a few times as things will when a man questions himself and his life story, the meaning of it all.' He laid both his square hands on the table like the paws of a lion and thrust his head forward. 'He lived! That was your point, the screw lived! A hole never opened up in his uniform, he never fell! *He* laughed at me, standing there when they'd got the cuffs on me and it was safe to laugh. Instead of lying down and dying he stood up straight and laughed because of a fault in the revolver. He laughed and he lived.'

'Yes, I believe that was so.'

'Those two both lived, didn't they?'

'Did they? I forget.'

'You know they did. That was your point, that was what you said to me that day. You said, "It is quite simple! Either, Marcovicz, you did not mean to kill; or else, you were not *meant* to kill," and then you said, "And after thinking it all over, *I* believe you never meant to kill." '

'That was my opinion,' Chance agreed.

'And that is where we disagreed, where we still disagree.

You said I had no right to kill and I said that I had a right
to kill because I was as I was made and had lived the life
laid out for me. That's right, isn't it?'

'It is arguable,' said Chance. 'I mean, we could argue about
it, I think.'

'We won't argue now though, not now. I've had enough of
arguments. You said, Doctor Chance, that I had no right to
kill, not the girl who would have betrayed me, not the screw,
the *wärter,* and not——'

He paused, suddenly dropping his knife and fork on to his
empty plate.

Chance raised his head.

'Not whom, Marcovicz?'

'Not the old woman.'

'Which woman?'

'The last one, a year or two before the War when I was a
steward on the *Dusseldorf*; an old woman, old and ill. You
wouldn't remember much about her. You can forget her; she's
not important.'

'I never read your case-notes very fully, I'm afraid. Perhaps you could refresh my memory?'

Marcovicz was dull. 'I was in the stateroom. I'd nearly
finished. Then, just as——' he faltered.

'Just as what?'

'There was an interruption; I forget what. But——'

'An interruption?'

'It's not important; it proves nothing one way or another.
They never got me that time. I was caught for an entirely
different job six months later but escaped to Scotland where
they soon had me for burglary and traced my record through
Interpol. That was the injustice of it, I was sentenced on my
past and not on my future. But for that I'd have been given
shorter sentences every time I was caught. As it was, every
Scottish judge——'

Chance interrupted casually, 'This woman lived, then? I
mean, she was saved was she, as the others were saved?'

'No, she died, Doctor Chance.' Marcovicz picked up his

glass and drank from it. 'She was the only one who did die—
and she died before the pillow had touched her face. I know
that because there was a post-mortem and they found it was
her heart, they put it down to bad weather on the crossing.
There was no proof I'd so much as touched her or her pillow.
We put it back just as it was.'

'We? Was someone with you?'

'I was alone, I tell you. I put it back under her head. When
they caught me I was half-way down number three deck on
a thick carpet and I think I was laughing because it must have
been about then that I first saw that I was right, that I'd
made my challenge and been taken up on it. Each time except
the last, I'd failed; the last time it had been done for me.'

'I see.'

'You don't see, Doctor Chance! You think I never meant
to kill. I tell you I did. You say, "You are not exceptional."
You falsify me, you try to turn me into a small man with a
loud mouth, a little criminal who shakes behind a knife or a
gun and dodges at the last moment. But I say that I am
Marcovicz, and that if I have not killed it is because I am an
instrument of God and that he will not let me do wrong. We
disagreed all along and I told you that one day I might have
to prove it to you, show you that I could kill and I would
kill. Do you remember that?'

'Yes I do.'

'That was why you called me a very vain man, wasn't it?
You always called me that afterwards and I would say, "No,
I am a very humble man because I trust God even with a gun
or a knife." '

Chance pushed away his plate and stood up.

'Is that all you wanted to say?'

'No, it isn't,' he remained seated. 'I wanted to ask you
something; I wanted to ask you if you'd changed your mind?
It's very important for me to know. Do you believe that if I
tried to kill again I would intend it, Doctor Chance?'

'I believe, Marcovicz, that *you* would believe that you intended it.'

D

The older man sat very still. 'That is your last word? You do not believe that I am dangerous?'

'I think that you are very dangerous but not because of your fancied intention; only because of what might happen if you were misunderstood, if someone, *not* God, took you at your own valuation of yourself, that then indeed you might kill again. Accidentally.'

A waiter approached and Chance took the bill and paid it. He stood there for a few moments looking down at the close-curled, greying hair of the other's head.

'I think I'm going to take a walk through the Town,' he said at length.

Marcovicz rose slowly.

'With me,' he stated, smiling.

'No, alone.'

'It might be dangerous for you to go alone. You may have wrong ideas about things and you say that wrong ideas can lead to trouble.'

'They can indeed.'

'That was what you told Magda. You said she might be in danger.'

Marcovicz slid his arm through the crook of the Doctor's and walked beside him springily. Linked thus they made their way out through the foyer and through the open entrance into the street. They turned right towards the tall white wall of the Medina.

'You think it is very dangerous to be wrong in one's ideas about God,' he repeated. 'Oh! Doctor Chance you take God very seriously, don't you?'

'I hope so.'

'So do I, so does Magda. Oh yes I know Magda does.'

'I don't think so,' said Chance.

'But she does,' went on the Jew with a shout of laughter. 'She trusts God with what she calls her sins. Very patient she says He is and that, like a true lover, He can afford to wait. She trusts me too; God and Marcovicz! That's good, isn't it?'

They were walking along beside the wall of the Medina

towards the Moorish archway which gave entrance to the central square of the Arab quarter. A blue jasmine was in flower and a tall plant with flowers like giant cockscombs. There were orange and melon stalls in the roadway and beyond the arch they could see the Public Gardens where the Arabs in brown and white sat drinking glass after glass of mint tea.

They passed under and through the hot shadow of the archway and on towards the railings enclosing the neatly laid beds of the Public Gardens.

Hundreds of small tables were green as aquariums with empty glasses and their contained stalks of mint; flowers burned in the red soil, and in the centre of the square a Victorian bandstand sheltered tiny children crawling and wailing round the feet of their suckling mothers.

'The difference,' he went on, 'is that *I* can't afford to wait, Doctor Chance, and that's why I was so glad when I saw you. You were like an answer to a prayer, our prayer, mine and Magda's. You'll shorten everything, make it easier; you *could.*'

'Could I?'

They had sat down at an empty table. Beside them, on the stone sill into which the railings were set, the Arabs, Riffis, and Berbers, squatted smoking their pipes of *kief,* talking briefly, disquietingly unobserved.

'Oh yes, you could if you chose to—or you could end it all! Instead of making it easier for me, you could tell her everything. You could say, "Marcovicz, a financier? A man of substance, a merchant banker who had bad luck, a widower, a divorced man? A bachelor who devoted his life to making money and who kept women, exclusive mistresses, in three capitals until the Crash came? Why! Marcovicz is none of these things! *I'll* tell you about *him*. Marcovicz is——" '

Chance was tranquil, the sudden stillness of disquiet.

'But which of these things is true, Marcovicz? You can't have told her that you're both a financier and a banker, a bachelor and a widower.'

'What does it matter, what I've told her? I might have been any of them, all of them, how is she to know what pattern my life has formed?'

'I agree, Marcovicz; but on the other hand I would like to know exactly what you have told her.'

As he spoke Chance was looking at the entrance to the Medina in the southern wall of the square. Through it, the whitewashed walls of shops and dwellings which flanked the narrow gullies looked cool, the white burnouses of the distant women dyed with shadows as pale as smoke. The archway was seventy yards away, he thought, perhaps fifty.

Across the table Marcovicz took his hand and held it compulsively.

'I have told her all of it,' he said, 'or, if you like, none of it. I've left it in her keeping; not the facts, just the ideas for her to make what she likes of. From what I have told her, she could believe any of the things I've outlined.'

'And *my* life, Marcovicz? What have you told her of my life?'

'Nothing! A hundred things! Just the possibilities, again. That you are a specialist, a great nerve doctor, a brain surgeon; a deeply religious man, a medical missionary whose wife died in Nigeria of blackwater fever, vowed from now on to celibacy. I've suggested that you are a rich eccentric, a philanthropist, a doctor who was struck off the Register for having an affair with a patient in Chelsea.'

Chance smiled. 'You are very inventive.'

'I have had to be. A man has got to be like God, he has to use his mind all the time. You know that yourself. A man has to make what he can of the facts. He must never stop.' His grip on Chance's hand tightened. 'Why if she were to know! If you were to say! If you were to tell Magda—you'd be altering the facts wouldn't you?'

'I don't understand.'

'The facts of the future, Doctor Chance. Instead of the bar, happiness, prosperity and a beautiful wife I should have—

nothing? If you were to tell her, I should become, I should be——'

'Tell her what?'

'Only the things that have so far happened and which could become untrue even at this moment. That you were nothing more than a prison doctor in Scotland, a gaol-quack, and that I was a recidivist, a so-called paranoid who tried to strangle a Berlin *nûtte* and shoot a prison officer. You'd be tampering with the future. How are we to know that you *won't* be a medical missionary, a famous man? that I won't make a fortune, get hold of money, of thousands of dollars, in just six weeks' time? It might all be true, all of it. In a few months' time, in a few weeks or even days, we might find that it was true, mightn't we?'

'Yes, Marcovicz.'

'There's only one man who could stop it,' said the other, very taken with his elaboration, '*you,* Doctor Chance! And I might lose her—lose her for ever.'

Abandoning Chance's hand he turned up his palms and gazed down at them as they lay loosely before him on the table; only his knitted forehead, upper eyelids and their brows were visible to the doctor who sat watching. After a moment the latter turned his head and once again glanced quickly sideways at the dark blue entrance to the Medina. Marcovicz looked up too, his gaze momentarily full on the Doctor's face; then his mouth opened and released the great wilderness of his laughter.

'Oh!' he shouted with dry eyes. 'Ah! That argument we had, that last argument about whether or not I had ever intended to kill my fellow man, and how I said to you that one day I might prove it to you—no!—that I *would* prove it to you. Oh it's good! it's very good! it's funny.' He jumped to his feet. 'Supposing I did? Supposing I did prove it to you?'

The doctor watched him intently but said nothing; and the other stood there very flat on his heels against a gently moving background of Mohammedans.

'Supposing I proved it by killing *you,* Doctor Chance?'

He held out his hands a little way in front of him, and round his neck the muscles began to swell, the enlargement spreading downwards slowly to the thickness of the shoulders and the great pectorals of the chest, to the biceps and the forearms, until even the cushions in the palms of the hands began to stand out round their hollows. He took a pace forward towards the younger man who sat there for these last instants watching him easily and with apparent laxity until with great suddenness he too got to his feet, and said:

'I don't think it will be necessary, Marcovicz.'

'Not necessary?'

'No. We must learn to accept the facts as they have been if we are to do them honour as they might be.'

'You mean that you are going to tell her? That you are going to give Magda the facts? That you are going to warn her?'

'Look, Marcovicz!' Placing his hands on the table between them, the Doctor leaned across it. 'Get us some coffee and I'll try to explain. We will talk it all over as we did in the old days—now get it quickly.'

'You will wait? You will not move from where you are? You will not run back or say a word to her before we have talked, before this evening?' The crippled man too leaned forward, his mouth smiling, his eyes half-closed by speculation as he looked into the Doctor's face. 'Let us go together,' he said at last, 'across there, to that little Arab café. Let us go arm in arm, like brothers, as we said we would.'

'No, Marcovicz.'

'Here! I'll take your hand, Doctor Chance: give me your hand.'

The Doctor took the table in both hands and threw it over. The sharp edge caught the German on the shins and he fell to the ground among the fragments of splintering tumblers

though nothing had happened. But above him the girl was leaning out of the window: he saw her eyes black with hostility searching him out through the medley of leaves and flowers.

He got up and lowered himself over the coping, clung on until the last moment then let himself fall into the open street-way. An old Arab, sandals in hand, glanced at him and then over his head at the leaning girl. She shouted to him but he was deaf; and Chance, dusting himself free of whitewash, walked swiftly away, leaving them to their surprise.

He knew his direction; had seen the brightness of the Public Gardens from the high window; but he was feeling sick. He saw a shop selling pottery: water-jars, amphoras for oil, and earthenware bowls. With one hand he grasped one, with the other he held out a hundred-peseta note to the vendor. Unable to speak, he pushed past the man into the darkness of the shop and squatted down on the floor beside a thin cat and a tiny child and vomited in the bowl.

The child and the man watched him silently until he had finished, and then the child started to laugh. Chance picked up the bowl.

'I'm very sorry,' pointing to his stomach, 'very sorry.'

The man indicated a bench and took the bowl from him. 'Ciento,' he said, 'ciento peset'.'

His handkerchief to his mouth, Chance expostulated.

'Give me back my change.'

The man stood to one side clearing the exit into the street. 'Go,' he said. '*You*—Go.'

Chance got up, swaying, and the child's laughter was re-doubled.

'Salaam ou ali khum,' said Chance.

The arab smiled distantly at the tourist and touched his shoulder.

'Ou ali khum salaam,' he said.

Chance walked out into the street and beyond it into the central square. He found an Espresso bar and drank a glass of goat's milk very slowly. Beside him was a man with yellow hair. He was wearing an open-necked shirt, grey flannel trousers and a glittering Swiss wrist-watch.

'Español?' he asked.

'No, I am English.'

'From England. I am Danish but I have been in London.'

He had a pleasant smile. It reminded Chance of a stock-broker he had once looked after, a star prisoner.

'Have some coffee with me?'

'Thank you. I like very much to drink coffee.'

'Good! So do I, but unfortunately——'

'You are—sick?'

'Yes. My stomach. It's very easily upset. Just now I was very sick. Absurd really! But I had to buy something to be sick into and then I didn't know what to do with it.'

'No?'

'I gave it back to the shopkeeper.'

'Yes?'

He was very solemn this man. About thirty-two, perhaps even younger; but lined and hungry-looking; a knockabout of some sort, not sure what he was doing nor what he wanted.

'You do not look well,' he said reflectively. 'No you do not.'

'I'm all right really,' said Chance. 'At least I shall be in a few minutes. I think I'll have a very weak coffee with you.'

'That is good.'

They sat and drank it in silence and the younger man made many small ragged movements.

'You are on holiday?'

'Yes, just a holiday.'

'It is very late for a holiday: everyone has gone home. The hotels are empty. You are from the Zone?'

'Yes.'

'You like it?'

'Yes, fairly well. Do you live there?'

'Yes I am in business. I buy cork for an American firm.'

'I see.' Chance offered him a cigarette. 'Have you been very long in the Zone?'

'Long enough,' said the man. 'You must forgive me but I have soon to go. My car broke down and I wait here while they mend it; but now it must be ready.'

'And then you are going back to the Zone?'

'Immediately.'

'You couldn't give me a lift could you? I have my passport of course. I would willingly pay for the petrol. You see I do not want to wait for the bus. My stomach——' as he spoke Chance produced his wallet. This man wanted money very badly; he would do a great deal for money, and the wallet was very full because Chance had cashed a large traveller's cheque only the day before.

The Dane smiled.

'Oh that is all right—er quite O.K.,' he said watching the wallet. 'As long as you have a passport.'

Chance was insistent. 'Please,' he said, 'take this, please do.' He opened the wallet to extract a note and his rosary fell out. It writhed on to the bar as though it were alive and he pocketed it quickly.

'Thank you,' said the Dane stiffly. 'But it is not necessary, not at all necessary. My name is Thaaren, you are——?'

'Chance, William Chance.'

'Pleased to meet you.' He extended his empty hand and they shook. 'And now we must go.'

The car was an old Ford V8 which Thaaren drove fast and initially in silence: but when, after crossing the Frontier, they had reached the outskirts of the Zone, the first white blocks of flats in the American section standing far behind the bay and the old town, he became quite voluble.

'These lands,' he said, waving at the vacant building lots, 'you see them?'

'Yes.'

'All to have been commercialised, many buildings, factories, warehouses, much capital: and now—nothing. The town stops. It has ceased to move. The money has gone. Look! There are the roads they had built: many Arabs working day and night. There are the notices of the companies who had bought the land: they are two or three years old and they mean nothing—they are only names: the companies are spending their money in some other part of the world.'

'Why is that?'

'The peace! For a time all was well, the Zone was in a boom, you understand? A very good boom, and then there was Korea; it was very useful, it helped a great deal, but now it has run out and in the Zone the war has started.'

'You mean the riots?'

'Yes, yes, the first was upon March the 25th, 1955—a terrible date for the Zone; but apart from the riots it is the war of those who have no money against those who have. You should not carry so much about you just now in Zone, it will be taken from you, it will disappear.'

Chance nodded. 'You know the Zone well?'

'I married here in the Zone after the War: a Moorish girl. We have children; but you must remember that no one lives here—that is to say no one from Europe lives here unless they have to. It is not wise to stay very long here. How long are you staying?'

'Oh not very long.'

For the first time Thaaren smiled.

'One thing I see you already have learned,' he said, 'not to tell so much as you are asked. Yes?'

'Yes,' said Chance, adding, 'Perhaps you will tell *me* something?'

'If I know it, yes, I will.'

'Well, do you know most of the Europeans here?'

'Who *live* here, you mean?'

'Yes.'

'Certainly! If they have—settled. One cannot know such men or women who come because they are in trouble for a short time; but anyone who stays here long, who is in *money*, you understand, I will know him because I too am in money.' Thaaren was very serious; solemn.

'Then I wonder,' said Chance watching him, 'if you have ever heard of a man named Fraser?'

Thaaren drove very carefully, his light eyes calculating the width of the road and the intentions of an Arab on the pavement wafting incense from a swaying brazier.

'You know this man?' he asked.

'No,' said Chance, 'I was wondering if *you* did.'

'An Australian?'

'I don't know.'

'A fat man, very fat, whom you meet in The Botticelli Bar?'

'I don't know if he is fat,' Chance replied, 'and I have never been to The Botticelli Bar.'

'Then if you have never seen him, how do you know him?'

'I don't.'

Thaaren drew up outside the Samarra Restaurant. 'Perhaps you will get out here,' he said. 'It is very convenient, it is central; the food is good.'

'Er—certainly! Thank you very much.' Chance collected his things.

'Then you don't know him?'

'Who?' asked Thaaren.

'This man called Fraser.'

'I have never heard of him. In the Zone there are many people, they come, they go: one cannot know everybody.'

'No, of course not.'

'And even if a man could know everybody it is not wise perhaps to do so, you understand?'

'Yes, I think so.'

'If I am you I am being careful *not* to know everybody; if I am staying only a short time. Otherwise I might find I stay too long. That can happen, you see?'

'Yes.' Chance shook his hand through the open window.

'You can find your way all right now, Mr. Chance?'

'Yes thank you.'

'To the Hotel de la Gare you can go down the steps past the Church of St. Francis.'

'And The Botticelli Bar?' asked Chance.

'You go there?'

'Yes, later. I have to meet someone.'

'You must ask someone else,' said Thaaren. 'It is not easy to reach from here; it would take me much time to explain how you must go.' He produced something from his pocket, the money given to him by Chance.

'I think you had better take this back.'

'Certainly not! It was most kind of you, please keep it.'

The notes fluttered on to the pavement as the car moved forward.

'It was nothing—a favour,' called Thaaren. 'You paid me nothing, you remember, nothing.'

Jostled by the Arabs, stock-still on the pavement, Chance watched after him as the car accelerated fast and turned off towards the Old Town. He stooped to pick up the two notes; but they had already gone, an earnest of the remote, abiding, goodness of Allah who was not begotten and did not beget. It would have been useless to question anybody even if he had known the language; and so he went back to the Hotel de la Gare to change.

He ran down the long corridor of the open steps to the Rue d'Espagnole and hurried in through the front entrance of the hotel to find Mademoiselle looking pretty again: her hair sleeked into a tiny bun, a few tendrils escaping at opportune places as she sat there behind the bar watching the waiter laying the tables.

'Ah ha!' Chance said. 'Tonight it is business again?'

'Every night,' she said curtly; and then interrogatively, 'Monsieur Chance?'

'Yes?'

'Someone has called for you, a gentleman.'

'Oh. What was his name?'

'No name, monsieur. He said you would know.'

'But I don't.' He took the key of his room from her hand. 'What did he look like?'

'Oh,' she said, *'Homme fort, un boiteux.'*

'A cripple! *Impossible.*'

'*Mais non, c'est vrai.*'

'Now look,' he said. 'It just cannot be. I left that man in Shibam, in the Medina, you understand, and came back by car. Marcovicz cannot have got back before me.'

'Marcovicz?' she asked with her head on one side.

Chance's irritation led him into a naïve sarcasm. 'You don't know him of course. Oh no. Marcovicz probably knows Mademoiselle Lucie—but intimately! All about her complete genealogical history, taste in clothes, scent, lipstick and pesetas. But Mademoiselle Lucie has never even seen him, his name is new to her. She is bewildered, *embourbée,* she has never heard of this Marcovicz.'

'Ah, Monsieur,' disclaiming with both her hands. '*Vous-parlez trop vite. Qu'est-ce que vous-avez dit?*'

'Oh never mind,' he said. 'I'm getting sick of this. Lies, lies and lies.'

'*Comment?*'

But he ignored her and ran up to change in his darkened room. He drew back the curtains, threw open the shutters and the fly blinds, and looked out into the yard. It was empty; but Aminah's fire in the washhouse still smoked, and over the wall he could see the steps leading up past the Church of St. Francis to the top of the old town. The cats were coming out on their evening hunt for garbage. They snaked out of the Arab Cemetery through holes in the crumbling walls and sections of leaning railing, emaciated, shadowy, wary, determined to stave off death for another night, to sleep safe through another day. Half-way up the steps, a tiny figure in brown knickerbockers watched them; an arab boy sharp as the cats. From the tower of the church a bell struck slowly. Benediction? the Angelus? Chance didn't know; but he crossed himself just the same. No harm. No harm either in transferring most of his money to a space between the wash-basin and the wardrobe under the linoleum: the passport too, and some letters.

He shaved for the second time that day and took two pills

to stave off pain, then wondered about Magda; whether she would manage to keep the appointment or not.

When he was ready he went out by the side door and started the ascent of the steps slowly. A partnership had been established at the bottom to ply the evening trade: a stove in a biscuit tin, one Arab skewering diced meat from a white bowl the other fanning the charcoal. There were fat boat-shaped rolls of bread on a piece of newspaper—the *Zonal Gazette* he noticed.

He was very hungry: not hungry, he decided, but empty: like a void receptacle. He bought a roll. The cook sliced it with a sharp knife and filled it with shazlic rolled in spice, ten pesetas.

At his approach the cats scattered into the disused cemetery: a sea of grasses, bamboos, wild jasmines and cactus where, on the undulations of old graves, the cats copulated, fought, and died of their diseases.

Surreptitiously he opened his roll and extracted a square of meat; he lobbed it in through the railings. For a moment there was silence, and then the vegetation began to shake, stirred up by the current of the cats moving in from all directions. He heard them snarling and coughing as they fought for it out of sight in their miniature ocean. He wished that he could differentiate: the one needing least might get most by being strongest; but these were Mahommedan cats and Allah did not differentiate.

He was about to throw in the remainder of his meat when he was hailed.

'Mister! Mister! I American, speak good Oxford. Hungry.'

The boy he had noticed earlier was racing down the steps towards him, one hand extended. Chance waited.

'You want it?' he asked.

'Sure,' said the boy. 'I've not eat two days, buddy. I sure hungry.'

'No,' said Chance, 'it is for the cats. Allah directs me to give it to the cats. All of it.'

The boy's teeth gleamed.

'You give to me?'

'No.' Chance pointed to the sky. 'Allah wants it for the cats.' He threw the contained meat high over the railings and they heard it fall like manna into the still surface of the cemetery. 'See?'

The boy looked up at him then into the darkness through the railings. He tried to shrug but he was still bewildered.

'You not American?'

'No.'

'English?'

'No.'

'You German? From Germany? Yes. I work for the Heinies very good pals. He have ship in Bay and give me photograph here and writing.' He brought a dirty envelope from the bodice of his knickerbockers.

'No,' said Chance. 'Not German.'

'Where you from?'

Chance said nothing. He tore off a piece of the roll and ate it, resuming his slow progress up the steps.

'Where you go?'

'Oh go away.'

'You tell me and I take you,' said the boy flapping along beside him on his naked feet.

They went on like that to the very top. Chance silent, munching away at the dry bread, the boy insistent, thoroughly roused and questing: searching round him like a dog at a covert, determined to find a way in.

Chance leaned against the wall of the church to get his breath back. Below him, the hem of the town and its white apron of bay swayed gently in the light of the falling sun. He must get to the Botticelli Bar quickly and have a long drink and then something innocuous to eat; he had done too much today. Tomorrow he would rest all day.

'You give me pesetas, mein herr,' said the boy. 'I, Haleb, good friends with all Germans. I not know Allah. No. I Spanish.'

'Liar!'

'Two. Zwei. Duo pesetas, signor: then I clean your shoes. Yes?'

Chance extracted a five-peseta note.

'Allah directs me to give you cinque pesetas,' he said. 'Now, *go!*'

The boy pouched it quickly as a hamster, his eye on the open wallet.

'Where you go?' he asked. 'I take you. I wait and come home with you to la Gare and be there tomorrow to clean shoes for you.'

Chance closed his eyes and keeping his back to the church wall swivelled the boy round to face the steep fall of the steps.

'Please,' he said. 'I beg of you to go. Eat. Mangez— shashlik: down there.'

The boy sat down cross-legged on the top step.

'I wait,' he said simply. 'You go pray. I wait.'

'Oh all right,' said Chance. 'The Botticelli Bar. Take me there.'

The boy jumped to his feet. 'The Botticelli, sure I know where The Botticelli. You American, bud?'

'No.'

'American! Sure you're American,' said the boy. 'You go Botticelli, you American.'

He walked on ahead, his fists clenched and swinging at his sides, full of purpose as a cab that has been hired: busy, direct, rattling away to himself. At each intersection he paused and waited for Chance to come up to him and then he took his sleeve as though he were navigating a blind man round corners or across thoroughfares. They left the Old Town well behind and came into a European area of broad tree-lined streets with a frontage of grilled banks, restaurants, vast garages, and antique shops. The evening parade was starting: thousands of girls, young and undulant, in twos and threes, in pale dresses and cheap jewellery, foamed down the pavements like fish in a tide of froth and light. They were threaded through with dark knots of men, who drove against them like

E

war canoes, alert, savage; their eyes searching for the answering glance, the brief moment of advantage.

On the margins, sunk in the black abstractions of the cafés, older men sat and watched: uniformly large, stable and assured, drinking from tiny cups: strong tea and Espresso coffee.

At first there was not an Arab to be seen: the people were exclusively European: Greek, Spanish, Italian, Gibraltese, Serafino: the indigenous population of the white zone; but, as they passed towards the end of the avenue, the Amritzar Gardens, the Spanish Wall and the Sultan's Casbah crowning the top of the hill, the burnous again appeared. Short women, old, shrunken by the years and child-bearing, lumpy and ungraceful. The air changed, the smells of the Mediterranean shore giving place to the raw smell of Africa: the scent which made credible both the lion and the desert.

They turned off left and the street was quiet, emphasising the rustle of the parade still faintly heard, which ascended from the Avenue Grande into the startling sky.

Haleb stopped and waited.

'You not like girls?' he said.

'No,' said Chance.

The boy spat on to the pavement.

'Boys!' he stated. 'Yes?'

'No,' said Chance.

'You go Botticelli?'

'Yes.'

'You like Arab boys?'

'No.'

'I take you Black Cat.'

'No,' said Chance, 'The Botticelli.'

'Then you like boys?'

'No,' said Chance. 'Lead on!'

The boy was puzzling it out: he kept pace with Chance, no longer walking ahead and contriving by some means to suggest conspiracy and an air of the confidential.

'You like drink? Whisky?'

'Yes,' said Chance.

'When you drink *then* you like girls?'

'No.'

'Boys?'

'No.'

The boy shook his head: 'I your friend,' he said. 'You tell me why you go Botticelli.'

Chance was thinking about Marcovicz. He could have forestalled him, just, if he had had resources: a fast car taking him direct to the hotel from Shibam. But why go and announce himself in the Hotel de la Gare? Why give the show away? There could be only one reason: to frighten.

He had wanted to frighten him, to let him know that though he might move quickly, Marcovicz had it in his power to move even more quickly. Yes, that was it. It explained the theatricality of it all, the refusal to leave a name, the florid touch of the 'he will know', in Mademoiselle's message.

He had wanted to alarm and he had succeeded. It was a typical prison manœuvre. He would be determined to prevent and forestall the possibility of any second meeting between Chance and Magdalena. Complex as his fantasy was, absurd in so many respects, he had such conviction that given the essential time he would probably end by involving the girl emotionally. Once he had succeeded, his enormous vanity and guilt, his excessive scrupulousness, might combine, and he might kill her. She must certainly be warned. And if tonight Marcovicz had prevented her from keeping their appointment at The Botticelli he, Chance, would have to seek him out again in the hope ultimately of meeting the girl alone.

He had thought of going to the Rendezvous, but remembering the hostility and suspicion of its owners, had decided against it. A note delivered by the boy would be uncertain, a letter also uncertain and too late. In any event, he realised, he did not even know her surname. It would be wisest to go to The Botticelli with the object at least of finding out more about Fraser who was apparently an habitué of the place.

'Money,' said the boy. 'You go Botticelli talk money.'

Chance missed his step, he stumbled.

'Yes, of course, money.'

The boy was intuitive, he thought; he could be used. If Marcovicz was watching his movements, then it might be as well to employ the child to keep the ex-convict under observation. It would be disconcerting to find him awaiting his return to the de la Gare after so tiring a day.

The boy was awaiting some further response, watching his face intently. He did not know how to smile, but something crossed the eyes in the round unwinking face.

'I figure things out,' he said. 'Find out.'

'Yes,' said Chance, 'yes.'

'You not go Botticelli, no good I know,' he returned in one breath.

'Yes—now. Quickly! I must have a drink and find out.'

'No.' The boy's face had grown smaller in its obstinacy.

Chance took his hand and held it firmly.

'Which way do we go?' he asked again, 'please.'

The boy looked down at the pavement; his hand, sinuous till now, became limp and his shoulders fell.

'Here,' he said, 'here is Botticelli.'

Chance turned round. Cut into the wall were narrow steps, a pathway, and at the far end the bulk of a house rising from bare terraces. Only a little light was visible, a glow of profound orange hovering like pollen inside a porch crowned with flowers. Looking away from it Chance spoke to the boy with sudden intensity. 'You are my friend.'

'My friend, yes,' returned the boy. 'You buy me passport; only twenty pound! Tres mille pesetas, trois mille huit cent francs. I come Berlin with you. We two stay always together; I work and look for you, clean shoes in London, Paris.'

'Later, yes perhaps later. But now you must do something for me while I am in there,' Chance whispered. 'You find out things for me and then I will pay you.'

'Arabs not have passports but my mother give me to you and you come with me and pay money and we go together from the Zone.' Haleb spat. 'Malo! The goddam Zone no good. I leave for ever with my friend.'

'Yes, yes, but first——'

'I understand! I go and find out things you want to know. You tell me soon I will come here and wait.'

'Good.' Chance leaned down to him. 'Go back now to the de la Gare, let nobody see you, but you see everybody: all those who come to speak with Mademoiselle.'

'I watch! When anyone speak with Mam'selle Lucie, I will run in and clean shoes, I hear.'

'No, not everyone, only *one* man—a strong man who shouts and dances and laughs.' Chance swelled out his neck muscles and danced on the pavement.

'You know him?'

'Sure I know him. He's a bad man, he works for Mr. Fraser.'

'Then tomorrow we will meet at the spice stall in the little Socco and you will tell me——'

'Tonight, I tell you tonight, I sure wait for you all night until morning here by The Botticelli.

'But first go and eat,' insisted Chance. 'Take this money and eat well.'

'Tomorrow,' said the boy.

'No, tonight, now.' But he was gone; making no sound as he ran down to the turn on his naked feet; and it was a moment before Chance realised that the ten-peseta note which he had held in his right hand, had gone too.

Loneliness assailed him; it spread inwards isolating him from everything by which he had been surrounded so that briefly he seemed to be not anywhere at all. But before fear became quite conclusive, he moved; ascending the steps at a run and going straight through the lighted porch into the room beyond. There was no one behind the bar; he had the impression of a black frontal, of metals gleaming, flowers and tall candles. The sense of ceremony, latent but inevitable, drew him up standing as he sought for the cause of the impression.

He saw the tiled floor, the actual flowers at one end of the bar, and identified the vestiges of recent incense; but was still not reassured and continued to search the wall with its reredos of bottles, for some explanation of his impressions.

Someone stood up, and he turned: a man all in brown rose from a table in the far corner and stationed himself behind the centre of the bar. The floor must have been stepped or he would not have appeared to be quite so tall as he waited there facing Chance, giving no attention to the three interrupted people whom he had left seated at the table: not on the other hand giving direct attention to Chance; seeming only to wait reflexly in the way a vain woman may wait, lost in the attention she perpetually gives to herself.

Chance sat down on a fixed stool and lighted a cigarette. He did not smile.

'I believe you're American?' he said.

'You do?'

Behind him one of the three tittered, and conversation, quite inaudible, was resumed.

'I am English,' said Chance, 'a doctor.'

'That's nice.'

With delectation the man placed a glass on the counter, dropped ice cubes into it, a large measure of whisky, a little soda, and stirred it with a slender spoon. He raised and drank half of it carefully, a ring on his little finger shining like his pale brown eyes.

'I wondered,' said Chance, 'if you served food here?'

'We do just that.'

'A little fish, for instance?'

'That might take time,' he drawled. 'That might take all of fifteen minutes.'

'Of course,' said Chance.

'Of course?'

'I only meant it would allow me time to enjoy a drink: a long one, say a whisky and soda, with ice, like your own.'

The man smiled. 'Sure, I did that nicely.'

'Salesmanship,' said Chance. 'How much is a large whisky?'

'That depends. I charge my friends double; but you're not a friend so you'll pay treble.'

'An expensive place!' said Chance. 'I was warned.'

'Is that so?'

'Yes.'

'About what? That's to say, *who* warned you?'

'A man named Marcovicz. As a matter of fact I'm supposed to be meeting a girl friend of his here. She hasn't turned up, I suppose?'

'I wouldn't know,' said the man, 'I don't know any men named Marcovicz—and that'll be just two hundred pesetas for your Scotch.'

'You were serious? About the treble charge?'

'Sure!' He took the notes and slid them into a flat wallet. 'I told you: The Botticelli is expensive: that's the way we keep it exclusive.'

'To what?' asked Chance. 'Or should I say *from* what?'

'I don't get you.'

'I wondered whom you excluded, or included; that's all.'

'Well,' said the man. 'We go for introductions—on the whole.'

'In that case, my name is Chance, William Chance.'

'Call me Heber,' said the man. 'How would you like espadon, Chance? It's rather exclusive, it doesn't grow other places.'

'Is that some kind of fish?'

'What else?'

'Thanks—Heber.'

Heber moved over to the left and hissed: an Arab boy, pomaded and very sleek, took the order, glanced at Chance and then disappeared into the kitchen again.

'Staying long?' asked Heber.

'That depends.' He looked into his glass.

'You know, I don't think I care for you, Chance!' he said. 'You don't look well.'

'I'm not.'

'You look kind of—eaten up.'

'I am,' said Chance. His eyes traversed the wall at the back of the bar and noted a small crucifix hanging near the base of the canopy. 'I suffer from a variety of affections.'

'In which case,' said Heber, 'you'd better be on your way: we've just gotten over the gastro-enteritis hereabouts, but it's never too early for the winter epidemic of virus pneumonia.'

Chance eyed him: the brightness of his hostility: the set of the brown cloth tie beneath the doughboy complexion, the lazy mouth, the brown stone ring on the manicured finger.

'I said "*affections*" not *in*fections.'

'So you're screwy too?'

'Everyone told me,' said Chance, 'that I ought not to come here.'

'They were dead right.'

'So perhaps after all, I think I may leave you.' Chance got down from the stool.

'So soon!'

'Yes.'

'And your fish?'

'I will pay for that.'

'Now, that is polite, Chance! and it will cost you just 400——' he broke off: his face fell into a smile as his voice rose into the high tone of badinage. 'Oh, Christ! it's Columb! and Hello, Anna! As I was saying, Chance, just 400 pesetas and mind the step——' His attention was still for the new arrivals. 'Come on in, you sweet things, and tell your lonely Heber all of the news.'

'I've changed my mind,' said Chance, sitting down again, 'I'll have my fish if you've no objection.'

He swivelled around on his stool to see them both: a short man wearing a grey silk tuxedo, with much forehead below curling hair, and a woman or girl, with thick amber hair and a face as white as a mushroom.

'I do mind,' said Heber with his easy smile, 'but it's your fish.'

The new American saw nobody: he was talking elliptically and without conviction. He propelled himself to an empty stool adjacent to Chance, ordered drinks by gesture, marshalled the girl by invisible reins and transfixed the bar-owner with unseeing eyes all through a blurr of gossip.

'But they wouldn't have been in yet, they only dropped over by plane this evening and called us up to say they met Humphrey in London yesterday. When somebody tells Humphrey what's in the *Gazette,* and somebody *will,* Humphrey's going to be awfully hurt. Those two skunks know it would be libel anywhere else, but what can Humphrey do?'

'What'd they print, Columb?'

'I don't know. Say, Anna! What did they write about Humphrey?'

'I know they said he'd never make London via Spain if Franco's police quizzed his passport,' said the girl from Columb's left. She was standing quite still in an off-white dress; very composed, deep-voiced.

Her escort emptied his glass gazing blankly over it at Heber. 'Say, what's happened to Norton, Heber? Monday's his night with us but he never got along for the game. Is he sick or window-dressing at the shop?'

'This is Sunday, Columb,' said Heber with a half-smile at the girl, 'and Norton's not sick, he's just suicidal. Shall I give him Scotch again, darling?'

She nodded. 'Poor Norton,' she said deeply, 'is it his liver, Heber?'

'Norton hasn't got a liver, he cremated it five years ago. Norton just gets depressed.'

They half-laughed and the man named Columb went on, 'But he'll make the party on Tuesday: Zoe and Robin want us to have drinks with them down at your place and go on to the Scheherazade afterwards, so we'll be along if that's all right with you?'

'Thanks a lot for telling me. I like to know who I'm having and what I'm going to do,' said Heber.

'Poor Norton,' the girl repeated into her reflection on the counter, 'he does just hate to be missed out of things. He gets so suspicious.'

'Anna darling,' interrupted Heber, 'do you want these drinks adding to the I.O.U. or are we paying tonight?'

'Do that, Heber,' she acquiesced.

Columb looked up, 'Pay for them.'

'But darling, we can't——'

'For Christ's sake, Anna,' his head lurched on its short neck, the silvery eyes swayed round and met those of Chance, 'I saw George,' he said still with his gaze on Chance, 'do you understand, *I saw George!* so pay it—all of it.'

'Well, why didn't you say, Columb?' she said, opening her white bag.

He ignored her. 'Heber, who's this thin man with the Donatello face?'

'I wouldn't know, Columb. We didn't get introduced and anyway he wen' out five minutes ago unless he changed his mind. *E*xcuse me! He must have changed his mind, he's still here.'

'Well, who is he? I kind of like his face.'

'He's sick, Columb! He's a Doctor Chance, but he's sick and I don't like sick doctors or pregnant women, they upset me.'

'Pregnancy and illness,' said Chance hesitantly, 'there *is* a connection somewhere.'

'He's nuts, too,' said Heber, 'I forgot to mention it.'

'Look! I want you to meet my wife.' Columb raised his voice, 'Anna, come over and meet the doctor.'

'Anna,' said Heber sideways, 'is the sort of girl that everyone calls "darling"—especially women.'

'Oh, Heber!'

'Not like that, Anna,' said her husband, 'shake hands, I want you to like him. He's sick, too—we're both sick.'

But she was unmoved, intensely private; she was apparently interested only in Heber and they went over to a table, talking.

Columb's glass rose to his lips, 'What do you mean about pregnancy and illness, Doctor? You shouldn't say things like that in bars.'

'Why not?'

'It's conversation, that's why.' He banged his glass down. 'In bars we don't converse—we talk.'

'I'm sorry.'

'What d'you mean then? There's no connection.'

'I think there could be,' said Chance. 'Illness and pregnancy are—productive, they refine—a sort of innocence may appear.'

'It depends,' suggested the American.

They were silent. A little Arab crept in, he carried a one-stringed instrument, he squinted and smiled, he bobbed at them diffidently and the girl called out, 'Columb, he's come back. Oh, isn't he cute? Play for us Hasan. Play for us!'

Her husband said, 'My name is MacGrady by the way, and I'm going to tell you about things, Doctor.'

'I shouldn't,' said Chance, 'not now.'

'You're not a doctor, Chance; you're a Catholic aren't you?'

'What makes you think so?'

'Anna whispered she thought she saw you at Mass this morning in the Franciscan Church.'

'Yes, she must have done.'

'Well, for God's sake listen to me, then, I'm dying.'

'I suppose we all are.'

'But not fast, I'm dying fast, I've got cancer.'

The Arab started to play; a small whispering tune of perhaps twenty or thirty phrases; in the background the girl called softly, 'Oh, isn't he sweet, Heber! Say, there are times when I don't think I could ever leave the Zone. Where else could this happen? a little man walking in—play some more, Hasan, play for us.'

She threw him pesetas and the Arab bobbed and bowed afresh then looked down at his silent instrument as though consulting it. He played again, repeating the tune three times, each time a little faster.

'That's enough,' said Heber, 'skeeter, vamoose.'

'*Ghadan,*' said the Arab, '*Ghadan.*'

'Yes, tomorrow, Hasan.'

'They found it in Madrid,' the American was saying. 'I went there to a clinic and I told them and they said, "It seems as though you have got yourself a growth, Señor MacGrady. We shall have to X-ray your lungs." Next day I went along and they X-rayed me in a dark room. They laid me on a table and took skiagrams and then gave me a cup of black coffee and a cigarette while they developed the pictures. I sat around in a white dressing-gown and they came in grinning——'

'*Look!*' shouted Heber to the Arab. 'Get out! We don't want you. All finished. Buzz!'

'*Ghadan,*' said the Arab bowing himself out, smiling and squinting.

'—the doctors came back happy—they're Spanish Catholics, of course, and they just love death—they patted me on the back and shook my hands. "Señor MacGrady!" they said, "we were right! You have got a growth in the mediastinum. See, it is here on the films. You are going to die——" ' MacGrady broke off, 'What are you drinking, Chance? Heber, we want a couple of Scotch.'

'I am talking to Anna, Columb. It's not important because I just love talking to Anna about anything.' Heber's voice became femininely emphatic. 'So it's *so* important.'

'Oh, get us all a drink, Heber darling,' she said.

Beside Chance, her husband glowered. 'Anna, I want you.'

'Now, don't get sulky, Columb! You go on talking to your new doctor man.'

'Is he still here?' Heber swung into the bar and filled the

glasses. 'He takes some discouraging; he seems to like being disliked.'

'I find it painful,' said Chance.

'A masochist, Anna! This doctor guy's a masochist. He likes pain so he stays for it.'

'The doctor's a Catholic, Heber,' put in MacGrady.

'No difference.'

'Oh no, Heber.' The girl looked at Chance directly for the first time. He saw that she had large eyes encircled by clean black creases at the margins of the full eyelids. Large as the eyes were, violet-coloured, very slightly oblique, they lacked depth as though some third invisible eyelid, a gauze, were permanently in place behind them.

'You see, Doctor, Columb is hoping to convert Heber who's just teetering on the edge. He's already got a crucifix behind the bar.'

'An' underneath I got the Koran, so what!'

'He can't make up his mind,' she said. 'Can you, Heber darling?'

'I don' have a mind when you're about, Anna—I'm all body.'

She did not smile but they sat down together again: the girl glittering and remote, Heber holding her white-as-marble arm loosely in his lap.

'He's homosexual,' muttered MacGrady, 'that's why I don't worry, Chance.'

'Of course not.'

'Is it that obvious?'

'I have always noticed that they love women,' Chance replied, 'I mean, to be near them.'

'Yeah!' MacGrady was momentarily distracted. 'Now what was I saying?'

'You were talking about your health.'

'I know that, Chance, I don't forget my health, I can't afford to. Look! let's get out of here, I want to talk to you. You're the man I've been expecting. Anna! this man was *sent,* do you understand? He's going to help us.'

'Yes, Columb,' she said, 'go on, Heber, tell me more about Norton.'

'Does your wife know?' asked Chance.

'Of course she knows: that's what I want to talk to you about.' He lowered his voice, 'She's all I worry about, there's eighteen years between us, Chance. I've got money in America, I've got 120,000 dollars in the States and a heap more to come; but right now I live on the interest, and it's tight. There are difficulties in getting it through and it won't stretch. That's why I live here with Anna in the Zone, where it's cheap. But I want to get out, Chance, I want to get out.'

Heber moved over. 'When he starts on the Church Sorrowful,' he said to Chance, 'just let us know, will you? Then we'll call a taxi and we can all get along to bed.'

Chance smiled.

'In the meantime,' Heber went on, 'have another drink; but don't mutter! We don't like people to mutter in The Botticelli. We like to know what goes on!'

'Doctor,' said MacGrady, 'you can come with us. Where are you staying?'

'At the de la Gare.'

'Christ!' said Heber. 'D'you hear that, Anna? The Doctor *was* staying at the de la Gare but he's now moving in on the flat. You've got yourself a guest, Anna.'

'No,' said Chance, 'it's very kind of you but they expect me back.'

'I'm sure they do. Isn't that swell for the Doctor, Anna? Someone expects him back.'

He sloped back to her, alert and vindictive, fondling the same hand cruelly.

'If you don't come,' began MacGrady. He produced a handkerchief. 'That's not alcohol, Chance, that's blood.'

Chance looked at it.

'I didn't see,' he said. 'Is it from your lungs or from your stomach?'

'I told you—my lungs. What's the matter with you? Are you drunk, or aren't you a doctor at all?'

'At last the jackpot question,' put in Heber. 'The question *I* would have asked an hour ago.'

Chance ignored him. 'I'm not drunk. I *am* a doctor.'

'Well, then, you're coming tonight?' MacGrady insisted.

'No, not tonight.'

'God rot your immortal soul,' said MacGrady. 'Who is this man? Who are you? Tell me someone before I get mad . . . Look, I'm dying and you're a Catholic and a doctor and I ask you to come to my flat and you refuse.' He got off the stool and, shouting incoherently, started to wrench at it. 'We've prayed at High Mass and we've said the Rosary— there's your own bedroom, your own bathroom. I'm bringing up more blood every day. There's Anna, and you're a Catholic and you won't come. Chance, I hate your guts and you're in mortal sin.'

'You won't get that stool up,' said Heber, 'they're all fixed. We don't like accidents, not on the premises, but you *will* get a haemorrhage.'

'I'll try and come in the morning,' said Chance to Anna, who had moved silently across the floor to hold her husband's arms in her hands.

'This man's a trouble-maker,' said Heber. 'He's sick and he won't admit it. He sticks his neck out and goes where he's not wanted; let him get out peacefully, without assistance from anyone.'

'Columb, darling, come on home now. I'll call up Dr. Friese in the morning.'

'Call him now,' said Heber, 'only get this damn Chance out of my bar. I didn't like him when he came in and I like him even less an hour later—which is ter say *now*.'

Anna was partly whispering to MacGrady, 'You can't invite total strangers round to the flat, darling—not in the Zone. I don't mean to be rude, but you do see how it is, don't you, Mr. Chance? Columb isn't well—and well——' Her arm encircled MacGrady's shoulders.

'And well! and well!' said MacGrady, lowering his head, 'and well! I'm ill; I'm not well. This man *knows*! He's come because we prayed. Someone always has come! They never let me down, do you understand? Never!'

'When in trouble,' said Heber, 'send for Joan the Wad— she never fails. Nobody's ever seen Joan the Wad but when clouds gather she's right there.'

As though about to embrace him, Columb lunged at him; like a man who protects aggressively.

'For God's sake, Heber, don't speak, I want to think; don't say any words that you don't know how to use. There's something I want to ask the doctor.'

'Call a taxi, Heber darling, I'll have to get him home.'

Some signal was exchanged between them and the tall man moved through the archway into the kitchen.

'There,' said MacGrady, rocking between Anna and Chance, his too small chin on his bow-tie and his forehead taking all of the light beneath his curling hair.

'I'll send for you in the morning, Chance,' he said. 'You must come in the morning, if you don't . . .' his lips moved upon the rest of the sentence finishing it secretly and unsaid.

'It's Rue President Hoover, Veinte Cinco,' said Anna. 'Maybe you'd better come, Dr. Chance.'

'I will,' said Chance, 'if you're sure?'

'I'll tell the fatima to make up a room in case you have to stay. But in any case——'

'I understand.'

'Columb will be different in the morning, Dr. Chance. He has a doctor you know, right here in the Zone. If you like, I'll get him around too so that you can discuss the case with him? That's what you call etiquette, isn't it? I wouldn't want——'

Her husband lifted his head. 'I heard *that,* Anna. Tell him the other way! Talk to him! Tell him you don't believe him. Ask for his opinion, ask him where he majored, let him know you'll fix him first off with a genuine doctor and show him up; and, while you're at it, tell him what we owe that hell-quack of Norton's for payment for injections and whisky.' He took hold of Chance's lapel and drew himself over to him. 'That's about what she wants you to know, Chance; that's what she's saying. But she wasn't saying it on Sunday, on any Sunday; and last night—Anna's a Catholic, I tell you.'

'She's very young,' said Chance.

'But she prays! she prays, don't let her make you think——' MacGrady broke off, his face dulling visibly. 'What'll you charge me, Chance?'

'I shall have to think.'

'I've got money. I got 120,000 dollars in the States and given time I can get what I want. You've got to help me, Chance. If that taxi comes back empty in the morning, you'll go down, you'll have committed a sin, you'll have failed mortally. When it's your turn, you'll be finished.'

'Well, isn't that nice,' said Heber reappearing. 'How I do like to hear Romans having a friendly little talk about dollars and sin;—it advances my conversion by at least a coupla decades. The taxi will be here by the time we finish that last drink.'

In the pause Chance said, 'I think it's very difficult to avoid vulgarity when you're as vulgar as we are. In the twentieth century——'

'He's drunk,' Heber cut in, 'the Englishman's drunk.'

'Not entirely,' Chance said.

'Well, come on then, Limey, what about the twentieth century? What about the *American* century. Let's hear you say it—and it's your turn to pay for the drinks, by the way. You don't get your fees in advance in the Zone, you know. We're not nationalised here.'

'I was only thinking,' said Chance, 'that we had, at last, succeeded in vulgarising it—sin, I mean. There's not really much left.'

'You know, Columb, I'm beginning to realise why I dislike this man. He's like the scorpion—he's even more dangerous than he looks. He'll have to be squashed very flat very quickly before he gets up somebody's trouser leg.'

F

'No one will kill him,' said MacGrady. 'He's too sick. Look, I love this man, I love him.' He kissed Chance on both cheeks. 'This man represents the Church Sorrowful, the martyred Church; the Church gagged and bound in Poland, Czechoslovakia, Hungary, Rumania; the Church Missions bleeding in China—d'you *understand*?'

Heber groaned and put his handkerchief to his mouth. 'Excuse me,' he said, as he disappeared through the doorway again.

At the entrance the taximan waited, browner than the night beyond the porch. Columb stumbled past him quickly, Anna smiled at Chance and followed. He heard her address the man in unruffled, rather amateur Spanish. He caught the repetition of the address, viente cinco, Rue President Hoover before he finished his drink and stepped out himself into the night.

Beside the steps the boy was awaiting him.

'No man come,' he said. 'I sure watch everything until the big bell makes twelve in the Church of St. Francis. But Fraser's man not see or talk with Mam'selle, he fix racket with many guys who change money in the Avenida Salazar.'

'You saw him then?'

'No bud, I don' see; but my kid brother watch town while I watch the Gare and he see Fraser's man talking to the boys who sell money as usual.'

'As usual?'

'The one-leg collects from them regular always for all time in a bag.'

A tout, thought Chance. An agent taking percentages from the one-man businesses throughout the European section? Presumably, then a syndicate with capital behind it. It gave him a new conception of the sharp faces flanked by blackboards on which the exchange rates were hourly chalked. He had always felt a little sorry for them; but now their importunities, the steady self-confidence in slack hours, struck him differently.

'Where do the men who sell money for money get the first money?' he asked the boy.

'Not catch on. I don't figure about money not much.'

No, of course not, thought Chance.

'Allah give or not give,' said the boy. 'He give, you live; he don't, you die—is cash.'

'Yes!'

Difficult within the range of their vocabulary of pidgin American to find out much more. He tried again.

'And where does Fraser's man take the bag when he has collected from the sellers of money?'

'He goes by my kid-brother of the taxi to a great joint in the President Hoover. And he——'

'The President Hoover? You're sure?'

'I sure am sure. Veinte cinco President Hoover. My brother of the taxi take him many months always the same to the big man in the President Hoover.'

In the darkness Chance smiled.

'You seem to have a lot of brothers.'

'Otto,' said the boy holding up his two hands with the thumbs clenched. 'And sometimes we sure do all eat at once together. Sometimes.'

'And what then?' asked Chance. 'Does Fraser's man go inside with the bag?'

'They see that guy coming right on along and the woman of two small girls, who sweeps for the Americanos unlocks the glass gates so that he may knock upon the inner door until it opens.'

'Who opens it?'

'The man from Australia. The friend of many Americanos.' Chance watched him. 'George?' he suggested distinctly.

'Si,' said the boy. 'The George guy from Sydney.'

They moved in silence down the dry bed of the steps past the cemetery of the cats. Here and there an Arab slept on the stone swathed in his burnous, his knees drawn in and his feet protruding. As they passed, Chance glanced into the cemetery, but it was untenanted.

The cats were about their business in the yards and soccos working hard in their search for scraps of decayed meat and fish. In the middle distance, perfectly still in the moonlight, perhaps on somebody's terrace, perhaps on a plinth in the cemetery itself, he saw grey statuary rising above the level of the grasses and shrubs: a man and a woman, life-size, heavily draped, placed only a few inches apart with their arms on one another's shoulders and their shadowed faces for ever gazing into the stone eyes confronting them. As he looked, they moved; the arms of the man dropped to his side and stepped backwards away from the motionless figure of the woman. Chance gasped.

'He make love to another guy's wife,' said Haleb. 'Such things are to be fixed in the night acting dumb.'

'Yes.'

But she could not be more beautiful than the wife of the man he had met an hour ago. For a moment he dwelt upon her beauty, the great indifference of it; for only a moment, and then he gave Haleb more money.

'You have done well. Take this and buy food. Tomorrow I must go from the de la Gare.'

'Where go?'

'The President Hoover veinte cinco, to the Americanos.'

'I see you.'

'Yes—perhaps. Before long.'

He left the boy standing there on the steps as he had found him; then, letting himself into the hotel, went straight up to his room. In the darkness by the open window he prayed for nothing in particular. There was a sweetness to be had, but tonight it eluded him and he was glad: response always aroused so great a distrust. It was always enough to have prayed while one could. In life only the Saints were equipped to suffer the terrors of supernatural certainty.

He lay quite still under the white sheet and summarised the day's encounters: Marcovicz, the Dane, George, Columb MacGrady, Heber, an enemy of people perhaps, and lastly, Anna: a cypher.

That left Haleb, the girl with the monkey, Mademoiselle Lucie and himself. In thirty years? In fifty at the most? He wove patterns and the people danced: they moved across the plenitudes of his mind like the Moors on the sand: arabesques, confrontations and linkages played out in black and white against a perfectly neutral sky.

And shortly, he slept.

Monday

A<small>ND</small> shortly he slept to be awakened by the women in the yard quarrelling about something. He pulled up the blind and leaned upon the sill to watch them. Two older women, squat as ducks, were raging at Aminah as she scrubbed imperturbably at her washing board.

'Salaam,' he called; but they gave him only impatient glances before waddling back into the house and leaving Aminah alone.

'Aminah! Aminah! A beautiful morning to be young in. Oh lovely! Come here and talk to me. Tomorrow I shall not be here. It is time we met.'

She could not understand a word he was saying and did not wish to. 'Listen!' he called, 'last night I met a most beautiful woman. I will describe her to you: she had thick hair and a white face which looked as though it had never been touched either from the inside or the outside. Her eyes were open but asleep. She had the proportions of loveliness to such a perfection that I dare not think about her or contemplate myself. I'm filled with a rage of pride because I'm a poor forty and there is no one whom I can properly tell.'

The girl moved into the wash-house with the same gesture of dismissal he had known when importunate and young. But he continued to talk out of the window.

'You tell me that I should go to my Confession, that this is an intimate matter. I *shall* go to my Confession; I'll find a Spanish priest who understands little English and it'll therefore be unnecessary to say too much.' He could scarcely see her within the darkness of the shed. 'Or perhaps you think that I am mad? A mad infidel who looks out of the window and speaks to the air? Perhaps so, but I can tell you that all men of forty would speak like this if they dared. I have seen men at clinical meetings——'

He moved away from the window, packed his bag quickly, and went down to Mademoiselle Lucie for his breakfast of coffee and stale croissants. At 10 o'clock the taxi arrived; he got in and was driven efficiently to the wrong address: the office of a Gibraltese dentist at No. 24 Place Nasser. The taxi-driver spoke no English but made it clear by gesture that he had been summoned by telephone and given orders, presumably in Spanish, to bring a gentleman to the dentist at this address. He made it even clearer that he would drive no further until he had been paid. Chance paid and pacified him and was then driven off in the opposite direction towards the American Section of the Zone lying just below the hills which surrounded the town. He was deposited there with his case outside an eight-storey block of curving flats which stood alone in one of the otherwise empty development lots he had been shown the day before by the Dane, Thaaren.

A little girl wearing ear-rings and dressed as neatly as a doll opened the glass door for him and showed him into the foyer. They stood there together on the tiled floor between the door of the concierge's apartment, which was open, and the closed door of the flat belonging to the Australian. He noted the name beside the bell-push:

George Fraser

before knocking on the open door opposite. The child's mother appeared with another, younger, daughter in her arms.

'*Señor MacGrady? Si!*' She confirmed. '*Numero siete.* Maria will take you to the lift.'

'*Gracias.*'

In the lift, ascending very slowly, clicking off the numbers of the floors, Chance whistled to himself. He felt gay. At the fourth floor he stepped out on to the terazzo, closed the gate and watched the lift descend again in response to an unheard summons from some other floor. He rang the bell, and in a few moments, precipitating himself into Chance's speculation, the American opened the door. The impression was one of parquet, rugs, and wide windows with the American standing very small and yellow-pale in front of it all. His mouth hung upon its smile as though he were teething, his hands shook, he was swaddled in a silk dressing-gown with his hair curling cockatoo-like above his forehead. He was unshaven.

'I'm glad you were able to make it, Chance! I thought—— Come in! You must forgive the way we live: we just got out of bed. The fatima didn't have a chance to make your room yet; but she'll be in any time.'

'Oh that's all right.'

'Here! Let me take your bag.'

'No, no. It's not heavy.'

They stood there for a moment struggling with formalities.

'Anna! You out the shower yet? It's the Doctor.'

'Well show him into the sitting-room, darling. I'm just going to fix coffee.'

'Come on out, Anna. I don't know which room you want him to have.'

'I told you, show him into the—Oh Columb!'

Hearing her laughter they moved through a door on the right into a long white room. Inside, Florentine chandeliers glittered among eighteenth-century portraits in oil; outside the sun was invisible in the sunlight already flaying the hills.

'What a day!' said Chance, going to a french window.

'We keep the blinds up, it saves electricity—at night of course.'

'At night?'

'Yeah! We play cards a lot; not cards—a game called Scrabble.'

'You're pretty high here. I suppose that's the Shibam direction is it?'

'Must be. D'you like it?'

'It's extraordinary.'

'I *don't* like it.' Columb left the window and wandered between doors in the opposite walls.

'No?'

'We play with Norton Sax—he's a friend of Heber's—three nights a week. You'll have to meet Norton; he's interesting, he's just crazy about this game.'

'Oh.'

'We play nights, before dinner, we don't dine till midnight here.'

'Really?'

'We have lunch somewhere about two o'clock, maybe three, then we sleep till seven, six if we've a party here, then perhaps we play Scrabble or go around to The Botticelli or the Marchita before dinner.'

'And dinner is at midnight?'

'That's right.'

'What do you do after dinner?'

Columb had halted in front of a portrait, wigged, haughty and entirely secure in Georgian pink.

'You see, Chance, we have an arrangement about this flat with Godfrey. You'll have to meet Godfrey, he's an extraordinary man.'

'In what way?'

'This is one of his ancestors, he has an awful lot of ancestors, I guess. He was a Colonel of the Brigade of Guards, who retired young, for private reasons. He left England years ago, he does a great trade in bloodstock, owns the local racecourse, and runs these flats for a syndicate in Dublin. He speaks Arabic and Russian—and he collects.'

'How interesting! My father was a great collector—butterflies and birds' eggs. He had one of the finest collections of butterflies and moths in the north of England. When I was young he was always wanting to take me on a trip to Africa to——'

'Godfrey's a specialist. He doesn't collect butterflies, he collects black women. When he's home he lives in the flat above this one or else in his villa on the Island, midway

between here and the Base. He's got a launch in the harbour.
He travels a lot in Africa but right now he's home and you'll
have to meet him.'

'I see.'

'You'll have to meet Godfrey and Norton Sax—and
George.'

'George?'

'He lives on the ground floor flat. He'll want to know you.
George is a very interesting man.' The American paused, 'I
can't think what's keeping Anna. Look Chance! You sit
down and we'll have breakfast in a few minutes.'

'Splendid.'

'You'll find this divan very comfortable. Put your feet up.
What'd you like to read while I go and give Anna a hand?
There's plenty of books here, Norton Sax brings them in for
Anna. Anna likes to read novels: you can take what you
want.'

'Thank you.'

'You're all right then? I mean you think you're going to
like it here?'

'I think it's extremely kind of you both to ask me. I——'

'You can ignore us Chance. We live the way we have to
live, the way we like to live. You don't have to live the same
way, but this is the way we live because we like it. You
can do as you like while you're here. I want you to be comfortable.'

'I'm sure I shall be.'

'We don't do any cooking here, we eat out. We don't have
the English breakfast, we just have the continental breakfast;
we have coffee or juice, grapefruit, pineapple, tomato and, of
course, orange. If you don't mind, I'll just go and see what
Anna's doing. Anna is very young, Chance; you said that
yourself and it's true. I could give Anna all of eighteen years
and we'd still not be level——'

They both turned as Anna came in. She was not dressed;
her light negligée was held high to her throat as though

clipped together with the full-scale cameo of her hand. She smiled at them both.

'Will you bring in the coffee, darling? I couldn't find anything but biscuits in the refrigerator. I just hope the doctor's not too hungry?'

'As a matter of fact,' said Chance, 'I had breakfast at the Gare before I left.'

'The fatima's just arrived and she's doing your room for you. Would you like to put your case in there?'

'If you could move this li'l table, Columb could put the tray by the divan, I think. We mostly have our coffee in our room.'

'Certainly.'

'You must have been up very early, Dr. Chance. I guess I don't ever wake up until after lunch; I'm just terribly sleepy.' She regarded him intently out of her enormous oblique eyes. She was very serious, as polite as a person half-asleep.

'Are *you* a good sleeper, Mr. Chance? Let's sit here shall we, in the sun? I jus' love the morning sun in the Zone.'

'Yes,' he said. Her pathos bewildered him; pathos and such beauty together.

'I don't sleep very well, do I Columb? You could put that tray just there, darling.'

'Anna gets nervous,' said her husband, adding, 'I'll sit with the Doctor. You take this chair, Anna.'

Still one-handed she rose. She rose as delicately as an aphrodite rising from her sea-shell: neither her white feet nor the thick hair, untouched by recumbency and the night, were safe from Chance's regard.

'Anna doesn't sleep well because she gets nervous,' Mac-Grady repeated, glaring at his black coffee. 'Anna is very young.'

'Yes of course.'

'She sleeps when she has to; sometimes she sleeps all day, maybe two days. She makes up that way and then she's all right again, aren't you, Anna?'

'I—atone, I guess, for all the late nights,' she said. 'We

often don't get to bed till four or five, and then after a week
or two I jus' have to sleep. I believe I'm gettin' that way now!
But it's terrible fun, I love it.' Her voice was very even, an
accompaniment to the gentle gestures with which she dis-
pensed the coffee, sugar and milk.

'Anna loves the Zone, Doctor. She loves it—that's why we
moved out of Spain, away from the *rabble*.'

'The *rabble*!' repeated Anna gravely, imitating the venom
of his tone. 'Columb took me away from the rabble, didn't
you darling? Didn't you, sweet?'

'We used to come here before we got married; but only for
a few weeks. From now on we're going to live here because
we like it. Anna likes the life, she just loves it: she likes to
meet interesting people, people with ideas: writers and
thinkers. Why! only yesterday Zoe and Robin arrived here.
You'll have heard of Lady Zoe Seebohm, who just got herself divorced again.'

'Er, yes,' said Chance.

'Well, you'll meet her. She and Robin are staying at Heber's
house in the native quarter and we'll be going there for drinks
this evening. Robin's some kind of an observer on the
American missile project—self-appointed I guess. Anna likes
to know people like that, real people whose village is the
world. That's why she likes to live here in the Zone and
that's why we will live here till we have to clear out.'

Chance looked up, the American was crouching over his
coffee, his head lowered, his blue slapped-looking eyes fixed
on Chance's face. He seemed as though he were about to
weep or shout. Anna got up: she inclined her head to Chance
so slowly and with such deliberation that not a hair of her
head was disturbed as she left them facing one another over
her cooling coffee.

'Is that likely?' asked Chance, repeating it again after a
decent pause. 'Are you likely to have to clear out?'

'What d'you say, Chance?'

'I asked why you thought you might have to leave the
Zone?'

The American did not reply for a moment. Chance was about to change the subject when he began to speak.

'This place is rotten,' he said. 'It's going rotten. It's not like it was. Godfrey knows. He'll tell you. Godfrey speaks Arabic. Godfrey's the only white man who has the franchise of the mosques, he's even been in the mosque at Mozambique; but he just doesn't do that any more and he doesn't have his Arab friends to his flat any more or to the villa. Because they won't come; they won't speak to Godfrey.'

'Does that worry him? I mean is it a recent thing?'

'It *is* a recent thing.'

'Do you think there are going to be more riots then?'

'*Riots!* D'you think I'd move for a riot? This place runs on riots; there's got to be blood and noise occasionally, it's the heartbeat, it's slow and irregular but it drives the Zone. I don't mean riots and Godfrey doesn't mean riots; a riot gets forgotten but what's coming up now will only be forgotten because there'll be no one here left to remember it.'

'A war?' Chance suggested.

'Not a war, but *the* war.' MacGrady paused, his little mouth vehemently closed over his baby chin. 'You think I'm dramatising, don't you, Chance?'

'Yes.'

'Well you're wrong. You're damn wrong. Why the hell should a man dramatise on his honeymoon?'

Chance sat very still. 'Honeymoon? Oh, I didn't realise——'

MacGrady's exasperation was immediate. 'Last night I thought you were bright, Chance. I had the impression you said some good things in The Botticelli, that's why I wanted you to come here. I thought you were my sort of Catholic. I didn't think I could be wrong—I didn't figure I was drunk— because I *don't* get drunk.'

'No, no, of course you weren't drunk. I'm sorry if I seemed a little slow. But nobody told me you were on your honeymoon—I thought you'd been married for some time. I assure

you I'd never have accepted your invitation if I'd realised
that——'

'We *have* been married for some time—for two weeks,
Chance. You've got eyes haven't you? Does it look as though
we'd been breeding? Does it look like the porch, the playpen
and the furniture instalments and the Life Policy? Does it?'

'No—but——'

'Use your eyes, Chance. Be civilised. But don't get misled.'

The American got up and began to move round the sunlit
room restlessly. Chance smiled. 'I don't think I've known you
long enough to be misled by you,' he said.

'That's bar talk! I don't like that sort of remark, it doesn't
mean anything. When I tell you not to be misled I mean I
want you to know things. Until you do know things you can't
help me and I know that you're meant to help me.' He
brought his fist down on the little table and the cups jumped.
'I *know* that!'

Chance was silent. In the hall, through the open door, the
fatima, a young girl with bright conjunctivitis, was lifting
the Persian rugs and sweeping the parquet soundlessly with
a soft brush.

'You've got to know everything before you start. You've
got to meet everybody that I meet and there's not a lot of
time. That's why I wanted you here.'

The fatima's movements and activity were entirely silent.
Through the open door Chance caught the faint smoky smell
of her burnous.

'Are you listening, Chance?'

'Yes, I'm listening.'

'And you might as well know that there won't be any
children. There just won't be any. Anna knows that; she
stayed with me a considerable time before we got married
in the Catholic Church a fortnight ago and Norton Sax was
best man and she knew and Norton knew there'd never be
children.'

'I see.'

'And it's not because I'm sick—we'll talk about that later—

an' it's not because I don't have the money. If you get to thinking that it's my health or my income you'll be wrong from the start. That's why I'm telling you this. I'm not that sort of a man. I wasn't ever meant to be worried about money and I'm not worried about money and that's why you have to meet George.'

Chance was dry, 'I'll put him on the list.'

'What you say?'

'I said I'd put him on the list,' Chance repeated. 'By the way, where does Norton Sax fit into all this?'

'Sax? He's a Jew. Every man needs a Jew in his life.'

Chance started to laugh.

'What's so funny about that? They got scattered, that's all. They got hit by God and disseminated over the face of the Earth. There are Japanese Jews, Indian Jews, black Jews, white Jews, German Jews, yellow Jews. They were the first Christians and they'll be the last. If you don't understand the Jews you can't understand the Old Testament and if you can't understand the Old Testament you can't understand the New Testament. Catholicism begins and ends in the Jews, Chance, and they know it. No one should ever laugh at the Jews— when a man starts trying to define a Jew he defines humanity.'

'It wasn't precisely that,' said Chance. 'I was laughing only because it struck me suddenly that it was going to be rather exhausting if I have to piece you together from all these different sources: this man Godfrey, for instance; or Norton Sax, or this man George. I was wondering if there wasn't a short cut of some sort for both of us?'

'What do you mean?'

'Well, first of all there's your health, isn't there? We'd have to discuss——'

MacGrady stumped over to him.

'You're not too well yourself, are you, Chance?'

'No.'

'But you're a Catholic, we're both Catholics, aren't we? We can start from there all right.'

'Yes we can. As a matter of fact that is just what I was going to suggest.'

'What were you going to suggest?'

'Well, that what we both need perhaps is a priest. I mean as a first step. A priest might save us both an awful lot of——'

'Oh for God's sake! I *live* here. I know the priests. They're all rotten—Spanish peasants in soutanes, corrupt and ignorant. Do you think I'd be in this state if I was in Rome or London?'

'London?'

'Farm Street, of course! But forget it. You sound to me like a convert, and you can't expect to understand the Church yet awhile. When you're older you'll know that there's a priest for every Catholic. In Ireland or Spain one priest can answer for a thousand scrub faithful: but *we* need, each of us, a Jesuit in a hundred.'

'Do you think so?'

'Chance I don't want to argue with you. You've come here to help me. We've got to talk about my disease and, later today, you've got to help me to decide about it. But in the meantime I just want you to listen to me and to everybody that knows me and after that you can speak and I'll listen.'

'I may not have anything to say.'

'Yes you will; and when you tell me, I'll do it, you understand?'

'Very well.'

'I'm going to take a shower and shave now. Is there anything you want? Let me take you to your room and show you a bathroom. Give me your bag.'

In his room he sat down on his bed, exhausted with words, and attempted not to think of Mrs. MacGrady. To know that she was the wife of the American had helped; to know that she might not, in any save the sacramental sense, be his wife at all, explained things but did not help at all.

He was in the same house, must see her through a whole

succession of days and nights with no more equipment than
that of one of the—what was it? Scrub Faithful.

A good phrase, he thought: vulgar, painful and enduring.
He must try, himself, to remain like that: quite isolated and
sufficient, watered from deep roots which cheated the desert
and the enormous aridity of the sky.

He was very disorganised; but forced himself to unpack
methodically, as though he had arrived for the week-end in
an English country home.

He went into the adjacent bathroom, inspected the stall-
shower, the pink porcelain and the cork floor. The window
overlooked the back of the flats; they fell down vertically,
alternating white balconies and dark windows, like an iced
cake. At the bottom lay a tiny patch of derelict garden.

Near a copse of hibiscus he saw an old Arab woman searching a pile of ashes for unconsumed cinders; saw the brown
bird-hand steal out swiftly to pick up its trifles with care
before transferring them to a little reed-basket by her side.

Longing suddenly for the Hotel de la Gare and the wash-
house yard, he began to clean his teeth for the mere distraction of it. He switched on the shower and drew the plastic
curtains round it, ran the water from hot to cold and back
again and in the process got his head wet. There was no
towel so he stripped and had a proper shower: hot, cold, hot
and then cold again: as though he were the American.

There was no towel in the bedroom either; but there was
a cotton counterpane. He was drying on it when the door
opened.

'Oh,' she said, 'forgive me! I just thought——'

'It's all right.' He wound the counterpane round him. 'I
couldn't find a towel. I hope you don't mind. I was going to
hang this thing over the balcony to dry.'

'I'm awfully sorry; I jus' wondered if the fatima had
brought you towels? I didn't know you were in here. I'll go
and get you one.'

He tried to hide his chest. 'Thanks.'

When she had gone, he slipped his trousers on. In a moment

she was back with two enormous towels, fleecy and white as a pair of new lambs; she stood there in the doorway with them, looking quite unsad but nothing else.

'Oh, thank you so much.'

'You're awfully thin,' she said, 'aren't you?'

'Yes—do come in. I'm quite decent.'

She left the door open and sat on a corner of the bed— very serene but upright, her hands still holding the mouth of the pale negligée close to her throat.

'I hope you're going to be all right in here—Doctor. I'm not a very good hostess, I'm afraid.'

'It's a delightful room,' he said. 'Delightful! And the bath-room——'

'Columb loves bathrooms. Right now he's taking a shower, he'll be in there for ages, he jus' loves to take a shower when it's hot.'

'Yes.'

Far away, down the passage, they heard him singing through running water:

> From Memphis to St. Jo
> From Chicago to Santa Cruz
> A woman's a two-face . . .'

'He sounds cheerful,' he said.

'He sometimes likes to sing when he's alone.'

'Does he?'

Her hand fell to her lap and the negligée drooped open. His eyes rose to hers, as solemn as a child's.

'You mustn't let him worry you,' she said. 'You won't let him worry you, will you?'

'No.'

'Has he worried you, Dr. Chance?'

'I don't think so—not yet.'

'And you can help him?'

'I'm sure I can—about his health.'

'That'd be wonderful. It really would, it'd be jus' wonderful.'

'He hasn't told me very much about it yet,' he said. 'Somehow, just now, I didn't get a chance to broach it. He was talking about—other things.'

'He does that,' she said. 'He talks for hours at night, hours and hours. I listen but I never really know what's bothering him. But if *you* listen, if you're patient, if you don't get——' she hesitated.

'Frightened?' he suggested.

'Why, that's it.' He saw her first real smile, one that was not intended, and she looked away hurriedly. 'That's it, what I meant to say.'

He did not reply.

'He does frighten people,' she said. 'He frightens them away and they don't come back.'

'No?'

'It's because he's frightened himself. I guess it must be, mustn't it?'

'Yes.'

She got up. 'Well,' she said, moving to the door, 'as long as you're comfortable.'

Along the passageway the sound of the water ceased without warning, as suddenly as if it had been cut off at the mains.

'I am,' he said, 'I couldn't have asked for a warmer welcome or a kinder——'

The cough came along the passage like a cry, violent and sustained. It went on for moments extending into minutes, an exhausting paroxysm which prevented either of them from speaking. When it had finished her hand was back in position and she was once again very polite.

'Let me know if there's anything at all you want. I'm sorry if I disturbed you. I guess I should've knocked, but I thought you were back in the sitting-room.'

He was suddenly decisive. 'Wait! I want you to tell me something, two things: they're both important.'

'If you've anything for the laundry,' she said as she moved into the passage, 'the fatima will do them for you at home. She collects from the baskets every morning.'

He followed her out and caught her free hand in his own. She followed him back into the room and he half-closed the door.

'Only two things—Mrs. MacGrady,' he said, 'and they're not very personal.'

'What things?'

'First, has he got a growth? Second, do you really want to stay in the Zone? Is this the life you like?'

'What do you think?'

'Tell me.'

She withdrew a pace. 'You tell me,' she said. 'That's why you're here isn't it? That's why you came—to tell us. We don't know. I don't know, I didn't even know Columb was ill till I married him two weeks ago. We never—shared a room—before that.'

'But you must know if you like the life,' he insisted, *'the Zone.* You must know that.'

'I don't know anything yet, not anything at all, except that it doesn't come into it, *my* liking or not liking. I guess you'll have to talk to George if ever you get to meet him: George and Norton Sax.'

'Have you talked to them?'

'They're men,' she said, releasing his hand, 'like *you.'*

He heard her go into her bedroom.

A dozen retorts occurred to him: 'Have you no women friends? Why are you frightened? Don't you trust men? Like them?'

But that, of course, was how it *would* go: back to the personal, the adolescent, the aching vanity, the childish things. The first question, the dull question, was the only mature one.

So he just dressed and went along to the sitting-room. Pointlessly, the sun illumined the landscape and the outlying scatter of the Zone. Even the brown hills and the near trees, tamarisks, palms and sumachs, looked incandescent. He was reminded of a burning-glass exactly focused upon an ants' nest: the grass blades and the ants momentarily white before they curled up into thin smoke.

At the foot of the President Hoover, in a partially excavated vacant terrace, he saw an Arab encampment: a whole family under bamboo scaffolding and felt rugs. Through a gap in the roof he saw the children crawling, the old men and the slow women, all in white like the doomed ants.

Behind him, MacGrady came in. He was wearing a towel round his loins, he had a fat little chest with a dusting of hair between his breasts. He was very pale but his hair was wet-curled above his big forehead.

'I jus' brought up some more blood, Chance.'

'Yes, I heard you coughing. Was there very much?'

'Not a lot, not more than usual.'

'How long have you been coughing like that? No, wait a minute, you'd better tell me everything—clinically, I mean: the whole story. If you leave anything out I can always ask you.'

'What'll you drink?'

'It's a bit early, for me.'

'Wait while I get the Scotch. Do you like Red Hackle? It's cheap here, there should be plenty in the kitchen.'

He came back with a tray: a jug of water, ice, a full bottle, and two tumblers. He filled a tumbler a third full with whisky.

'Half that for me,' Chance said.

The American tipped some of it into his own glass, added ice and filtered-water to both and handed a brimming glass to Chance. He slacked over to the divan and lay back against the head of it, relaxed and chubby.

'Two years ago in Madrid they X-rayed me——'

'Yes, you told me,' Chance said.

'Well, I'm telling you again. It wasn't large and they said they could treat it with X-rays and that I should improve. I took the course and it did improve: I lost the cough that'd had me for eighteen months, I got back my wind and pretty quickly I felt better. The specialist told me I'd need another dose in two years' time, either that or an operation which might or might not work. I said I'd never let them cut me and it was left that I should go back for more X-ray at the end of two years.' He drank generously. 'For the last six months the cough has been coming back and the short wind. I get dizzy, I feel as though I had got a baby in my chest clutching my windpipe and I've been bringing up blood every morning for the last fourteen weeks.' He drank again. 'That's about all.'

'And you're not going back to Madrid?'

'No.'

'Why not?'

He let his wrist flop over, he uncrossed one fat leg and examined his toes. 'I don't believe they know the hell what they're talking about. I been seeing this doctor of Norton's: Friese. He's all sorts of a man. He's a psychiatrist and a homoeopath. He's some other things as well. Maybe he's some kind of a pervert and something more than that too. He owns a night-club round about here—I'll take you there. He smokes the *kief* a lot, you'll understand, and he likes his Arab boys. I know he's a very clever man, he's so clever he must have got himself struck off somewhere else and taken to running this place here in the Zone. When you meet Friese you'll understand why I haven't asked him very much about things since he told me I'd got no growth, that if I'd had a growth I'd have been dead by this time; not smoking and drinking and putting on weight. He tells me I'd be a damn fool to go back to Madrid for more X-ray. He says that where doctors are concerned it's always more dangerous to be rich than it is to be ill.'

Chance waited quite a long time watching the American sprawling there: an equivocal hint of discomfort lurking somewhere beneath his composure.

'That's all, is it?'

'That all, Chance.'

'That's why you don't go back?'

'Nobody wants me to go!' He threw an arm across the head of the divan. 'They wouldn't like it. Heber wouldn't like it and George wouldn't. Norton and Godfrey wouldn't like it.'

'I see.'

MacGrady thrust his head forward. 'They're my friends, Chance. They know all about me, they understand me. I've been mixed up with them for a long time. They watched me get married.'

'Yes?'

'What do you mean—yes?'

'Well, one's friends usually——'

'Usually what?' MacGrady flung his legs over the edge of the divan, the towel slipped down to his hips but he disregarded it. He leaned forward and his voice thickened. 'What're you hinting at?'

'It's only that I don't see, that I can't see why the opinions of your friends should stop you going back to see the doctor who originally diagnosed the condition. It seems——'

'You don't have to see. That's not what you're here for. You're here to give me advice, medical advice and nothing else yet. I manage my own affairs, if I don't want to go to Madrid you have to accept that. And I told you I *don't* want to go to Madrid and that's got to be enough for you. If you want your fee you start from there: you don't go prying into what doesn't concern you and asking a lot of foxy questions.'

There was silence. Outside, far below the white flats and the town falling to the shore of the inland sea, somewhere beyond the roads, an incoming ship called once; and the sound, softened by distance, threaded through the sharper barks of the motor horns in the Avenue Grande.

'This is all rather boring,' Chance said. 'I mean *you* are being boring. It's very boring when people keep on lying at a time when lies aren't necessary.'

'Just what am I lying about, Chance?'

'I couldn't say really. One never knows what prisoners, I mean patients, are lying about.'

Squat, rather frog-like, MacGrady sat up on the divan. 'Prisoners? What prisoners?'

Chance moved in his chair. 'I was thinking about something else.'

'And you think I'm lying?'

'Oh yes! Undoubtedly.'

'About what?'

'I've told you; I simply couldn't say at the moment. You haven't been lying long enough, I suppose. You see there's a certain consistency about the inconsistencies of falsity which only becomes apparent over a long period. I'd have to send you away and see you again tomorrow and so on. Gradually, the truth which is being avoided would become obvious from the pattern of the lies.'

MacGrady was impatient. 'You're a strange man, Chance. I'd like to know just what you think I might be lying about.'

'Oh well! You're frightened of course.'

Fat and rosy in the morning light the American plucked at his towel. 'That's just damned arrogance. I don't want sympathy; but I do expect insight, and I ask you, wouldn't you be frightened if you were dying in mortal sin? If you had a growth moving slowly, spreading out in you while you walked and slept? Stalking you day and night when you hadn't the time or the mind to prepare yourself for what might be coming?'

'I would of course; but we've discussed all that—I mean the physical side of it. The moral remedy is not my concern and I really don't think it has very much to do with your lies or you'd have done something about it before now. You must be frightened about some other thing which you can do nothing about.'

They both heard a door open and close in the other part of the flat: an incursion of the normal which provided an opportunity they ignored. After the lapse of generous moments, Chance concluded, 'Your friends, I imagine.'

'Why in hell should a man be frightened of his friends?'

'I'm not quite sure, but I've noticed that my patients often are very nervous of them. After all, one sees so much more of them.' Chance sipped at his drink, 'I mean, more than of one's enemies. I suppose you could be in debt or something.'

'I am not in debt,' MacGrady spaced out his words, 'do you understand, you damned fool? *I am not in debt!*'

All the sounds coming in through the window, the movements of the town, the markets and the quays were neutralised by this vehemence. The speakers themselves were forced to await the deaths of echoes they could not hear. The American was very sullen; he made no attempt to excuse himself by any further remark; his continuing silence most scornful of justification.

'Prisoners——' Chance began, 'people, I mean, don't usually react viciously unless——'

'I am not a prisoner either,' MacGrady bellowed, his face blanching. 'What the hell's gotten into you? This is the Zone, it's not a prison. We're all free here. I'm a rich man; everybody here is rich. I don't know any poor people; I don't like them. All my friends are rich.'

Chance appeared to be discomfited by the hand holding his glass of whisky; he frowned as he observed its trembling. 'I was wrong then; there must be something else.'

Without looking over to him he sensed more than heard MacGrady's standing up; but from long practice kept his chair and betrayed no physical interest.

The short man stood in front of him waiting for some acknowledgement of his challenge.

'It's about time I knew just what you're talking about, always supposing you know yourself, that you're not some kind of a crackpot who thinks he can spread his own crooked ideas and pass them for straight truth in situations he's not big enough for. Just what do you mean when you say it must be something else?'

'I mean only *that*!' said Chance. 'That I believe that you're lying out of fear, and that if your fear is not connected with your friends then there's something else you haven't told me.'

He looked up at the American, saw the scornfulness of his mouth and the sudden tautening of the puffed lower lids before he replied.

'Or you could be just a very low-down prig, Chance, a medical prig who sits there talking to himself, frightened to come out in the open and hinting at cowardice on the other man's part. I don't like that sort of a doctor and I don't like that sort of a man; it takes an honest man to be an honest doctor. Why can't you come out with it? Why can't you get on your feet and if you've got anything to offer let me have it now before either of us grows any older?'

Chance was watching the minute movements of the whisky brim inside his glass as it rose to the encircling droplets and fell back again time after time.

'I'm warning you, Chance, that you'd better speak up before we go any further or we may not go any further. I'm beginning to think it's essential from the start for you to prove yourself if you're going to help *me*.'

The silence was prolonged. 'I want to know, straight out, what *you* think I'm frightened of.'

'There is nothing to say.'

'It's not money, is it?'

'Very often in my experience it's blackmail of some sort.'

MacGrady was beginning to breathe heavily. Although quite still, his inner exertion starved him of air. He seemed about to cough, his voice grating in his larynx so that he was forced to repetition in order to make himself heard.

'Abou' wha'?' he coughed. 'Blackmail about what?'

'Something you've done I suppose, or that they think you've done.'

'Done? They? I've done?' The cough enveloped him again bowing him down like a great weight beneath which he was forced to crouch, his fat calves tense, his knees trembling, his face invisible to Chance. At the conclusion of the spasm he came up again slowly, rising like a diver from depth. His face was covered with sweat; there was something in his left hand and thin blood on his chin.

'Chance! You'd better get out!'

Chance got up slowly.

'I made a mistake,' whispered MacGrady.

'I'm very sorry.' Chance turned; his back was to the window as he began to move over to the door.

'I made a big mistake,' came the pursuing whisper and the

pause, until, by the door, the question came again: 'Against whom, Chance? Blackmail against whom?'

Chance turned to face him. 'It could only be Anna—if you care for her.'

MacGrady moved quickly. 'That's it then,' he said as he came across the floor. 'You'd better get out right now. If you don't——'

The whisky from Chance's glass slopped on to the rough Spanish parquet as the shorter man grasped him. The fat arms ran round his waist like a cook's, the towel slipped to the floor as they stood there wrestling; the glass was broken. Chance was forced back across the room out through the french window and on to the balcony high above the empty road.

'Just that,' MacGrady grunted. 'A mind full of poison—what Heber said: a scorpion and you got up my trouser leg. You know things—you get talking when people are in the bathroom and then you jump from a long distance and you sting—but you won't sting anyone else.' With immense invalid's strength he pushed and levered Chance inch by inch across the terrazzo of the crescentic balcony to the balustrade.

'The usual convert crawling with self-love,' he whispered, 'graceless, putting his neighbour before God, and his own lousy little soul before his neighbour. You talk about fear, other people being frightened, but right now you're more scared yourself than ever I was—and for as rotten a reason.'

'Stop!' Chance shouted. 'You're mad, MacGrady! You'll kill me.'

'Outright, admit your fault. Admit you've got your eye in ours—that you're trying to taste *us*.'

'If you do,' Chance called, 'we'll be where we were. It will be as though I had never come and we had none of us ever prayed.'

There was no reply. Chance saw only the façade of the upper stories quartering the horizon and the immense depths of the sky.

'You're wrong!' he shouted. 'How could *I* care for *you*?'

The grip round his waist slackened instantly. He stood upright at once, wiped the moisture from his lips and cheeks and stepped forward towards the open window and the darkness of the room. The American ignored him, his chest moving unevenly, the right side slightly higher than the left. He was looking across at the hills as he drew in the air.

Chance passed him quickly and sat down on the divan. In the bathroom he heard Anna singing disjointedly. Outside, MacGrady recollected himself in complete nakedness. He might have stepped out there to do exercises; a man pausing between one exertion and the next. As Chance watched him his head fell, with an ungainly movement he barged back into the room knocking his shoulder on the closed window and went over to the glass he had left on the floor. As he stooped to retrieve it he said, 'You'd still better go.'

The Englishman got up and walked unsteadily across to the bureau on top of which there was a plate of soft water-biscuits, one of which he took and ate as he waited.

The American finished his drink, picked up his towel and strapped it round him again. He shut the window and let the venetian blind fall loudly over the sun and the burned hills.

'I always hated them,' he said, standing back from the blind, 'and now I know why.'

Anna had her shoes on, she must have carried them into the bathroom and put them on there because they heard her going quickly, perhaps gaily, back to her room. And this time they both acknowledged the inference of her presence.

'To do that,' Chance said, 'was no explanation. It's a thing that's worried me, the fact that action always delays explanation.'

'What I was saying about evil, Chance. You think you know what it is, don't you?'

'No, never until it's too late, until after it's happened. I suppose really it's just an interruption—of good; and that's probably why we can't anticipate it or know very much about it until it's happened.'

'We'll leave that if you don't mind,' the American said

heavily. 'What I'd like to know is why you came here in the first place?'

'I don't know, for a holiday.'

'Do you think you'll ever get away?'

'I'm beginning to wonder.'

MacGrady did not smile, neither did Chance; but the idea of smiling was no longer inconceivable to either of them.

'Well I'll tell you about that: I know now that you won't! You'll never get away.'

'Will *you*?'

'Yes. By Christ I shall.'

Chance took another biscuit.

'My plane leaves in six days,' he said. 'I have a return ticket.'

'From the Base, Chance! Don't forget that. It's your first trip to the Zone, isn't it?'

'Yes.'

'It's a pity somebody didn't tell you a bit more about it before you came. When people arrive here they talk very surely about their date of departure. A lot of my friends have done that—some of them for the past ten years.'

'I see.'

'You've got to get yourself across to the Base, that's all isn't it? From the Zone to the Base.' He laughed. 'It's a very little distance but you can be pretty sure you'll never make it. So maybe in one sense you were right when you figured you might be a prisoner.'

'*You* sound very sure.'

'I'm not that sure, but give me till tonight and I'll *be* sure.'

Chance watched him as he refilled his glass with about the same quantity of whisky.

'Why, what's happening tonight?'

'You're going to meet people, that's all.' Still breathless, MacGrady drew breath, 'Norton Sax, Friese, maybe George Fraser. You'll have to be careful about George, by the way; he has habits.'

'And tonight will decide something, will it?'

'Yeah,' he was near smiling, 'it will decide *you*, Chance.'

'I may be a prig, but you are very arrogant I think.'

'I can afford to be, I'm a cradle Catholic.'

Chance was amused. 'I'm glad that friend of yours in The Botticelli didn't hear that. It might further have delayed his conversion.'

'You mean Heber?'

'Yes.'

'Heber would have liked the little balcony scene all right.'

'Too short,' Chance said shakily. 'Inconclusive.'

'I'm sorry about that, I mean I'm sorry I went for you. Sometimes I get that way when I drink in the mornings.'

'Is that often?'

'No,' MacGrady said a little absently, 'probably only when I'm under very considerable stress.' He looked up. 'Were you scared?'

'Very! But more afterwards than when it was actually happening. I've noticed that before. When one is in danger of immediate death one is merely irritated. For instance, it never occurred to me to pray.'

'Don't be Protestant, Chance.'

Chance took another biscuit. 'To tell you the truth I was worrying about my stomach. You haven't a glass of milk, have you?'

'I'll go get you one. Would you like it warm or cold?'

'Warm, if you don't mind.'

'You look pretty washed up.' The American paused by the door. 'You'd better sit down on the divan while you wait.'

'Thanks.'

'Try and not look so sick. If Anna comes in and sees you looking lemon-green she might begin to think you'd been upset. I don't want you to let her know just how we've been talking.'

'Don't worry, I won't mention it.'

'She might think I was kind of inhospitable—she was educated at a Sacred Heart convent in New England.'

Chance was straightening himself, stroking back his hair

with the flat of his hands, bracing his shoulders, and attempting alertness; he caught MacGrady's eye and they laughed. Chance went on laughing on the divan very quietly; he locked his legs together and held his head. In the kitchen he could hear MacGrady laughing and coughing alone. He heard Anna go in there and ask questions which were answered by more laughter through which he waited, trying to control himself, in case she came in.

She was dressed and earnest; she stood over him with a minute frown between her smooth hair and wide eyes.

'What goes on? I heard you two shouting at each other. I was just terrified.'

He bit his lips hard and tried to relax but could say nothing.

'Gee! I didn't dare come in at all,' she went on. 'What's he been doing to you?'

'We were discussing his health.'

'Really! Is it that good?'

'I don't know,' he managed, 'I didn't get much time to think about it——' MacGrady had come in with the glass of milk.

'The Doctor got more interested in his own and we'll not be getting around to mine again until he's had his milk.'

'He looks awful pale.' She was gazing innocently at Mac-Grady. 'You haven't been scaring him, have you Columb?'

'No!' Pause. 'Now get out while we finish.'

'But I want to go shopping,' she said still with her untroubled eyes, 'I want nylons and Lanvin and lip-rouge and some more books and that new dress at Hepzibah's you promised for Zoe's party.'

'Zoe doesn't have a party! Zoe only got here yesterday.'

'Well Heber's party.'

'Heber likes trousers.'

'But MacGrady, *you promised.*' She screwed her face up and put on a parrot voice, 'Zoe-doesn't-have-a-party-an'-Heber-likes-trousers,' she intoned 'Heber-likes-trousers-and-Zoe-doesn't-have——'

'Oh all right,' he said. '*Go* shopping! Let everyone know you're shopping and spending. Go and enjoy yourself and let George know on your way out.'

'Why darling, I'm just positive we'll be all right now. I'm just positive we're going to find our way out.'

'That's what I'm telling you,' he said, rounding on her, 'I meant it. *Go* shopping!'

'I'll be very discreet, sweetheart. We mustn't muss it up at the last minute.'

MacGrady seemed to have forgotten her. In his towel he looked like a statue half-completed. His wife's blank eyes found and lost him and then moved swiftly to Chance and away again.

'I'm not kissing you,' she said. 'Where're we lunching——?'

'The Capuchin.'

'But that's expensive! Why that's the most expensive,' she began to parrot again, 'the-most-expensive-restaurant-in-town.'

'Oh get out, Anna!'

'Do you want any more Scotch, darling? I could get you a bottle of Scotch, I could get two.'

'No.' Loudly.

'O.K. I'll meet you both in the Capuchin then at a quarter-past one.'

'No.' Chance intervened from the divan. 'If you don't mind I want a swim before lunch. I'll eat somewhere quiet and cheap. The Samarra perhaps.'

They both looked at him, possibly surprised because they thought they had remembered his presence.

'You're not coming with us?' she questioned. 'They do an awful nice fish at the Capuchin. The very best thing for doctors' stomachs.'

Chance was looking at MacGrady. 'Why that's just swell of you,' he said in his sort of American, 'but if you've no absolute objection——'

'You're sure?' she said.

'Yes.'

H

She spoke over her shoulder as she drifted towards the door, 'The water's awfully cold. In October it would freeze an acclimatised eskimo. But then of course doctors know best—about everything.'

They heard her go down to the bedroom, humming some song, heard her return and insert the key in the outer door, still humming, 'From Memphis to St. Jo, from Chicago to Santa Cruz.'

'That tune dates,' MacGrady said as the outer door clacked in the hall, 'I don't like it. When I was twenty-five I liked negro stuff a lot. Maybe you did too?'

'Yes.'

'It's god-awful to be forty, Chance, but it's worse to be nearing fifty.'

'Yes.'

The monosyllable made the American restless. He was aggrieved.

'You feeling better?'

'Yes thank you. Shocks seem to do me good. I feel much better than I did when I got up this morning.'

MacGrady grunted as a way of apologising for returning like this to himself.

'Well what d'you think about me then, now you know the whole story? Do you want to examine me clinically?'

'No, it would be pointless. What you need is machines; a full chest investigation: X-rays, tomography, bronchoscopy, possibly even a biopsy.'

'Biopsy? Of what?'

'Well the growth, if you've got one.'

'And where's that to be done?'

'That depends.'

'On what?'

'The money situation. If that doesn't worry you, if you've got plenty I mean, you could have it done in New York, Rome, or Madrid. If you're short I should imagine you'd have to have it done in London, or for that matter, anywhere in England. You could get it done on the Health Service, or better still pay half—an amenity bed. They're pretty prompt without being grossly expensive.'

MacGrady sat down slowly and with all the care of a man gingerly distributing a heavy burden.

'If you were going to arrange it,' he said, 'if you or your London doctor recommended cutting, if it's an operable growth . . .' He made no attempt to complete his sentence and Chance came in quickly.

'Oh it almost certainly is. I'm sure your friend Friese is right as far as that goes. If it were not operable, by this time you'd have been either dead or too ill even to stand up.'

'Yeah! There's no need to return to the balcony. I was only saying *if,* Chance! *If all these things,* then if I could get to London, then maybe——'

'You mean the things we haven't discussed?'

'Just those.'

'Well it may be cowardly but I hardly like to press them again quite so soon.'

There was no answering smile. He was distressed, pale, plump and pitiable suddenly; a real nakedness only now apparent; his cigarette-free hand coming up to wipe his lips.

'It would be no good pressing me because I just can't tell you. What I said about crawling to my friends and enemies was what I meant, though I was sore at you at the time. You were right when you said I had my remedy and hadn't used it. I've been to no priest and so I have to accept the indignities of Protestantism.'

Chance waited and was rewarded.

'You'll have to meet them, all of my friends, wisely. You know that in the spiritual sense a man's life isn't like that, he can't hand it to you like a rotten apple. You have to see it as a whole tree with roots in the dirt and branches in the air. If you want to mend it you'll have to see the whole of it— by grace, if you're in it.'

'Yes, I see.'

'If I'd wanted another lumber-jack I'd never have spoken to you in Heber's bar.'

'It all sounds very perilous to me.'

'Of course it's perilous,' MacGrady shouted with immediate loss of his pathos. 'You dumb ape! Don't you know that, even within the province of the Church and the priesthood, we dwell on the edge of ruin?'

'Oh yes, I think I see that.'

'And you're only wishing to God I'd picked on someone else, another Catholic?'

'Not necessarily a Catholic; someone a bit stronger. There are plenty of them about.'

'It's your weakness that is God's strength, you damned fool. For God's sake! d'you think I wanted a hero, some natural man with an Everest complex? I'm a Catholic and only a Catholic can help me, a man in grace, a man supernaturalised. When you pray you get what you want and you want what you get. I got you—so you're the answer.'

'I hope you're right.'

'Yes, and I hope you went to Mass last Sunday and that you're praying regularly and that you're going to your Confession on Friday whether I'm here or not.'

Chance had immediate difficulties with the glass of whisky which he had decided to drain and MacGrady crouched over at him with high indignation.

'And that's nothing to exercise your phoney British sense of humour over. How the hell can you be of any help to anyone, let alone a case like mine, if you're not in receipt of grace through the Sacraments?'

'It's just that it's an idea that had never occurred to me.'

'What had never occurred to you?'

'The idea of one Catholic cashing in, or profiting I should say, at another's expense.'

'That's just your rotten post-reformation background,' Mac-Grady continued. 'Don't you know anything about Indulgences? The treasury of the Church down the ages which posterity uses from now to eternity. What's the use of the perfection of the saints if it's all been buried with them? It's a pity you can't stay longer with me, because you obviously need further instruction if you're going to travel around the place claiming to be an English Catholic.'

Chance's glass was empty and he spoke lamely, 'Well, I'm perfectly willing to do all I can, but I can't help hoping that you're right—about me I mean.'

'If you do what I've told you to do and what you know very well the Church tells you to do, then I can't be wrong.'

'No, no, of course not.'

'Well, I'm glad you've got that straight. By the way, would you like me to get you a rosary? Have you got one?'

'Well, I had but I'm afraid I may have left it in Shibam. I thought I put it back in my wallet but I couldn't find it this morning.'

'What were you doing in Shibam?'

'I went there with someone.'

MacGrady was obviously resisting a variety of questions, he merely said with a shake of his head, 'That's bad! I'll have to lend you mine and I don't like travelling without it and that means I'll have to borrow Anna's which will leave her without one.'

Chance: 'I could always use my fingers.'

'And when did you have your fingers blessed? Didn't anyone ever tell you that a rosary blessed by a Dominican has more indulgences attached to it than a rosary only blessed by an ordinary priest?' He was hurrying down the corridor as he went on. 'My rosary's been to fifteen European shrines, Chance; it's been blessed by the Holy Father himself and by Padre Pio, I've never lent it to anyone else before.'

Chance heard him routing about in the room adjacent to the dining-room; the sounds of more rummaging when his continued search had taken him into their own bedroom. It was embarrassing for him to know that the open door made him a party to MacGrady's carelessness. But in a few minutes, triumphant and still a trifle admonitory, he returned with an enormous rosary constructed of oaken beads and a golden chain, from the base of which hung a large ivory crucifix.

'I've got to go and get dressed,' he said as he handed it to him. 'You should do at least one decade daily with a Salve Regina at the end. Friday you should always do the full five Sorrowful Mysteries.'

He went out, leaving Chance there in the mounting light, the rosary draped around his knee as he lay half-recumbent on the divan.

When he had finally gone, when the door had closed behind him and the lift, heard faintly, had hummed into silence, Chance got up and toured the flat. In addition to the long sitting-room, the kitchen, two bedrooms and bathrooms in use, it consisted of a dining-room heavily furnished in Spanish oak, another small bathroom with cupboards spanning one of its corners, a separate lavatory, a dressing-room adjoining the main bedroom, and an unused bedroom filled with cases and cabin trunks.

For a time he wondered about the labels; but beyond noting that they were fresher and more various on one set of luggage than on the other, he drew few inferences from them. The pieces had travelled far, some had shuttled backwards and forwards between the opposite coast and the Zone, others had moved over the Atlantic once, had circled Paris, Rome, Venice and Madrid, and then settled down to a similar monotonous junketing between Europe and the African coast. Now they were together; abandoned, empty, but together.

He made his way along the obtuse-angled hallway which gave access to all the rooms, collected his wallet, swimming things and the flat key which MacGrady had left on his dressing-table, and went down in the lift.

In the entrance hall, midway between the doors of the flats belonging to George Fraser and the concierge, a little Arab girl of perhaps eleven or twelve was standing. She carried an empty straw basket and was wearing a tiny brown burnous with the hood pushed back from her face. Her feet were naked and dirty, her face thin and secretive; but there was a sureness, a lack of intimidation, in her stance which halted Chance outside the doors of the lift.

He saw that she was unawed by it all: the tall building,

the smooth lift bringing the stranger down to her, the greatness of the space enclosed between the terrazzo, the marble
and the teak.

She let her basket hang above her naked feet, she stared at
him boldly and he smiled.

'Salaam,' he said.

'Bonjour M'sieu,' she said carefully.

She looked him up and down, his clothes, his shoes, the
top of his head, and then glanced at the closed door in front
of her, the one with the name of George Fraser above its
single bell-push.

'Vous-parlez Français?' he said, moving towards her.

'Oui.'

'Combien de kilometres à la plage, Mademoiselle?'

She shrugged. 'Sais pas,' then, 'M'sieu?'

'Yes? I mean Oui.'

She came up close to him, she left her door and approached
him as though she had suddenly made up her mind about
him.

'M'sieu,' she said, and he noticed that the ends of her black
hair were dyed with henna. 'Demeurez-vous ici?'

'Oui, Mademoiselle.'

'Tout seul?' she whispered with a smile. 'Tout seul
audessus?' And she pointed towards the well of the caged
lift and beyond it up the black and white marble of the staircase to the high roof and the distant dome of glass through
which fell the white light of the day.

'Tout seul?' He repeated foolishly.

'Mais oui.' She came even closer to him so that he was able
to see that her eyes were as expressionless as those of the
marmoset. 'Vous et moi,' she breathed, 'tous seules dans
l'appartement au-dessus.'

'Non!' he said loudly, his voice echoing up the lift shaft,
'no, no!'

Frowning, she took a pace backwards; her basket began to
swing to and fro as her small fingers twisted upon its handle.
Her eyes darted sideways as she heard the door of the con-

cierge's flat open. Above her head Chance watched the door; he saw the woman come out and stand there for a moment, taking everything in. He saw her skirts ruffled and the head of one of her tiny daughters appear beside her knee, the doll-like face with its gold ear-rings and centre-parted hair likewise gazing out upon them both. The mother's hand came down gently over the child's eyes, the head was turned and the little body thrust backwards into the room a moment before her mother too turned and followed her.

In front of him the Arab child still waited. She did not hold her chin high, she scarcely looked at him, she did not sniff; but beside her naked feet the basket swung faster and faster.

'Why are you waiting?' he asked in English; but she ignored him.

'Que faites-vous?' he said, 'Mademoiselle! What are you doing?'

She looked up at him without defiance. He had the idea that she was bewildered by his vehemence. She was twisting her basket now with a rotary motion, watching it in the way a child will watch a trifle and see only that.

Suddenly, as though she had drawn an answer from somewhere, from the very movements she had given to her basket, she looked up at him and smiled quite happily before moving forward towards the closed door.

'Eh bien!' she said with little interest as she rapped three times on the wood and waited placidly as though she were alone.

Chance moved forward. 'Mademoiselle! Je vous prie, Mademoiselle!'

But she ignored him. She was perfectly still. Even her basket had ceased to swing. Chance was about to catch her hand when the door in front of her opened; and at that moment she did turn. She turned and glanced at him with great swiftness and with intense hostility out of quite black eyes before she entered in and the door closed behind her.

Chance remained where he was for a moment. He looked

from one door to the other, up to the glass dome in the high roof and then out through the glass doors into the empty road. Automatically, he put his hand into his pocket and felt for the bulk of MacGrady's rosary where it lay over his hip. He pushed open the swing doors and walked out into the roadway where the sudden heat sheathed him like a pall. The road sloping downwards towards the old town wavered before his eyes. He saw the purple of distant bougainvillea breaking like a wave against the staring whites and blues of walls and buildings, the squat Spanish tower of a distant church over to his right. On this he fixed his gaze in order to recover his sense of balance in the heat before he set off down the hill past the vacant lots and fading billboards.

He never saw the boy approach, he gave his appearance no thought but accepted his presence, the shower of his questions, the small angular extra shadow, and the flap of his naked feet as though they had been there all the time.

'I sure wait all the time. Where you been? You got passport yet for me? You been talking money from Americans for passport, yes? You not see this George guy? You go get friendly with bad people and forget all things?'

'No, I haven't forgotten. I've been working.'

'What for? Why you work? You been making racket with the Fraser's man?'

'No,' Chance said. 'He's not important. I think I'd nearly forgotten him. I don't think I've eaten anything since last night. I don't feel too bad, you understand? It's a question of just something, some fish and a little bread and then some coffee.'

'You hungry? I show you place.'

'The Samarra,' said Chance. 'It looked nice, not too expensive. We'll eat together and then I'll swim. I shall swim out a very long way. I shall get clean and cool. I feel——'

'Sure better not go Socco,' said the boy. 'It's off limits for today.'

'No, no, of course not; out of our way. We'll get the first taxi and drive straight to the restaurant. After that——'

'No taxis here, not today.'

'We'll walk then,' said Chance. 'It's very hot of course, and I must admit I'm not well; but many people—in China people starve if they don't get money from somewhere. Children have to eat.'

'I show you quick way. We need not go through Arab quarter. We cross dead places to new town.'

The boy took his arm and together they struck off the road, skirting the Arab Quarter tumbling down the hill to the harbour and the sea. Ahead were the trees of the public gardens and the curve of the Avenue Grande with its banks, garages and western cafés.

As they stumbled over the broken stones of incomplete foundations Chance thought: it seems impossible; and it would be if things were isolated. Although I've dealt with such things at second-hand for so many years, this is the first time I've been directly involved. It's very difficult to explain; but it comes down to this question of evil.

In his preoccupation he addressed the boy directly.

'You see, if you could carry out an act in a vacuum, I mean a literal as well as a philosophical vacuum, then of course if it *were* wicked it would be achieving pure evil; but of course you can't. You have to do with things which *are* and are good. I mean you can't get to hell until you are there. That is what MacGrady meant. I thought he was just being Catholic-glib, but he must know something not remote at all, but very near.'

'You a doctor-man?'

'Yes,' Chance replied absently.

'Well, what you say?'

'What?'

'What you go on about, Doc?'

'I can't explain it really but sometimes in the prison I've caught the sense of it. I've seen how necessary hell is if we're to set ourselves over and against it. I think I see that we do need the danger of it at first hand. In the West we've put our faith in psychiatrists, many of whom are more bewildered than their patients. In America——'

'Movies!' said the boy.

'That's not what I meant,' Chance said.

He allowed himself to be piloted through a dark alley, up some steps, and through a deserted garden in which the bees alone were singing; but he continued to talk aloud because he found it consoling.

'Because one sees so little crime in a prison,' he said. *'That* struck me as worse than most of the things I've seen at home. I suppose we've been forced to make a religion of childhood, but really we should be far more concerned to suffer the children that are in us all to be safe——'

'We're just about there now. Today you sure talk a lot and I don't get it. We just got to go through here and we come to the road of the Samarra.'

'Good.'

'And we give the Socco complete miss, not go near it at all.'

'I see, a short cut.'

They crossed the road and hurried together under the orange trees to the restaurant hung with nets, glass floats and festoons of fisherman's cork.

They were shown by the waiter to an upstairs room and sat alone at a table by a window.

'Eat only one fish,' said the boy, 'and I take what you leave.'

'The town is very quiet today,' Chance said.

He looked out of the window at the void street. Many of the shops were shuttered and the banks had their ornate grills clamped tightly to the pavement like black teeth. The waiter, he remembered, had appeared hurried and distracted; he had not objected to the presence of the boy.

'Perhaps,' Chance went on, 'it is a Jewish fast day, or an Arab one.'

'It is the day of the great congress in the Soccos,' said the boy. 'Many people chew fat there and here El Glauoi Pasha from Marrakesh have speech. You give that place the big miss today. Tomorrow, maybe O.K.'

Below them in the street a French girl hurried along the closed frontage, swung up the white steps of a block of flats, and disappeared behind swing doors. A large open car slewed past with two uniformed Arabs in the front seat and a tall blue-suited man in the back accompanied by three veiled women.

On the pavement, a policeman in fez, blue knickerbockers and a short Scottish-looking jacket, saluted, crossed the road and entered the restaurant.

'We will have our coffee, I think, and then go and have a look at the Socco,' Chance said suddenly. 'She—I mean they —may have decided to see what's happening. We might meet them there.' And he added to himself, 'Unless they have gone to bed again.'

'No,' said the boy. 'Sure better stay right put, all Americans sleep it through in hotels.'

Chance turned to call the waiter and saw that he was already on his way, coming up the stairs at a run.

'*Monsieur!*' he said, '*Il faut que vous-partiez.*'

'Comment?'

'Partez, vite!' the waiter replied, hissing with impatience.

'Cafés—deux!' said Chance irritably. 'Vite, s'il vous plait.' He attempted to explain in his dreadful French, 'Dans quelques minutes—O je vous assure, nous ne serons ici que cinq minutes.' He pointed at his watch and held up his out-spread hand.

'*Impossible, Monsieur! Le gendarme la-bas a commandé au proprio de fermer le restaurant toute de suite.*'

'Mais——'

'*Il n'y a pas de "mais," Monsieur*. The police waits to see you go. I am sorry but it is a situation.'

'What's happening? I mean, que se passe-t-il?' He tried to think of the French for 'riot' but failed.

'So far, Monsieur,' he clicked his fingers, '*rien de tout*. It is usual. For many months we have such orders and always

—nothing. A few windows *peut-etre*, a few dead dogs, an assembly of the *Conseille Legislatif,* and a bribe, *vous savez, un petit cadeau* from one *conseilleur* to another *et tout sera tranquille.'*

'Well, why should we hurry? Surely if this is customary, we can at least finish our meal? After all your war has been going on for months.'

'It is not'—the waiter began with desperate patience—'*Ce n'est pas seulement une question de guerre.* There are what you call *canards* of an agreement between the French Government and the White House for a bomb in the desert.'

'The bomb?'

'A trial only, but of *la bombe atomique la plus grande du Monde,* to be exploded in the desert. *Enfin!* There is a religious unrest amongst the Arab peoples which has united them and their sheikhs.'

From the ground floor the proprietor's voice rose up to them:

'Gaston! Gaston! Dépechez-vous, vite!'

The waiter stood back, scribbling on his bill-pad, a thin sweat on his forehead. 'I've heard nothing about it, Chance said. 'It wasn't in the newspapers.'

'The war of Monsieur Eden was not in the newspapers either until the bombs were dropping.' He pocketed his tip. *'Merci, Monsieur.'*

'You live here?' asked Chance as they followed him down the stairs.

'My wife is alone in La Rue du Mexique.'

From the ground floor they were shown out into the street by the Zonal policeman. They watched the proprietor hook down his slatted grille in front of himself and his nets, saw him peer out a moment from the peephole in the central wicket gate; and then turned and walked together along the nearly empty street.

'In Trafalgar Square on a Sunday, one might if one were a foreigner get the worst impression and I must say that his point about Eden was well made. It is very difficult to know whether or not I should get out now while I can. And quite apart from that of course there is Marcovicz.'

'Bad man,' said the boy.

'Very obviously we will have to see for ourselves,' Chance persisted. 'There is something very frightening about this place and I only wish to God I could find some perfectly ordinary person with whom I could discuss it.' He turned to the boy. 'Take me to the Socco.'

'Sure thing! Tomorrow.'

'No, now. Today! Quick!' He shook him viciously, 'or no passport. I will get another guide, a boy who does what he is told to do.'

'If the Riffis get mad, if they bump you off, bud, no passport not any time anyhow.'

They had passed the El Sayyid Hotel and entered the narrow streets of the Arab quarter. Passing through the Spanish Wall and rounding the last corner into the open space of the Socco, they were brought to a standstill by a wall of Arabs. They stood there in their thousands filling the enormous space of the Market Place: a vast bird colony of brown, grey and white stretching as far as the cliff walls of the Sultan's Palace on the far side.

They were quite silent, so silent that the dry murmur of the flies above the field of covered heads could be heard as a constant undertone scoring the words of the man to whom they were listening.

He sounded as though he were coughing: the words floated across the Socco like the injunctions of an invalid, a compound of invective and pleading to which thousands of men listened with the stillness of a single person. Here and there, the roofs of market stalls, rickety scaffoldings of poles and straw, stood above the multitude of cowls and turbans like the masts and sails of foundering feluccas. In places smoke still ascended from the neglected fires of the fish-fryers, and in the far distance, high up on the walls of the Palace, the tiny figures of sentries could be seen standing motionless against the white sky.

On the outskirts of the crowd there was some movement,
a whispered coming and going as the older men made their
way to and from the Moorish cafés on the perimeter of the
Socco. In one of these, unnamed, dark and airless, Chance
and the boy took their seats at a table by the wall.

They drank tea, sucking the sugary water through the leaves
and stalks of the green mint amid the silence of the aged.
Outside, the voice of the speaker could be heard only as part
of the sunshine: a cicada at noon emphasising the peace and
darkness of shade.

Chance scanned the walls; as his eyes accommodated to
the shadows, he made out murals painted over the roughcast
in sharp greens, oranges and mauves. Western men and
women absurdly like English seaside postcards played out
their follies on three sides of the room. The artist had shown
the women as dominant; their great breasts and nipples thrust
outwards through their tight dresses towards men attenuated
and impotent-looking: drab fetishes in crumpled suits being
dandled or lifted up to suckle at the busts or become lost in
the gaping lips.

There was a French billiard-room scene: green-faced
goateed men in berets played snooker with hatching eggs. In
the foreground a man in the haze of delirium tremens tried
to slake his thirst at the neck of a decapitated chicken, while
under the table, a cameraed American, also drunk, held an
Arabian cat stretched out beneath his chin as he prepared
to take a mouthful of its starved loins. Everywhere, in all the
scenes, were the emptied bottles and the managing meno-
pausal women—one to a man.

A few feet away, at the next table, an old man caught
Chance's attention. He found himself held by the bright contempt of the eyes in the old face and watched him as he
removed his bamboo smoker from his mouth and gestured
with it first at the pictures on the walls and then high up
above at a portrait on the top shelf of the bar.

The photograph there was flanked by triangular banners
embroidered with the crescent moon and star of Islam; the

face looking out from between them framed in a shallow white burnous from which the powerful features seemed to project outwards and downwards upon everything.

The old man got up and strode out, light and erect, to the doorway.

'Ben Youseff,' he said distinctly, and opposite Chance's table he spat on the dirty floor.

Haleb clutched Chance's sleeve, 'Scram, bud!'

Chance gave him ten pesetas to pay the bill and together they made their way through the seated Arabs to the narrow doorway.

In the Grand Socco there was silence. The speaker had finished and the crowd was beginning to move. Through the door of the café Chance saw the pattern of the brown, black and grey shifting from the centre. Thousands of faces became visible as they turned away from the rostrum: from the middle, eddies of movement spread outward, the prospect of burnouses and faces swaying as though a gigantic dance were starting. As the pressure increased, groups on the perimeter were hurled suddenly outwards to burst against the chairs and tables of the cafés and the shuttered fronts of the shops. Men began to shout; thick cries and indistinct slogans unified from some secret impulse into an alternating rhythm: Sidi Mohammed . . . Mohammed . . . Ben Youseff . . . Sidi Mohammed . . . Ben Youseff.

Behind Chance the proprietor opened the door of his bar and, running, passed between the tables to where he stood with the boy. Before Haleb could give him any warning he was thrust out alone into the pack of bodies reeling back against the tables on the pavement, a corps of Arabs instantly closing in behind him.

Out in the centre, fez, stones and sticks rose into the air, poles torn from the market stalls sprouted like a sapling forest and through a dozen narrow sorties the crowd began to pour back from the Socco into the Old Town.

Surrounded by old men from the periphery, themselves helpless in the pressure of the young, Chance was forced down the Street of the Goldsmiths towards the Harbour. Beneath the narrow strip of sky and the airing poles jutting from the upper windows he was tumbled past the crowded doorways and the glittering windows of the little shops.

Half-way down the hill from a point where he could see the donkeys at their tethering posts in the Rue d'Espagnole, he was seized by the arm and held from behind against the doorway of a shop. Relentlessly, the Arabs crushed past him as he stood there pinned against the wooden jamb. Rents appeared in his shirt as hands clutched at him and old fingers with long nails clawed at his neck and chest. The seamed faces surveyed him in their passing shouting at him incomprehensibly as they were swept onwards down the hill to the sunshine and donkeys waiting under the palms.

The grip on his upper arm tightened, the limb was dragged slowly backwards, a steady traction on the ligaments of his shoulder-joint excruciating as a slow saw. He felt his shoulder-blade ride round the edge of the door as he was drawn backwards until his head, twisted half-round, was compelled to follow his arm into sudden painless freedom.

In the small shop in which he found himself, Marcovicz, grey and grinning, wavered before him.

'All right?' he asked. 'All right, Doctor Chance?'

'All right, Marcovicz.'

'Here, sit down! Sit down in this chair.'

He was led to a barber's chair and pushed gently into it. In the mirror he saw himself: the triangular rent in his blood-smudged shirt, a grotesque swelling of his nose, and his over-long hair fringing his forehead like a woman's; behind him, Marcovicz in a singlet and jeans, a grey mask of shaving soap surrounding his mouth and ears.

'And to think that you didn't trust me! That it was you who ran away just when I was beginning to trust you.'

'You know very well why I left you.'

'Ah, Magdalena? You were worrying about her? You were beginning to doubt my motives?'

I

'Have you got a cigarette, Marcovicz? I left mine in a café.'

'Of course I have.' He inserted one between Chance's lips and then lighted it. 'I was right, wasn't I? You were very taken with Magda, you saw her sweetness, her innocence, her great wisdom?'

'I think she is a very interesting girl.'

'She liked you too, Doctor Chance. She wanted to see you again; she was very disappointed when I told her I didn't think it would be wise just yet.'

Outside, the crowd was still herding down the street. A small stone cracked the window and fell amongst the brilliantine, contraceptives, and advertisements for aphrodisiacs within the display counter.

Marcovicz paused in his shaving. With the open razor still in his hand he moved over to the door, locked and bolted it.

'They won't want any more customers this afternoon. They got nervous when the riot started, their hands were shaking so much I decided to shave myself. "I'll look after the business for you—for what's in the till." That's what I said. I picked up a couple of razors and they all left, very quickly —customers included.

Chance was watching him in the mirror: there was something of the circus about Marcovicz which he had not noticed before. He combined the unpleasant athleticism, the deformed dexterity with the capacity for the sinister, which is the mark of the clown born. Behind him as he capered, was the oval of the window beyond which a stream of cowled heads and distorted faces flowed like a muddy river in spate. Younger men, more active than the old, were now in evidence, their mouths open as they shouted and cursed. He saw nobody bleeding or injured, but guessed that some of the older men must by this time have fallen to carpet the cobbles over which their sons swarmed. A few of them were carrying torn cotton strips fixed to the ends of bamboo poles looted from the stalls in the Socco.

'Don't you think it might be a good idea, Marcovicz, to put the shutters across the windows?'

'Oh yes, Doctor Chance! A very good idea, if the shutters didn't happen to be on the outside.'

'I hadn't realised.' Chance drew on his cigarette. 'What are they going to do, do you think?'

'What they always do. They'll run along the Espagnole to the big hotels behind the bay, they'll break a few windows, smash up the bathing huts and end by playing Riffi football on the beach.'

'There is no danger then?'

'Danger!' Marcovicz laughed, he tossed the cut-throat up to the ceiling, caught it by the blade as it fell twisting and shaved his left cheek with a single flourish. 'How easy it would have been. Oh brother! In a mob like that. And yet they didn't even trouble to knife you. Why! If it had been intended, I could have done it myself as you passed, couldn't I?'

'Very easily.'

'I was there as I was there for Magda, as I was there for the old woman in the *Dusseldorf,* as someone else was there for me. Everything was arranged, we were brought together in the right place at the right time; but there was no directive from above.'

'Or from below, Marcovicz.'

The Jew bounded with delight. 'Do you know that Russian poem about the Devil on the swing? "To and fro, to and fro, higher, higher, higher!"' His voice cracking into laughter, he drooped suddenly into meditation. 'But what a foolish thing to do when I'd been looking for you all morning: the Gare, the bars, the harbour, the airfield—everywhere. You've moved, haven't you?'

'I have.'

'Where to, Doctor Chance? Where have you moved to? What's your new address?'

'I'm staying with some friends.'

'Ah! friends. Are they rich? Have they plenty of money?'

'I think so.'

'They'd feed you? Wouldn't let you go hungry, look after you for the rest of your little holiday?'

'I should imagine they would, if it were necessary.'

'Of course they would.' Speaking compassionately, he moved over to the basin and sprayed himself thoroughly with the flexible rose. 'That's what friends are for, isn't it? You turn to them when you're in trouble and they say only one word—"Yes." They say "Yes, Marcovicz; yes, Jacob! Yes, Doctor Chance!" Don't you agree?'

'It depends.'

'On what?'

Marcovicz was now towelling himself. His big hands flew round his face and over his grey-fleeced head. He threw the towel into a corner and poured face lotion into his left hand, massaging it into his bruised shaving area meticulously as he scrutinised himself in the big glass.

'Ah!' he went on, changing his approach, 'this is refreshing! Since I believe a complexion is as important to a man as to a woman, would you understand me if I were to tell you I used to dream of this too? Of having my face shaved, my whiskers pruned like a rich man, pomades for my scalp, lotions, brilliantines, shampoos, mud-packs, vibro-massage, manicures—the lot?'

Chance smiled.

'I made it a rule the night before a job always to go into the Adlon and sit down there amongst the pigs, Doctor Chance. It was an observance with me, I believe in these things. Before Hitler came to power there was a Lutheran padre in the Hamburg prison, or it may have been a psychiatrist or a priest, I forget which; but one of them told me that my trouble was the Jewish trouble, that I was a ritualist without a ritual. What do you think of that? That's good, isn't it? That's a deep remark.'

'It is profound.'

'Yes, Doctor Chance. Outside, we take these things for granted, but not inside. I used to send myself to sleep sometimes thinking of myself in the saloon at the Adlon, or it might even have been your Harrods in London, on the night of a big robbery. I'd order everything, I'd choose my attendants, sometimes a man sometimes a woman—sometimes both? It would depend how I felt——' He broke off and sat down on the other chair with his arms akimbo. 'About friends! You wouldn't say it depended on their gratitude, would you?'

'Gratitude is a grace.'

'Ah, the Grace of God. That's good! Oh I like to hear you say that because I want to borrow from *you*.'

'I see.'

'How much have you got on you?'

'Nothing, Marcovicz. I left my coat and wallet at the—at my new address.'

'After all, I might have saved your life, mightn't I? You can't say that one of them mightn't have stuck a long knife into your ribs as you passed. Such a thing happened only a few weeks ago.'

'Did it?'

'Oh yes. An Englishman shopping in the Street of Little Wishes with a big knife in his back—it came out through the nipple. You must have read about it?'

'No, I don't think so. I don't read the papers very much.'

Marcovicz transferred his hands to his knees and leaned forward. 'We'll strike a bargain. You'll lend me fifty pounds and I'll let you see Magda again. You'd like to be sure that she's going to be safe, that she's in possession of all the facts, wouldn't you?'

'I would.'

'You had to let me go from the prison. You could none of you stop me, could you, because the law is always a step behind, because man makes the law but God makes man?'

'That is very true.'

'And, after all, you and Magda share the same religion and she liked you, she was interested in you.'

'So you said.'

'Exactly. She's a strange girl. She's going to wait for me, Doctor Chance. She believes that one day money will descend on me out of Heaven; and she's right; it will. In a few weeks, months at the most, I shall have money; thousands of pounds which I am owed for something I did.' He tilted his head back and laughed up at the yellow ceiling where the flies darted in their angular figures. 'Something I did. Or perhaps something I didn't do. That's good isn't it? To be owed money for something you didn't do? Is that Capitalism or Communism, is it interest on shares or the five-day week? Answer me that!'

'I have no politics, I'm afraid.'

'Of course you haven't. You're a Catholic, your Church stands above politics. If it was founded by God, it will laugh at politics. Why! Money pours into the Church which you and Magda share, and like all Catholics you both believe it's all due to the providence of the Most High, don't you?'

'That plus a little coercion from the priesthood.'

Marcovicz clapped him on the back shouting with laughter. 'Realists, with one hand in Heaven and another in the world's pocket, that's what I like about Catholics. A few more weeks with you and you'd convert me. Imagine that! Imagine me in the Catholic Church. That would set them thinking. They'd feel worse than the Governor at the Loch the last time I was sent back there.'

'I don't think it would worry them very much.'

'Oh I was only joking. I don't want to tire you; I didn't mean to offend you.'

'You didn't. As far as the bargain goes, Marcovicz, I can't lend you fifty pounds, but I will give ten to Magda when I meet her.'

'That's very generous. It makes me feel generous because generosity warms a man. But believe me I never worry much about such things. I'm a beggar and a beggar is the only man who is really free to choose.'

'Where am I to meet Magda, and when?'

'Tomorrow. It was her suggestion if I found you. She wants you to meet her tomorrow in a church.'

'In a church?'

'Magda is praying in the old French church—Notre Dame de la Guerre in the Rue Belgique. She'll be there for nine days on end.'

'A novena?'

'That's right, a novena.'

'And at what time does Magda want me to meet her? Time's getting short and I shall have to be getting back.'

'At twelve-fifteen. It doesn't matter if you're late, she'll still be there. Magda prays like a good Jew, Doctor Chance, like a Statue of the Buddha, an hour at a time—when once she gets started. She'll wait for you.'

'Good.'

Marcovicz went over to the window. 'What did I tell you? It's all over; 'Exercise' is finished. They're going back to their peters to bang themselves up—the others will be associating on the beach. I'm going to clear this till because I deserve it, Doctor Chance.'

'I'm very grateful to you.'

'Don't be grateful to *me*! Be grateful to God for Magda. After what you did to me yesterday I might have made a different decision, mightn't I?'

'You would have regretted it.'

'Oh no, not here. This is the Zone. We're all free here, we're on the edge of the desert where the world meets, we're on the edge of time and in the centre of beliefs.' He paused. 'You won't forget the ten pounds will you, and the address?'

'The address? I'm sorry, Marcovicz; but I can't promise to give you my address. I'm supposed to be having a holiday, I only want to be satisfied that Magdalena——'

'Forget it! Forget I ever asked you. I understand; you've

moved up in the world as one day *I* shall move. You've left that cheap little hotel. You'll be staying at the Sayyid with some wealthy Catholic you've found, or you'll be in the American quarter, or making love to *eine reiche geshiedene frau divorcée* in the Casbah. You don't want to see Marcovicz. You don't want to be reminded of the nick, of the dead facts, any more than I do. You're like me, God-driven! But we will meet again, won't we?'

'I'm very much afraid we will,' Chance said as he shook his hand.

'Of course we will. I'll know your address within——' he passed his hand over his eyes, 'yes, within six hours, Doctor Chance.'

'In that case it would be pointless for me to tell it to you.'

'But I'll keep quiet about it. You never know. You may be glad I was here, that I knew it, that we met again.'

'It's very possible.'

'Good-bye, Doctor Chance. The Zone is yours. I'll let you out.'

'Good-bye, Marcovicz.'

The cripple pulled back the bolts and unlocked and opened the door, he clapped Chance once on the back and stood there behind him whistling in the doorway as he watched him ascend the narrow street slowly in his torn shirt.

It was a quarter to seven by the time he slipped his key into the lock of the flat.

Along the passage-way he could hear them talking in their bedrooms: the sounds of movement, of drawers being pulled open, cupboards opened and closed. They must be dressing for the evening. He tried half-heartedly to remember the programme MacGrady had sketched out for him and failed. He believed in any case that the American would by this time have forgotten it himself. Listening for a moment by his closed door he heard him pad along into the kitchen: the clink of ice and glasses, the blinds going up in the sitting-room. He washed and put on the only decent suit he had brought with him.

Anna was in the large bathroom, he heard the shower running and caught the drift of her Lanvin in the corridor.

'That you, Chance?' MacGrady called.

'Yes.'

'I want to talk to you. Come and have yourself a drink. Where'd you eat?'

'The Samarra; they——'

'Did they close up on you?'

'This sort of thing often happens, does it?'

'At the Capuchin they don't get frightened so easily. You should have come with us; you were invited. Anna was—disappointed.'

'Sweet of her.'

The American made little of it. 'She's like that about people —a kid.'

He was sitting on the divan, the falling sun coming in full through the balcony windows making him look healthy, very composed. Yellow whisky, yellow cuffs and shirt, pale-yellow linen tuxedo, near-pink hands and face.

'What you been doing since?' he asked formally. 'I got a lot to say to you before Norton Sax arrives. Anna an' I feel we want to get this business over with quickly.'

'You mean your X-ray?'

'The whole thing, a definite diagnosis. It'll have to be in London if you're sure you can get it for me cheaper there.'

'When did you think of going?'

'Day after tomorrow.'

'*What!*'

'I said Wednesday, the day after tomorrow. You'll have to cable that consultant of yours, the thoracic surgeon and tell him to expect me. We'll have to get my photograph into your passport.'

'I don't understand.'

MacGrady moved over to the decanter and refilled his glass. 'Go get Anna. Tell her to come in here in her skin if necessary, tell her we've got just ten minutes before Sax shows up.'

'I'd rather you did that yourself.'

MacGrady laughed. 'You know I like you, Chance, I love you. You want time to think, don't you? You're scared stiff about it all but you won't admit it. You just want to get by that window and work it all out and then when I get back you'll know it all. I've watched you, you're a man who likes to get into a corner and get somebody's wavelength. You're all brain and a rotten little body and if you can get time on your own you know things, don't you?'

'Sometimes.'

'Well this time I'm going to save you trouble. George Fraser has my passport and my debts. He has an interest in me, he doles out an annuity on what I've got and what I expect to get when my father dies. He takes a very great interest in my health and my whereabouts. If I go places he likes to go with me and if George prayed, which he doesn't, he'd be praying for a short interval between my father's death and my own. He's got his eye on some sort of a clock and it's going to be just too bad for him if it gets jammed up.'

'Oh.'

'But George is generous too, and it would probably interest you to know he just lent me another two thousand dollars last week-end to pay off a few other debts. There'll just be enough left over to make London and fix this doctor of yours, provided he's not too expensive.'

'I met a friend of his this afternoon,' Chance said. 'A man named Marcovicz.'

'A friend of George's?'

'Yes.'

'It doesn't connect. What's he look like?'

'Oh, a cripple, but very powerful. As a matter of fact, I knew him, that is to say, I'd met him once or twice in Scotland some years ago.'

'Yeah? Go on, describe him.'

'Well, he's very powerful——'

'You said that. What else about him—age, colour, nationality?' MacGrady swilled the whisky round his glass, easily; very clean in his shining tuxedo, very fit in the golden beams of the descending sun.

'German-Jewish, I believe,' Chance said, 'though his name sounds Polish. About fifty-five, perhaps sixty-five. He's a man with such vitality that it's difficult to be sure. I knew him first during the War and yet today when I met him again he didn't seem——'

'So far we've got his nationality and his age, and the fact that he's crippled in some way,' cut in MacGrady. 'Maybe sometime we'll know the colour of his hair, if by that time he isn't bald.'

'No he's not bald, he has astonishing hair, quite grey, tightly curled as a wig.'

'Curled grey hair.' MacGrady stood up. 'And crippled?'

'Yes, and yet he still dances on his toes just as he did when I first met him, like a circus man, an acrobat.'

'Keller!' said MacGrady. 'You are describing Keller.'

'No, Marcovicz,' Chance insisted. 'I happen to know his name because——'

'Keller or Marcovicz,' MacGrady shouted. 'It's the same man I tell you! What the Devil in Hell d'you want to get talking to him for? Why can't you behave as I expect you to behave?' He swallowed the remainder of his drink and then went on half to himself. 'What are we worrying about anyway? It'll not be long before he's all washed up. He's been short-changing George on the Bureau collections and next time there's a riot nobody would be very surprised if something happened to him. I always told George that the Dane would be a safer substitute.'

'The Dane?'

'Yes. He was a collaborator in Denmark during the War; quite a lot of people back there would like to know just where

he is now, and that suits George all right. He likes to be able
to trust his teaboys.'

'I think I may have met this man too.'

'You do! Well that wouldn't surprise me at all. What was
his name?'

'Thaaren,' said Chance.

'Right again.' MacGrady smiled at him a little bitterly. 'I
can see there are things you think I shall have to tell you—if
you don't know them already. We'll get together later this
evening, but in the meantime don't make the mistake of
imagining Anna knows anything.' He leaned forward. 'Not
anything at all.'

'I understand.'

As she came in, they did not look at her, but MacGrady
got up immediately. He stood at the end of the divan, his face
curiously dark and childish, prematurely young, against the
stream of the incoming light.

'I was telling Chance here that I leave the day after tomorrow,' he said loudly, 'I'll have to travel on his passport
while he doubles up for me here in the flat. You can tell
everyone I'm sick again.'

'Yes, darling,' she sighed.

'You'll say the Doctor got scared about riots and that I'm
resting up for a few days and won't see anyone at all.
Nobody.'

'How long will you be away?'

'Four days, maybe five, if I fly there and back direct from
the Zone. I don't intend to get anything done at this stage.
I just want to know how long I've got, and what, if anything,
can be done.' He turned to Chance. 'Do you think he could
fix me up inside three or four days?'

'He could almost certainly make a diagnosis in that time
and give you some idea of the outlook.'

MacGrady refilled his glass hurriedly as the bell rang in
the hall. 'That'll be Norton. He's a man who can smell a dead
conversation from five minutes back. Anna, you'd better get

along to your room and look as though you'd been fixing your face.'

She watched him carefully, her eyes taking in Chance briefly. 'The fatima, darling! If we have to hold out here for three or four days, she'd know. She'd be a leak.'

MacGrady ignored her and they both watched him as he went out into the hall; then Anna too left the room, moving swiftly down the corridor to her bedroom. MacGrady waited until her door had closed and then let in Sax.

He came in ahead as though in opening the door Mac-Grady had sprung a trap letting a seasoned dog out on to the track. Neatly made, ribby, with a finely hooked nose and greying crew-cut hair, he ignored Chance walking past him to the divan as he cast round for something. Under a chandelier he turned on MacGrady who was following him flaccidly.

'For a moment I thought I was early,' he said. 'Now I know I was only premature.'

'We slept late, Norton, I want you to meet——'

'Your door was locked. I don't like to ring after knowing you so long—it might seem impolite; and anyways, in the Bronx we don't know these things, because we aren't taught them.'

'Look, Norton, this is Doctor——'

'Where's that lovely girl?'

'Anna's just dressing, she'll be all set in a couple of minutes.'

'That passes,' said Sax, taking the tone of the room. 'You haven't got the table ready, the chairs aren't out, the board's not out, there's one drink—not two. But that glass has Anna's lipstick on the rim, there's her Lanvin whispering loudly! In short, I smell strangers.'

'Yes, I told you, Norton, this is Doctor Chance. He's staying with us a few days. Just got in from the Base on a brief vacation and we asked him to stop along with us for a bit.'

Sax's eyes flicked off Chance and skinned something in the distance.

'Because I don't like strangers I had six drinks before I got here but that doesn't mean I'm not drinking before the Game, that is if we're going to play? If nobody's changed their minds about anything in the past five minutes?'

'Sure we're going to play as soon as Anna comes along. The Doctor here has played the English version of the game and he likes it fine, he's been looking forward to this.'

'With his hair that long he couldn't be looking forward to anything. What's the matter, has he been taking estimates from the hairdressers?'

Chance laughed.

'I saw Heber. He's worried about you; he thinks you're getting Anna into bad company. Robin and Zoe,' Sax lowered his voice. 'If you don't mind we'll talk somewhere else and with drinks.'

'I'll go and get you a glass,' Chance said, moving to the door.

'He's at home then,' Sax said to MacGrady. 'He already knows what's in the cupboards. I must meet him some-time.'

MacGrady said: 'I told you you'd like Sax, Chance. He was Woolcott's secretary.'

In his mimic American, Chance drawled. 'He should worry! Given time he'll live it down.'

Half-way to the balcony the older man halted. 'You know I think I'm going to dislike you even before your back is turned.'

'It was mutual,' Chance retorted. 'Last night, remember?'

'I didn't meet you last night.'

'Yes you did. You were calling yourself Heber then but I'd know you anywhere Sax.'

Sax appealed to MacGrady. 'Look, someone should have warned me, I'm an innocent antique dealer with chronic hepatitis and I upset easily.'

'The Doctor doesn't know many Americans, Bill, he's not used to the approach. When you ride him he thinks you're being rude to him.'

'He's dead right. And he's a doctor too, is he? I must bring him along my horse sometime. It's got piles.'

Chance laughed, a quick guffaw.

'Don't do that! Nobody's laughed at me in years and it hurts. I'm a very sick man, I expect to die very soon.'

'He keeps two knives by his bed,' MacGrady said on cue.

'What did I tell you. He knows! Everybody's been talking about me. It's got out that I keep two knives by my bed: one for opening the mail and the other for committing suicide.'

'One would do,' Chance said.

Sax rounded on him. 'You can go now, Doctor,' he said. 'We've finished with you. You can take my taxi. Columb, where's that girl? And when are we going to play scrabble, and why don't I get a drink? I haven't had one in ten minutes. If I get sober I begin to get nasty.' He walked out stiffly through the door. 'I'll get my girl and a glass. Whose bed-room's she in?'

'Now then, Norton.'

'Well I thought you said he was a doctor,' he called as he closed the door behind him.

'Chance, I think you'd better get yourself a drink.'

'I'll have some milk, I think: whisky later.'

'It's going to be a long night.'

'I should be sick if I started too soon.'

'Sax is real sick. He fights everyone. He's quarrelled with Heber but they still have a joint share in Godfrey's syndicate because they live by it. They'll split when Heber gets in deep enough with George. That's what Sax is waiting for.'

'George seems to be very powerful here.'

'What'd you say?' MacGrady was fumbling with his hands. 'Things are difficult, it's difficult to know just where they begin and end: everything's balanced, poised. My life's like that, morally and in time, everything's hanging on to something else. It's like the clock that George is watching, it's like that clock on the bureau only instead of a cupid swinging on the pendulum there's a universe involved, the universe of my immortal soul.'

'Don't you see, darling,' said Sax re-entering with Anna's hand and some glasses in his clasped arms, 'they talk together when I'm not there, they get up by the wall and whisper behind my back, making plans. You wouldn't do a thing like that to Sax, would you honey?'

'No, Norton,' she said, her eyes dusting Chance. 'Anna wouldn't cross Norton for anything: she loves him. She doesn't know why but she does.'

'If only I were different,' he said sliding his hand slowly up her white arm. 'If only I'd never gotten an Oedipus in the Bronx, why I'd eat you right up.'

'Oh Norton!' She collected her arm very carefully and moved to the bureau. 'Tell me about Zoe and Robin. What they say about the party?'

'You've hurt my feelings, he said taking the scrabble board from her. 'You changed the subject.' He questioned the room again. 'I wanna know what's been said. Sax wants to be in on it. *Who's going where and when?*'

'But darling,' she said moving to him very suddenly and kissing his forehead. 'We're all just here like we always are and nobody's been saying not anything at all; we're going to play scrabble just like we always do.'

MacGrady said, 'We'd better have a trial round for the Doctor to sit in. You two can have the divan, Chance and I'll take the chairs.'

'Why do you lie to me? Anna and I always *do* have the divan. You always *do* have the chair!'

They built up on the central word, Pilot.

'That word comes red-handed,' Sax said.

'No comment,' said MacGrady.

'How do you mean?' asked Chance.

'The guy I'm thinking of washed his hands in the blood of the lamb, or was it a goat?'

'You're thinking of Pontius, that's A T E,' said Anna.

'You don't say.'

Into the silence MacGrady said, 'I pass, I've got a string of consonants here.'

'And I can only make DOC,' said Anna, 'and that's slang, so it's your turn, Norton.'

'Talking of which,' he said. 'I've got a medical friend in Tottenham, a Jewboy like myself, who qualified at Aberystwyth. He's got himself a Bentley and a couple of Catholic mistresses from Ireland who work in a Whitechapel brewery. And he's done it all scribbling little recipes for aspirin and hormone at the Government's expense. He says it's a good thing he never knew any Medicine in the first place.'

'You do talk tonight, Norton,' said Anna gently.

Sax took her arm again: it lay passively across his thin trousers. 'That's because I'm unhappy, darling. I'm worried about Columb's health; I'd just hate him to get into the hands of quacks promising him quick cures in Limeyland. Why they might——Now as a London consultant, Doctor Chance, what do you feel about all this?'

'I'm not a London consultant.'

'Now now don't be too polite. I have *heard* of Liverpool and Sheffield and the University of Blaenau Festiniog.'

'I'm not a consultant at all. Incidentally, it's your turn, Sax.'

'I know that. I seem to be all on my ownsome tonight, I guess I'm going to win the jackpot.' He strung out a large number of short words on the board. 'You'll be telling me next you're a G.P. in the suburbs like my friend Stein with a licence to sling out cascara and Spanish fly on your little buff-coloured forms—I make my score 105, anybody check?'

MacGrady got up. 'It's time you had a drink, Doctor.'

'Thanks, I will.'

'Don't let's talk any more,' said Sax. 'I don't like conversation. I lost my faith in words when I was four. I like to play with my little bricks. I believe in the alphabet, the only begotten word: G-O-D spells God, D-O-G spells Dog, S-O-D, etc. On my night off I like to come around here and play with letters; so let's not all talk at once but let's do it with full glasses.'

K

Anna sighed: she turned it into a yawn, withdrawing her hand from Sax's lap to damp her unrouged lips as they parted slowly in the failing light. They all looked at her: the thickly white cheeks were dabbed with colour like a doll's, the hair drooped over the oblique eyes.

'I guess I'm just awfully sleepy,' she said. 'I was this morning, wasn't I, Columb?'

'You've been washed out for days. Why don't you get yourself a rest, darling?'

'If she does that,' said Sax, 'I shall get out my suicide knife. I come here to look at her, she soothes me.'

'She looks extremely tired,' Chance said.

'*You* look very fresh—so does a motor accident. Nobody's stopping anybody *else* retiring.'

Anna rose carefully: she kissed Sax's forehead again. 'You'll just have to forgive me, Norton. I feel terrible. I'll have to lie down for a bit or I don't think I'll ever make Zoe's party tomorrow.'

MacGrady said, 'I'll ring Godfrey and Pearl and tell them not to come around—we'll be seeing them tomorrow anyway.'

Sax spoke: 'When you're in bed I'll come and sing to you, darling. I'll be nice, I'll be polite, socially very desirable. Things just haven't gone right this evening, I didn't have enough to drink before I got here.'

She smiled at him dizzily. 'If George comes up——'

'He will!'

'If George comes up, tell him I was awfully sorry—that I felt all washed up and just had to get along to——'

Out in the hall the bell rang.

'That's him now.'

'Well I'll go right away. I love George always, but——'

'George'll understand, sweetheart,' said MacGrady. He put his hands on the gentle curve of her hips and guided her to the door.

'Good night,' she said.

'Sweet dreams, Anna,' Sax was a little restless. 'I know

what I am. You don't need to tell me. I just get this way, I guess I lived too long; I was a nice kid before I learned how to talk.'

'It's not you at all, Norton. It's just that—oh I don't know.' She turned, yawning again.

'I do know and I might even be sorry.'

'G'night.'

'Good night, Anna darling.'

'That girl,' Sax continued as soon as the door had closed, 'leaves me feeling like Oscar Wilde on his first night in Reading Gaol.'

MacGrady said: 'Why are you so vicious tonight, Norton?'

'If you want to know; it's this doctor, he gets in my back hair.'

'I'm sorry,' said Chance.

'Don't interrupt! Can't you see we're talking about you? For Christ's sake will somebody go and let George in before I start screaming.'

Accepting MacGrady's nod, Chance went to the outer door and George Fraser came in beaming: a great loose man in looser clothes, with pulled lips hanging round leaning teeth.

'This must be the Doc,' he said in a Sydney accent. 'Delighted to meet you, Doc, hope you're liking the Zone?'

'I'm glad I came.'

'Good oh! Evening, Norton. God bless you, Columb. 'Allo! where's the fair bride, where's Anna?'

'She heard you were coming,' said Sax. 'She took sick.'

The heavy eyebrows, bold against the silver hair, went up. Jovial concern showed in the lips.

'That's too bad. Is she sick, Columb?'

MacGrady filled a glass for him. 'You know how Anna is, George? She just gets pale and edgy if she doesn't catch enough sleep, and she's been getting ragged ever since the wedding. Tonight—she just packed up.'

'Well, ain't that a cow! She's just climbed into her bed, has she?'

'About half an hour ago,' said Sax.

'We'd better not talk so loud,' said George closing the door and tiptoeing back to them. 'I know what it's like trying to get to sleep with a party on the go. If yew don't manage it in the first ten minerts you don't get off at all. Well, I *am* sorry.'

'She'll be all right,' said MacGrady. 'She's just nervy that's all.'

'No trouble?' said George subsiding comfortably into his own girth. 'I mean nothing in particular, no little disagreements or anything of that sort?'

MacGrady: 'No.'

Sax: 'Not so's you'd notice.'

The blue eyes in the big face moved quickly from one to the other: the lips played out a cosy smile. 'Mind if I use your telephone a moment? I've got an idea.'

'Go right ahead.'

He tiptoed out and shut the door behind him.

MacGrady: 'Grapes.'

Sax: 'No, peaches from Godfrey's villa. George is very attached to Anna; we all are.'

MacGrady: 'She only wants to sleep—that's all. She wants to be left alone.'

Sax: 'In that case why land her up with strangers on her honeymoon?'

MacGrady was glooming at his own feet: he did not appear to have heard the remark and Sax drew himself up. His nostrils flickered.

'That's what's the matter here, this flat's not the same: it doesn't smell right. There's something going on. If you,' he turned on Chance, 'if *you* had any manners you'd not be occupying so much air around here and covering so much of the floor space. You'd take a hint, you'd get cracking and packing. Right now you'd be in your bedroom or in the hall ringing for a taxi.'

Chance fiddled with a button.

'You don't hear me?' said Sax. 'Is that right? You're both deaf, all waxed up? Well I'll say it again more quietly, I'll whisper it to make sure you get me.' He drew in a breath and shouted falsetto, 'The doctor must get out—vacate—scram.'

'Godfrey doesn't like people shouting, Norton.' MacGrady turned to Chance: 'You heard what he said, how do you feel about it?'

'I'll leave if you like.'

'I don't like.'

'I'll stay then.'

'You creeping cat!' The white saliva in the corners of Sax's mouth reminded Chance of Marcovicz as he had known him. 'What do you think you're going to get out of it? What's in it for you? Don't you see you're only upsetting everybody? Don't you see that nobody wants you to waste your time here?'

Several times Chance undid his wrist-watch strap and re-inserted it through its retaining loop.

'Well?' Sax shrieked.

'I have thought about it,' Chance said. 'I remember your partner: he gave me the same advice the moment I entered the bar. I've wondered why.'

'Maybe he was sober—he sometimes is.'

'That's where you should laugh, Chance,' MacGrady said.

'But,' went on Sax, 'you don't look right. You don't even smell right. In a revival meeting you'd be good theatre, but here we expect people——'

MacGrady intervened strangely. He put an arm round his friend's shoulders. 'Norton's a great friend of mine, Chance. You should have seen him best man at our wedding. Why if you'd seen Norton at that nuptial Mass——'

Sax shook himself free of the encircling arm. 'Since we're apologising for me, maybe nobody minds if I join in. Say, Columb, what's that little game you and Anna play with the counters?'

'Do you mean scrabble?' Chance suggested.

'Did somebody speak? No I meant the other little game with the girls, Grace and Mary, you know, the rosary.'

'I don't like that, Sax,' MacGrady said.

'I think——' Chance began.

'Nobody asked you to. You look sick as it is.'

'Norton, I don't think you can be too well tonight. What do you feel about it, Chance?'

'Well unless this is how he always behaves——'

'You dirty little ponce,' Sax interrupted, 'creeping in on the party card to nose around another man's wife under cover of the Catholic juju——' He swept up Chance's whisky glass, measured the distance carefully and jerked its contents into the opposing face. Chance mopped himself with a handkerchief and MacGrady stepped between them.

'I think one of you'd better get out,' he said.

Sax turned on his heel and sat down on the divan. 'You owe me money, MacGrady. I want it.'

'Two days, Sax.'

'I want it now.'

'How much?'

'All of it.'

'How much is that?'

'You know how much.'

'I'll go get my cheques.' MacGrady drew a cheque book out of a pigeon-hole in the bureau, sat down and started to write carefully.

'If you want to thank anyone for bitching up an arrangement that suited us both, if you want any religious reason for the turning of your luck, MacGrady, if you want to know why you're getting yourself an enemy out of a friend——'

'What do I tell them, Norton?'

'Oh forget it!'

MacGrady was handing him the cheque when the Australian returned. He was spanned by a vast pannier of roses: white, fully out, and of exhibition size.

'I bought these late roses. I thought Anna——' He stopped in the doorway his eyes on the cheque—'What's this, business?'

He put the basket down on the divan and stepped forward very quickly, taking the cheque from Sax's hand.

'A little settlement,' said MacGrady. 'Norton wanted his money tonight—all of it.'

'This is interesting,' said George sitting down beside his roses. 'Noub'dy told me anything about this. I thought we were having a jolly night. You know, a buck's night to meet the doctor and down a few drinks.'

'I'm through, George,' said Sax. 'I'm clearing out. Heber takes over. It was nice while it lasted but there's a new factor. You may not have noticed him.'

'I notice everything,' said George beaming, 'and I don't lose weight on it.'

'He's the bad influence, the nasty something you can't quite trace until it's too late—unless you've got a sensitive nose.'

'Now now, Norton, sit down a bit. You're over-excited, let's get down to cases. What happened?'

'I think I can explain,' said Chance.

'I'm sure you can, Doctor. Let's all have a drink. You know, I must be getting old: I'm losing my resilience. These days when I leave a room where all the bucks are friendly and come back ten minerts later to find people dripping whisky, other people writing out cheques and still other people talking about clearing out, I don't react as quickly as I used. I get confused for a minert.' He drank. 'Was it religion, Doctor?'

'I may have been a little tactless,' said Chance.

'He's a convert,' said MacGrady. 'I don't know where he got his instruction, but the Doctor's all right; Anna and I like him——'

'Of course you do.'

'He'll only be staying a few days, but Sax here——'

'I know! I know!' said George. 'Norton's not been too dinkum lately. He gets worked up. I see it all. Now let's have a look at this.'

He glanced down at the cheque. He started to laugh. He put it down in his closed fist beside him on the divan and shook gently. He looked at it again and rocked, his great belly billowing in and out like a black sail.

'Oh,' he groaned, 'oh, just listen while I read it to you: *"Pay Norton Sax, Atheist, ten thousand days plenary indulgence of temporal punishment. Signed: St. Collum Call of Ballybunnion."* '

MacGrady sat silent by the bureau and Sax grabbed at the cheque. But George was too quick for him.

'No,' he said, 'I'm going to have this frimed. It'll be up in my office. Columb you're a scream.'

Sax said, 'Give me that cheque.'

'Later, Norton, later,' said George. 'Downstairs in about ten minerts. I want to talk to you, Norton, I'm worried about you. I don't like my friends to make financial mistakes, do you, Columb?'

There was no reply.

'He doesn't,' went on George. 'You can take it from me he doesn't. Why even if Columb *had* ten thousand in ready cash, and we know he hasn't, why even then——'

'I'll see you down there,' Sax said. 'But I'm warning you, George, that this doctor man——'

'Now now,' said George. 'You trot down to my flat. Hasan will let you in and brew you a good strong coffee. I just want to get these flowers along to Anna and down my drink with the Doctor and I'll be with you.'

Sax went out swiftly.

'Well,' continued George. 'I'm very glad I dropped along.' He turned to Chance. 'I expect for a moument you really thought he was owed money by Columb there, didn't you, Doc?'

'Well——'

'Until of course I read out the cheque. Why I don't mind betting *he* owes *you* ten or fifteen dollars for drinks, doesn't he Columb?'

MacGrady was dull. 'What you say?'

'I was telling the doc here you don't owe Norton a cent,

not a single cent.' He was looking at the American with intense good humour. 'Do you, Columb?'

'I guess not.'

'The trouble about Norton's jokes is that he gets to take them seriously himself. He takes his jokes seriously, you see what I mean?'

'It was a fantasy,' said Chance.

'That's the word.'

'I began to think it must be,' Chance persisted. 'The sort of people who'll lend you ten thousand of anything, aren't the sort of people who are going to——'

'Cut up rough in public,' finished George. 'You know, Columb, I *like* your friend. How long are you staying, Doc?'

'Oh just a short time.'

'Good oh! Expect you'll be moving around quite a bit? Shibam, Cairo, Marrakesh—if that's not too far. Churchill, now, did a lot to popularise Marrakesh. You ought to try and fit it in.'

'I did think of it.'

'You pint?'

'Pint?'

'Yes—pictures. Churchill pints.'

'Oh I see. No, I'm afraid not.'

'Of course,' said George, 'there's a lot to see in the Zown if you've only got a week or two?'

'Six days,' said Chance. 'No, five.'

'Ow! that's different. You ought to let me get you a guide, oughtn't he, Columb?'

'Anna and I were going to tote him around.'

'Now, Columb! The poor little girl's whacked out. Let us fix him up. I could find a little girl or boy; they don't charge so much. You like children, Doc?'

'They fascinate me.'

'They do? That's bonzer. Know anything about Arab children?'

'Not very much. They're very beautiful, wild—like animals.'

'No,' said George, 'not animals. Oh dear me no. You

wouldn't say they were like animals would you, Columb, not the young Arab girls?'

'What you say?'

'The young Arab girls,' said George slowly, 'you wouldn't agree they were like animals—I'm not discussing the boys at the moment—but the girls, Columb. Yew wouldn't say they had much in common with animals? You wouldn't think of comparing the young Arab, the girl of say ten or eleven, they mature at twelve here you know, Doc, you wouldn't say——'

'No,' said MacGrady suddenly, 'no, I would not.' He looked across at Chance. 'You going to last out, Doctor?'

'You see,' went on George, 'that's a Western notion. In the West they don't understand children, they measure the mind by the body. If they see a body that's not fully developed, they infer that the mind inside it is in bud, whereas of course the body grows out of the mind. Why the Jesuits know that, and the Russians.'

'Yes?' prompted Chance.

'I don't like to talk religion,' said George shyly. 'I know too much about it. Oh I'm quite safe, you know, I don't get steamed up like poor old Sax. But the Colonel's the man to talk religion. Godfrey's been through Catholicism and come out on the other side. Just wait till you get Godfrey on the subject of the Arabs and the desert.'

'But about the animals?' Chance protested. 'Why is there no comparison between the Arab children and the animals?'

George yawned. 'You know you oughtn't to draw us out on this, ought he, Columb? It's getting late—or early; another day'll soon be coming up.'

'George, the Doctor here hasn't eaten since luncheon.'

'But,' said George, 'as Columb will agree, it's a question of innocence.'

'Innocence?' asked Chance.

'You see animals can't be innocent: oh dear me no! They don't know enough. Children *can* be. That's the fundamental difference, that's why there's no real comparison.'

'I see.'

'They can be,' said George, 'but they're *not,* especially not Arab children; and that's where we came back to religion again.'

'How?'

George began to chuckle, a preliminary tremor crossed his full black trouser top. 'I don't suppose, coming from the Old Country, that it's ever struck you innocence may not be a virtue? In practice, the Arabs don't believe in it; for them, innocence is something to be got rid of, they don't equate it with wisdom; they certainly don't trouble to preserve it, not sexual innocence anyway; it's not encouraged. Those little Arab boys and girls; why——'

'Look, George! I don't want to hurry you, but the Doctor here——'

'Hurry me?' said George. 'You hurry me on this particular topic? Now don't say that all your little weaknesses are a thing of the past just because you've taken the jump into matrimony.' He grinned amiably at Chance. 'You just ought to have heard us, Doc. At one time Columb here was getting some very interesting views. You draw him out one evening when you're not so hungry.'

MacGrady interrupted decisively. 'Look, Chance, if you want to eat at the Capuchin I'm going to call them up and book a table.'

Against the sun falling swiftly behind the hills George gathered up his roses. He swaddled them in short black arms and managed, in a crippled way, to extend a hand to Chance.

'Be seeing you, Doc. Drop into my place tomorrow. I'll just put these in Anna's room, be pretty for her when she comes to. They don't need water, Columb, they're in deep moss, lovely stuff, yellow as a wattle bush.'

'Thanks a lot, George, don't wake her.'

'I'll take my shoes off.' George kicked them off in the hall. 'I've got rubber feet! And Columb, don't worry about Norton.'

'I'm not.'

'Better warn the Doc to keep off religion though; it's Bill's soft spot. Yew and I will get a chat in the morning, so bring the Doc down, will you?'

'I'll see how Anna is. I'm not feeling too good myself right now.'

'It's important, Columb.'

'I doubt if I shall manage it tomorrow morning,' Chance said. 'I've letters to write.'

'I know, I know!' George was sniffing at his roses through his scarlet nose. 'I've got letters too. You wouldn't believe the number of letters I've got tucked away downstairs, would he, Columb?'

'No.'

'I'll see you in any case,' said George, 'on business at ten-thirty.'

'Eleven,' said MacGrady.

'Eleven it is.'

'Good oh! and thanks for the drinks. I'll pick up my shoes on the way out. I won't put them on, not worth it. I can go down in the lift. It's nice to live so close.'

'Yeah.'

Two minutes later the light went on in the hall, like a signal announcing something. They stood there in the sitting-room filled with the red flare of the sun and watched George tiptoe hugely to his shoes. His fingers to his gaping lips as he picked them up, still on tiptoe he let himself out to the lift.

'Do you really want to eat?' asked MacGrady.

'No, not much. Whisky makes food seem rather distasteful.'

'Have some more, then.'

'Thanks, I will.'

He helped himself, a large one, and then warm zonal water to the top of the tumbler.

'Well, what d'you think of George?'

'He's very frightening.'

'Just so, Chance. If we're going to beat him we've got to think fast.'

'Yes. It's probably best to confine ourselves to practical

arrangements. I'll cable the chest surgeon tomorrow and write you a letter to take with you. You leave the following morning, Wednesday, and return on Saturday or Sunday, bringing back my passport so that I can get out of this place.'

'You realise you've got to hold them off for those three days here in the flat?'

'Yes.'

'Who, Chance?'

'All of them I suppose: all of your friends.'

'And Zoe and Robin. They're not dangerous but they might let something slip if they discovered I'd left, and then it would come to the same thing.'

'And what is that?'

'I'm not just sure, that's what I want to know. It's what I'd most like to know. They'd get hold of Anna, I guess, and send someone quick to London, Heber probably, or maybe after tonight, Norton Sax. Think you can bring it off, Chance?'

'I think you'll have to tell me more. I mean, supposing one of them gets to you in London how could he force you to return? What would his hold be?'

'It would be a good one.'

'What?'

'They could get me arrested by the English police. They could bring up the past and bury Anna.'

'You'd better explain.'

'Look, Chance, I'm not telling you.'

Chance stepped across and closed the door. 'You appealed to me in two ways, MacGrady, both as a doctor and as a Catholic: in both capacities I've a right to your confidence. If you don't choose to give it me I'm under no moral obligation even to try to help you.'

'I'm not worried,' MacGrady said.

'You should be.'

'No, Chance. *You* should be.'

Chance was silent.

'Because,' said the American, 'you know you'll never leave the Zone until my problem has been rightly solved.'

'What have you done?' asked Chance.

MacGrady let the blind fall before the open window and the dying sky was sectioned by the silhouetted slats into a hundred red pieces. He stood back and on an impulse pulled over the white shutters and bolted them across. He switched on the chandelier and behind him the blind began to rap as the evening wind caught and blew its ladders against the wooden shutters.

'Chance! There are some things a man doesn't like to discuss with another man; he's not meant to.'

'I agree.'

'Don't interrupt! Look, Chance; the Church understands guilt, she knows how to handle it and you're only a Welfare State doctor from the provinces——'

'No,' said Chance, 'as a matter of fact I'm in the Prison Service.'

'The Prison Service?' MacGrady stood there blankly.

'Yes, ever since I came out of the Army—slightly over twelve years ago.'

'You mean you've been handling convicts exclusively?'

'Yes—a few of the officers and their families of course; but mainly criminals.'

MacGrady refilled his glass and sat down heavily on the edge of the divan. Against the shutter, the knocking of the Venetian blind measured out the silence.

'I had intended to tell you,' said Chance.

MacGrady said, 'You'll have talked to murderers—known them intimately. You'll have seen men under sentence of death.'

'Only two.'

The American put his glass down on the floor, one of his plump hands came up to his chin and held it as his eyes wandered to the shutter.

'As a matter of fact,' Chance went on, 'that was how I

knew Marcovicz—or Keller, if you like. I looked after him
for a year or two in Scotland during the War.'

Caught by a sudden movement of his foot, the other's glass
rolled across the floor leaving a trail as it circled a corner of
the Persian rug.

Chance picked it up, went over to the table and refilled it.
He handed it back to him and sat down again. He crossed his
legs with care, unobtrusively, not looking at the man opposite
him.

'Marcovicz has been trying to find out my whereabouts. I
saw him this afternoon and he alarmed me. He is a very
dangerous man I should say; far more—unpredictable than
anyone I have so far met——' and he added, 'Here, I mean.'

MacGrady reached down for his drink and half emptied the
glass between pale lips.

'He happens to have a strong sense of the Divine,' Chance
went on, 'and although he is a lapsed Jew he's unfortunately
not a materialist. That is really why I consider him to be so
very dangerous——'

'I'm hearing you.'

'I've nearly finished. We understand one another. I mean
we do have to do with sin; we recognise it as a reality.'

'I thought you were talking about crime, Chance?'

Chance hesitated. He shrunk back into his chair and
seemed to the other to become momentarily smaller and even
less robust.

'No,' he said, 'no. I don't think I meant to give you that
idea.'

'Then why rake up your job? Why try and mix me in with
Keller?'

'I don't know, MacGrady. I'm sorry——'

'I dislike your perpetual apologies,' MacGrady said, scowl-
ing at him.

'I think I may have been trying to trace a connection. I may
have thought there was a connection. Sometimes I get an idea
I don't know much about until I've said it.'

'If you think you can reduce me to the status of a common criminal and mix me up with a petty jewel-thief like Keller, a blackmailer lurking in the background on a rotten hunch he drew from one incident——'

'You know him then?' Chance interrupted quickly.

'No, I *don't* know him. I've no call to know Keller. We met, that's all; once, only once,' MacGrady was nearly shouting again, 'and *you* should never have met him. You should have kept yourself to yourself and not gone lunching around the Zone when you are my guest and Anna invited you to the Capuchin.'

'I met him before I met you. I met him the evening of the day I first went into The Botticelli; as a matter of fact, we went to Shibam together.'

'Then you should have told me,' MacGrady bawled. 'Why the hell didn't you put me wise to it, Chance? My God, am I to get no rest——?'

Again the silence intervened, spinning itself out to the metronome of the blind.

'I'm filling in no blanks,' he resumed more quietly. 'I don't know how much he told you or how much you already knew but I am not going to tell you what I did or did not do. My intentions are between myself and God.'

'I only wanted to know as much as was necessary to help you—that's all.'

'Then find out!' said MacGrady. 'Ask everybody. Crawl around piecing it together from my friends and enemies. I am bigger than my sins, Chance; I am a giant in comparison with my crimes. Whatever I have done, I tower above the act and I demand to be treated in scale with myself. I am a man made in the image of God, privileged to Hell and to Heaven, I'll not have myself mixed up with twentieth-century penology and the lousy doctrines of Freud. I'll not be dwarfed to the status of a criminal like Keller and if you've any idea of connecting me with him, then maybe you had better leave in the morning.'

'I'll think it over,' Chance said.

MacGrady, the door open behind him, left him sitting there in the dimly illumined room with the blind still knocking speculatively as fingers against the shutter. He heard him enter Anna's bedroom and close the door as his mind returned to the past.

He gulped the remainder of his whisky and stood up. Perhaps MacGrady was right; perhaps the confusion in his mind between the two men, between Markovicz and MacGrady, his religious inexperience, precluded him from making any useful judgement. He was, he knew, very tired; perhaps, now, just a little drunk.

Turning round, he saw MacGrady in the doorway. He was in his pyjamas and looked cool.

'You won't forget the light, will you?'

'The light?'

'Yeah. We get awful bills if it's left on. The tariff's pretty steep here in the Zone.'

'I see. No, I won't forget it.'

'You're all right, are you, Chance?'

'Yes, I'm all right.'

'But you think you may have taken on too much?'

'Yes, I was just wondering whether to go—or stay.'

'Well, that's very good,' said MacGrady, 'I like to hear you say that. That means you'll have to stay.'

'Does it?'

'Yes. A definite decision one way or other would have meant I should have been forced to pack off in the morning—with apologies of course.'

'Oh.'

As Chance moved over towards him, MacGrady switched off the light and when they had reached the door of his bedroom, said:

'I've got a present for you.'

'A present?'

'From Anna. She thought you might be needing it. It's a sleeping capsule.'

'Oh.'

L

'Maybe you don't take them?'

'I think I will tonight. Will you thank her?'

'Sure. She left something else for you too—it's in your bedroom.'

They said good night and Chance went into his room. He saw George Fraser's roses at once, standing on his dressing-table against their own vast reflection in the looking-glass. A card was propped up in front of them inscribed in American capital script.

He picked it up and it was faintly scented.

I FOUND THESE DISTURBING. I HOPE YOU TOOK YOUR PILL?

A.

For a moment he held the card tightly in his two hands and then very deliberately raised it to his lips. Through his closed door, through her open one, he heard her break off in the middle of a sentence before MacGrady closed the door.

He dropped the card and lifted the roses. He switched off the light and stepped through his open french window on to the tiny balcony and hurled the white basket and its cargo far out into the moonlight.

Too late, but long before it had reached the cinder patch and the shrubbery, he heard the voices: the gentle rumination of conversation on the ground. Leaning over the balcony, he watched the roses receding, tumbling out like a giant confetti as the basket somersaulted down to land at the feet of the two men by the little shrubbery.

They looked up: white roses strewed the grey grass and the hibiscus. He saw the two faces; George Fraser's fat with momentary astonishment, Sax's sharp and bright as a dagger. For an instant they beheld one another, separated only by the great height of the building, and then the laughter welled up from below; George bellowing and stamping over his dark shadow, Sax capering round him silently in the bitterness of his delight.

To shut out the noise, Chance ran back into his room, closed the windows and bolted the shutters. For minutes he remained in the bathroom before he remembered the capsule. He swallowed it, undressed and climbed into his bed to sleep the night through dreamlessly.

Tuesday

DREAMLESSLY into the next day, when he rose and dressed early. He did not know how early because his watch had stopped. But the fatima, who came at ten, had not arrived; the flat was quite silent and dark, dark at the back where his room was, where the cold shadow of the western morning was stamped on the grass and the thrown roses like a film of ink; dark at the front where the bedroom doors were all closed and the drawing-room shutters bolted upon the East.

Shoeless, he walked through the hall and swung the shutters open. Below him, the Arabs were about: the women going off to the markets down the side streets, the men as always walking slowly and very erect, perhaps to the mosques, perhaps to the cafés to drink mint tea. He wondered when they ate, and what; wondering, he realised that he himself was hungry. It struck him that he had not thought about his stomach for many hours, that he had had no time to do so. Vaguely he wondered what might be happening to it: it seemed to have slipped out of his immediate thinking.

Outside the hall door he found the milk, newly delivered, and in the kitchen a grease-proof packet of sliced toast, very stale: Macgovern's Jeely Pieces, Glasgow, prepared by Manchard et Fils, Marseilles. He ate six of them without butter because he could find none and then heated milk and coffee on the little Agipgas stove in the kitchen.

When it was ready he prepared a tray: three cups and saucers, a coffee jug, a milk jug: the last four slices of Macgovern's Jeely Pieces, a glass of orange juice from the refrigerator for Anna and a tomato juice for MacGrady. As an afterthought he added a bottle of Red Hackle and a jug of warmish water from the filter.

He still did not know what time it was although he had decided that it must be about eight o'clock. There was an hour's difference between the Zone and the Base, there was about two hours' difference between the Base and London: it was very confusing but immaterial on a day like this.

They would have to wake up when he knocked: it was unfortunate but necessary. He assured himself that it was very necessary to disturb them. There was the cable to send, the letter to write to Sir Gladwyn Dyce, both *his* responsibility; but they had to decide on the details of what he now thought of as the siege: how much food to get in to save shopping during the three or four days, what to do about the fatima, the passport business, MacGrady's plane tickets and the party tonight.

If they were going to Robin and Zoe's party it would be as well for MacGrady to start his illness during the course of the evening: the symptoms must be agreed upon, not acute enough to warrant a visit from the man Friese, but serious enough to confine the American to bed. His own departure, too, must be made to seem credible and clean: nothing left in his own room which might arouse the suspicions of the fatima.

Obviously, the longer they could hold off the others, the longer MacGrady's start, then the better their joint prospect of success. He personally did not greatly care if they did run him to earth within a few hours of the American's return: that would be too late, the action would have been accomplished and the change forced: afterwards, nothing could ever, in the Province of God, be the same again for anybody.

But with all this to determine, with so much delicately to be done, they could not be allowed to remain lazing in bed until their usual hour. They might have headaches, be half doped and wholly annoyed by his interference; but they would have to accept it.

Alert, a little irritable, he knocked on the door and waited.

He waited for quite a long time listening closely. Of its own accord his free hand rose to the wood again but before it could knock he withdrew it. They must have heard it, yet they had not replied.

Why had they not replied? He put the tray down gently on the floor, and it creaked; cups and saucers knocked and rattled and through the door he heard MacGrady groan.

Anna called out, 'Is that you——?'

'No,' he called, 'it's the doctor, it's Chance.' He wondered to whom he was referring. 'It's me; it's Bill here.'

'Is that you, Norton?' she asked. 'Oh dear! I just don't know who it is. Who is it?'

There was silence and he heard her yawn: imagined her arrangement of herself on the other side of the two inches of wood between them. He was quite certainly angered by the sudden airlessness of the passage and the wing-like beating within his forehead.

'It's me,' he called out, harshly. 'I don't know what the time is but I've brought you some coffee and orange juice.'

'Oh!' she sighed as though she were turning over or perhaps sitting up and making quick mirrorless adjustments to her hair and nightdress. 'Oh! It's the doctor. It's you, is it? I thought—I don't know what I thought. What's the time?'

'I don't know the time. I've brought you some coffee: I mean, I think we ought to start on things. It might be late.'

'Coffee?' she asked. 'Did you say coffee?'

'And orange juice.'

'What?'

'Orange juice.'

'Oh.'

There was silence again. He believed momentarily that he was himself asleep: words of the previous night's conversation returned to him. He heard distinctly the knocking of the venetian blind against the wooden shutter. The coffee steamed upwards from the tray at his feet and MacGrady spoke.

'Why don't you lie down, darling?'

'There's someone at the door, sweet, he says he's got coffee. I believe it's the doctor.'

'What d'you want, Chance? Oh, go let him in! What's he want, for God's sake?'

'No, darling, wake up now. You let him in. He's got coffee —sounds as though he's got a tray.'

'For heaven's sake, lie down, Anna.' The voice was slurred by a sheet or pillow.

'Can't you wake him?' called Chance.

'No, I can't. Why, I guess it must be very early. Have you really got coffee there?'

'Yes.'

'Are you dressed?'

'Yes.'

'And shaved?'

'Yes.'

'Are you fully dressed?'

He laughed.

'Yes, of course. Everything.'

'Well, then, I shall just have to wake Columb. I'm just as God made me. Whatever's the time, Chance?'

Chance imagined her naked: the tray which he had picked up rattled in his hand. 'I don't know. You see, the clocks seem to have stopped. The eight-day one isn't going, and my watch—but the milk's arrived.'

'Columb, wake up!'

'Don't *do* that!'

'But, darling, the doctor's brought us coffee. Go let him in.'

'He can let himself in.'

'No, Columb! Put on your dressing-gown. You look just awful.'

'You don't look so good yourself—What d'you want, Chance?'

'I've brought the coffee and some whisky and stuff. I thought we ought to talk before the fatima gets here. There's that cable to work out—a dozen things.'

'Did you say whisky?'

'Yes.'

'Well wait a minute.'

He heard him get out of bed and picked up the tray again expectantly.

MacGrady stood there. 'Bring it in,' he said.

'Are you sure it's all right?'

MacGrady rolled back to the bed without answering directly and Chance followed him in. The room smelt of garlic and talcum powder.

'Pour out that whisky, will you? I can't, I've got a morning shake. What the hell's the time?'

'I don't know.'

'Well, get me my watch. It's on the dressing-table.'

Chance handed it to him.

'It's two-thirty.' MacGrady shook the watch. 'No, that must have been last night. It's stopped. Oh what the hell!'

'What about Anna's coffee,' said Chance looking at the tall twin mirrors of the wardrobe door.

'Leave it for me,' came her voice from beneath the bedclothes. 'I'm not fit to be seen. Columb says I look like a New Yorker drawing in the morning.'

MacGrady said: 'Pour the whisky in my coffee, will you? What's this stuff?'

'Oh, Macgovern's Jeely Pieces,' said Chance. 'It was all I could find.'

They heard Anna's muffled laughter. 'Why that stuff's three months old—we left it for the mice.'

'You'd better take yours to your room,' said MacGrady. 'She won't come up until you do. Leave the doors open, we can talk like that, but not for five minutes. I've already exceeded my dawn vocabulary by about three hundred words.'

Chance filled his cup and then went across the corridor and sat on his bed.

He heard Anna emerge and the clink of her cup as she filled it.

'I think that's just very thoughtful of you, Chance,' she

said. 'But you shouldn't have done it. You should have called me. Why! I know where everything is.'

'Pipe down Anna, you're making my head ache.'

'I won't pipe down. I like to talk in the morning; *this* morning. I feel just chipper today, ready for anything. Say, Chance, where did you find the milk?'

'It was outside the door.'

'Was it? Well that means it's long after seven-thirty. They deliver at seven-thirty hereabouts. Did you look at the eight-day?'

'Yes, I told you,' said Chance, 'it had stopped.'

'Oh, Columb! You forgot to wind the eight-day. You promised you'd wind it every Sunday.'

'I did wind it.'

'Well, in any case,' Chance called, 'if it's as late as all that we'd better get down to things. There are lots of things to arrange if MacGrady really intends to go through with it.'

'Look, Chance, you've known me for a long——' he coughed violently, 'long enough to call me Columb.'

'Well then, why do *you* keep calling the poor man "Chance" all the time?' came Anna's voice.

'That's different! He's an Englishman; he expects to be called by his surname. I'm an American and I don't.'

'How d'you know? For all you know he might like to be called Bill.'

'Anna, you're annoying me. What were you saying, Chance?'

'I was thinking that we ought to get on with fixing up our arrangements. That is, if you still intend to go through with it.'

He heard the sounds of the stale toast being crunched.

'Do you?' He called again to MacGrady. 'Do you intend to do it? Do you want me to get that cable off and borrow my passport? Or have you changed your mind?'

'What's that, Chance? I can't hear what you're saying. I'm eating this toast stuff and it makes a buzz in my ears.'

'Of course he does, don't you, darling?' came Anna's voice. 'You haven't changed your mind about it, have you? The

Doctor's worried in case you changed your mind. Tell him you haven't, tell him you're going to get right away to London and get yourself all fixed up so we can all get away from here and have things like we always wanted them. Everything. Tell him, darling.'

'He knows!' said MacGrady dully, and then called out loudly, 'Don't you, Chance?'

'Yes,' said Chance.

'Well, what's to do then?'

'Well, I've been thinking it out,' Chance replied. 'If it's not too early for you to absorb it, I think we ought to divide things up.'

'Do you want another cup of coffee, Chance?' called Anna.

'Why do you keep calling me Chance this morning?' he asked irritably.

'Calling you what? Columb, I wish you'd quit eating that stuff and take him another cup of coffee. The poor man's been up for hours.'

'Aw! let him come in and get it.'

'It's all right,' Chance called. 'I'll heat up some more when you've finished.'

'What did you say about dividing things up, Chance? Can't you come a little closer, I'm deafening myself in here yelling at you.'

'You're deafening *every*one,' said Anna. 'You've got smokers' laryngitis. Your voice is like a buzz saw when you raise it.'

Chance moved out of his room and camped on the floor outside their door.

'I'll tell you what I thought,' he said.

'Go on, then,' said MacGrady, unnecessarily.

Chance frowned into his cup.

'Well,' he said, clearing his throat, 'Anna will have to get in food and stuff for three days——'

'Jeely Pieces,' she said. 'You both seem to go for *them*.'

'I shan't be here,' said MacGrady, 'maybe Chance doesn't like them.'

'He'll have to.'

'Also,' said Chance patiently, 'MacGrady, I mean Columb, will have to have his passport photograph taken. We will have to steam my own one off and we will have to think of some way of making him sound and look less American—his clothes, for example.'

'What's the matter with my clothes?'

'Well, nothing, but——'

'That's all right, Chance, I was only ribbing. I've been working on this myself. I lived in Cavendish Square two years. I can give a pretty good imitation of a London Englishman when I want to. I've even got a bowler hat somewhere if the moths haven't eaten it. Say, Anna, where's that bowler hat of mine?'

'Don't interrupt him, darling. What were you saying, Chance?'

'Well, there's the question of your plane ticket. If you're flying from the Zone you had better get it booked, hadn't you? And what happens if you're seen making for the airport?'

'Don't worry about that. I'll book the ticket in your name on your passport before lunch. I'll catch the early mail plane for the Base and go on from there direct by the first connection. Return journey, I'll book through from London Airport to the Zone. It will be Saturday night, and there's always a plane that night. If, for any reason, I'm held up in London, I'll cable' you or telephone. You'd be able to give me a day or two's grace if I needed them, wouldn't you, Chance?'

'Well——'

'What d'you say?'

'I was only thinking that under existing circumstances I would wait: but—it may not be under existing circumstances. In fact, it won't be. I mean things will be very different by Saturday. Each day after that is going to increase our difficulties.'

'I just don't know how you can think of that extra day,' Anna said. 'Chance and I boxed up in the flat, living on Jeely

Pieces with George and the others nosing around like wolves.'

'We've covered all that! Chance has got it sized up, he understands the situation and he's ready to go through with it.'

'There's his passport,' she insisted. 'You'll have to bring it back by Sunday at latest. Why! He just won't be able to move without it. Suppose something went wrong at home for him and he was wanted quickly in England, he'd be helpless. We got to think of *his* life too, darling. We don't know anything about him except that he *is* a doctor. Maybe his stand-in or maybe his family, if he's got one, maybe they——'

'Look! Has Chance mentioned his stand-in or his family?'

'No, darling. But——'

'Chance is a praying man,' said MacGrady. 'That's why he's come here and that's why we're using him. Don't be so god-damned faithless, Anna. If he has any worries he leaves them to God; he sees his life as it is, balanced brilliantly in Eternity. He's not worried by a day here or there because he sees the connection.' He turned on Chance, 'Don't you?'

'No.'

'That's because you're washed out.' MacGrady's emphasis ignored Anna's laughter. 'You're a tired man, but you're not going to let your weakness stop you; you'll hold out whatever happens.'

'Maybe the poor man's a prophet too,' she said. 'All the charismata; one jump ahead of everything before it happens. Maybe he knows what day you *will* be back and just what I'm going to wear Sunday.'

'Chance isn't interested in what you wear or don't wear. He's not that sort of a man. You recognise the sanctity of marriage, don't you?'

'I haven't really thought about it much.'

'You what?' MacGrady called.

'Oh stop badgering him, darling. He doesn't want to make his confession to you. And in any case there's no time for it now.'

'All right! All right! I just want to know if there's anything worrying Chance. I want to get it absolutely clear he's willing to hang on till Monday if necessary. What's the answer, Chance?'

'I suppose I will if I have to.'

'An' there's no extra snag as far as you're concerned?'

'I'm not sure.'

'Is it Keller?'

'Not entirely.'

'Heavens! Where does *he* come in?' came Anna's interruption.

'Will you be quiet, Anna? What's the consideration, Chance?'

'I'll discuss it later.' As Chance moved away from the door, he added, 'I should imagine you'd better be getting up.'

As he turned into the sitting-room he heard MacGrady following him and moved across to the window to wait for him there. He heard the rasp of his breathing and the soft sound of his naked feet as he padded up the polished floor of the corridor. Tracking through the bright room enlarged by the morning sun he slung the door to behind him and stopped in front of Chance. He was very pale, his pyjamas hung open over his fat chest and from beneath the lighted forehead the dull eyes glowered upwards.

'You've got an eye for Anna, haven't you?'

'Yes.'

'An extra day's going to screw you up so tight you might bust out at the seams? A primary situation: every hack movie from Gish to Garbo and onwards; only worse.'

'Why worse?'

'Because you happen to know we don't quite have a complete marriage and that's an element it's difficult for any man to stomach. It just cries aloud to be remedied by every damn fool that comes along even when a female's good and satisfied with what she's got.'

'I didn't think she was.'

'And that's just where you're right; but you're not such a dead-brain as to think you could help her without helping me, are you?'

'It's very much more difficult now.'

'Exactly. You happen to know that if there's a hack scene then *we* put it there and we get the slow clap when the audience walks out.'

'You seem to have got God very well organised,' Chance suggested.

'That's a cheap remark; it suggests you don't believe what I know you must believe as a Catholic. Only Protestants are capable of that sort of cheapness. We know very well, whatever the appearance, that we don't do the organising and that it's not so easy to sin your way right out of it. I've been trying longer than you and I know what I'm talking about.'

'You're suggesting that your marriage was made in Heaven too?'

'That is quite certain,' MacGrady said slowly. 'Anna was made to want me because she knew I was liable to go rotten without her and the rest doesn't matter at all.'

'Even the things she didn't know?'

'When we got married, Chance, there were several things she didn't know but only one of them weighed up to anything; and that's why you came along.'

'You mean your health?'

'When did she tell you?' MacGrady asked so quickly that Chance believed his own question must have been most welcome.

'Yesterday.'

'When I was in the bathroom?'

'Yes.'

'You should have avoided that, Chance! I'd like to be sure when I'm gone that you don't discuss me with Anna—all seduction begins with words.'

'No, with looks,' said Chance.

'So far as I am concerned you two can look at each other until you're spinning dizzy, but if you talk it'd better be about the time or the weather.'

Chance could see the tightness of the jaw beneath the puffy cheeks. 'I don't promise.'

MacGrady ignored it. He was fat with thought as he stood there in front of the taller man. Speaking without emphasis and probably with sincerity, he muttered, 'We only want time, that's all. I lied in my head when I let her think she'd got that, but only because we both know that time is the last corrective. In hell everyone is always under the compulsion to hurry: time continuously shrinks for the man in hell; for the saint it ceases to exist.'

'And if you are given it, what will you do with it?'

'I don't know. Maybe I'll go on as I have done, maybe not. I might change; I might be what I knew I could be when I was young.'

MacGrady moved over to the eight-day clock and lifted the glass bowl carefully between hands which trembled so that the cupid pendulum started to swing backwards and forwards between the ormolu pillars. He wound it and set the hands at nine-thirty.

'In a sense it doesn't matter,' he went on. 'A little more time and I'll know I'm not finished with yet—not yet. But I make no promises one way or another, I ask only for time to be in a position to make or not make future promises.' He turned round. 'All I might have to say when *I* come up for judgement is that I never bargained.'

'Then you take the opposite view to Markovicz,' Chance stated tentatively.

MacGrady rounded on him, 'Leave Keller out of this! I've told you before to forget you ever met that man. He'll get you all mixed up and he's an inessential.'

'I'm not so sure.'

'All right then! You'd better go your own way—we didn't choose.'

'Choose?'

'It might have been someone else, in some other bar on a different day of the week. It happened it was you, in The Botticelli and on Sunday night; that's all.'

'And you make no terms where I'm concerned.'

'I don't have to, not if I'm going to be consistent.'

'It's a pity in a way——' said Chance.

'That is the first discovery of the catechumen, that it's not good to be on your own, that it can be very unpleasant.' The American moved over to the door. 'Where are you lunching today?'

'The same place if it's open.'

'It should be. By the way, don't forget the party tonight. We're having drinks here first with Godfrey. I want you to meet him, he's a very interesting man, if you're getting worried about riots he's the man to ask. He knows it all.'

'What time?'

'Oh, round about seven-thirty. We'll possibly be leaving here about eight-fifteen.'

Chance heard him go into the bathroom, the sound of a violent self-induced coughing as he freed himself of the accumulated mucus of the night. As he waited there Anna came in.

'That clock's all haywire,' she said. 'I finally found my watch and it's only nine o'clock. You got us up awful early, Chance!'

He watched her repeat MacGrady's manœuvre with the clock but said nothing. As she slipped the globe back over the mechanism she glanced up at him. Her forehead was very smooth, her eyes wide and serene, but there was a certain questioning laxity about her lower lip. He stared back at her easily and then abruptly left her and went along to his bedroom to collect his things: camera, traveller's cheques, bathing-suit and towel.

Some time later, when MacGrady had dressed and gone he paused outside her door. He could hear no sound from the other side and wondered if perhaps she had climbed back into bed again. She might of course be in the kitchen, the bathroom or the sitting-room. Perhaps she was lying on the divan reading. He could not imagine her cooking or cleaning: it was impossible, he realised sharply, to imagine her doing anything very definite at all.

He went along the corridor slowly, glancing discreetly into

M

the rooms as he passed. The bathroom door was open: the sitting-room, dining-room and kitchen were all empty. He was sure that she had not gone out with MacGrady, and by the telephone in the hall he waited speculatively. From some-where a very faint sound reached him. He retraced his steps to the far end of the passage and listened outside her closed door. She was humming very quietly, somewhat breathlessly, with sufficient interruption to suggest that she might be dancing. He heard her song briefly discontinued as she jumped or high-kicked somewhere between the end of the bed and the wardrobe.

As he stooped to hear more clearly, the strap slipped from his shoulder and his camera fell to the floor with a clatter and she called out wildly:

'Who's there? Is that you——'

But she did not commit herself.

He left the camera where it had fallen and went down the passage very quickly and let himself out on to the landing.

Fool! he thought as he walked down the steep road into the town. I should have picked it up; she will not only know in which order we left the flat but she will know that I have acknowledged something. I should have said who it was and made a joke of it or I should have said, 'It's Chance here; it was my camera. Sorry if I startled you.'

As he turned a corner he heard the boy calling him.

'Say, wait for me. Don't go so fast, bud.'

'Go away.'

'I've been hanging around all morning. Sure got tired wait-ing for you, Doc!'

'Buzz off!'

'You been getting in big with the Americans?'

'No.'

'You been petting that American dame? While Señor Mac-Grady get downtown?'

'Go away, you little pest.'

Chance kicked him hard on the seat of his pants, the boy tripped and fell on his face. On the other side of the road

an old Arab doubled up with laughter and Chance strode on
to an Italian café in the Rue de Belgique opposite the Church
of Notre Dame de la Guerre.

He sat down and ordered a white coffee. While he was
waiting for it he got up and strolled back down the main road
and into the side street through which he had come; he hoped
it was the right one but he could not identify it because he
had observed nothing. For some reason he was walking with
his head down and thus noticed a patch of blood on the
paving stone from which there trailed away red asterisked
drops fallen from only a little height. He followed them for
a fair distance and then returned slowly to the café.

He saw with annoyance that in his absence someone had
taken a seat at his table, a man with grey centre-parted hair
wearing tinted spectacles. His clothes were expensive and
foreign, his nails well-manicured and his slender hairy wrists
enclosed in lawn cuffs held together by gold cuff-links.

Chance said, 'Excuse me, I believe this is my coffee.'

The man might have ignored him or he might not have
heard him: without seeing his eyes which were invisible
behind the sepia lenses, it was impossible to be sure.

'I was sitting here,' said Chance.

'You are speaking to me?' he replied without looking up.
His voice was as characterless as a bad recording: the words
perfectly enunciated but lacking inflexion or vitality.

'Why yes! I left my table for a moment. I thought you
might think it odd if I——'

'I never think anything odd,' he replied very precisely, 'and
I was in any case aware that you were about to sit here; that
is why I selected this table.'

He turned round sightlessly and appeared to study the
entrance to the café. As at a summons, Marcovicz came out
and limped quickly over to them. In front of Chance he
stopped, seized his hand in the long spongy grip, and smiled.

'Was I right?' he asked. 'Didn't I tell you I'd trace you
within a few hours, Doctor Chance? And what a coincidence
that your friends should be mine, that you should have moved

to the flat in the President Hoover. Why, it's just like the stir: we meet, we move on, we separate and then we meet again. This is Doctor Friese, another friend of mine, a friend of the MacGrady's too. Here in the Zone we all know each other.'

Chance freed his hand. 'In other words, Marcovicz, you have been following me?'

'Oh no, Doctor Chance, waiting for you, that's all. I was outside the President Hoover when you came out but you didn't see me. I nearly came up to you and then I saw that you looked as if you had something on your mind. Harassed you looked as though you'd heard from the Governor that there was going to be a smash-up over the food or as though you had a job to do in the topping-shed. When I saw your face I was sure of it and later when I saw you kick that kid I said to myself, "Now that's not like *him,* that's not like Doctor Chance. He'd never kick a kid——" '

Chance sat down. 'What do you want, Marcovicz?'

'I want nothing, nothing from you.' He gestured at the church. 'I only wanted to tell you that, after all, Magda will not be there: she has left.'

'She has gone back to Belgium, you mean?'

'Not likely! She wouldn't do that; not without me. She's left the Rendezvous. You won't see her again. Even I can't see her for the next few months. She's moved up in the world.' He glanced at Friese. 'I told my friend the Doctor here last night. I said, "Doctor Friese, it's very wonderful, yesterday I met an old friend, a doctor like yourself. A fine doctor, a man of humility who was willing to help even me." I said, "I want you to meet him, I'd like you to know him, he will be at the Notre Dame de la Guerre tomorrow morning between eleven and twelve. I know he will because he's a man who never breaks his word." And so together we came; we decided to wait for you. It got late, we waited and waited but you did not appear——'

Friese spoke. 'We would in any case have met later today, Doctor Chance, for in a sense I understand you are to be my guest, perhaps I should say my patron, at The Scheherazade this evening. I think you will enjoy yourself; but it will scarcely be the moment for intimate conversation—I have a rather amusing cabaret arranged—and there are certain facts I feel sure you should know about a mutual friend of ours.'

'Oh?'

'That is,' the Doctor continued, 'before you commit yourself in any professional sense.'

'I don't think you quite understand. I think you have made a mistake, Doctor Friese; I am merely a guest of the MacGrady's.'

Friese took off his spectacles and polished them gently on a piece of chamois leather.

'Even so,' he said, 'as a colleague of yours and an acquaintance of his I think it might interest you to know something of his background. It's as well, I always think, to know exactly where one is in such cases. In this part of the world, Doctor Chance, it can prove inconvenient to be under any misapprehension about casual acquaintances. Very inconvenient.'

Chance was impatient. He looked round him restlessly as though seeking, without rudeness, for some means of escape.

'In a few days or even sooner,' he said, 'I shall be leaving, so I don't really think——'

'I am very glad to hear it.'

'Oh yes,' cut in Marcovicz, 'that's what I said to you from the first, isn't it? I said, "You've come here for a holiday, Doctor Chance, you must relax, you must enjoy yourself, you mustn't get involved." ' With great frankness, a smooth and open advocate, he turned to Friese again.

'The Doctor is a very religious man, you know; I've heard that he's a convert and that he has come to the Zone to retreat from the world and think over the great step he has taken.'

'Quite. But from his own point of view, Keller, I think that a few further days might be a little too long for the Doctor.'

Chance said, 'I think I'm capable of deciding these things for myself.'

'Indeed!' replied the doctor, 'but you see, through no intention of your own, you've become involved in a very delicate situation; very delicate. My patient MacGrady is a very sick man——'

Chance got up and Marcovicz put a hand on his shoulder. 'It is like this, Doctor Chance; let *me* explain.'

Friese interrupted, 'If you don't mind, Keller, I think that my explanation would be preferable. I know that Doctor Chance will not be so foolish as to refuse to hear me out. I have access to no less than two members of the Secretariat in London. Both the senior ranks of the Police Force and the Home Office seem to enjoy a little holiday in the Zone which has become very fashionable of late. The somewhat highly-coloured reports of the activities here attract the enquiring mind. And of course my own little club, the Scheherazade, is exotic enough to have become a "must" for the short-term tourist. Perhaps, Doctor Chance, you are familiar with my name? At one time I had a rather exclusive psychiatric consultant practice in Wimpole Street. You may remember my evidence in several of the more lurid murder trials immediately prior to the War? Possibly you will be familiar with my little work *Recidivism and the Psychopathic Personality* which became something of a classic in the 'thirties? You might even recall my evidence for the defence during the trial of the Peak District murderer?'

'I don't think so,' Chance said sourly, 'because at that time I was taking my first M.B. at Trinity College, Dublin.'

'It is immaterial, quite immaterial! What I wanted to point out was that it would scarcely look well if it became known that a Prison Medical Officer had been spending his, no doubt well-earned, leave in mingling with his former charges and,' he tapped the table with his long fingers, 'staying as the guest of a person who had himself been an accessory *to the murder of his own wife.*'

'You are talking about MacGrady?'

'I am glad that I have made myself so clear. Don't misunderstand me; fortunately for my patient and yourself there has as yet been no trial in this case. I am not attempting to prejudge a man—but the facts are unusual. Perhaps you recall that my patient's first wife was a very wealthy woman, rather elderly and rather sick?'

'I know nothing about her, I did not even know that Mac-Grady had been married before. In any case I don't see that it has any bearing on my visit.'

'That is precisely why I wished to meet you this morning, Doctor. I wished to persuade you, if I could, that it had a very *direct* bearing on your visit.'

'You're telling me, in other words, that you're blackmailing MacGrady?' Chance said suddenly, 'You wish to exert pressure on me to leave his flat?'

'Precisely! I am happy to see that you can be so direct. Perhaps now, Keller, you would explain.'

'But it's not necessary,' said Marcovicz, as he seized a banana from the next table and began to eat it voraciously. 'The Doctor knows it all. He knows! crime and sin, sin and crime, he recognises them. He's a religious man and he knows where they begin and end, don't you, Doctor Chance? You've studied them in yourself and in us, and since I slipped up that day in Shibam, you've been working on it in your head, haven't you? And by this time——'

'I think we must avoid irrelevancies,' said Friese carefully. 'Here in the Zone we recognise neither sin nor crime. They are meaningless terms. In England, a vaguely Christian ethic combined with a bastardised Roman Law ensures that the terms are still temporarily valid and er—even distinctive. Despite the rather woolly humanism of certain of the Prison reformers, psychiatry as a penal science has not yet come into its own. The dilemmas of Behaviour, in the purely social sense, which of course is the only sense which ultimately matters, are——'

'He doesn't agree with you,' Marcovicz interrupted excitedly. 'I can see he doesn't. We'll have to tell him everything; we'll have to explain. Let me——'

'Some years ago,' Friese continued smoothly, 'our friend Keller was burgling a stateroom in a German liner in mid-Atlantic, when the occupant, an elderly diabetic, awoke. I need not tell you that Keller is a man of very considerable tension, Doctor; and that, in addition, he is a true compulsive who has always wanted to kill, to be what he calls "the instrument of the Most High." '

Friese's forehead was smooth, his voice precise and passionless. Marcovicz did not interrupt, seeming to be as spellbound as a man in the hands of an accomplished masseur.

'As you will understand, the two disorders, in this instance, led to the inevitable result. The moment the lady screamed, our friend decided she must be silenced in the only way which seemed to him likely to be permanently effective. He seized a pillow and——'

'I ran over to her,' Marcovicz was acting it all out by gesture. 'She was screaming ruin for me; she was my past and my future too, the future that God had ordained for me—fuller than all my dreams. I put the pillow over her face and held her down. I was going to leave it there, I was going to count as I always do count when I'm deciding something; but when I'd reached three, I heard something; I heard a noise in the room. I looked round and I saw him; I saw the American man in the doorway of the other cabin watching me. I didn't move; I stopped counting; my hands came up with the pillow still in them—leaving her there purple and gasping, but alive; still alive! I thought I was going to fix him first, when I saw he had a revolver in his hand and that he was not even pointing it at me, that it was hanging there from his hand like a toy pointing at a pattern in the carpet. I was foxed; I didn't understand! Then, as he came past to look at his wife, I smelt his breath and I saw the look in his eyes; a floating look as though he didn't know where he was or what he was going to do. And then, suddenly, I knew he didn't care, that he didn't know enough to care because he'd reached that great moment where a man may do one thing or the other, where there's no time because there's no decision, no *fix!* I decided to make his mind up for him. I turned on him and I said, "How long have you been out there? I forgot

to lock your bloody door! You could have been there a long
time," I said, "watching me at my work."

'He said nothing, he stood there like a fat ghost. He was
watching his wife die. Oh yes, she was dying all right; nice
and cleanly of shock—a natural death. It didn't take long and
when it was over I started to collect. I'd got enough there to
retire on, nearly all of it fastened up in a crocodile suitcase
I'd found in a cupboard. And then, when I smiled at this
American in the sort of way I can smile, he aimed his gun.
"You can leave that," he said. "All of it. You take nothing."
I wondered what he meant. I didn't like it; I was going to go
for him, but I thought better of it. "Why you dirty Yank," I
said. "You're not even drunk." And do you know what he
did? He crossed his wife on the forehead and he prayed and
then he crossed himself. I thought he'd forgotten me until he
looked round at me and said in that Yankee drawl of his, "No,
not drunk. Now get out! Get out the way you came in or
we'll neither of us ever leave this ship."

'I understood him perfectly! My father, a schoolmaster, had
brought me up to speak English even before he taught me
Yiddish or German; and I went. But before I went I told him
I'd got an accomplice, the night-steward, that if he was going
to send me down for murder we'd book him as an accessory—
standing there watching me start to do it for him. He said
nothing. I didn't know whether he was going to laugh or to
cry but I thought fast. I saw it all, everything, Doctor Chance.
I realised that we had each other, that we were trapped under
the hand of God.'

'Keller,' said Friese evenly, 'behaved very prudently. His
calculation was humanly exact. He left without the proceeds
of his crime and he held his tongue. It was not, in fact, until
many months later when he was convicted of burglary in
Hamburg that he had time to think the matter over clearly.'

'That's right! Time!' said Marcovicz. 'Time to think; time
to realise that I'd never been paid, that I'd solved somebody
else's problem at the expense of my own; that I was owed the
money, every cent of it, because I had been used, used. Mac-

Grady crossed himself; he thanked God, or he said he was sorry; yet he had done *nothing!* and I had *got* nothing. I made up my mind then; I said, "I'll do my bird* but when it's done I'm going to collect. I'll follow him, I'll follow that Yank into the Sahara Desert if necessary; but I'll have what he owes me —every nickel of it. I'll have what God owes me.'

Friese laughed, a weary titter.

'Doctor Friese laughs at me,' went on Marcovicz. 'But you don't laugh at me? You see, don't you Doctor Chance, how it has all come true? You understand how I trusted in God and how I waited. How, in the end, I tracked him down here to the Zone and caught up with him. How I found the man who was no better than I was, but safe beyond the law. A man with no greater Faith than my own but a dirtier sinner, a blacker criminal than any unbeliever.'

Friese produced a cigar case and proffered it to Chance.

'No thank you, I don't smoke cigars.'

He removed the band from his own, clipped the end and lighted it. 'I think, Keller, you have said all that is necessary for the present. As an educated man, Doctor Chance will I know agree that medical men the world over have never been averse from profiting by the decease of their patients when once it is seen to be inevitable. There was a notorious case in England some time ago I believe——'

'Oh but I'm sorry, believe me I'm sorry,' said Keller peering into Chance's face. 'I'm sorry, Doctor Chance, that it should have all have ended like this. I wanted you to meet Magda again; but it wouldn't be wise, I know it wouldn't be wise; and in any case she, like you, has moved on. She has left the Rendezvous and I've no objection to giving you her address. She is engaged for three months at the Sultan's Palace, if you wanted to see her you never could. She's in purdah, Doctor Chance, in *purdah*—she has taken the veil.' He shook and bellowed with laughter and then bounded away down the pavement to the Arab quarter.

'An interesting case,' murmured Dr. Friese, as he prepared

---

* Prison slang for sentence.

to make his departure. 'It is unfortunate that there should be such a predominantly sexual element in his paranoia. I have often thought that it is interesting to note that it is invariably a *young woman*—er—naked and even virginal who is rescued from the dragon and so proves to be the undoing of the knight.'

He slid his hands into his yellow gloves, picked up his malacca cane and with no smile strolled off towards the French quarter.

Chance sat on for a few moments and then crossed the road and entered the Church of Notre Dame de la Guerre, MacGrady's rosary swinging in his joined hands.

That evening he awaited their appearance with great impatience. He heard them take their showers at about six o'clock and tried to keep his eye off the slow revolutions of the cherubs on the pendulum of the eight-day clock by reading *The Comforters* which he had taken out of Anna's bookshelf beside the bureau. But he was in no mood to appreciate its delicate satire about Catholics like himself. Physically relaxed after an afternoon passed alone on the white sand below the Villa Hutton, he was mentally on edge; his mind returning recurrently to speculation about MacGrady's first wife. Her emergence in the conversation with Friese had troubled him. He flicked over the pages of the novel and read, on page 39 :

'At this point the West of Ireland took over, warning them "Converts have a lot to learn. You can always tell a convert from a cradle Catholic. There's something different." '

Hit by its aptness he dropped the book on the floor as the bell rang in the hall. He was recalled from St. Philumena's and the dilemmas of the convert heroine. The present shrilled through the flat and from the bedroom door he heard Mac-Grady call Anna in the bathroom. 'That'll be Godfrey, darling. I don't have any clothes on. Ask Chance to go let him in.'

'It's all right,' Chance called. 'Do you want me to give him a drink?'

'Sure! Give them both a drink; Pearl will be with him unless he's been thrashing her again. We'll be right with you —you'll like Godfrey. He's an aristocrat and he speaks Arabic.'

Pearl came in first, very dark; purple-black as a grape and with a pomegranate lipstick. Her long nails were silver-lacquered; she wore a baize-green dress and a rolled-gold locket on her sooty breast. Behind her, Godfrey Tyghe, the last in a long line of soldiers; a white man, pale and drawn together, his facial skin scoured and ageless as old chamois. About fifty, he had little pigment: pale clay-coloured hair, grey irises, bleached lips eyebrows and eyelashes.

They all three smiled at one another. Pearl fragile. Her nose was wide but quite straight; the whole face miniaturised; the negroid idea refined and compressed to become not merely presentable to the West but immediately acceptable. The wide lips parted before the exquisite teeth, as white as peeled nuts, with great agreeability; all the movements from the ankles to the dark vernacular of the face had the new grace of a child's. This too was how she was dressed, with little expenditure; a slavey's dress, a cheap bangle and a heart-shaped locket; yet her speech, though precise, was free of the usual rubbery consonants, the parted purple lips giving breath to a voice as light as a débutante's.

When they had introduced themselves she at once sat down cosily, crossing her legs at the ankles as though a royal photographer were present. Because she did not want gin or whisky Chance gave her a glass of lime-juice; but her husband accepted a large gin and stood with it formally, his back to the long window.

'MacGrady tells me you speak Arabic,' Chance said.

'Yes?' he questioned or stated.

'Did it take you long to learn it?'

'I have been here fifteen years. I think I became fluent after five.'

'It is difficult, I imagine?'

'The pronunciation, yes; the syntax, no.'

Chance drank and Pearl giggled. He tried again, 'You have travelled a lot in Africa? It must be tremendously interesting.'

'It was.'

'Oh I see, you've given it up?'

'I have.'

'You're going to settle down here?'

'Circumstances,' said the Colonel stiffly.

'Godfrey thinks there is going to be a war,' said Pearl precisely, 'a world war in the desert.'

Her husband frowned briefly; he moved forward so that he stood more over her.

'He thinks the Americans want it that way,' she said happily. 'Oh yes he says they will not spend enough money on bases to frighten the Arabs and Russians because it would suit them to use the desert for their big bombs. Godfrey says that is why they are going to have a rehearsal any day now.'

'*Pearl!*' said Colonel Tyghe looking down at her and then quickly up higher than Chance's head as is the habit of short men in the presence of taller ones.

Chance took his glass. 'The same again?'

'Thank you.'

'How very interesting!' said Chance over the decanter. 'Do you really think that?'

'Certainly! But Pearl has expressed it badly. Pearl——!'

'Yes, Godfrey,' she said smiling delightedly at Chance.

'Pearl, I have told you before that you are not to précis my private opinions in public.'

'No, Godfrey. But you did say that you think there *is* going to be a hydrogen war in the desert, didn't you? to lots of people?'

'I am fascinated,' Chance intervened. 'I wish you would talk about it.'

'He will,' she assured him. 'When Colonel Godfrey has finished his drink he will talk about it; but you must just come and sit beside me, Doctor Chance, and be patient. I will tell you about my mother.'

Chance sat down on the divan beside her and she immediately snuggled a black shoulder up against him. The Colonel parted his lips coldly at them.

'Won't your husband sit down too?' Chance suggested.

'My husband?' she tinkled with a laughter in the high key of Africa. 'My *husband!* The Colonel Godfrey is not my husband. I am a kept girl.'

The one-time soldier coughed into and then drained his glass.

'I wish,' he said with petulance, 'Pearl, I wish you would behave yourself. If you don't, my dear, I really think you had better not come tonight. I think you will have to go to your room.'

'Oh no, Godfrey, oh please! I want to come to the party. I will be very good, I will not say another word, I will not talk at all. I will just tell Doctor Chance about Mother——'

'There will be time for that later I think,' said the Colonel as Anna and MacGrady came into the room.

'You had a drink and got yourselves introduced?' the American said.

Anna kissed Pearl, smiled at Chance and Colonel Godfrey, and then drifted over to the drinks.

'Does anybody know what time Zoe and Robin are expecting us? I already ordered a taxi for seven-thirty, but maybe that's too early.'

'There would be room in the Buick, Anna,' said the Colonel.

'No, Godfrey, it's simpler to separate,' MacGrady said.

'I would like us all to be together,' Pearl interrupted. 'Then he cannot be angry with me in the car. He is angry because I wanted to tell Doctor Chance about the war in the desert.'

'What she say, Godfrey?'

'Pearl's English is improving, one has taken considerable pains with it, but she is still inclined to paraphrase badly.' Still looking at MacGrady and in the same tone of voice, he went on, 'She must not attempt to report speech. Do not, I beg you, Pearl, do this again tonight at the Moores' party.'

'Even at second hand,' Chance said, 'I found your theories fascinating—about the desert I mean.'

'I told you, Chance,' said MacGrady. 'Godfrey speaks Arabic. He *knows* the desert; he has more friends amongst the Arabs than amongst the Europeans, don't you, Godfrey?'

'At present, the atmosphere is not good. One might say with truth that it is particularly bad. My Arab friends do not often visit me, nor I them.'

'Godfrey, you know, Chance, has lived in the desert, haven't you, Godfrey?' said Anna with brief animation.

The Colonel grimaced, a quick raising of his chin. 'The Arab is a great walker,' he said suddenly. 'He will walk five hundred kilometres to buy a febrifuge for his camel.'

Chance: 'Really?'

Anna: 'You don't say?'

MacGrady: 'Don't interrupt him, Anna; Godfrey knows the Arabs.'

'I met one a hundred miles north of Gao where there is a small oasis, a post office and store, a mere wooden shed, you understand, where the desert peoples may pick up their mail and trade in their gold and diamonds. This particular man had——'

'Gold and diamonds?' asked Chance.

'Certainly. There is a good deal of surface gold in that area, diamonds too in the windy season. They lie in the sands in regions known to the Arab. This man had ordered medicine for an ailing camel. The parcel had not arrived and I overheard his conversation with the storekeeper. I was on a reconnaissance of my own at the time and I asked him what he would do. He said, "I will go on to the Zone and return!" He meant it. I saw him fill his water skins and set off quite by himself and in no hurry. The Arab never hurries.'

'But the poor camel!' said Anna.

'That would die of course. In fact, it had probably died some days before I met him; but since he had no means of knowing this it seemed reasonable to him to continue his journey even though the return distance might take him three weeks.'

'Extraordinary!' said Chance.

'It is Islamic,' said the Colonel, 'quite an attractive religion.'

'Godfrey's family were all Roman Catholics for hundreds of years,' Pearl put in excitedly. 'Many of them were roasted by a Protestant tribe, but Mother's a Methodist; she was converted by a missionary in Takaradi——'

'Pearl, do not interrupt!'

'But about the Arab and the camel,' Chance insisted. 'Surely——'

Colonel Tyghe spoke with controlled scorn. 'To the Arab the death of the camel is a secondary consideration to his first intention of travelling in order to preserve it. He says to himself, "I will procure medicine incidentally to my walking many miles over the sand. When I return I shall have accomplished a purpose by doing what I set out to do and in fulfilment of the will of Allah. No matter what the outcome I shall have lived a significant period of my life in doing what seemed to me to be good." '

'I see,' said Chance.

'I do not think so.' The Colonel regarded him with light hostility. 'It has taken me fifteen years to see and to reject it.'

'Godfrey speaks Arabic,' said MacGrady glaring at Chance.

Anna kissed his forehead. 'Darling, you seem to have got Godfrey's Arabic on the brain tonight. It's not poor Chance's fault.'

They all laughed.

'In Christendom, a woman crosses the road to Boots,' said Colonel Tyghe with nausea, 'to buy worm capsules for her pug. In the middle of the road she is disembowelled by a bus. I think one need say no more. I left London fifteen years ago and I have no wish to return.'

'Godfrey leaves everything,' said Pearl. 'He left England because it is so insular—full of vegetarian restaurants. Godfrey says that until they become civilised and open cannibal restaurants too he will never go there again.'

'A joke of course. But Pearl has told it badly and quite out of context.'

'But, Godfrey——'

'I will admit that in the jungle some years ago I did for a time acquire the taste for it.'

'Mother cooks wonderfully,' Pearl insisted. 'She has a recipe for corned beef——'

'Pearl!'

Anna was by Chance. She leaned against him for a moment laughing helplessly.

'Oh, isn't she cute? Oh, Pearl darling!'

They all began to laugh. Even the Colonel tittered briefly through straight lips. 'I think it is time we left, MacGrady. Pearl, I wish to remind you that you are to remain silent at the party this evening. Nobody is interested in either you or your mother. Go and wash before we leave.'

Getting up obediently, she assured them, 'Tonight he will whip me. He is a very cruel man and he is jealous of Mother. If I were your girl you wouldn't whip me, would you Doctor Chance?'

'Pearl!'

She flashed him a smile and slipped from the room.

In mitigation he said, 'Pearl is a little stubborn. It is true that one has to get out the whip occasionally. It is the only thing these girls understand.'

'But, Godfrey?' said Anna.

'I do not believe,' the Colonel concluded, 'that the practice would be sympathetically received in America. The West does not understand its women.'

'Godfrey has lived with the Arabs, Chance,' said Mac-Grady when they were all in the lift. 'He has absorbed all of their values. He speaks Arabic fluently. He reads it, he writes it. Much of their philosophy——'

'Was he a Mohammedan?' Chance was embarrassed, 'I mean, were you a Mohammedan, Colonel?'

N

'A monotheist merely,' said Colonel Godfrey. 'Pearl, do not meddle with the lift buttons.'

In the taxi they followed the Buick into the Arab quarter. Driving round the Socco through the old wall and the wide archway of the Medina, they drew up on a cobbled court-yard facing the Sultan's palace.

Blue was predominant; the walls through which they had driven, pale; the sentry outside the fretted entrance to the palace, stygian blue; and the women passing silently in snow-blue burnouses beneath the luminous gentian of the night sky.

Talking, gathering together between the cars, they turned from the façade of the palace into the warmth of a narrow street. They turned right and left, laughing and walking loosely through the blueness and then climbed stairs through the inner wall of the Medina to a higher level. They threaded their way through narrowing alleys scented with smoke and spice where many dark entrances gave access to the Arab dwellings within the wall.

Once again they ascended, and at the top of the steps, not far beneath the hacked battlements and antique cannon of the fortress wall, entered the doorway of Heber's *rez-de-chaussée* perched over its courtyard half-way up the inside of the wall.

'It's just beautiful!' said Anna to Lady Zoe, an ageless mauve-haired woman with wild eyes. 'I haven't been here since Heber first took it over and I'd never have recognised it. Why, that archway in gold!'

Lady Zoe kissed her. 'Heber took out all the doors,' she said in a voice which just missed the timbre of the hunting field, 'but I must say I shall dream about this floor. It's glass you see or possibly polythene. We're over part of the court-yard. Robin darling, they've come! Robin's simply dying to talk to you, Colonel. He wants to pick your brains about the desert for an I.C.B.M. project he's working on.'

She led them into a tiny room illumined principally from lights in the courtyard below. These threw shadows of vast

leaves, ceramic birds and slender vases against the frosty glass
on which they walked. The room was warmly dim and seemed
to be very crowded. People sat on ottomans bordering the
walls or stood clustered by the empty arches of the many
doorways leading into other tiny rooms.

Robin, Lady Zoe's third or fourth husband was a used-
looking man with a painstakingly impeccable accent and
manner. The newness of the Moore's arrival, their host's half-
completed interior decorations and their studied ease with one
another gave everything the air of a bridal housewarming
through which, in less foreign circumstances, the guests would
have moved carefully.

Chance had time to note Doctor Friese in conversation with
Heber, who ignored them, in one of the archways, two or
three American girls from the American air base discussing
American air supremacy avidly, and the white bulk of George
Fraser in deep conversation with a smart young Arab. But
before he could come to any more clear appreciation of the
party, he was being introduced to Lady Zoe.

'Oh yes,' she said, 'you're the Doctor. Now do tell me what
is all this about thingummy's chest? I never can remember
his name, the American man with the adorable wife.'

'Well, as a matter of fact, I don't really——'

'We will sit down,' she said, 'I do so like to sit down when
I'm talking. That could be a sign of middle-age I suppose; one
sees lists of them in *Vogue.*'

She sat him down beside her on a divan, so masterfully that
for a moment he felt as owned as her husband. 'Don't worry
about any of these other people,' she went on. 'They're just
people, charming you know and so interesting; but *you're*
English, aren't you?'

'Yes,' he said.

'You have interesting eyes. Very interesting.' She appeared
to study his face closely but he had the impression that she
had left it far behind even before she started. 'Are you just
a little bit mad?'

Chance accepted a drink from Robin Moore and then

looked into his wife's eyes; they were greenish and quite mad.

'Because I am,' she said. 'It's a frightful nuisance isn't it?'

'I don't know,' he said dully.

'But you must talk; you simply must talk to me. I want to know all about you very quickly.'

'So that you can forget me equally quickly?' he put in.

She didn't laugh. For the smallest part of a second she became even more earnest and then forgot that too. 'I think I'm going to like you. Where do you come from?'

'Petersfield. But I live, or rather work, in Scotland.'

She looked pained. 'What county, I mean?'

'I really don't know, my father was born in Warrington and my mother in Worthing.'

'Ah, Warrington of course,' she began, and then thought better of it for a moment, until, having caught the polite incredulity of his glance——

'I used to stay there. She's a kinswoman of mine. Her sister was quite beautiful; my father went to Paris with her aunt. He was an eccentric you know,' she winked, 'like us! In other words, my dear, mad.'

'Really?'

'Now come on, who else? The Sevenoaks, you'll know them and the Pearses, they've got land in Ireland too.' She appropriated the county in three sentences and then moved on to Buckingham Palace.

'And would you believe it? Nicolette used to sit on Edward VII's knee. Even at that age she suspected his motives and she didn't like his beard I remember, so he didn't get very far. Robin, by the way, yearns for the days of Edwardian diplomacy; but I always tell him his height would have been against him even then. Now why can't you doctors do something about that? I mean, just imagine Robin at a levée.'

Chance obediently searched him out but couldn't see him. He had disappeared behind a press of guests.

'Now *you*,' she was saying as though she were trying to fix

him in her mind for a moment, 'do tell me if you're staying
with that nice American couple indefinitely?'

'No,' he said with an effort. 'As a matter of fact I'm leaving
tomorrow morning—quite certainly. I have to get back fairly
soon and——'

'Too bad, but whatever for? Oh of course you're a doctor;
though surely they have frightfully long holidays, don't they?'

'Not nowadays.'

'You don't look in the least like a doctor. Not in the very
least.'

'You think there's a type?'

'You look sensual. What my mother would have called
passionate. It goes with the other, you know.'

'Oh.'

She gave her head a little shake as though she were waking
up from a doze and then got up abruptly. 'I believe you
remind me of a friend of Robin's, a writer. He's a darling but
alarmingly croyant.'

'You mean religious?'

'Dreadfully; an R.C.' She signalled to someone whom
Chance could not see. 'Well now you'll have to talk to Colonel
Tyghe and Pearl, but you must sit next to me at dinner
because I think I rather like you.'

She moved away youngly, her mauve page-boy hair shaking
round her once-lovely face as she thrust the Colonel and Pearl
down on either side of him.

The Colonel looked as pale and detached as ever. He was
patently one of those cold men who become even more remote
under the influence of alcohol. Only the increased tilt of his
chin betrayed him, giving the impression that his self-esteem
had grown so tall that he had difficulty in seeing over the top
of it.

Pearl said, 'Colonel Godfrey is getting quite drunk, Doctor
Chance. I like him to be drunk because then he is too far away
to punish me.'

The soldier smiled disdainfully.

'I promise you,' she went on, 'that all he will tell me tonight will be "Be quiet, Pearl!" You will hear him saying it all the evening.'

The Colonel spoke: 'I hear you are leaving in the morning?'

'Yes.'

'A pity! I had hoped to show you my photographs; they are quite unique.'

'Brown girls!' said Pearl. 'No good brown trash all of them. Me, I am soot-black on the outside but red on the inside, aren't I, Colonel Godfrey?' And she laughed again—a sharp cry this time, a sound from the kraal which monstrously and momentarily cut through all conversation. In the silence Chance fidgeted, but Colonel Godfrey only gazed haughtily ahead of him as Pearl burrowed her small behind further into the cushions, delighted with the pause she had effected.

'Pouff!' she said, 'looking at *me* like that! Do they think I care? I know they are none of them married; they are kept girls, all of them, second or third time round. In Africa they couldn't get a nigger in a woodpile, no they could not, not in Johannesburg.' Suddenly, before they could stop her, she sprang up and pirouetted in front of them in her little green dress. '*They* couldn't get a Colonel of Brigades with a racecourse and a flat in Germany Street!'

'*Jermyn* Street,' Colonel Godfrey corrected her, a pale gleam in his eyes. 'Pearl, sit down or I shall send you home.'

She shook herself, appeared suddenly meek. 'I'll be good, but I won't sit down. I will go and talk to Mr. Fraser very quietly because he likes me and sends postcards to Mother.'

Following her glance, Chance watched the Colonel's face. He saw no change in the expression; but she evidently discerned something, a tiny movement of the neck muscles, perhaps, as his chin was lifted a fraction of a degree higher. She left them happily but the next moment she was back again with a tray of glasses.

'Serving girl,' she said. 'I know my place.'

When she had gone for the second time, Colonel Godfrey glanced at Chance.

'I do not care for this sort of thing,' he said. 'Do you?'

'No.' Chance's agreement was hasty.

'For what?'

'I beg your pardon?'

'For what do you not care?'

Chance hesitated. 'Parties,' he said firmly.

'Precisely.' The Colonel appeared to examine their accord very carefully before he made his next remark which was again a statement.

'You are a Roman Catholic.'

'Yes.'

'A convert?'

'Yes.'

'A recent one?'

'Fairly. I was received into the Church a year ago; but I was only confirmed a few weeks ago.' Chance corrected himself. 'Good God no, I was only confirmed four days ago. How extraordinary! I seem to have been here months.'

'Not at all. You have merely experienced Africa.'

'I have?'

'You are a monotheist as are the Arabs and the Jews; both, I might point out, desert peoples. You should live in the jungle for a time. You would soon become a Hindu.'

'I don't understand you.'

'The trees!' said Colonel Tyghe. 'They make polytheism inevitable. In the desert it is different. There is only the sun to look at, monotheism is therefore inescapable.'

'You think that religious belief is merely a question of geography?'

The Colonel smirked, an affirmative smirk.

'Surely,' Chance concluded, 'that's a little old-fashioned.'

'Not more so than the Koran or the Old Testament, I think.'

'You are not a theist at all, then?' Chance suggested. 'I mean, you don't believe in God?'

'I have no need to, since, if He exists, I consider it to be His function to believe in me.'

Chance laughed.

'Tell me about the war.'

The Colonel was silent for some moments, long enough for Chance to suppose that he was going to ignore the request but at last he said:

'The West has made the great mistake of teaching the Arab the time.'

'Yes?'

'Since you understand me so well I see I need say no more.'

'I was hoping you *would* say more.'

'I was going to have added that one cannot teach people the time without giving them a sense of history.'

'That is interesting.'

'As interesting as it is obvious,' he snapped. 'It is the mistake the later Roman Emperors made in the colonisation of Northern Europe.'

'But they were dealing with barbarians.'

'Precisely! As you will agree, the West in foisting pan-Arabism upon this century have not that excuse, since they are themselves the barbarians of our time.' And he added in his coldest tones. 'They will pay the price. A leader will arise and unite the Middle East with South Asia. The enormous wealth and military potential of the Islamic communities will be harnessed *not* to the effete values of Christianity which are totally unacceptable to the philosophy of Islam, but to the new, saner and more compatible values of Marxism. The war will be fought.'

'You mean the war in the desert?'

'Not in the desert.' Colonel Godfrey helped himself to Chance's drink. 'Out of it.'

'Out of it?'

'Certainly! The war will be fought out of it, on the edges. The *casus belli* will have come out of the desert like your single God; it will lay waste the green places and enlarge the deserts in which already little can grow. There will be no fighting in the desert, only out of it, always on the periphery.'

Lady Zoe paused in front of them, looking at them as

happily as a good hostess who sees that an introduction has been a success. They both ignored her.

Chance tried to seize a solid fact before it was too late.

'You mean the North African coast?'

'I do *not* mean the North African coast. I mean the desert into which we have wandered, the twentieth-century desert of Western values which we carry with us and upon the edge of which we like to imagine we are living. It is a little unfortunate for you, I think, that the New Dialectic should have——'

'I'm sorry, but what do you mean by the new dialectic?'

'I prefer not to be interrupted; as I was about to say——'

'But surely,' Chance insisted. 'All this involves you too, doesn't it?'

'I have made my choice,' replied the Colonel with finality. He looked up as MacGrady came over to them, and his glance seemed to convey faint boredom and impatience with the conversation in which he had been forced to indulge.

'Don't let me interrupt you, Chance. I've been wanting you to talk to Godfrey; but we're moving on to the Scheherazade.'

'You're looking a little pale,' said Chance pointedly.

'Yeah, yeah, I'm not feeling quite the thing, but don't let that worry you now. How did you get on with Godfrey?'

'Oh I found——'

'Godfrey knows things, he understands the Arab mentality. If you'd left in the morning without seeing him you'd have been wasting your time in the Zone. You might just as well have stayed home.'

'Are we leaving now?' inquired the Colonel.

'Just as soon as we can get everyone together. If you want to finish your conversation with Godfrey, Chance, you could come along with him and Pearl; Anna and I are going with Zoe and Robin.'

'Always provided you can get in,' chimed in Lady Zoe from behind. 'It's a rather small motor-car.'

The house inside the Spanish Wall was emptying. They stood there, an island amid the haste of departing guests and last-minute assignations. Chance noticed most of the American women from the Air Base had disappeared and with them the merry bulk of George Fraser and his shadowing companion from The Botticelli Bar.

He turned to MacGrady. 'I never saw Friese. Where is he?'

'You wouldn't know Friese even if you saw him, so——'

'I forgot to tell you, I met him this morning at a café.'

'You did?'

'Yes.'

The American's head fell forward on his bow-tie. His eyes closed and opened again to search Chance's face. He smiled socially and with obvious effort.

'He's gone on ahead I guess,' he said smoothly, 'to oversee the kous-kous.'

'Oh.'

'You had a talk with him?' he asked as Anna joined them.

'We did talk. It wasn't very interesting.' Chance appealed to Anna. 'You know I'm not sure he oughtn't to go back to bed, he's looking very pale isn't he, Anna?'

She took him up very quickly. 'He just won't do it, Chance; and we can't argue with him in the middle of a party, can we?'

MacGrady put his head down and broke out of the circle in his bull-like fashion.

'I'll be all right,' he roared, 'if only you'll all leave me alone. It's my belly again. It's not my chest, you understand? It's nothing to do with my lungs; they're finished anyway and I get along without them. If I'm not right tomorrow I'll get rested up for a day or two as soon as Chance has gone.' He paused inside the golden archway and turned on them. 'That's all I need: a little rest and not too much to eat or drink and I'll be ready to go on dying on my feet again for another couple of years—if that'll satisfy everybody.'

There was so much of belligerence in his expression at the conclusion of this speech that Chance was quite unable to decide whether he were sincere or simply dissembling very cleverly with the cue they had provided him.

Zoe Moore laughed; it was a deep snigger involving the

diaphragm and the nose, so comically inelegant that they were all quite effortlessly able to join her.

Colonel Godfrey said: 'Look here, MacGrady, if you don't feel fit in the morning I'll send you something down from my drug-rack. I have a rather effective native remedy——'

'What is it?'

'It's a pigmy cure I picked up in the jungle primarily used for yaws but effective in gastric conditions as well.'

'I don't *have* yaws! If I want anything I'll get it from the chemist, or from Chance before he leaves.'

'He doesn't trust Colonel Godfrey,' said Pearl as they made their way out into the courtyard where Robin Moore was awaiting them in a tiny car with the accelerator pedal pressed hard down.

'Robin has always wanted a Bentley with a three-inch exhaust pipe,' his wife shouted through the noise. 'But since Dudley got most of my money when he divorced me he's always had to buy his motor-cars off the peg.'

'You see,' said Pearl as she and Chance got into the back of the Colonel's Buick. 'What did I tell you, Professor Chance? She is worse than a kept girl. She has to buy her lovers.'

They followed the little car through the streets and Chance tried to draw out the Colonel on the subject of the desert.

'I was very interested in your theories about God and the desert.'

'No doubt.'

'You implied that the physical desert has its counterpart in the mind? That, like the Arabs, we are most of us living on the margins of consciousness.'

'Nothing of the sort.'

'I beg your pardon?'

'The Arab does not live on the edge of his desert. I believe I related to you the story of the Arab and his camel?'

'Oh yes you did, but——'

'A simple illustration. When people no longer voluntarily seek the desert, the desert will seek them.'

'But for what reason?'

'According to the old mystics it is the precursor of the divine.'

'I agree,' said Chance.

'But according to the new,' concluded the Colonel, 'it must precede the discernment of The Ultimate.'

'And what is The Ultimate?'

The Colonel blew his horn. 'The new dialectic,' he said with finality.

From beside Chance, Pearl provided the postscript:

'I want Colonel Godfrey to take me to London,' she said. 'He could not whip me there. He would be put into prison wouldn't he, Doctor Chance?'

'Yes I suppose he would,' said Chance happily.

'Imagine the Colonel Godfrey in prison!' She gave her kraal-cry. 'Just imagine.'

The Scheherazade was tall and dark, illumined inside by mosque-lights of intricate metal which hung on chains from a high black ceiling. The walls also were black but covered all over with tiny enamelled designs of mandalas flowers and foliage through which painted beasts, birds and reptiles peered and crawled. Here and there, heavily fretted screens in the Moorish tradition gave access to shadowy alcoves furnished with wide ottomans and floors covered with fresh rushes and herbs.

At one side of the main space a group of Arab musicians squatted within a small raised enclosure carpeted with woven palm. They played continuously and without any intermission: sounds as indeterminate as those made by soft winds in their passage through thin shrubs and cereal. When the instrumentalists sang, their singing voices, though so near, sounded as if they came from far away: isolated calls and cries as sad and suggestive as those which may be heard at dusk when children stay up late.

Through all that followed the Arabs sketched in their notes of music and song very casually, providing the accompaniment as from a world no more than half asleep.

'Friese feeds them *kief*,' said MacGrady, who had been waiting for them. 'He has it run in from the country by jeep once a week.'

'I just love that smell, don't you, Columb?' said Anna.

'You don't want to get too fond of it or you'll be in heresy like the rest of them.'

They walked to the further end of the room where the Moores were already reclining before three low tables drawn together against a side-wall.

'The Doctor!' said Lady Zoe. 'He must sit next to me. I hear he is leaving in the morning and unless I am muddling him with someone else he intrigues me.'

'That woman has a wonderful face,' MacGrady told him. 'Her second husband was an earl. You do realise that, don't you, Chance?'

Chance caught Anna's glance, both of her obscurely violet eyes. She hung back momentarily as the others moved forward to take their places in a long row against the cushioned wall.

'Can you light my cigarette? No, from your own will do.'

He held it out and she took his hand in her fingers until the cigarettes touched. She drew slowly, a mere breath which set the tobacco burning brightly. He was about to withdraw his hand when she retained it pulling it closer so that the lighted end of his cigarette was ground delicately into her own as their brightness increased.

She let a little smoke drift from her mouth as she passed him and sat down between her husband and the Colonel. She did not thank him, and a little bewildered he remained there a moment too long, conspicuous.

Behind him Dr. Friese emerged from the kitchens; he came forward as softly as a creature emerging from its own good place, and at his coming there was a perceptible change in everything, an organisation of everybody. A few more lights were switched on, the uniformed Arab in the doorway peered in and signalled something to the musicians who sank their notes to a level of secrecy as nearly private as their reveries.

Moving on past Chance with a nod of recognition, the Doctor greeted Lady Zoe, who smiled at him briefly.

A waiter appeared carrying a demi-john of the palest wine.

'A consignment I must ask everyone to sample,' said the Doctor. 'It reached me only this morning but I believe it will have travelled well if a little surreptitiously.'

'Smuggled,' said MacGrady.

Friese raised his glass. 'Let us drink to all frontiers.'

They drank and Anna said, 'Poor Chance, why doesn't someone tell him where to sit?'

'He has been told,' said Lady Zoe. 'I am insisting on his sitting next to me but he's most reluctant about it because I have told him I am passionate.'

'If you remember,' said Chance taking his seat beside her, 'I didn't believe you.'

'No,' she sighed, 'they never do, until afterwards.'

Everyone laughed and Pearl in the clipped tones of the Colonel said, 'White women are invariably frigid.'

'The Esquimaux,' began Lady Zoe, and sniggered. 'Oh dear, how dreadful, all that fur! Robin tells me they never take it off.'

Three waiters were bringing in the food; covered dishes heaped high with flocculent mounds of semolina in which were embedded black olives, almonds, raisins, peppers and breast of mutton.

'I'll have to insist on soup alone,' said MacGrady to Friese, 'and not too spicey. I'm not eating tonight.'

'My dear boy I am sorry. Are you not well?'

'It's my belly, nothing serious; but if I don't watch it it may develop.'

'I see, that's too bad. Perhaps you had better let me look in on you tomorrow morning?'

'Thanks, I'll call you if I need you; but I think if I rest up for a day or two I'll be ready for anything by the week-end.'

'But you've got a doctor. Or don't you trust him?' Lady Zoe's glance wavered over Chance. 'You're too thin, my dear. I mean, as a doctor; they should always be plump.'

'Chance is leaving in the morning,' said Anna. 'This is his farewell party and I'm far more worried about him than about Columb. He doesn't eat as much as a humming-bird.'

'Oh for God's sake,' interrupted MacGrady. 'Send me in some soup and start the cabaret. We came here to be amused not to talk about our health.'

'Ah! The cabaret. Alas! My girls have left me as a result of a most profligate offer on the part of the Sultan. As a matter of fact I'm expecting his brother, Yacef Ali, at any moment.' As Friese spoke the far door was opened by the porter and Magda came in followed by a smart middle-aged Arab wearing a dinner jacket. They were shown by the head waiter to one of the alcoves on the opposite side of the room.

Friese excused himself and with his stick ported beneath his left arm bowed them to their table. He remained with them a few minutes and then clapped his hands casually and took up his original position beside Lady Zoe.

'What an enchanting man,' she said, 'and just at the interesting age. Who is the gal, Doctor Friese?'

'A Belgian I believe. I fear the traffic at the Palace is a little too rapid for one to recall names. The Sultan's brother has a Westernised palate and the income to indulge it.

'I know the girl,' said Chance. 'I met her on Sunday.'

Anna: 'My my, I must have misjudged you, Chance.'

Lady Zoe: 'My dear, you must introduce me to the Arab, he looks so elegant.'

The musicians had changed their tempo: a more staccato melody, louder, filled with cymbals, small bells and hand-drum beats. As the brighter lights were dimmed, two young Arabs entered from a doorway at the back of one of the screened alcoves. They were dressed in pink silk and pearls and wore tiny bridal caps over their painted faces. From these, diaphanous veils trailed down to their naked feet. Their loose bloomers, pale as wild roses, were fastened tightly above their ankles with flowery clasps to emphasise the perfect conformation of their feet and toes, the nails lacquered with gold.

They bowed deeply, stood slowly straight again and then began to dance rigidly. Perfectly still in the one place they rippled almost imperceptibly, their slender hips flickering behind the silks. They started to circle one another deftly and delicately, their eyes wide, brown, and moistly hostile, fixed always on the row of faces for whom they danced. In the grip of the music they drew slowly nearer to the tables, weaving down their entire length and back again, their simulated excitement growing as their proximity allowed them first to touch then to rebound away again. Their red lips, heavily painted, parted with mock desire, their lids dropped until their lashes rested on their dark cheeks, and their hands sought convulsively the floating silk which always receded from their grasp.

On the tiny dais the musicians watched them; much older men with sun-flayed faces and fixed eyes whose heads moved in unison as they followed the weavings of the dancers down the lighted table. The pace increased, the dancing boys shuddered and wept tears of perspiration down their powdered cheeks. At a final crescendo of bells and tambourines they paused before falling suddenly to their crossed and flowered ankles, their young necks bent in submission beneath their veils.

There were a few hand-claps, somebody threw a hundred-peseta note and one of the boys tucked it like a cockade into a fold of his pink silk cap. They bowed themselves out but returned in a few moments with a tray of mint tea, a bundle of long pipes and goatskin pouches of *kief*. MacGrady got up.

'I like to smoke lying down,' he said. 'Let's get settled on one of the ottomans, Anna. You come too, Chance.'

'You did not care for my boys then?'

'No,' MacGrady said with finality.

'A pity,' Friese murmured, 'but there is no accounting for tastes, is there, Colonel?'

Pearl giggled. 'Colonel Godfrey allows everyone to be rude to him except me, don't you, Colonel Godfrey?'

But the soldier only smiled his cold smile and, rising, drew

her into one of the alcoves where he lay down and waited
for her to fill his pipe.

Chance said, 'MacGrady, I'd very much like you to meet
Magdalena. Do you think the Arab would mind if I introduced you?'

'She must have made a big impression on Chance,' said
Anna. 'You go on over with him, Columb, and tell me just
how she looks and where she dresses. I caught only a glimpse
of her when she came in.'

'And afterwards,' said Lady Zoe, '*I* shall insist on meeting
him.'

As they crossed the floor MacGrady said, 'What's the idea?'

'It's a second string,' Chance whispered, 'in case of any
delays in London. I think we might get the entrée to the
Palace for Anna if not myself. You must back me up.'

MacGrady fumbled with his cigarette case to gain time.
'You don't know quite where you're walking, Chance. You'd
better keep right off George, they don't like some of his
activities at the Palace.'

'But it's a good idea?'

'It might be.'

Magda rose first, she was wearing black paper-taffeta and
was most delicately made up, looking no more than eighteen
in the oldness of the colour. On her breast a cross of seven
moonstones held the light. Her escort was a little heavy about
the chest and stomach, his dark face was splendid and his
false teeth cleverly filled with gold. When the introductions
had been made he became extremely courteous and with his
cigar between his teeth drew out the table so that MacGrady
and Chance might sit down one or either side of the girl. A
scent which he had used lay heavily in the confined space and
was not unpleasant.

Chance said, 'I hope Magda is a little better, Your Excellency? I prescribed for her on Sunday morning.'

'That was kind of you. Western Medicine has much to
recommend it. I think she already looks a little better. She
has a complexion more sensitive than the sky.'

o

'Yacef is a poet,' said Magdalena. 'He says very beautiful things. Are *you* a poet, Mr. MacGrady?'

'I read it constantly but I don't drink enough to write it.'

'Perhaps on the contrary you drink too much,' said the Arab. 'It is the great failing of the West.'

'If you had lived in the United States, *you* would drink too much,' MacGrady retorted.

'That would entail a change of religion. It is matter I have already discussed with Magdalena who is a Catholic.'

'Colonel Tyghe has a neat equation about that, he got it from a Frenchman. He says that Mohammedanism equals no alcohol and as many women as you like, while Christianity equals only one woman and as much alcohol as you like.'

'Neither my brother nor myself have ever cared for the French,' said Ali. 'Their colonial methods are deplorable and cause my people great suffering.'

Chance intervened: 'Indirectly that was why I was so anxious to meet you, sir. I am at present staying with Mr. and Mrs. MacGrady as their doctor.'

'We called him in,' said MacGrady, 'because we needed his help badly.'

'He will give you good advice,' said Magda. 'I think he may have saved my life.'

'For that,' said the Arab, 'I am deeply indebted to you, Doctor Chance. At the Palace we are usually well aware of the shifting patterns made by our guests in the Zone. When Mademoiselle Lebrun told me of her conversation with you, I realised at once how narrow her escape had been.' He drew on his cigar. 'Although we have to keep open house in this part of the world we are not without a most efficient filing system. The person in question is a most unwelcome visitor and we hope to find means of curtailing his activities quite soon.'

'I don't get all this,' said MacGrady, 'but I don't suppose it matters. Chance, you're not to be too long. It looks rude.'

Chance addressed Ali. 'Well sir, it is going to be necessary for MacGrady to go to London for a short time for vital treatment of a lung condition. I have undertaken to look after his wife——'

'The tall girl in white?'

'Yes.'

'She is a beautiful woman. I have a remembrance of meeting her somewhere, Madrid or Rome?'

'Anna has visited all the Southern capitals,' put in Mac-Grady.

'Then she has contributed to them; her walk is a history in itself.'

'She dresses well,' said Magdalena.

The Arab enquired of Chance, 'I can be of service to Mrs. MacGrady?'

'I wondered if it would be possible for you to receive her at the Palace if things became difficult in the town? I may have to leave before MacGrady returns and I understand there's a likelihood of some political trouble over the week-end?'

'The Doctor's been very good to us both. It's really on my behalf that he's putting himself to the embarrassment of interrupting your evening, sir.'

'What is your present address, Señor MacGrady?'

'Oh we rent one of Colonel Tyghe's flats in the President Hoover.'

His Excellency Yacef Ali was displeased. 'That is a pity. I do not wish to be discourteous, but I know that the Sultan would prefer his guests to have lived elsewhere.'

'It would really be a question of sanctuary,' said Chance.

'Indeed, Doctor Chance, it would. The American section is likely to become a focal point in the event of a riot. Foreign propaganda for some months past has centred on the influence of Washington within the Zone. Madame MacGrady might even have been safer in the French Legation where a few stones would have been the most she would have had to fear.'

MacGrady ground his cigarette out and got up. 'Well that's just too bad. I'm sorry we should have wasted your time like this, Your Excellency. I guess I shall just have to try and fly

Anna back to my father's place. I'd better get a cable off to the Investment Trust right away.'

'The connection, Señor MacGrady?'

'Oh it's not important, my father's a sick man at the moment and all his personal business is handled by the Chase Manhattan Trust in New York City.'

'I see.' The ash fell from Yacef Ali's cigar, a white flurry on his immaculate lapel. 'I know the Corporation well, they have interests here, I believe?'

'Oh they only have about three billion invested in the Zone and they don't easily get frightened. They'll be much more worried about Anna's whereabouts—to begin with.'

The Arab's smile was golden, a glittering disclosure of fillings between the pre-molars. 'It is fortunate, then, that it can so easily be arranged.' He rose to his feet a moment before MacGrady. 'If things should become in the least uncomfortable for your wife, do not hesitate to contact Mademoiselle Lebrun at the Palace.'

'What you say? You must forgive me, I don't feel so good tonight. The Doctor and I are really supposed to be entertaining our guests.'

'She would, I know, be delightful company for Mademoiselle who finds the mornings a trifle long.'

'I'm so very grateful to Doctor Chance, I wish he were coming too.' Magdalena lay back against her velvet cushion.

'Of course, but we shall have to exercise some discretion. During these disturbances my brother's diplomatic sense is severely tested. Sir Anthony Eden's ignorance of ancient issues has aggravated our position. It would not be too difficult to extend our hospitality to a lady.' He bowed. 'But an English gentleman's arrival would not pass unnoticed by the staff.'

'You are very good, sir. I think if you could take care of Mrs. MacGrady our minds would be set at rest.'

'Only if it is necessary,' MacGrady said. 'The whole thing may turn out to be a storm in a teacup like the Coca-Cola riots last year.'

'That was a question of the possible alcoholic content. My people were not to know——'

'Yeah, yeah, they got steamed up as a result of rival advertising.'

'I take it, then, that Doctor Chance will communicate with us in your absence?'

'Yes, you'll do that, won't you, Chance?'

'A short note, a telephone call is all that is necessary. We have three armoured cars at present and the Palace guards are equipped with most effective sub-machine guns.'

'Yeah, American stuff.'

His Excellency said kindly, 'The present issue is a Soviet contribution, and an improvement I think.'

They parted politely and leaving the alcove strolled back across the floor to their own tables.

MacGrady said, 'I am not a patriot, Chance, until it is necessary.'

'You handled him cleverly.'

'He's only a heathen.'

Chance sat down beside Lady Zoe who was talking desultorily to Dr. Friese.

MacGrady went smoothly on to join Anna, Robin and Pearl sprawling on ottomans in an enclosure at the far end of the room.

Lady Zoe seemed pleased to have Chance back but Dr. Friese excused himself and wagging his cane disappeared in the direction of the kitchen.

Sensing his companion's vagueness, the capriciousness of her attention, Chance watched the others curiously. They lay beyond the screens, foreshortened; MacGrady's head invisible behind the bulk of his chest, Anna a pale drift beside him, her head with heavy hair and half-shut eyes like still-life upon an emerald cushion. She seemed to look back at him out of the darkness with slow speculation, sharing her pipe with the American, drooping over it, loosing invisible puffs of smoke into the shadows. Beside them on either side of the Colonel, Pearl and Robin Moore also reclined, both small and dark in the lapse of talk. One of the Arab boys, a pink idol, squatted in there on the rushes filling and refilling the pipes whilst the other remained attendant upon Chance and Lady Zoe.

'Used you ever to play sardines, Doctor?'

'I beg your pardon?'

'The tragedy is that as one gets older one is so easily attracted, don't you think? If the old had more energy they would make bigger fools of themselves than the adolescent. Take my great-aunt for example, and doddering old Von Stellansee. Did you read her memoirs?'

'Yes, I believe I did; the Baron was eighty, wasn't he?'

'No, ninety-five, my dear; a mere fifteen years older than Tante Nicolette. They wrote hundreds of tiny love-letters to one another, most of which she included in her book; they always began most passionately but by the third sentence they only had strength left to sign their pet names—Booby and Flops.'

Chance drew on his pipe. 'Can you tell me what this stuff is supposed to do?'

'According to the Doctor it makes the intolerable tolerable.'

'You don't like him?'

'My dear, one doesn't like or dislike doctors.'

'Oh.'

She passed him her pipe. 'I'll be back in a few moments but don't smoke too fast. Doping is like marriage, one must keep level. You go and find us a nice sequestered ottoman—alone. They're far too crowded in there.'

'Would you like to join His Excellency? Or have you changed your mind about that?'

'He's too swarthy,' she said. 'I still have my prejudices.'

Chance walked over and stood in the archway looking down at the others and puffing ineffectually at his pipe.

'For God's sake, Chance, why don't you sit down?' asked MacGrady. 'What you on the prowl for?'

Anna: 'He's waiting for Zoe, aren't you, Chance?'

'I suppose I am.'

MacGrady: 'What do you mean, *"suppose,"* you either are or you aren't.'

'Don't bully him, darling. How are you feeling, Chance?'

'A little restless. This kief stuff doesn't seem to have had any effect on me at all.'

Pearl was giggling. 'Lady Zoe will look after him while I look after her husband. Tonight everybody is very tired of everybody. We are all children playing a game, aren't we?'

MacGrady propped himself on one elbow. 'Chance, you're too damned scrupulous. Why don't you lie down and relax somewhere with someone? What you afraid of?'

'I'm not afraid of anything.'

'You've got too much pride, you're not a proper Catholic at all.'

Colonel Godfrey spoke: 'What is a proper Catholic? I am fifty. I have yet to meet one.'

MacGrady sat right up. He levered himself on fat white sleeves and beside him Anna closed her eyes sacrificially.

'There you are,' he bellowed, 'you're letting down the Church. You're too damned mealy-mouthed, always watching points, your mean little self. Catholicism makes a man big enough to be safe wherever he is and whatever he does so that he doesn't have to go on always being so careful. You annoy me, Chance, you make me mad. What the hell you standing there for watching everyone?'

'Darling,' said Anna sleepily. 'I keep telling you, he's waiting for Zoe.'

'He's not, he's not waiting for anyone. He's only waiting for himself. He's a stuck-in-the-button English Protestant. He's wondering whether he ought to have come. He's full of censure; he's making prayers for our immortal souls while his mind's fixed on his own precious flesh and his own lousy little desires. Why don't you move on in, Chance? Why'd you go on behaving like an existentialist?'

Chance turned away.

MacGrady: 'And don't say you're sorry or I'll get mad.'

Chance: 'I'm not sorry.'

MacGrady: 'Well go and be not sorry outside somewhere. Don't drool in the doorway. Get yourself an occasion of sin so that you can love God instead of yourself!'

'MacGrady,' said the Colonel, 'you are a most interesting man.'

MacGrady rounded on him. 'You be quiet, Godfrey. You're only a damned little lapsie, one of these hen-brained twentieth-century gnostics and this is nothing to do with you.' He lowered his head and his voice. 'This is the Church Sorrowful and you can thank your rotten stars it still exists and *will* exist long after all the little traitors like you are quivering in Purgatory bleating against the implacable love of God.'

Anna leaned forward and took one of his hands. 'Darling, you're really being awfully rude to everyone. Now come and settle down again with me. Nobody wants to quarrel with you; and the Doctor's going in the morning, you know he is.'

'I do know he is.' MacGrady sat down again beside her, his eyelids puffed above his starting eyes. 'He's running out on us all the time.'

Lady Zoe reappeared and slid her arm through Chance's.

'My dear, you seem to be making everyone very cross. I told you to find a nice cosy niche for us.'

'I thought perhaps—your husband——' Chance began.

'Oh please,' she said, 'don't be dreary.'

MacGrady: 'God Almighty!'

Chance turned and looked at Lady Zoe. She was not so very old; thirty-six, forty-six? In the pink light he observed the dyed hair, the insatiable green eyes, the drowned debu-tante beneath the thin fat, the witty lips. He wound his arm slowly about her shoulders and kissed her long and angrily.

'Ah,' she said, 'you *are* married, then?'

Anna was sitting up again. 'I always say that when they don't say they're not, they *are*.'

'But what a surprising person,' said Lady Zoe. 'He's really succeeded in making me feel rash.'

'I would say you're quite safe now,' said Anna with fatigue.

'My dear it was not you he kissed.'

Anna: 'Chance, come on in here, I want to talk to you.'

MacGrady: 'You're talking to no one. Pass me that pipe and relax.'

Followed by Lady Zoe, Chance moved off to an adjoining chamber and they lay down beside one another. The Arab boy followed them in and Chance turned on him.

'Go away, we don't want you.'

'No we don't,' she chimed in. 'We think you're quite revolting.'

'Disgusting,' said Chance, 'and what is more this is a foul evening. Everyone is so painstakingly eccentric.'

The boy changed feet, glowing like a blush rose in the archway until Lady Zoe lobbed a cushion at him, when with a twist of his eyes he disappeared.

'Your trouble,' she suggested, 'is that you're homesick?'

'It's a little vaguer than that. If you can understand, when I arrived here I had some idea of who I was and what I wanted, but after only six days of this place, I'm beginning to feel like a ghost.'

'My dear, you're so lucky, I've been like that for years. I just float.'

'I think you've always been too rich.'

She sniggered and he moved a little further away from her.

'That's a trifle. The real trouble is that I'm mad and that I know it. That's what I mean by floating. Sometimes I rise and sometimes I sink. My life is a pointless pilgrimage without milestones. I bump into things. I got stuck with Robin for a time so I married him, and I dare say all my marriages were the same, they were only temporary pauses.'

'It's the place,' he said, 'it's the Zone. No one here makes any pretence of sanity.'

'And are you an exception?'

'Only just.'

'And you're leaving in the morning?'

'No,' he said, 'I mean yes.'

'Anna will be disappointed.'

He lay very still. The mention of her name offended him

and he remembered that throughout his marriage he had always been unable to discuss his wife with other women.

'You are in love with her, aren't you?'

'I don't believe in it.'

'Really?'

'It's not cynicism,' he said sitting up, 'but I detest the state of "being in love." It has happened to me so many times and accomplished so little that I take as much trouble to avoid it as I take in avoiding ugly illnesses.'

'And how ill are you at the moment?'

'Oh, malaise you know, the beginnings of a headache, a neurotic wish to take my temperature twice a day.'

She laughed. 'You know of course that she is very interested in you?'

'I haven't thought about it.' He stood up. 'I don't want to spend the rest of my life exploring purely mortal relationships. It doesn't matter for a lot of men, but it matters for me because I have a constitutional weakness, I enjoy desire and when I feel it I put up no resistance and waste real time.'

'My dear, d'you believe time is ever real?'

'I think it's real when we've discovered what it is we want. On the other hand, it can *seem* most substantial when we're consuming it in pursuit of what we don't want.'

'And for you, Anna is an impossibility?'

'Well, she is, isn't she?'

She was irritated. 'It all sounds frightfully pious, but then of course you're a convert, aren't you? And they're always a little enervating.'

'I know what you mean but I'm not sure that I don't prefer to be like that.'

'And that's why you've decided to go in the morning?'

'Yes.'

'We're very different. In your place wild horses wouldn't get me out of the Zone.'

'Perhaps when I have gone,' he said without smiling, 'you will remember me and admire me *so* much.'

She was momentarily startled and resorted to politeness.

'But perhaps you've got very good sense—for other reasons. Robin and I have been wondering whether we were wise to come and stay in the Casbah. Godfrey's been alarming us about his Arabs all evening. Heber's even been thinking of selling up everything; his beautiful glass floor, his ringdoves, his *azulejos*. If I were able to care it would break my heart.'

A shadow fell and they looked round. Stick in hand, Doctor Friese stood in the archway. They saw his face, pale and ceremental, with its two dark-spectacled holes. He was swaying slightly.

'My dear Lady Zoe, do nothing precipitate. I assure you I am very much more in touch with the situation than Colonel Godfrey, who, I sometimes think, has spent a little too long in the desert for the comfort of anyone save his current predilection.' He coughed. 'I refer of course to the female nigger who shares his bed and board if not his blood.'

The Lady Zoe stood up.

'He's been drugging again,' she said loudly. 'This is very tedious.'

'Correct!' Doctor Friese rose on his toes. 'I must ask everyone to leave. We are about to close. I have heard that there is a certain amount of unrest in the native quarter and whilst I have enjoyed your company I have every intention of continuing to do so in the future, which is why I counsel you to do nothing hasty about leaving Heber's charming little *pied-à-terre* in the Casbah. Simply return to it coolly, with that peculiarly British—er we must stand firm.'

Behind him the Arab musicians changed their tempo. One of them stood up and began to sing sharply, his voice pitched to the black roof and the embrasures so that its echoes mingled with his long-drawn wails and cries.

'What goes on?' It was MacGrady's voice.

'Doctor Friese is drunk, my dear,' Lady Zoe called. 'He says we're going to be raided.'

The others filed out sleepily and stood behind Friese. Anna was yawning. Pearl's teeth shone and the Colonel paced the floor smiling his high smile. There was no sign of his Excellency Yacef Ali or Magda.

Friese stood to one side and allowed Lady Zoe to pass him, but before Chance could do so he blocked the archway again.

'A word with you, Doctor Chance, in connection with our talk this morning.'

'I have nothing to say to you. Move!' Chance pushed him to one side and joined the others.

Friese smiled warmly at MacGrady. 'Your guest is in a hurry, MacGrady. He hastens to return to his home. As I may have been about to explain to him this morning it is a concept which means little to me. But what is home if it is not the place of fulfilment? And to whose home does Doctor Chance wish to return, and for the fulfilment of what desires?'

Lady Zoe said: 'The man has been eavesdropping.'

Friese leaned upon his stick elegantly, his dark lenses directed fully at MacGrady. His calm, the precision of his tones, held them all there before them. Though drugged or drunk, inspired or merely confused, he had, with his background of the singing Arabs, so much the quality of an oracle that for the moment no one was able to move in the direction of the door.

'Home,' he said, 'not to the vast spiritual domicile of the Church, nor to his own home. For why should he have left it only in order to return so soon and in such haste? For what does he hunger and—er thirst? My dear MacGrady——'

'What you getting at, Friese?'

Lady Zoe: 'The man is quite evidently and most boringly drunk.'

'Touched,' said her husband. 'I think we had better be going.'

Pearl twirled. 'But *I* think this is such fun. We ought to make him dance for us. At home we would make a circle and he would run round it. In the old days we would have sacrificed a chicken.'

Anna moved. She walked past Friese with the smallest of smiles on her downcast face; a figure, from the powder of sequins on her shoulders to the paste buckles of her shoes, white and glittering.

'I really don't know what we'd better do about the bill,' she said to Zoe. 'He'd never even remember whether we'd paid him or not the way he is tonight.'

'He's overdone it. He can't hold his *kief*. They always get this frightful flight-of-ideas thing when they take too much.'

The Arab porter held the door open for them and with the exception of Colonel Godfrey who talked to him for a moment, they came out into the moonlit street and gathered round the Moores' car.

The Colonel hurried over to them. 'Let me know how you are in the morning, MacGrady. I know a rather good man if you should need one.'

'I don't want a doctor. I'm quite all right. I only want to get home and stay there with the blinds down.'

Anna yawned, 'I'm so sleepy.'

They got into the Buick and said good night to the Moores through the windows. The Colonel let in the clutch and the car moved off fast towards the American section.

Back at the flat Anna immediately went to bed and Mac-Grady brought out the Red Hackle. He slumped on the divan:

'You don't want to talk any more, do you, Chance?'

'No.'

'Neither do I.'

Chance smiled.

'But you're all set?' the American went on. 'You're sure you'll go through with it?'

'I'll have to, I suppose.'

'Yes, you do have to.'

'I don't quite know why.'

MacGrady ignored this; he said: 'I suppose you want to know where you stand?'

'Very much.'

'Where *you'll* maybe have time to find out, *I'll* not.'

'Too bad.'

MacGrady grinned, a sentimental grin. 'I know what you're thinking and it's rotten sorrow for you. But you can't blame me, I have to take what's offered, don't I?'

Chance said, 'I don't suppose I've any right to ask it really, but did you go to Communion last Sunday?'

'No,' said MacGrady shutting his mouth tight, 'I was sick ... I wasn't well.'

'Confession, then?'

MacGrady controlled himself. 'Since when has the Vatican laid it down that the Easter Duty is insufficient? No, don't get excited, Chance!' His voice rose, 'I'd be interested to know, that's all. It occurs to me that maybe you've got advance news on it, a cousin who's a nuncio, or a member of one of the Sacred Congregations? Maybe you had tea at Castel Gandolfo on your way over? There's been a change which nobody else knows about, a Papal pronouncement, an encyclical, a bull? It's been laid down that the faithful have to go to Communion every Sunday. High Mass has been abolished and High Mass Catholics like myself——'

'For God's sake remember that you have to be up early.'

But MacGrady was on his feet touring the room. 'I object very strongly to ignorant interference in the matter of my personal interpretation. Why don't you realise, Chance, that it's all in the providence of God what graces a man is given. Even I know what I should do all the time; I just don't do it, that's all.'

'It seems to me,' Chance said with equal control, 'that no Catholic can continue to know what's right if he's not making use of the Sacraments.'

'You're not a priest,' MacGrady shouted. 'You're a green convert and I'm not going to have you telling *me* what to do.'

'I didn't think it would work. I was pretty certain you'd start shouting again. It was just that I didn't see why I should have to take all the risks I am taking for as rotten a Catholic as yourself.' Chance drank. 'That was all.'

MacGrady refilled his glass. He was conciliatory:

'You don't have to worry about me, you don't have to worry about God or the Church; as long as *you* make use of it, you're doing all right always.'

'I'm glad we're agreed on that.'

MacGrady was over by the bookshelves. 'I don't have time to instruct you now, even without that little book of mine. But I'll put it this way; it's only your temptations that come from the Devil, your tribulations come from God'—he paused significantly—'and I'm one of them.'

'About the passport,' Chance said rudely.

'You're not listening, I'm trying to help you and you're not listening, you're bogged down in materialism.'

'Without it——'

'You'll get your passport from me on Saturday at latest. I got everything fixed. I'm used to moving in a hurry; but that's not the point. What I want to tell you is that though you had a right to ask me what you did ask me, it's one you should never have exercised. If you were as good a Catholic as you're going to need to be, you'd have known that. You'd just have got on with it.'

'With what?'

'Praying for me, of course,' he bellowed. 'You ought to be praying for me night and day!'

Chance moved hurriedly. He hid his face by pretending to study the eight-day clock on Anna's bureau.

'Are you praying for *me*?' he asked.

'I'm in no condition to pray for anyone. You know that. How the hell can you expect me to pray for people in my present state?'

'You could pray for yourself.'

'That's not enough, I need everybody's prayers. The continuous prayers of the Church——'

'Sorrowful,' Chance finished for him.

'You're right, you're dead right, that's my devotion, it's my role. They've got to have them like me: taggers-on, men who can follow the Church intellectually but not with the heart. Men who, though they were never ill-disposed, lacked grace at a moment of decision; and have had to await it ever since. I tell you there are thousands of us who got started and then stopped, never to move again in our own time. We wait, we stand at the doors of the shrines and the gates of the treasuries of grace accumulated in centuries by the saints. We find our only recompense there and in the Church Sorrowful where men weaker than ourselves have suddenly known glory under the whip and grace in their own blood-loss. We don't look to the contemporary Church and we don't look to the fat Church. We look backwards to the ages of faith, across continents to the decades of martyrdom on the other side of the Iron Curtain. We're like the twentieth-century Church itself, attending in luxury its Eastern blood-bath and sitting complacently on its past holiness—the sanctity it knows must come again from the East.'

He put out his hand carelessly for his glass, his fingers fumbling absurdly in the wrong place. He frowned; and then, noticing Chance's expression, said suddenly:

'Well what d'you think? D'you get my drift?'

'I think so.' Chance was very still. 'It's disturbing—terrible in a way.'

MacGrady livened at once: 'For *me* Chance, not for you. You're a convert; you can't expect to think such things, feel them, be them as we are. By predilection you're a suffering man yourself. When you're older you might be given the spiritual tribulations I've had thrown down on me. But not yet. You're new to the Faith, it's flowering in you as it once flowered in me and my kind and that's why you were sent. So don't fall into false pride, don't start imagining you can live the way *I* have to.' Finding his glass, he brought it to his lips and drank gloomily. 'Why, what's the matter, Chance? Why do you look so black?'

'I'm tired—depressed, I think.'

'By what I said?'

'I don't know yet; but it's very compelling. That phrase, "the fat Church," is destructive.'

MacGrady yawned. 'You're out of sorts, that's all; you had a long day.'

'Possibly.'

As though he were moving fast away from some shameful commission, the American warmed to his new emotion.

'You think I don't notice you, that because I instruct you and make demands on you, I don't care a damn about how you're feeling or looking? You think I don't worry about anyone but myself?'

Out of his discomfort, the contention of his anger and fear, Chance whipped him once.

'It suits you, MacGrady,' he said.

'What's that?' The American hesitated momentarily, but the great mills of his sympathy had been set in motion. 'When I'm back in London,' he said, almost softly, 'are there any messages you'd like me to give to anyone?'

'No thank you.'

'Are you sure about that? Your wife, for instance?'

'She's dead.'

There was a silence in which Chance stood shrunken in the one small place; as though it were dark; but the older man was lumbering somewhere not very far away. He was something large in the thicket which the Englishman had drawn round him, and such sorrow as the mourner sustained was redirected towards the man he had dumbfounded. For this reason, and because he regretted his earlier irony, he continued:

'I think if you don't mind, MacGrady, we both ought to go to bed.'

'What's that? Oh yeah, you're dead right. We've got to be up early. Don't wait for me, I'll stay here a little longer and finish my drink.'

They said good night as people will when words have died, a little formally, and Chance went along to his room.

P

Wednesday

WHEN he awoke he remembered at first very little. He was not sure whether or not he had awakened before on that day, had a memory of MacGrady coming in dressed for travel, white and jubilant; saying something, even sketching out a blessing from the doorway. Or had he dreamed this? But certainly, now it was very late; the hands of his stopped watch standing at eleven-thirty, the opposite wing of the flats bright white through the blinds, and the shadows beneath their illumined balconies very short.

If MacGrady had gone then he had missed his departure and to have missed it, if in fact it had taken place, was in a sense to have been cheated of a lifetime. The acts of any moment might be the culmination of a lifetime, and therefore of final significance; but few were so purposefully contrived as had been this one act of his on this one and particular morning.

For some reason his agitation centred about his passport. It distracted him from even the briefest of prayers as he lay there half in and half out of his bed.

Getting out he crossed the floor and peered between the downcast slats of the blind, but could see nothing of the ground; only the topmost flats black and white against the sky, their verandas empty save for an Arab girl hanging up washing on a balcony opposite. He dared not tilt the slats downwards in case MacGrady had left; for in that event no one must glimpse his face for at least a further seventy-two hours. And yet, with powerful obstinacy, he now wanted to see the ground: the hibiscus in its dry soil, the single Arab woman who sorted the cinders, the solidity of foundations and a glimpse of the concrete road. He bent down to the bottom slat and set his eye to it; it vouchsafed him only another higher balcony and, beyond its end, the infinite distances of heaven, cloudless, sunlightened and terrifying.

He opened his door and listened in the hall. The small Persian rug lay ruffled on the parquet; and that was all. No sound came to him from the MacGrady's room or from the kitchen, so that he was assured of even the fatima's departure; for she left at eleven, he remembered, and it was now nearly midday. As soon as it was safe and he had seen they would have to change bedrooms: Anna moving into the spare room at present filled with cabin trunks and he himself taking over MacGrady's room.

Overcoming his reluctance to begin the day by moving out of his room, he closed his door behind him and in stockinged feet went along to the kitchen. It was comfortless and hygienic as usual; the cupboards closed, the tea towels hanging on the rail, the refrigerator door half open; but the room smelt strangely, he recognised the herbal smell of a burnous and hurried back to his room and locked it from the outside.

From the sitting-room, pierced with razor edges of sunlight from the hiatuses between its tight shutters, he moved into the dining-room and found a note. It lay propped against a tray covered with a white cloth on the heavy oak table.

'11 a.m. We just didn't have the heart to disturb you. I waited around till the fatima had gone and had my coffee when you continued to show no signs of life and then after this *early* morning I just had to go back to sleep. We can change rooms when we're both awake at the same time! Columb left you his love and blessing and said not to worry about a thing.

A.'

She was careless he thought: there was no word about burning it. She could have wakened him herself and explained to him without taking risks of this sort. He read her words through again and attempted to ignore the sudden complete distaste for food which overcame him at the thought of her care for him.

He shredded the pasteboard and burnt it in the kitchen and then returned and lifted the cloth from the tray she had left for him. It disclosed a half-bottle of burgundy, a fresh un-opened packet of Macgovern's Jeely Pieces, some butter, a goat's milk cheese and an unripe avocado pear.

Remembering the bare look of the sky, he said a grace and crossed himself. Then he drank half the wine slowly, peeled and stoned the avocado and ate it all, finished half the packet of toast slices and most of the butter and managed in this way to pass nearly an hour. Finally, when he had finished the wine, he went back into the sitting-room and lay down on the divan.

In the half-darkness his boredom began. He felt the dead hand of it upon his mind, as subtle yet certain as the premonitory symptoms of the migraine to which he was occa-sionally subject; first the sudden soundless flick or click some-where behind the eyes, then the white spot hovering blind-ingly in the centre of the visual field, and finally the cold grip of the mounting headache. A pain which made it impossible to indulge in even the most trivial activity. But with boredom there was not even the pain to contend with; only a paralysis of the attention which might last for hours, or rarely, for days at a time, and which had to be countered immediately.

To begin with, he got up off the divan and switched on the light. He went over to the bureau and watched the movement of the eight-day clock within its glass case: the cherubs swinging on their revolving seat, their pudgy hands clasping the metal ropes, their legs crossed an inch above the pedestal as, two days ago, MacGrady's had been crossed before he dragged him out on to the balcony.

The key lay where the American had placed it after the last winding, just inside the canopy. Without further attention the cherubs would continue to swing and the hands to record the passing of time for another seven days; that was to say, until Tuesday next.

He wandered over to the bookshelves, his eye passing along the titles swiftly and without interest. On the bottom shelf a row of paperbacks momentarily attracted him. He saw: *Buddhism for Beginners, The Bhagavad Gita—A Commentary, The Life of Benedict Joseph Labre, Orthodox Judaism, The Koran—Newly Translated from the Arabic,* and still in its wrapper, *Why I am not a Christian* by Bertrand Russell. He drew them all out, shuffled them with his eyes shut and spread them on the floor in front of him. He selected the third from the beginning of the row and sat down on the divan with it. With his eyes still closed he selected three pages and turned down their corners. He decided to read only one paragraph on each page. Opening his eyes he turned to the first one. It read:

'It was to reveal the Truth that He has created the Heaven and the Earth. He causes the night to succeed the day and the day to overtake the night.'

The second paragraph read:

'Seek out your enemies relentlessly. If you have suffered they too have suffered: but you at least hope to receive from Allah that which they cannot hope for. Allah is wise and all knowing.'

The third paragraph advised:

'If a woman fear ill-treament or desertion on the part of her husband it shall be no offence for them to seek a mutual agreement; for agreement is best.'

He thought about this last for a long time: one of the private nearly interminable reveries of the convert attempting to find some way out of the dilemmas of conduct where only one course of behaviour is as certainly right as it is distasteful. Drowsing, he put his hand into his pocket and pulled out MacGrady's rosary: Wednesday, the Glorious Mysteries. He repeated the paternoster in Latin as an aid to concentration. He got as far as '*sicut et nos dimittimus debitoribus nostris*' when behind the practice of the words he heard very distinctly a sentence of MacGrady's. 'Chance, as a Catholic I know what's right—I just don't do it—that's all.' He made three further attempts to repeat the first paternoster and then returned the rosary to his pocket.

He went along to his bedroom and collected all his things together very scrupulously leaving nothing, then repacked his suitcase. He dumped it noisily in the passage directly outside MacGrady's bedroom and then clattered back along to the sitting-room. He switched off the chandelier and leaning by the door watched the sunrays creeping like flame up the wall to the ceiling. Out beyond the hills the sun must be falling fast but he could not see it. He remembered something else MacGrady had said: 'I see that sun coming up in the early morning when it promises a man nothing and its voice is loud.'

She could not possibly sleep all day. He would give her only one more hour and then he would waken her. They would have an evening meal together, early. Afterwards they would talk.

He went along to the kitchen and set about the preparation of the meal; rationing out the time to each task as he had seen the prisoners do when they were confined to cell.

First he set the table in the dining-room: auratum lilies from the bowl in the hall, a trifle faded and nearly scentless, but, once the oldest were removed, still new enough to deceive: silver for three courses: soup, something else, fruit—tinned or otherwise—coffee and the goat's milk cheese if she wanted it.

She might not care for cheese of course. He knew so little about her; only how she looked and spoke, nothing of her tastes or desires. Once she had said something to him about 'drinker's food.' And by that, presumably, she had meant something highly spiced and very complicated: curry, lobster in sauce piquante or tunny cooked Lisbon fashion with peppers, gherkins and tomatoes.

Tonight she would have an omelette; it was all he knew

how to cook and there were three eggs in the refrigerator and a tin of fines herbes on the top of the cupboard.

He put the eggs to one side, greased the frying pan with butter and soaked half a teaspoonful of the herbs in a wine-glass full of milk. He opened a tin of apricots and then separated the cream from the tops of three bottles of milk and whipped it up for twenty minutes until it was exactly right when he returned it to the refrigerator to chill. Lastly, he opened a tin of chicken soup, added milk to it and set it to simmer on the stove.

There was a quarter of an hour to go. He would allow him-self one drink of MacGrady's whisky and then he would knock on her door and rouse her. He would tell her that supper was ready. He poured himself a stiff one, about three fingers full and drank it in the dining-room as he circled the table.

MacGrady had said, 'Get yourself an occasion of sin and love God instead of yourself, Chance.'

Wrong of course and yet how like a Catholic to say it.

But what did MacGrady deserve? He asked himself as his eye fell once again on the clock. He might have been one of those four boys on the pendulum; immature, arrogant and protected, rocking away time for his victims: presiding over their defeat behind the glass of his transparent indifference. He would have no human redress if one day someone who had entered his life began suddenly to betray him on the other side of it whilst he rode his pendulum rotating backwards and forwards until the spring gave out.

Abruptly, Chance went along the corridor. He was very quiet. He picked up his case and took it into his bedroom. He found a bottle of sleeping tablets, extracted two or three one-and-a-half-grain tablets of sodium amytal and swallowed them quickly. In the hall the telephone rang. The noise of the bell rang down the lighted space like a stream of bullets seeming at this moment to ricochet physically off Anna's door and his own person.

Without thinking, he ran along to pick up the receiver and

answer it; then half-way there, on the blue Persian rug he remembered in time, and halted.

Behind him he heard her door. He saw it open, he saw its surface brighten under the light of her bedroom before he moved into the sitting-room and began to gather up the books he had left on the floor.

'No, George,' she was saying, 'he just can't bear to see any-one . . . *I*'m banished to the spare room.' There was a pause. 'Yes, Chance left this morning. He seemed awful vague but I think maybe he was going on to Marrakesh . . . Yes you can, George. I know Columb would be very grateful if you'd just put out a little bulletin that he's gone to purdah for all of three days and that even enquiries are most unwelcome.' She laughed. 'But, George, I like moody men, they make me feel alive. If it would help him get better I'd lock myself up with him for a month.' Again the laugh. 'But I wouldn't ever stop praying, once I'd started that is, that afterwards one of you'd persuade him to go see someone real tops on chests, say London or even back in New York . . . What you say? Well if they do start rioting here, we'll just all leave together; but it won't have to be before Saturday, because right now Columb wouldn't move out of that bed even for an earthquake.' Chance heard the clicking of her nails against the receiver as she talked faster. 'No, I don't know him. Are you sure he can be watching our flat? But, George, I don't know any little Arab boys. Where's he stand? Oh how cute! I'll go look later; right now I've got to go heat soup in case Columb calls out wanting it . . . Yes I loved the roses, it was just lovely of you to think of me . . . *Throw them out?* . . .' She was non-plussed. Chance moved into the hall and signalled for her attention but she ignored him. 'Well I guess it was that girl, she does do unaccountable things . . . Now, George, don't go round in a circle. I don't know where the doctor's gone . . .' Her voice thinned off and in her eyes focus returned. She was questioning Chance as she listened to George, one hand covered the mouthpiece as she whispered, 'What shall I tell him?'

'Nothing. Just cut it short,' Chance whispered back. She nodded . . . 'Now stop it, George, I'm cold and tired. I just got out of bed, I *don't* know where the doctor's gone or why an Arab boy should be planted in the vacant lot. Yes, George, you can call again but not too soon, now good night!' She replaced the receiver.

Chance watched her collect herself: a coming together of the body and of sentience as delicate as a cloud forming over hills.

She smiled at him. 'It was the flowers. I'd clean forgotten about those roses. You threw them out, did you?'

'Yes.'

She began to watch him but thought better of it. 'I could use a drink,' she said as she moved past him into the sitting-room and sat down on the divan. 'He says there's an Arab boy watching the flats. Could that be you too?'

'Yes I think so. Shall I get you a drink?'

'I'd just love it, a long one.'

'What? I mean whisky or gin or tomato juice?'

'Not tomato juice,' she said. 'Get me what you've had yourself.'

'But you don't usually——'

'As far as that goes you don't either. But tonight you're swaying all over the place, aren't you?'

He went into the kitchen and poured her a weak whisky, topping up the tumbler with sterile water from the filter; remembering before he returned to turn off the gas below the soup.

'It must be very late—or early,' she said, sipping her glass. 'Did Columb ever wind up that clock?'

'Yes, he did it yesterday.'

'Heavens! Was that yesterday? It seems like last year. This day seems to have gotten itself all mixed up, doesn't it?'

'I was thinking the same,' he said.

He was a little uncertain where to place himself. He was wishing that the earlier failure had not ended in a resort to the amytal. He stood about between the closed shutters and the open door into the hall, where the telephone was, watching her as she sat there on the edge of the divan in the dressing-gown which a blade of scarlet sunlight sliced from her waist to her chin; a line of light which so dazzled his eyes that he could hardly see the parts of her lying on either side of it.

'If you're hungry,' he said, 'I made you some supper: soup and an omelette of sorts.'

'I know you did.' She seemed to be very amused. 'I heard you clattering about half the night in and out the kitchen and up and down the hallway.'

'You mean half the day.'

'I couldn't figure what you were doing at first, or why. I played a game making it all up out of the sounds. You were awfully busy, weren't you?'

'I thought you were asleep.'

'No, I wasn't asleep.'

'Reading?'

'No, I wasn't reading.'

'Dancing, perhaps?'

She looked up at that. The line of sun caught her left eye and she moved her head impatiently sideways so that her right eye was momentarily impaled on the bright blade. She leaned a little over and away from him.

'What you say? *Dancing?*'

'Yes.'

'And why should I have danced?'

'I don't know.'

'What have I got to dance about?'

'You danced yesterday?'

'Did I?'

'Yes.'

'Well, that was yesterday, wasn't it?' She took another sip from her glass. 'Why don't you sit down, Chance? You look very funny swaying about there in front of the clock.'

'It's the soup. It might boil over. I can't remember whether I turned it off or not.'

'You cooking soup?'

'You haven't had anything since breakfast, have you? I was going to do an omelette. I have it all ready mixed, so as soon as you're ready——'

'There's no hurry, Chance. I'm enjoying this drink. I feel very happy right now and I'm just awfully grateful to you.'

'Why are you happy?'

'Why not? Don't you ever feel happy?'

'I don't know—I've forgotten.'

'Because you're so old,' she said, 'is that it? Well I'm not; I'm quite young and I always do feel happy when something's just going to happen. When it's got to.'

'Even if it's unpleasant?'

'Oh you're a man. You like to make things happen; but I'm a woman and we like to be happened to. It makes us feel good. I'm very happy.'

Chance sat down on the arm of a chair and steadied himself by leaning against its back. He lighted a cigarette.

'What else did he say?' he asked suddenly.

'Who?—George?'

'Yes, Fraser.'

'Oh, he went on and on, he was very suspicious. Why, he was most suspicious about you and the fatima and Columb, and Columb and you and the fatima—oh, and the little Arab boy, *your* little friend.'

'Were you worried?'

'Very, but what's the good? It's all started now: Columb's gone, he's on his way. George says there's going to be riots here in the Zone, the worst ever. Somebody, maybe those Russians of Godfrey's, has been spreading rumours that we're going to carry out atom tests down by Timbuktu of all places.'

'Did he say anything else?'

'You're very interested aren't you? Why worry about old George? He's not the big bad wolf and we're not the two little pigs. He can't eat us up even supposing he wants to. You mustn't worry so much, Chance; that way you'll never get fat.'

'What else did he say?'

'Well, if you want to know, he said Godfrey and Pearl are thinking of packing and Zoe's wondering about leaving Heber's place in the Medina and that's about all. I've forgotten his old conversation. I managed to brush him off easily and that's all that matters.'

'You aren't worried at all then?'

'I really couldn't say. *You* tell me! Go on, Chance, tell me!'

'I wish you'd stop calling me Chance.'

'I know you do. You frown every time. What name'll I call you by then?'

'I don't know.'

'You wouldn't like me to call you "Bill"? would you?'

'No, I would not.'

'I just like to call you "You," it's how I think of you. You're just someone I know and yet I don't know. You haven't given yourself another name.'

'I see.'

'You still haven't told me why I'm worried, Chance. Now come on. You sit back and tell me just all we both have to be worried about and frightened of and why the big bad wolf will get into our little straw house and eat us up before we've done a thing.'

'I can't,' he said. 'I'm very sorry but I'm half asleep. In fact, you may even have to cook your supper yourself because I'm exceedingly tired.'

She looked up quickly. 'Yes, you look tired. Why you look as though you're going to slip off that chair any minute.'

'As a matter of fact I was thinking about something Mac-Grady said last night. It has depressed me but I think if I go to bed early I shall feel better about it in the morning.'

She was too interested: 'Was it after I went to bed last night, when you were talking together in here?'

'Yes.'

'What'd he say then?'

'I want to think about it.'

'But what was it about? Was it anything to do with me?'

'No.'

'You, then?'

'It was about the Church Sorrowful. I'd never taken it seriously before; but after last night——'

A little boredom stole into her face and tone. 'You think too much, Chance. As Columb said at Zoe's party, you ought to do more and think less.'

'Did he say that?'

'He surely did. And what's more I agree with him.'

Feeling the old, immediate, thickening in his mouth as he eyed her, he said only: 'I wonder.'

Stealthily she sensed his doubt, desire, creeping up on it shuddering like a cat on her divan as she went on:

'But, of course, if you insist you could come over here and lay down. That way you could still think or talk a little and sleep a little at the same time. And then, later, we could fix the soup and that omelette of yours.' She rocked her half-empty glass, watching its waves in the strip of sunlight. 'Couldn't we?'

He was banal, deliberately shallow. 'I don't think I'd care for your cooking. And in any case I'd be asleep too soon.'

'The divan would be fatal, would it?'

He didn't answer; but he looked across at her again. She was frowning. He noticed that on her bracelet, a thick gold slave-bangle probably bought by MacGrady in the Street of Goldsmiths, she had fastened a tiny blue Lourdes medallion which was swinging as she stroked her knee.

Without looking up, she said. 'Chance, I only want you to tell me why I'm not worried. You can go to sleep later, you've got all night to go to sleep in, but right now I want you to tell me all about me and MacGrady.'

'That would be rather difficult.'

'Well go get yourself another drink first; and then, afterwards, sit yourself down in your chair and just talk quietly.'

'No, I've had enough to drink.'

They smiled at each other, and momentarily he was able to shift the starving hunger of his thoughts.

'If you like,' she said, 'you can pretend I'm not here——'

If I could, he thought.

'——you can just think aloud like I do sometimes when I just can't get to sleep.'

'Well,' he said, searching for them, for all the minutiae and impressions which had impinged in three days, 'you've known MacGrady about two years. You must have waited about on him for two years and it grew worse and worse waiting for him and waiting for yourself, for your own decision. But you had to do it because you were bored with things, whereas he was never bored. He was rich, he drank, but he was interesting; he interested you continuously in your own possibilities. You had never met anyone like him before.'

'Yes?'

'And a Catholic,' he added carefully. 'You were both Catholics and they're not necessarily interesting socially. If they're lapsed, they're often finally very dull. But MacGrady was not dull. He was capable of continually surprising you. He was a little frightening and just possibly noble. Your convent days had probably made a very deep impression on you, you must at one time have had some sort of a vocation; young people often do at that stage in their lives if they are gracious enough to know the Church as she really is. So you thought perhaps that this nobility of his was for you.' He paused. She was watching him attentively and he saw that all her distraction had vanished. He told himself that she was not particularly young.

'I'd like you to go on, Chance, if you can.'

'It's so very easy to be wrong,' he continued, 'so much of it is guesswork and inference, things like the labels on your trunks. But of course we do know that women can act in this way. It is their splendour to be the means of bringing nobility into the world. So, even though you might have been unaware of it yourself, your feeling that this greatness in Mac-Grady was awaiting you could have been a very powerful motive. But as I say, there was a mixture of motives: apart from the nobility, the danger, the wealth and the pathos, there was your own beauty; and the fact, that as a Catholic, you'd have been more aware of its worthlessness than other women.'

She was silent; she had not finished her drink, it stood beside a foot from which the shoe had slipped.

'And then?'

'You married him without knowing that he was dying and more of a blackguard than you had imagined. You did not know at first that he was nearly impotent, and I don't suppose even that would have stopped you. But you found out about the growth soon after you got married. You found that the light was to go out, that no matter what you did, yours could never have the greatness of a great marriage and that consequently, so far as you could see, you had chosen utterly wrongly; and that there was nothing you could do about it except wait and pray.'

He got up and moved across to her. Somewhat unsteadily he sat down on the divan beside her. 'At the moment,' he said, 'you are not worried; even without a Faith it is in the nature of women to transcend the tragic. For you, MacGrady cannot come back the same; he will either be better or dead, but never the same. Something is happening for you. If you have no child nor any prospect of a child, at least you are getting the future out of it all. You have undergone a betrothal and a marriage which was certainly beyond your own choice; but, today, waiting is really at an end; and therefore you are not worried; and that is why you are not worried.' He yawned deeply and added, 'Though a man would have to be.'

She got up and kneeling, lifted his legs from the floor on to the divan. She took off both his shoes and placed a pillow underneath his head. She went across to the light switches and switched on all the wall brackets. Standing at the foot of the divan she looked at him intently.

'What did you take?'

'I had some whisky.'

'What else?'

'Amytal, a sedative, three grains I think; though it could have been six.'

'I'll get you some coffee.'

'I'd much rather go to sleep.'

'No, not now. You must talk to me.'

'I'm very tired of it. There are times when I wish to God I'd never become a Catholic.'

'Me too, Chance.'

'Tell me why you danced,' he said.

She sat down beside him and shook him, her pale hands on his shoulders, the great eyes near his own and her smooth hair shaken in a thick layer across her forehead.

'You great fool!' She was biting her lower lip. 'You'll just have to get yourself awake. You can't down amytal on neat whisky the very day I get the chance to talk to you alone. It's cowardly. *I* know because I do it too. But you can't slip off like this and sleep through till tomorrow when everything might be different. I've got to talk to you and it's got to be now.' She gave his hair a tug. 'Chance, get yourself up and into the kitchen, and we'll have dinner together. I can't sit here all alone with the wreckage and pray. I can't even wait. You said I couldn't. You said I'd done enough and been good enough; and I *have*! As good as I'm ever going to be.'

She left him then. She went across the hall and into the kitchen. In a few minutes he heard the clatter of cups and he followed her. In the doorway he supported himself against the jamb and watched her deftly preparing a strong cup of coffee. She looked back at him but said nothing.

'Your shoe's off,' he said.

'So are both yours.'

He looked down at his stockinged feet.

'When you've had this,' she said, handing him the coffee, 'you'd better help me get through this soup you made. I guess you'd better sit down to drink it, though; you're all at an angle.'

He was looking down at her naked foot. 'I'll get your shoe for you if you like. You left it by the divan.'

She came up to him and held the coffee cup to his lips, tilting it so that he was forced either to drink or spill it.

Q

'I suppose you're used to this sort of thing. I suppose you've had to do it often for MacGrady.'

For answer, she forced the remainder of the coffee between his lips and he choked.

'Part of the spiritual life—the ascent of Mount Carmel,' he said.

She took away the cup and he mopped at his tie clumsily. She was reheating the soup and cutting bread for toast. He saw the knife slip and cut her thumb. 'One gets very tired of it,' he went on, 'so I don't blame you at all if you've had enough of it.'

She poured his soup into a vacuum jug and cut the toast into croquettes. Blood from her thumb had soiled it, so she threw it into a dustbin beneath the sink.

'Especially since half the time one's not even sure whether one is right; or even if it is—good—to look after a drunkard, for instance, so that he can go on drinking. After all, why should anyone look after anyone for that matter? Unless there's been some very clear agreement which takes the future into consideration? Arabs have several wives. I was reading the Koran before you got up and do you know what it said? It said agreement is always best. I'll go and get it and read it to you.'

She put the soup jug, two soup plates, pepper and salt on to a tray and washed her hands under the kitchen tap; he saw that she was very angry.

He fetched the book and her shoe from the sitting-room and went straight into the dining-room and sat sideways on to the other door.

Carrying the tray, she paused in the doorway. He saw her take in the flowers and silver before she put the tray down on the sideboard. She poured out his soup and then sat down with her own.

He got up and sat down beside her on the floor so that he could slide her shoe gently on to her foot where it rested beside the table leg. Her skin was ice-cold and he knew that she had ceased to eat. He got up.

'Would you like me to tell you what it said in the Koran about agreement?'

She found a very small handkerchief in a fold of her dressing-gown and blew her nose.

'You'd better drink your soup,' she said, 'all of it.'

'You don't want to know, then? I agree with you, it's rot. It is a faithless absurdity.' He quoted, ' "If a woman fear ill-treatment or desertion on the part of her husband, it will be no offence for them to separate; for agreement is best." '

There was silence. She had finished with her soup and was waiting. The two doll-like circles of colour he had noticed a day or two earlier were reappearing on her cheeks and he watched them define themselves slowly as bloodstains on fine fabric.

'What have any of us got to fear from one another but love?' he said. 'If we love we must fear. Loving we fear, fearing we love; but if we knew perfect love we should have no fear.'

'Your soup,' she said.

He drank a little of it. 'They wouldn't understand that, of course. For them Allah is permanently in heaven and always has been. How could they hope for perfect love if there was no one to bring it into the world. They would always have to agree to separate some time or another, from the beginning, wouldn't they?'

'When you've finished.'

'But we don't. We agree never to separate, don't we, from the first? Never.'

His last word was loud and on her cheeks the colour deepened.

'Well, go on,' he said. 'Answer me! I'm right, aren't I? We give all that we know of ourselves and all that we could never guess to the other person for ever, don't we? We are joined in earth for our time and that is all that matters. To have lived at all is to have been married, spirit to flesh and flesh to earth. What do we know of ourselves beyond our promises of love? Though they're all we have to go on, they must be enough.'

He finished his soup and she took both plates and put them on the sideboard.

As she went into the kitchen she said, 'Who're you trying to convince?'

He made no reply and in a few moments she called out, 'You did say we were to have omelettes, didn't you?'

He was less unsteady on his legs; he was able to walk in now without difficulty and to speak more directly. 'Both of us. It is very important that we should both be quite clear about it before it's too late.'

'Too late?'

'Yes.'

Unthinking, she was breaking an egg into the pan. 'It was too late on Tuesday morning,' she said as the egg spilled its clear substance into the fat.

He took her hand and crushed it. The yolk and albumen flowed over their joined fingers, splinters of the shell crackled like a fire in the heated butter. He saw her lips widen with pain so that the tips of her teeth showed as she leaned against him.

'We've talked too much,' she whispered. 'Columb said to me I wasn't to talk to you.'

He drew breath and straightened himself. 'He said that to me too.'

Her eyes were closed. She was smiling, leaning against him still, her yolky hand on his shoulder and her lower lip bleeding.

'What you say, Chance?'

'I said, "Do something, make something"; the omelette— coffee.'

She stepped away from him, 'I'm doing nothing. I'm going to sit down somewhere. I'm going to lie down. You cook it; they're his eggs but it's your idea.'

'MacGrady's,' he said.

She was by the door. 'Why certainly. All MacGrady's; even *your* time, Chance.'

He broke an egg into the frying pan.

'And agreement is always best,' she called from the hall, 'and we've agreed, haven't we?'

He did not answer.

'Or if we haven't,' she called again. 'If we haven't agreed to give it all a rest, I don't know just what agreement is, nor anything about *you*.'

'No,' he said involuntarily.

'What do you mean, "no," Chance?'

'You talk like MacGrady,' he said, breaking the last egg.

'What you say?'

'I said you talk like MacGrady,' he shouted, 'like your husband.'

'Don't shout.'

'Nobody can hear.'

'But *I* can hear, Chance.'

'And you don't want to. You don't like to be reminded, do you? You don't like to be reminded of MacGrady. He trusts you.'

'He trusted you too.'

In the frying pan the eggs were congealing. He was going to have turned down the gas but he forgot. 'What do you mean *trusted*?'

There was no reply and he called out again. 'Why the past tense?'

He thought she was not going to reply at all but she did after a little pause.

'If you want to argue come in here.'

'We don't eat in there; we eat in the dining-room.'

He heard her laugh. His hands were shaking; but he turned the gas down and tested the omelette. It was nearly ready and he was about to transfer it to a plate when she laughed again.

He snatched up the frying pan and ran into the sitting-room. She lay sprawling as he himself had sprawled so many times in so few days, looking at her feet, both naked now in the light which came in from the hall, for she had switched off the main lights.

'My!' she said. 'That smells *good*. Are we going to eat it out the pan?'

'What did you mean, *trusted*?' he asked swiftly.

'I told him not to; I warned him all along. But where's the knife and fork, Chance? Surely you don't expect a convent girl to eat with her fingers, do you?'

'So that's it,' he said. 'There's nothing new about this for you. You anticipated it. While I've been going along from moment to moment, you and MacGrady, or you at any rate, have been seeing what I never thought of allowing myself to see. So you warned him all along, did you? You've been several days ahead? In the middle of the week when it was Monday, as someone else might be at the beginning of next week though it's only Wednesday for me?'

'For me too, Chance.'

He threw the omelette and the frying pan into the hall; saw the omelette fall out on its impact with the floor and roll fragmentarily across the rug.

'Goodness! You *are* angry, aren't you?'

'I have lost nothing,' he said.

'Haven't you?'

'No, nothing; not so far.'

'Oh, I don't know 'bout that.' She was still studying her feet, spreading her toes as though they were newly discovered fingers.

'Despite your damned intuition,' he said, 'everything is precisely the same for me as it was the day I arrived.'

'Four days,' she said. 'What a strong man. My, my, we get holy in a matter of hours. What about two years? What about seven?'

He looked at the closed shutters, at the portraits of Colonel Godfrey's ancestors on the walls, at the dim clock and its revolving boys.

'He knew very well what he was asking,' he said. 'Mac-Grady would never have expected me to find it easy; particu-

larly if you were behaving as you say you have been, preparing yourself for the apple before ever it was presented
to you.'

'Oh dear! Chance. Are we going to go back to original sin?
I'm so tired of it all—all those convent days. But of course
you're a convert and they're always just death on original sin,
they're so very tickled to have made the discovery.'

He brought her a bowl of apricots and cream and switched
on the lights. He stood beside her eating his own.

'And all the Sisters,' she was saying, 'late vocations too;
and so sure, from personal experience I guess, what was best
for us at seventeen, at twenty-five and for all I know at ninety-
five too. And the long female armies of the Church, making
me just shudder, all down through history, with a scarlet
martyr here and there and a host of irradiated virgins.'

'He's a blackguard,' Chance said, 'but he believes in me and
it is a very great compliment when a blackguard believes in
you.'

'How do they know what's best for us?' she said. 'Chance,
pour me a drink, will you?'

'I'm not suggesting it's your fault,' he said. 'It is nobody's
fault. It is just the way we are and have to be; but you should
never have implied that it was too late. In the world we can
never know whether it's too late. If it were too late he'd be
dead; MacGrady would be dead.'

'Well, that's nice of you, Chance; but if you won't get me a
drink, I'll get it myself.' She rose and tried to push past him
carelessly. He thrust her down on to the divan and handed her
a drink.

'I'm just awfully sorry,' she said. 'I know just what I've
done; but if I hadn't done it I don't think I could have gone
through with it at all. You do see that, don't you? I know
from all you've said, that you must do.'

'Yes,' he said.

She held up her glass. 'Have a drink,' she said. 'I'm just so
grateful to you.'

The telephone rang in the hall and she looked up at him.

'Shall we answer it?'

The bell rang on as he considered. Not an automatic line with a double ring and an intermission but a long staccato ground out by some Arab in the local exchange—or a French girl or a Spaniard.

'We'll leave it.'

The ringing paused and was then renewed more stridently. 'Let them wait,' he said.

'That's right. If they want us, they can ring again. It'll be Zoe, I know. I know it'll be Zoe wanting to know how you are.'

The bell stopped.

'You mean how MacGrady is,' he said.

'What'll we do if it goes again, Chance?'

'We'll have to answer it. We don't want anyone trying to break in.'

'No.'

'Is the fatima coming in tomorrow?' he asked, 'because if so, I'd better move my things into your room.'

'That's right.'

'And you'd better get all your things into the spare room as we arranged?'

'That's right.' She turned on to her side and pillowed her cheek on a ringed hand.

In the hall the telephone rang for the third time and she sat up.

'Yes?' she asked him.

'Yes,' he said heavily. 'You don't mind, do you, if I move into your room? I could sleep here as long as I could be sure of waking and moving down the corridor before the fatima arrives; but I think it would be a risk.'

'I should say not. You go right on and get into my bed and I'll bring you a warm drink in a few minutes and tell you all about it.'

She went to the telephone easily as though it were no interruption and picked up the receiver.

'I guessed it was you, Zoe. I said to Chance, to Columb, I

mean——' and here she laughed, and Chance went down the hall. 'Yes, Chance went off early . . . No, not for me at all, darling; I don't like them so thoughtful. But you know what Columb is . . . Well *he's* a little better this evening, but he still won't eat or drink a thing. I guess he'll start getting restless tomorrow and by Saturday he'll be raging to get up.'

Outside the bedroom door, Chance paused. He collected his case and put it on the bed; he left the door open for a moment and surveyed the room.

'No, I haven't heard a thing. Why today I didn't even dress . . . George called up earlier but he only asked after Columb; he didn't say much about the Arabs at all, but maybe that was because they didn't get warmed up till later . . .'

The bed was unmade, its light blankets and linen sheets pulled hard back: MacGrady's pyjama trousers on the floor where he had dropped them, the shape of his head on the left pillow beside the shallower concavity of Anna's: the dressing-table a scatter of cosmetics with a haze of powder on the black glass surface. He saw that the wardrobe doors were open, disclosing rows of dresses with a phalanx of slender shoes beneath them.

'Well, darlings, if you're really worried I'll try and make it. By lunch-time I might be good and hungry but nat'rally it depends on how Columb is. If he's restless he won't let me out the flat even to see the midday sun . . . But what does Godfrey say? Have you called him? If *he* gets breezy then I do believe it might be time to think of moving right out . . .'

Chance shut the door and undressed. He made up the bed and climbed into it. The scent she used had impregnated the sheets and the deep pillows; from where he lay he could see the clothes she had worn the day before drooping over the back of a chair; next to them, on a purple ottoman, MacGrady's lawn shirt, the cuff-links still in place and a pair of turkish sandals surmounting the pile.

He closed his eyes and opened them again perhaps a moment, perhaps much, later when he heard her knock. She carried a tray on which a large wineglassful of hot milk stood beside a plate of biscuits.

'I should have made the bed,' she said sitting down on MacGrady's side. 'But I just couldn't be bothered. That was Zoe all right; she and Robin are real worried about the Arabs. Robin's perfectly certain there's been no Franco-American agreement about any atom tests but somebody's putting it about that the democracies are threatening tests to cool off the Arabs for the French in return for oil concessions somewhere else. Robin's very well-connected and he knows everybody and usually has his ear pretty well to the ground so——'

'He's only rather a dreary little Cabinet toady,' said Chance.

She laughed. 'I didn't think you went for him very much at the party.'

'He ought to be running a golf club. We always get an epidemic of men like that after a major war. A little fighting goes to their heads. They join some second-rate West End club to hunt for politicians, or else attach themselves to one of the more deadly Sunday newspapers and start writing off-beat articles about game reserves, mountaineering, or native customs in Montego Bay. He's just the sort of man one would find here. If MacGrady was so friendly with him I can't help wondering why he didn't get *him* to solve his problems. If he knows all the diplomats he claims to know, he should have been able to smuggle him out in the Bag.'

'Now, Chance darling, don't start getting steamed up again. You know very well that Columb would never ask for help from an English Protestant. And besides a man like Robin would have been just horrified to know any of his friends was in debt.'

Chance was silent.

'If you can bear any more news, Zoe says that Heber's been spreading it around that Godfrey's been in Russian pay for years. He told Robin that all these reconnaissances of his with the different sheiks which we thought were part of his black-girl fixation were really arms deals for Friese and George with the Arabs. Zoe says it's quite certain there's been a steady trickle of rifles and ammunition across the frontiers into the Zone. Oh, and guess what?'

'I couldn't.'

'Robin says all the rifles and ammunition as good as have the red star on them. It's all very complicated but it seems the Egyptians have been shipping the stuff in for months through Saudi Arabia or somewhere and that it's all a present from the Soviet Union to embarrass Washington and London.'

Chance sat up in the bed. 'Did you ask Zoe if she's mended Robin's khaki shorts yet?'

'You just won't take him seriously, will you?'

'I detest reporters, particularly silver-plated ones. Did she say anything about leaving?'

'They're pretty windy but I don't think they've got that far. They've invested a lot of money in some business here and her alimony's not all that big. They want me to go and talk it over with them at lunch tomorrow at the Capuchin. I'm in a spot because they've asked me to see what Columb says, and of course I stalled and said he wasn't fit to talk about anything yet; but I can't go on doing that for ever and they're getting very friendly all of a sudden. They don't seem to trust anyone but us now, and though I'd like to let them in on things and invite them round here instead of letting them check in at the Sayyid for the week-end, I know Columb would never forgive me if it got about that he was not a free agent; and with Zoe being such a babbler——'

'They wouldn't believe you even if you did tell them. People like that float above corruption and never see it.'

'Columb said a Protestant aristocracy's a contradiction in terms.'

'Did he?'

She turned and smiled at him. 'You know, Chance, I just can't figure what it is that Columb ever did to get himself tied with George in the first place. I know it's not just the money; I know it must be something he did before ever I met him; but I can't get him to talk about it any time. Before I married him I used to care, I used to worry about his first marriage a lot. I used to say 'It's Helen': and then I'd think, 'No it must be more than that. It must be some crime. Something not awfully bad but bad enough to be worth something to George and to Columb.' Then I got to thinking that it must be something just terrible.'

'Such as what?'

'Oh well, murder you know.' She was looking at him in her blank way. 'I met such a lot of murderers since I came here. That sounds awful. Back home the people just wouldn't understand a thing like that. If you were to tell them, "I met a most amusing murderer at a party last night," they'd think you were heading for the Sanatorium. But since I met Columb and all these sort of people one meets in the Zone I've got to feeling that murderers are really comparatively respectable people: rich you know, and well-mannered——'

'When did you first get this idea about MacGrady?'

'Oh, it came gradually. The way knowledge does when you get to seeing more and more of a person. I got that I had to take more and more dope to get any sleep at all and I used to pray about it by the hour and do novenas in my bed. I even tried to break with him once and went away to Rome when we'd been sharing together in Barcelona. But I came back because I'd known he was bad from the start, and a little more badness in the past didn't seem to matter, it was only more for us both to do. It was as I may have told you before; this feeling that I didn't want a man or anything that wouldn't be a life-work in which I could lose myself. What you would call 'Mission-sistering' I suppose, a hangover from the Convent. But not only that; I could see my friends getting married young to tough smoothies from Yale and Columbia and having hygienic babies and watching their smoothies grow into fatties and practising polite birth control on the side an' keeping the Church's year in Stamford, Connecticut, an' joining the women's clubs and—getting just nowhere.'

She laughed; her abstraction vanished. She lighted a cigarette and passed it to him.

'Well, if you're not too sleepy,' she said, 'I'm going right on with my confession.'

'Do.'

'Well, it may have been very arrogant of me to judge, because nobody knows that it isn't better to live in Stamford and have babies than it is to go pegging around the Mediterranean with an alcoholic who doesn't seem to want even a Pekingese. All I'm saying is that in those days I was praying an awful lot and that when Columb came along I somehow couldn't ever get away from him again. I just loved something about him. I still do; and no matter what he's done or what he ever does do in the future I couldn't ever leave him, even though I might be tempted to—digress a little on the way! I began to see him as the one for my great marriage—I like that phrase of yours—and after all my shilly-shallies I was all set to start in on it when he told me about this growth and that he was dying.'

Chance's cigarette smouldered between his fingers untasted. He drew up his knees and she leaned against them.

'Well, can you imagine that?' she said flatly. 'I felt I'd been tricked by God. Here was I all set to love him and make him back from something soft and drunk into something strong and—conscious, only to find I'd married a dying man without even time on my side. After that, I cared even less what he'd done or hadn't done and I didn't care much about God any more. I believed in Him all right and in the Church; but I decided to be a passenger and leave it to the saints to get me to Heaven. I left off worrying and praying, praying anyway, and I told God "I never said I'd make sacrifices for nothing; if you're going to give me nothing, nothing that I can see grow good or touch or hold, not even the beginning or the middle of a man, but only the end of him, well I'm through. From now on," I said, "I'll make my own rules to fit whatever else happens." A tear of anger escaped her and hung on her left cheek. 'Or maybe that was what I wanted to say, even if I didn't actually say it.'

They were silent for a long time. Outside the windows,

below the place where they sat, somewhere at the bottom of the President Hoover, they heard a taxi go past, its horn blaring; from further away, a single, very soft explosion.

Anna got up.

'You don't want to let your drink go cold. You ought to have drunk it while it was hot.'

He took it and drank from it.

'I can't say very much, I'm afraid. It isn't that I don't care or that I can't see something you haven't said; it's only that I do care and that I do see and that I don't want to.'

'That makes two, doesn't it?'

'It does.'

When she was out in the passage he called to her. 'Are you going to go out to lunch tomorrow, then?'

'Yes.'

'But not till after the fatima has been? It would be rather nerve-wracking to be left here alone with the girl liable to ask me something through the door.'

'Don't worry. You'll be chaperoned.'

She put out the light and closed the door. He heard her go up the hall into the spare room; later, the whistle of the shower and the sound of some song which she sang softly to herself.

In the darkness he completed the appropriate five decades with MacGrady's rosary, and at the end thought of the dark tomb and despair, the young men in white garments, the Stranger in the garden; and he prayed for MacGrady.

She had said something about the boy Haleb, a detail in the pattern of her conversation which he had nearly forgotten. Getting out of his bed, he knelt on the ottoman and gently swung the shutter open.

Beneath the moonlight dammed in by the ring of hills, the soundless limits of the town lay like sunken shipping below him. He saw the black and white-blue of the commercial blocks linked by rectangles of smaller dwellings; here and there, cypresses standing straight as plumes of seaweed at flood-tide, and, beneath him, the Arab encampment tumbled like discarded shells on the dark bed of the vacant terrain.

In the roadway there was only one shadow thrown long and attenuated from the far kerb; the shadow of the boy who, with his back to the hills, waited for the least inkling of information from the flat on the fourth floor. As Chance watched he saw him pace slowly up the hill, turn and return, then remain motionless with his small face uplifted against the blank windows.

He climbed back into her bed again and, eventually, fell asleep.

Thursday

H<small>E</small> had lain all that morning in MacGrady's room inter-
preting fitfully the sounds of the fatima washing-up in the
kitchen and the unaccustomed noises from two of the adjacent
flats. Apart from Colonel Tyghe's, immediately above, and
the ground floor shared between George Fraser and the concierge, he had discovered that only one other was tenanted,
the one in the opposite wing, where the day before he had
seen the Arab girl hanging out the washing.

Remotely, for about half an hour, he had heard faint footsteps in the bedroom directly above his own; distant voices
too: the high commands of the Colonel, and once, the shriek
of a rusty castor piercing the steel and concrete of the fabric.
Then, as time passed, there had again been silence and he had
had the sense of persons moving overhead to a different
section of the flat, of a task concluded.

Later still, Anna had knocked at his door and for a time
they had talked warily.

'I fixed you some coffee and rolls,' she had said. 'The
fatima's gone and I've locked the hall door; so you're quite
safe and you can emerge now, unless you want to stay on in
bed. I've got to keep my date with Zoe and Robin.'

He had dressed quickly and followed her along to the
sitting-room. She had been wearing a two-piece suit of cloud-
grey linen, he remembered, and he had been struck by some
overnight change in her face; a darkening of the delicate
arches of her brows. Above them, her hair had been thick and
shining as usual; but below, though her cheeks remained cold-
white and her lips pale to greyness, she had darkened and

greenly shadowed the margins of her eyes. He had seen very distinctly that she was angry.

In the sitting-room the shutters had been folded back, the windows opened wide, and the venetian blinds let down. Through their slats air, light and sound entered the room; and momentarily he had had the impression that these things: the wind blowing from the hills, the ingress of daylight and the remote clatter of the town were all an intentional part of her protest.

He had drunk his coffee standing, while she, sitting on the edge of an ornate wooden chair by the window, had smoked a cigarette whose fumes rose grey through the sunlight.

'What time are you meeting them?' he had asked.

'Round about one at the Capuchin.'

'Oh.'

'But I'm going now. I've had enough of being penned up in this place. It feels like a year out of my life already.'

'I know what you mean.'

'I keep expecting to hear from Columb. The way time's creeping since he left, I keep forgetting he can only have been in London, England twen'y-four hours.'

'Perhaps this afternoon . . .' he had been muddled himself, 'what I mean is that he should be with the specialist, Sir Gladwyn Dyce, this morning, and I suppose the X-ray results and so forth should be available by two or three o'clock Greenwich time. Which means it's quite possible he'll get some sort of news then; in which case he might cable a preliminary report to us which would arrive early this evening.'

'In which case,' she had cut in abruptly, 'I've got to fill in time somehow. And that's just why I'm going out now.'

'So you said.'

She had glanced at him. From their dark-green margins, he had caught the venom of her eyes in a beam of sunlight.

'There are a lot of things I could do to pass the time, unless of course you're nervous about being left too long alone.'

It was at this point that he had moved over to the tray,

picked up a roll and tried to bite it, only to find that his false teeth were not sharp enough to pierce its crust. He had turned away so that she should not see his humiliation.

'If your dentures are blunt, you should use your fingers,' she had said. 'Don't worry about me, I'm used to having what the magazines call *mature* men about the place.'

He had been unable to reply because his mouth was full of the dried roll; but he had felt his own colour.

'For instance,' she had said happily. 'I could go shopping. I could buy some of the things I'm going to need for my new life when Columb comes back cured.'

'Cured?' he had managed.

'That's what I said.' She had drawn on the cigarette greedily and then blown the smoke into the sunshine, watching it slowly disperse. 'Or I could go to church; I could go to Confession.'

He had nodded.

'All said,' she had resumed, 'that's the right place for a confession; you go to a priest. Provided you're sorry, all you got to do's find a church with a priest in it and get into a box or up against the screen and get absolution. The Sacraments are there all the time like a river and you just have to jump in; you don't have to bleat about on the bank all the time like High Episcopalians or Buchmanites.' A pause. 'Protestants always get the Sacraments wrong, they start economising out of nerves or pride or something.'

'Do they?'

'They certainly do. Why there's times when I wonder if a Protestant can ever outlive his meanness to God,' she said as she rose impatiently from her chair. 'The bigger a Protestant is, the smaller he makes God.'

She had caught his intentional smile. He had watched her grind her cigarette into an ashtray as he asked:

'What time will you be back?'

'I'd just have to try and fit in God anywhere,' she had said, ignoring his question. 'Why! Imagine trying to fit God into a temporal universe. It'd just burst like an old egg. That's

what Columb says, anyway.' Over by the door: 'Is there anything you want in town?'

'Cigarettes. By the way, what time will you be back?'

'Couldn't say. Depends on a lot of things. Why?'

'I'll have to know what time to expect you so that I don't
show myself to the wrong person. I'm going to keep the door
bolted in case of accidents.'

'In that case I'll knock six times quickly—like this'—a quick
tattoo on the top of the bureau. 'How'll that be?'

'All right. But all the same——'

'You can get your own lunch and tea, can't you? There's a
mass of stuff in the kitchen.'

'Oh it's not that. It's only——'

'Yes?' He had sensed her eagerness.'

'MacGrady more or less——'

'Oh! Chance in the role of the Guardian Angel?' she had
said with a renewal of coldness. 'Don't worry about me. I'm
going to have a great time. I'm going to eat and drink and
talk and get absolution and do a whole heap of shopping.'

'And if the telephone rings?'

'Let it! Just don't answer it that's all. Why, *you* said leave
it the first time Zoe rang—last night. If your memory carries
you back that far?'

'It does. Supposing, though, it was a cable or a telegram
from London.'

Having seen the quick nip she had given her lower lip, he
had smiled at her brightly and followed up his advantage.
'You'll just have to be back fairly soon, won't you Anna?'

She had frowned, thinking very fast at the clock, calculating, not looking at him at all.

'It would be frightful,' he had persisted as she reset her
watch, 'if there was some news and we missed it, wouldn't it?'

From the doorway: 'I don't think anyone's going to miss
anything very much in this flat.'

'One of us might,' he had said, 'if only one of us is here
in time.'

'In time for what?'

'For a telephone call of course.'

'Well that'd be too bad.'

'Is that all?'

'Telephones have been known to ring more than once. They'd call again.'

'They might.'

'An' *I* might,' she had replied as she unbolted the door. 'Now are you going to get yourself out of sight before I open this, or do we have to go on wrestling in front of the whole block?'

'Good-bye, Anna.'

'Good-bye, Chance.'

And she had gone . . .

But that had been several hours ago: since then, nothing whatsoever had happened. He had half-expected the telephone to ring, a delivery of letters through the opening in the door, or, at least, the sound of the lift being used.

Lying on the divan, the empty tray beside him on the floor, a litter of cigarette-ends in the ashtray and three half-read novels at his elbow, it was for this sound in particular that he waited. The sound which might mean that, in a moment, she would be back, that he would hear her knock on the door and see her once again.

He had never known what it was to be starved of sound before. Sometimes, on a night call to the prison, he had become aware of its contrasted silence, of the dull buildings within the high walls beyond which the street-noises went up into the darkness. But even there the silence had been im-permanent because he himself had brought sound with him: the clatter of the hospital orderly's boots, the ring of key-chains and the voice of the duty officer raking the stillness in the cell where the prisoner lay.

Today, he discovered, even the town out beyond the win-dows was quieter than usual. He had to crawl close to them to catch the murmur of the crowds in the Avenue Grande and the faint cries of the vendors in the Socco Chico.

He returned to the divan and started to watch the clock. He found it was possible to be quite sure the cupids had ceased to turn if one caught them at the end of a revolution. It was a trick of timing: one had to look away and then look back again quickly. If one had timed it correctly the revolution to the left would be ending so slowly that it was imperceptible; the swing to the right would not yet have begun; while the quite sensible pause between the two would still be in the future. For moments it would seem that the clock had been arrested, whereas in fact there had been no failure of any kind whatsoever.

He succeeded in getting this effect several times; and then, try as he would, he could not recapture the knack of it. He decided that he must voluntarily distract his attention for a moment and then try once again with less concentration. He picked up one of the novels and opened it. Somewhere, within the flat, a door opened.

He closed the book. He had distinctly heard the click of a handle somewhere along the passage. Very quietly he leaned over the side of the divan and with one finger pushed the sitting-room door. It swung away from him slowly and soundlessly, completely concealing any view of the divan from the lower end of the corridor.

He got up and put his eye to the crack between the upper and lower hinges.

Framed narrowly, he could see the open door into the kitchen, a section of the Persian rug and the nearer end of the bathroom door. It was opening slowly, being drawn gently inwards by someone he could not see, by someone he would not see until they were half-way up the reception end of the corridor.

He closed the door completely and with no sound, and then took off his shoes, slid them under the divan, and moved directly through into the dining-room where he peered through the keyhole. He was exactly opposite the bathroom and he saw the child at once. She was dressed exactly as she had been three days earlier but she was a little older than he had imagined her. Her naked feet were quite soundless as she stole out into the corridor and disappeared from his view round the angle leading to the bedrooms.

Waiting, he heard her attempt to enter MacGrady's room, try the handle of the room he had first occupied and then go into Anna's room. He heard her trying the doors of the cupboards and the slither of the cabin trunks as she pulled them out to open them. In a moment she returned, he heard the minute sound of her feet as she came towards his end of the hall.

When she went into the kitchen, he crossed back into the sitting-room and, lying down, drew himself quickly under the divan. In a few moments he saw the door opening, and the small naked feet moving over the wooden floor a few inches from his eyes as she set about her tour of the room.

He held his breath when she came up closer to the divan, when her hand descended to pick up the ashtray in which his latest, incompletely stubbed, cigarette still smouldered and smoked.

He heard her gasp, the sudden hiss of an intaken breath as she waited there fractionally before dropping to her knees beside him to peer into the darkness where he lay.

He caught her by the ankle with one hand, heard the anger of the one sound she made, but felt no immediate pain when she transfixed his gripping hand to the floor. He merely grunted when he saw what she had done so very quickly: the short steel hatpin pushed hard home into the parquet at an angle between the bones of his palm.

In the moment of his amazement she had gone. He wrenched the pin out and wriggled back into the room. In the hall he wasted seconds at the still-bolted door and then remembered the bathroom. He thought he remembered the balcony vividly as he ran in there and threw open the windows to find that beneath him lay only the dead four-storey drop into the hibiscus patch. On the sheer white surface of the wall there was not even a pipe to be seen.

As he turned away, he was thinking or realising vividly

that she could have come in some minutes before he had become aware of her; that though he had seen her coming from the bathroom she might originally have entered from the kitchen. There was, too, quite certainly a balcony outside his own room; but where was the key and how in any case could she have reached the balcony? From where?'

This drew him up at the bathroom door. Only seconds had elapsed, a few swings of the cupids in the sitting-room. Neither for them had there been more than deception, yet she seemed to have taken advantage of that illusory pause and slipped out of the flat through a chink in time itself. And then he noticed the cupboard door above the washbasin, the cupboard which spanned the right angle between two walls and which he had thought was a linen cupboard.

One door was now open and was swinging as though in a powerful draught, and there were no shelves to be seen in the dark recess behind it.

He climbed on to the washbasin and kneeled on the soap-trays to peer down the dark shaft which carried the plumbing of the tiered bathrooms of the wing. Below him, he saw her silhouetted against the light which filtered through from the open cupboard in the bathroom of the bottom flat and was just able to discern her features in the light falling on them from his own.

He saw that she was exactly small enough to shin down the trunk of the effluent pipe to which she clung with her hands and knees. She would slide down from duct to duct, branch to branch, as though she were slipping down the stem of a smooth black tree with its roots in George Fraser's flat. She would pause at each junction to steady herself and then slither down a little further. As he watched, she looked up. He saw the sallow sharp little face with its black eyes and lank hair only fifteen to twenty feet below him and he shouted at her foolishly: an accusation, a threat, a recognition.

'Tu!' she shrieked back, 'Toi!' and the word reverberated in the empty space above his head, it's double meaning, for it sounded to him like the French 'thou' or the French 'tuer,' dismaying him as he crouched there.

She redoubled her pace and he leapt backwards on to the bathroom floor. He was trembling with rage and disgust. He filled a jug with water at the tap and was going to pour it down on top of her when he heard voices echoing through the open cupboard doors. With the full jug in his hand he scrambled back on to the washbasin and put his head into the hole. He could see that much of the light from the bottom opening was occluded by something, he could scarcely separate the proportions of the child from the black shadow into which she was lowering herself. It was not until he heard the rumble of George's laughter that he realised it was the body of the man himself which was blocking the original light.

She was nearly down and she knew. In a moment Fraser too would almost certainly know everything he had wanted to know. It was too late.

He poured the water down the washbasin and went into the kitchen to make tea. He drank three cups and then went back into the sitting-room and prayed that Anna would return quickly. It was not an organised prayer, it owed nothing to formal instruction; it was the sort of prayer wrung out of a man forced unexpectedly to appreciate the threat of another's death, the presence of final pain or the imminence of despair. For he realised that he could no longer be sure now that she would ever return. The man in the flat below, if he was as vicious and determined as MacGrady believed him to be, might act at once in the light of his new knowledge.

If Anna returned quickly before any decision had been taken, they might still, once they had communicated, pretend that he himself had returned briefly to the flat to pick up something he had left behind him. They might still insist that MacGrady himself was there, though confined to the room which the child had been unable to enter. But it was thin; there were half a dozen flaws in it. The child had taken nothing, she had obviously known in advance what she was about and had been sent up only to confirm or disprove the story they had told George. It was not likely that she would make any mistake in giving her account, though if she were honest she would have to admit that she had found two bed-rooms locked: MacGrady's and his own.

He looked at the clock: it was five minutes past five. In the hall he heard the quick tattoo of Anna's knock on the front door.

'Anna?' he called.

'Yes, it's me.'

He let her in, and she smiled at him. He smelt, in the warmth of her clothing, the heat of the day which he had not properly seen. The temper of the sun had made her paler, there was a fine dampness over her forehead, her cheeks and her upper lip; and he caught the sense of the sun, the heat and the light through which she had hurried, when he discerned the wine in her breath. She carried parcels with bright strings and ribbons on them, she held a white paper cone of tuberoses lying sheathed like pale fingers within the whiteness, and these too brought in with them a distillation of the out-side heat.

He stood back and she hurried past him down the dim hall and into the sitting-room. She dropped her parcels on to the divan and dabbed her forehead and her lip with a damp hand-kerchief. She pushed up the smooth margin of her hair from her forehead, and with eyes, as yet unaccustomed to the permanent dusk of the sitting-room, peered at the turning clock on her bureau.

'I got your cigarettes,' she said.

'Oh thank you.'

'Everything all right?'

'No.'

'No telephone calls or cables? Nothing exciting, nothing to celebrate?'

'No.'

She executed a half-turn away from him on the shining floor.

'Chance, I'm sorry I was that way this morning. I didn't mean to snap at you but I just felt so mad about everything.'

'You were rather short.'

But she swept on. 'Do you ever get that way? Do you ever get so you feel you just want to tear someone's eyes out, make them feel just so small and so worthless?'

She had dropped her handkerchief and he retrieved it and tucked it into the breast pocket of her suit. 'I'm so glad you're back,' he said, 'I was afraid——'

'Oh I had a great time. I had a bumper lunch with Zoe and Robin, then I went shopping; I bought some English make-up in case I have to go to England, the light's different there you know, and I got all of the news from them and I don't think I slipped up even a little bit on anything.'

'Good.'

'Oh, and I went to my Confession and I feel just great after it.'

'Oh.'

'What did you do, Chance? Did you make yourself some tea and read my books and write some letters to your friends at home?'

'I looked at a couple of books but I didn't write any letters.'

'Oh, which books? Not the Koran, I hope!'

'No.'

'Which ones then?'

'Oh a book called *The Comforters* and another one called *The Ordeal of Gilbert Pinfold*. They were rather disturbing.'

'Is that what's the matter with you? Why didn't you read something cheerful, or better still do something cheerful? Why didn't you write a nice letter to someone?'

'I didn't feel like it.'

'Whatever's the matter with you? Has anything happened that shouldn't ought to have happened?'

'Yes; I'm afraid that in one sense we're both wasting our time.'

She was taking little parcels out of her bag.

'How come, Chance?'

He told her briefly and at the end she said:

'Well that's just too bad, that's not nice at all. Let me look at your poor hand. The little vixen! Just wait until I see George!'

'You can't see George.'

'Can't I just?' She was looking at his hand. 'It's quite swollen, there's some antiseptic in the bathroom, you ought to put some on it.'

'I don't think it would help. I'm only hoping it was a clean hatpin.'

'Sending little cats up drainpipes into our flat!' she said, 'and stabbing my friends with hatpins.'

He laughed. 'You're astonishing, Anna.'

'Well I don't know 'bout that, but I certainly *feel* astonished. I bought these flowers because I thought we *ought* to have flowers, there's something very sane about them, about buying them and bringing them home and putting them in water.'

'They're beautiful,' he said. 'They're very beautiful. I think they are the most beautiful flowers I have ever seen.'

For an instant then she looked at him fully, seeming to transcend something she wished to communicate in her looking, and which they both acknowledged, by the manner in which she prolonged her gaze.

'You do believe that, Chance?'

'Yes I do.'

'I had a feeling you might like them, and that's why I bought them for you.'

There was a short silence before she moved and picked up the paper which held them. 'The things that have happened in this past few days!' she said. 'Why I'm beginning to wonder just what we're all playing at; and I don't mind telling you I've had just about enough of it all. What can they do to us even supposing they do know that Columb's gone to London to get himself cured and that you haven't got a passport and that I've compromised myself, sharing a flat with you for a few days?'

He said nothing and she sat down on the divan, slowly un-wrapping the tuberoses and laying them across her knees.

'What's come over us all? What are we frightened of? Why don't we——'

The telephone rang and she handed the flowers to him before going out into the hall to answer it.

'It's a cable from London, England,' she said fumbling in her handbag for pen and paper.

He moved out and watched her write the message down, repeating it aloud as she did so.

' "Neo-plastic growth confirmed stop Maybe benign and operable stop Right atalectesis supervened on journey"—does that make sense to you, Chance? "Immediate surgery impera-tive London Clinic tomorrow stop Writing and returning MacGrady's photographs etc by evening post today for Satur-day in Zone stop If necessary park Poor Clare as arranged Zoe's party pending my letter stop Above all hold everything and order Mass Friday Sorrowful. Sender: Chance." '

'That twist he's given the name is clever,' she said dropping the receiver back on to the bridge. 'What did I tell you? We've all been fighting a lot of dirty cobwebs and he's going to get better!' She took the flowers from him. 'What are we waiting for, Chance, darling! Let's tell everybody, let's get our friends praying for him, let's get out of this damned flat and out of this dreadful place and cross over to Europe tonight.'

'We can't,' he said.

She put her arms round him. 'Why ever not? What do a few old debts matter? How do we know what's going to happen any minute for the best. How do we know our lives aren't going to be changed overnight, even as we stand here talking and hoping?'

'We don't,' he said, thinking of Marcovicz in Shibam.

'In a few months, weeks maybe, we'll be able to pay off every cent he owes George and the others and not know the difference. We'll be able to laugh at them when Columb's father dies. He's a rich man, why he's a very rich man, one of the richest in Connecticut and he has no other children.

When Columb inherits it and when he's healthy why then he'll be able to——' she walked past him into the sitting-room as he asked:

'He'll be able to what?'

'Live right. He'll be able to get a fresh start, you always can in the Church. And that means *we'll* get started; our marriage will begin, won't it?'

'Yes,' he said, 'but only provided he breaks free.'

'Who from?'

'From George, from Marcovicz, from all of them.'

'Marcovicz? Who's he?'

'Keller.'

'Oh that little man. What has he got to do with it?'

He said, 'Come into the sitting-room.' And she followed him in; but they did not sit down, preferring to stand some little distance apart on either side of the bureau.

'What do you think made MacGrady let George have his passport in the first place?' he asked.

'Well I don't know. I told you, I used to worry about it but just lately I gave up. I didn't even think about it any more; I got to accepting it like you accept a heap of other things about people, like you might accept the fact that someone lost a leg or has ulcers. But I suppose I figured that he'd given it to him as sort of security for what he owes, maybe so that he could borrow more.'

'He's been borrowing from him for a long time, hasn't he?'

'I don't know. He knew George before ever I met him. I believe they were in some sort of business together after the War. George was buying up old stuff from the desert campaign, trucks and guns and things. For all I know he may still be doing that, he may be tied up in that racket of Godfrey's which Robin was talking about at luncheon today.' She thought for a moment. 'As a matter of fact that's why I was surprised the way Yacef Ali was so obliging when you and Columb tackled him Tuesday about me going to the Palace. The Sultan and his family have it in for George and Godfrey and their friends because they think they may upset the little game the Palace plays with Moscow, Cairo and Washington.'

'You mean golf on Sundays and cous-cous or whatever they eat during Ramadan. He was certainly a little cool to both of us and but for Magda and the fact that you are very beautiful I don't think he'd have consented at all.'

'It's too bad, Chance, we can't convert you into a nice slim Mayfair type girl and then we could both go together and stay there until things have settled down.'

Chance was restless. Catching his mood she said, 'But you were on about Keller?'

'Yes. Do you happen to know when exactly it was that MacGrady gave George his passport?'

'Yes I do know that because I wanted him to cross over to Italy with me to buy some things for my trousseau and he made difficulties about it then.'

'When was that?'

'Three months ago. But what has this got to do with Keller?'

'One more question,' he said. 'Can you tell me how long Keller has been in the Zone?'

'No, I only met him once and that was by accident. Columb didn't like him at all; he took real sick the day after we saw him, an' I was surprised because I thought he was just a very funny man, plumb eccentric, a character.' She looked across at him. 'Why, Chance, do *you* know how long he's been in the Zone?'

'Yes I do. He's been here just three months.'

She was frowning. 'You mean that Keller and Columb's passport——'

'There's a very definite connection. Until Marcovicz came, Fraser would have had to remain content with other securities. It's not every creditor who can get complete control of a man's movements, particularly a man who may be conveniently dying and who is likely to inherit a fortune before he does so.'

'So it's Keller who knows what I don't. Is that it?'

'I'm afraid it is.'

She sat down suddenly on the chair and watched the revolutions of the clock. She looked a little cat-like, like a cat half-watching the flight of a wasp or a bluebottle. Her large eyes, reflecting the green eye-shadow, were surmounted by a smooth forehead but there was a suggestion of squint in the gaze they directed at the pendulum.

'Just what are you trying to tell me, Chance?'

'Only that you've got to wait; that we all have to.'

'But what's Columb done? What is it that seemingly everybody knows bar me?'

'It's of no consequence,' he said carefully. 'I would be breaking my word if I tried to explain to you. I can only tell you that when he was here it was a question of personal morality but that now he's in England it could involve the police.'

'Here?' she asked. 'You mean the Zone?'

'Yes.'

She got up. 'I hate the place,' she said. 'I just loathe it. It seems to be suffocating me in my sleep. That's the way I feel, I feel I've been asleep for months with someone closing all the windows and starving me of air while I slept. I've been drifting, dodging, I haven't asked myself, I haven't thought. I've been lazier and less healthy than if I'd stayed in Stamford, Connecticut, with all the friends I affect to crab about.'

'One feels like that and one imagines it's very good of one,' he said, 'but really it's only pride because there must always have been a great deal of goodness in the past.'

'I'm not interested in the past and I'll tell you something else too. *He* hated it; he shuddered at it but he couldn't ever break away from it. When he wasn't drunk he used to wake up nights shouting that thing of Campbell's at me, something like:

> "*This is the desert,*" Anna,
> "*Where cigarette-ends are intimate friends,*
> *And it's always Sunday and it's always*
> *Three o'clock in the afternoon.*"

'Did *you* know he hated it, Chance?'

'Yes.'

'And you guessed that I did too, didn't you? Even before I entirely knew myself? Why that was the first question you asked me: if I liked the life here in the Zone? And I said, what did I say?'

'I think you said, "I don't know." You seemed to think *I* ought to know and that I'd come here for that reason.'

'*Is* that why you came?'

'I still don't know. It's only when a thing is over, an event, a whole phase of days, of years, that I can begin to guess its purpose; and even then I can only assess it by the way I'm behaving in the present. When I was young I had no idea that events had anything to do with me; but in the last few years I've become suspicious, fascinated by the most trivial happenings: a wrong number on the telephone, chance meetings, or a summer cold that prevents some appointment. Since I became a Catholic the excitement has grown; I've tasted time as though it were milk or a sea: something essential, nutritious, measured, or vast, fantastic and perilous. When I decided to come here I knew I was going to use a great deal of the measure, I was watching the sea and the sky for signs. When nothing happened I nearly went back; but the moment I met Marcovicz I was sure my decision—it was nearly a challenge—had been recognised. From then onwards I wanted, if I could, to possess my holiday by my behaviour at the time, and not later on; so that the moment it was over I should know what it meant.

'I had this feeling, certainty almost, that one day I might be terrified by the shortness of my life, that because time, experience and behaviour had never been joined there might be no part of it I could hold or value, that it might seem like some pointless and trivial holiday remembered only by a shell on the mantelpiece.'

When he had finished, had half-concluded what he was trying to say, he caught sight of her again. Like a ship on the ocean he had visualised, she grew slowly clear to him on a most remote horizon. He saw that she too had momentarily forgotten his presence, that she was about to respond as to

S

the idea by itself and not to him; but before she could do so the bell rang in the hall and their conversation was killed swiftly.

As they waited there was a knock, sharp and a little official; not repeated. They heard a key turn in the lock, and the door opened.

Colonel Godfrey Tyghe came in very neatly. He was exceedingly smartly dressed, wearing gloves and carrying a soft hat and keys in his left hand, a small ledger in his right.

'Good evening. I'm sorry I had to use my key, Anna. I wasn't sure just whom I should find here; there have been conflicting accounts. How is MacGrady?'

'Oh he's——' She was extraordinarily ill at ease. Chance thought that she must be experiencing an outrageous betrayal of their intimacy. He had never seen her so little composed. 'Oh he's—but Godfrey sit down. Let me get you a drink. You do know Doctor Chance, don't you?'

'We have met. I understand he had left.'

'Well no; you see——'

'I fear I haven't really time for a drink, Anna. I leave for Cairo in the morning.' He coughed.

'For Cairo, Godfrey?'

'Yes.'

'You amaze me. Columb will be——'

'Where is he?'

'Well, right now——'

'I have to see him. It's merely a question of the rent; the Irish Syndicate rather wish me to clear up affairs before I leave as I may be away for some time. I'd understood that your husband had been paying Fraser, who acts as my agent in matters of this sort; but he tells me that MacGrady has nearly a year's rent outstanding.'

'That could be.' She laughed. 'It sounds just awful, but you know how it is. One stuffs George's bills in a pigeon-hole meaning to do something about them before the next party, and then when the time comes nobody ever gets around to mentioning them.'

'Oh perfectly, perfectly. I'm having trouble with the Sultan over the race-course dues, too. Normally, of course, one wouldn't trouble about a couple of thousand dollars; but with things as they are——'

'Is that what's outstanding?'

The Colonel consulted his little ledger. He spoke coldly.

'That is what MacGrady owes me to date, without of course any question of—er the inventory which no one has had time to check. Strictly speaking, however, there will be the advance on the lease up to December which I'm also entitled to claim by the terms of the agreement Friese so kindly drew up—an additional five hundred dollars.'

'So that's two thousand five hundred dollars,' she said wanly. 'Well, Godfrey, right now that's just a little awkward.'

'Your cheque would do.' He looked at the clock. 'Is that the time?'

'Oh yes I think so. It is, isn't it, Chance?'

The Colonel straightened himself beneath a portrait of an eighteenth-century Grenadier in full dress uniform. Beside the face gazing out of the frame, his own was curiously dead and smooth.

'I have to see my heavy baggage on to the train,' he said. 'Also, since I shall have to visit my remaining tenants, who have decided to leave this evening, I am very short of time indeed. If you prefer it, I'll go and see MacGrady myself?'

'Well——'

'I think, however sick he is, that he might be glad if he saw me. I feel sure it would be advisable for him to make arrangements himself to leave this area for a time. I think it would be wisest.'

'To leave the flat? You mean you do believe there's another riot brewing up?'

'I fear it will be considerably more than a riot, Anna. It is more likely to be a small-scale civil war; possibly, a massacre.'

From his place beside Anna, Chance intervened. 'Of whom, Colonel?'

'Of the so-called Christian community,' said the Colonel

looking straight between them, 'which is to say of the Europeans.' His lips parted, 'And of the Americans.'

'In the very near future, you think? In the next day or two?'

'It will not be long delayed, I am sure. Personally, I have always made it my business to anticipate these events. I have been wrong on occasions: it has amused my acquaintances. I have no doubt that if you cared to ring up your consul you would find he's arranged to play golf with the Sultan on Sunday. That is his own affair. But, as I think I explained to you, Doctor Chance, I prefer to select my deserts in advance. That is why I have every intention of being in Cairo by this time tomorrow——'

Anna put in, 'And Pearl; is she——?'

'In Cairo, where of course dollars are at the moment as essential as they are in most other parts of the inhabited globe.' He looked over Anna's head. 'Pearl, you say? The girl is on her way back to her own tribe. My chauffeur deposited her at the frontier three hours ago. She is an excellent walker. She was not with me long enough to become physically corrupted by the Western cultus.'

'But she lives in Takaradi doesn't she? That's thousands of miles away.'

'Her mother lives in Takaradi. I bought her from a nomadic tribe, dyers in indigo, the Blue Men of the Gow area.'

Anna was at the bureau. 'I don't know just where Columb left the cheque book. You see, I wasn't expecting to pay out anything much till he got back. That is to say, I mean——'

'He has left, then?' enquired the Colonel.

'Well no, Columb hasn't left; he's gone away for a few days——'

Chance began to retreat from the room. 'A letter,' he murmured.

Anna spoke at him irritably. 'That's all right, Chance. You don't need to back out.'

Chance eyed Colonel Godfrey. 'MacGrady has gone to England. He should be back on Monday.'

The Colonel grimaced. 'He is very wise. For an American he shows extremely good sense; though I should have thought a somewhat longer absence would have been more prudent. You and Mrs. MacGrady, I presume, will be leaving for Spain by the morning boat? or will you prefer to spend a few weeks together in great Rome?'

Anna said, 'I've got the cheque book. How much was it we owed you—apart from moth balls and broken teacups?'

'Two thousand five hundred dollars.'

She wrote it out and tore the cheque viciously from its stub. 'You surely don't imagine, do you, that Columb has left me and that Doctor Chance and I——?'

'I imagine nothing; it's not a habit of mine. I merely deduce from the facts as they are presented to me.'

'And those are?'

'You tell me that your husband has left you alone in my flat, with another male, on the eve of a riot of which he must have known something; and, since I am aware of his professed beliefs, of the very practical casuistry of the Catholic faith, I make the obvious inference. However, it is not important; within a year or two at the most, Western values will be in only slightly less picturesque decay than the temples of Leptis Magna—a few broken pillars in the sands.' He smirked at Chance. 'It will not be a god who will rise out of *that* desert.'

Chance said, 'What makes you think there's going to be a riot, or should I say, massacre?'

There was no heat in the Colonel's eye. 'The Arab is not to be underrated once he has an adequate reason reinforced by an adequate means. Under these circumstances, he is that most dangerous of men, the contemplative-activist. A human force well understood by the men of the Vatican prior to the decline of Catholic power.'

'Polemics apart,' said Chance, 'when you say "means" you are really talking about weapons I suppose?'

'I am. I have contacts.'

'And when do you think it will start?'

'You are acquainted with the Mohammedan calendar?'

'No.'

'That is unfortunate.' He turned. 'I must go. I had not expected to remain here so long. My concierge and her family, by the way, have orders to keep the main grille locked; but provided her Spanish husband, a most devout Catholic, does not persuade her to evacuate my building—it *was* heavily insured—it should be possible to get in or out by ringing the bells.'

Chance walked with him to the door. 'Is Fraser leaving too?'

'That is precisely the point I hope to discuss with him later this evening—if I have the time.'

At the door he bowed stiffly to Anna and then let himself out on to the stairs. Chance locked the door behind him.

When he re-entered he saw that she was flushed and that she had poured herself a drink.

'Columb would have hit that man. He'd have picked him up by his nasty little neck and just booted him out the door.'

'Do you think so?'

'Columb may be all sorts of a blackguard and a drunk but he'd never have stood for that. He'd never have let anyone ride *me* like that.'

'Are you sure?'

She would not look at him. She had taken a cigarette, the second in three days, but had forgotten to light it. She snapped it about between tapering fingers.

'Of course I'm sure. If Godfrey had behaved like that——'

'That's what I meant. D'you think he would have behaved like that if MacGrady had been here?'

'Oh damn England and its cold backbone! Give me America every time—wet or dry.'

She handed him her glass.

'Finish that for me,' she said. 'Get yourself some morale!'

'Where are you going?'

'When I've packed I'm going right on over to the Casbah, to Yacef Ali. It's all arranged, isn't it? If anybody thinks I'm going to be stuck here in the middle of a mythical riot with only a dyspeptic between me and the Riffis——'

He waited there in the doorway; heard her slamming drawers and doors, rattling things in the bathroom, as he smoked the battered cigarette she had dropped on her way out. When she came back, her long strides stretching the narrow skirt, her nylons gleaming and her face tight and white, he said nothing. She dropped her case by the door and got out the key.

'And just let anyone try and stop me, just let that jellied sow in the bottom flat try and put his fat stomach between me and the nearest taxi!'

'Why don't you ring one first?' Chance was smiling.

'In America I wouldn't have to so long as there was a man within a hundred yards.' She pulled the door open.

'I wish you luck,' he called as it slammed behind her, and he listened for the lift.

When it had ceased to whine he counted thirty and took off his shoes and followed her down by the staircase. A minute or two behind her he waited on the last step, well concealed by the shadows thrown from the waiting lift. Without leaning forward into the dim light of the foyer he was able to watch through its glass sides and note all that she did and said.

She looked very civilised with her soft grey case, her sharp clothes and gleaming hair. She might have been the tenant of some expensive service flat as she took the concierge to task through the doorway of the right-hand bottom flat.

'But I want the key, Señora Redonda. You've got to let me out. Why, you've got no right whatsoever to stop anybody leaving the building. I don't care what Señor Fraser said and I don't care what Excellente Godfrey said, I want that key and I'm going to have it if I have to shoot somebody first.'

The door was closed slowly and soundlessly in her face and, guessing, she turned in time to see the opening of the door behind her. The square of additional light fell on the floor sharply with George Fraser's shadow balanced centrally within it.

'What a lot of noise,' he said. 'I thought for a minert the riot had really got started; but it's only you.'

'I want that key, George.'

'And with your bag too, all packed up and ready to go like the wives of the men with money.'

'I know you've got it because Señora Redonda told me so.'

George laughed. His face was quite invisible, a black symmetry crowned with silver hair. 'The Señora's gone. She was there when I opened my door, but she's not there any longer. It's like a conjuring trick, isn't it, Anna my dear? One moment you see her, the next minert she's gone clean as a Queensland ostrich.'

'The key,' she repeated.

'It'd be just too bad,' he went on, 'if everyone did that wouldn't it? We'd none of us know where we were. People vanishing out of flats, other people pretending they were still there when they weren't, and still others supposed to have gone turning up again like bad dollars.'

'George, I'm very serious about this. I want you to know that I'm giving you just sixty seconds to hand me that key.'

'But that's too long, Anna dear. I don't need sixty seconds for what I've got to say, five seconds will do me. How long does it take *you* to say "Two-hundred-thousand-dollars"?'

'You can discuss that with Columb when he comes back.'

'Now, that's generous of you. I like to hear a genuine offer.' He was amused, his merriment spontaneous. 'I'm owed two hundred thousand, without interest, and I'm told I can discuss it some time with someone somewhere *if* he comes back!'

She had not moved at all. She was very much taller than the Arab child when she had stood there a few days earlier, her case did not swing in the long hand. She was as rigid as the verticals of steel and stone enclosing the entrance beyond her. When she spoke her words were indistinct because her voice would not carry clearly so far as Chance.

'. . . sixty seconds and you've got just thirty left.'

The Australian, so much grosser than his shadow, ruffled

in some pocket and produced keys which shone like jewellery when he held them in front of her, dangling between fat digits.

'I don't like ifs,' he said. 'I don't collect them because you can't spend them. I like certainties. It's the way my old mother brought me up. 'Not,' he said, 'that you can control everything; oh dear me, no! Take my waistline fr'instance. I do exercises every night! Which reminds me, how's yer new boy friend, the little doctor man from back home? I bet he's not getting any fatter on the sort of exercises he's taking since MacGrady ran out.' He had retreated a little into his doorway, the shadow of his large head had withdrawn from a black to a white tile. 'But I'll show you the sort of exercises I do, Anna! Just you watch me very closely now.'

He was on his toes as she fired and his movement was so quick that his resultant change of position, small as it was, might have been that of some third person. For though the fat arm was back in place on the lintel of the door, the small revolver and the handbag which had held it had been hurled over his head into the hallway behind him. He threw the keys after them.

'And that's just what I was going to point out,' he said with no trace of breathlessness, 'that a spreading girth is a disadvantage at certain times. It gives you bulk, it means that people can't miss when they plug you at close quarters—provided they pull the trigger in good time.'

In a leisurely fashion, without moving either of his feet, leaning out, falling slowly towards her, he had her by both elbows.

'If you and I are going to talk business,' he said as Chance left the staircase for the opposite wall, 'and I think we ought to, then it had better be in my office. There may not be another opportunity. Everybody seems to be leaving and I've heard it's going to be noisier than it was in 1955. With me being so large and the Riffis being so clever with their guns I'm beginning to think it's about time I was calling for my Chrysler too. I have it all planned out, we'll travel first class, not roses roses all the way, because you don't like them; but we'll end up in England just the same and check in at Columb's hotel.'

Lazily he shifted one hand from her elbow to her knee as it came up at his paunch, hampered by the narrowness of her skirt. 'Now I didn't want to have to do that because full-scale legs were never to my taste. I like innocence, give me the girl-bride every time; so if it was a liberty, you forced me to it and I might be blushing. So do come in quietly, my dear.'

There were three steps spanning the foyer midway between the entrance and the staircase. There was a distance of about twenty feet between the bottom of these and the widely opened door into the Australian's flat. Chance crouched there momentarily and then hurled himself at the free side of the wood. It was perfectly judged since Anna in her struggle had forced Fraser within range of the door's arc of closure whilst remaining beyond it herself. The solid slap of the teak against the bulk of the man's body echoed dully in the enclosed space. The retch of his pain, the grunt he gave and the dead weight of his fall followed quickly.

Freed, one sleeve torn, but collected and agile, Anna ran ahead of him to the lift as Chance gave the door its final push and heard the lock engage on the far side.

They closed the gates and pressed the wrong button without dismay. To move as they were moving was sufficient. They neither of them observed the descent to the basement until the lift had come to a standstill against darkness. They knew then that they would have to pass the ground floor again and waited mutely for it to descend to them after the halt had ended. Neither of them was aware of having pressed the button marked with the red figure 4, but in their passage past the level they had left, both were greedy to the exclusion of all other observation for each accident of the foyer. Time did not stand still but was concertinaed, closed upon itself, as it may be when emotion translates it into terms of the physiological.

The door into Fraser's flat was still closed upon its owner, yet it was open and he was there looking up at them, blood running dark down one jowl as his eyes and laughter rose with the lift. The revolver of which he had possessed himself despite his pain, was also a measure of his strength against confusion: traversed by the heavy hand its short barrel followed them up, but it was not used.

In the flat the telephone was ringing. Chance closed the door and slid the bolts across, leaving Anna on the divan.

'You'd better answer it,' she said.

He picked up the receiver, 'Hello!'

'Hello,' the high voice sounded bewildered.

'Who do you want to speak to?'

'I'm sorry, I'm afraid I have a wrong number, I wanted to speak to Anna MacGrady.'

'That's right, this is the MacGrady's flat.'

'Oh is it? Well then could I——'

'I'm afraid she's asleep. She's not awfully well at the moment. Who is it speaking please?'

'Zoe Moore here, who is that?'

'Bill Chance, the doctor.'

'Oh, the doctor. I thought you'd gorn.'

'No, not yet.'

'You're still there?'

'Yes, I am.'

'How very confusing. What a very confusing time we all seem to be having, don't we?'

'Yes yes, we do.'

'So you haven't gorn? You're the same doctor I met the other night, are you?'

'Yes.'

'I just wanted to be quite certain. I *do* remember you!'

Silence.

'Hello, are you there?'

'Yes.'

'I said I did remember you.'

'Oh. I remember you too.'

'But of course.' Her voice went high again. 'Has Anna caught Columb's lung or something?'

'It's not catching, but she is ill, or rather, shocked.'

'How dreadful. Will you tell her when she wakes up or is better that Robin and I have quite decided to leave in the morning?'

'Certainly, I'll tell her.'

'You might ask her to call me back herself.'

'I'm sure she will,' said Chance.

'You see,' she went on in the way she would, so that his responses seemed superfluous even on the telephone. 'You see, we rather thought she and Columb might like to come with us and share expenses as far as Tripoli.'

'That's a long way.'

'Oh yes, we were thinking of going with that strange little man who goes in for black girls, Colonel Tyghe. But in the end Robin decided it mightn't look well so we thought we might buy a really large jeep or something and go by the coastal road in the morning. Robin thinks he would be in a very much better position to observe things at first-hand like that? What do you think?'

'It depends what he wants to observe.'

'What?'

Chance cleared his throat. 'What he wants to observe,' he repeated. 'I'm sorry but I forget what he was reporting on. Was it wild life, or b-ballistic missiles?' He was stammering with fatigue.

'I do hope you're not ill too!' came her voice. 'The *Arabs* as well, Doctor. Robin's covering all this pan-Arab movement for the Government.'

'Oh.'

'I thought you knew. Freddie Tyrrelstown got him the job, and with all these rumours and counter-rumours, Robin thinks . . .'

'Surely it would be advisable for him to stay here then, wouldn't it?' Chance seized his opportunity. 'I mean if he thinks the Casbah's a bit too near the Palace and so forth, you could both move in here until the riot's over. I know the MacGrady's wouldn't mind. Why don't you come over right away? I'll go and consult Anna.'

'No no, my dear, don't think of it. Robin wouldn't hear of it. He has everything arranged and he's always a little military about plans. He says you can't possibly get an impartial view of a campaign if you're too close to it and he's convinced we ought to get to Tripoli over the week-end.'

He sensed the return of her protective vagueness and let her run on and down.

'Well it's just too bad about the MacGradys,' she echoed. 'Americans are always so welcome everywhere at the moment. As Nancy Mitford says, "poor old perfidious Albion has to . . ." Don't you agree?'

'Yes, oh yes I do.'

'By the way, what do you think about it all?'

'I think,' he said distinctly and inanely, 'it's all a bore, don't you?'

'I do so agree, that's exactly what Robin thinks.—What are you laughing at?'

'I yawned.'

'Oh well, that's different.'

'Yes it is.'

'And you're staying with the MacGradys?'

'Yes.'

'Well I do so hope you'll be all right.'

'I hope you will too.'

Her 'good-bye,' was not unfamiliar, so short, so uninflected that it seemed to deny the existence of any conversation or communication at all.

Anna did not look up as he entered and surprisingly she was not drinking:

'Don't tell me about it; I heard.'

'Good.'

'They backed out pretty fast, didn't they?'

'They're very sane people,' he said.

'No, not sane, they're just English, that's all.'

'No, not English,' he insisted, 'they're MacGrady's people. They're your people, ours, like bones in the desert, they have no nationality.'

Their eyes found one another and between them the cherubs in the eight-day clock revolved smoothly and soundlessly within their glass circle.

Friday

Very early, Chance was roused by a violent movement of his bed. He had nearly awakened several times before this, but had contrived by various means to evade full consciousness despite the fact that the previous day, long and physically lazy, had made full sleep difficult. Now, as the bed shook and jerked beneath him, seeming to jar first the floor, the entire room, finally the building itself, he sat up at once in the succeeding stillness. The following sound-wave of the explosion reached him as he fumbled for the light-switch: a single deafening clash as sharp as an overhead thunderclap.

He did not bother about the light, but from his bed unbolted the shutters and dragged them inwards; he thrust the window open and leaned on the sill.

Over the hills a cold light was breaking: it touched the tops of the mosques and the towers of the Sultan's Palace above the harbour and then thinned to lose itself among the thinning stars in the east. Overhead, the midnight indigo still rested; and beneath it the cut shadows and façades of the town stood against the margins of a sea heavy at the coast but glittering in the West where the moon declined upon its horizon.

Beneath him, between the Palace and the American section, grey smoke hung high over the basin of the hills. As he watched, it climbed higher into the sky drifting slowly in the dawn wind towards him, and brought with it the dry smell of expended cordite.

He was looking for its source, some flash of flame or glow of fire in the packed buildings of the central hollow when Anna came in.

'Whatever was it?'

'I don't know. Something's obviously been blown up but so far as I can see at the moment there's nothing but smoke.'

She kneeled down beside him on the bed. 'I can smell that all right; but where does it come from?'

He pointed: 'Somewhere about there I think, between the Imphala Gardens and the Palace; but I can't see any damage.'

Her face was blue-grey beside him as she leaned out into the air. He noticed that to see more clearly she opened her eyes a little wider and that they reflected the clarity of the dawn.

'D'you know why?' she asked.

'Why what?'

'Why there doesn't seem to be any damage? It's because there isn't any. They've just blown the Legislative Building higher than dynamite—there's nothing left at all. Why, you shouldn't be able to see the Harbour from here, only the Bay and the Villa Hutton.'

'Are you sure?'

'There isn't a brick or a roof standing. They must have just picked it out cleanly, unless it was a bomb from the air, and planted tons of high explosive underneath it.'

'I think we'd have heard a 'plane if it'd been done from above. What's so odd is that nobody seems to be doing anything about it. There's nobody shouting, no firing or sirens——'

'Later on there'll be shouting all right. The Arabs always shout like mad when they get excited. By the way, did you try your light switch?'

'Is it off?'

'There isn't a light anywhere; they've either damaged the cables with the explosion or sabotaged the generators in the Rue Marconi.'

'Look!' he said. 'Flares, down there in the Socco Chico.'

In the Arab quarter they saw points of flame moving slowly past street intersections, one by one: to the right, in the direction of the Avenue Grande the prick of headlights; from somewhere came the faint wail of a siren.

'What does it mean?' he asked as they sat down beside one another on the bed.

'I don't know. This place has been so thick with rumours ever since I've known it it's just about impossible to pick out the truth even over big things.'

'This is big enough, surely. In the political sense it involves just about everybody, doesn't it? Even Russia?'

'Russia's got a seat on the Assembly, but it's empty. Then there's the United States, France and England and four little countries. It'll certainly be enough to make the cables hum when the foreign correspondents start flying in.'

He slumped back on to the pillow. 'One thing's quite obvious. You'll have to get out of here today. I'd like to get you over to the Palace this morning if possible.'

'That's just ridiculous. I'm not leaving you here alone.'

'Somehow I feel it's almost inevitable. I don't know whether it's an irrational compulsion of some sort or whether I get that feeling simply because of the difficulties.'

'In that case you'd better have a work-out. It's what I've often had to do in the past when I've been trying to sort things out.'

'You see,' he went on, 'without the passport which could easily arrive today I'm quite helpless even if the Palace people change their minds. It's scarcely likely, of course, that they'll want to harbour Western nationals *now*; but, quite apart from that, there's my passport. It'll be of no use to me whatsoever until I can get MacGrady's man to unfudge his exit visas. They'd hold me down at the Harbour or the Airport. They'd want to know how on earth I got back into the Zone without an entry stamp.'

He shivered a little in the wind from the window and she draped a blanket over his shoulders and then handed him a lighted cigarette.

'You get any sleep at all tonight?'

'Not much, did you?'

T

'I was thinking about everything. It just doesn't seem solid does it? It doesn't seem like any particular time at all.'

He made no reply.

'Wake up, Chance.'

'I was thinking about Hiroshima,' he said. 'A book I once read giving a description of what happened to a few people immediately afterwards. There was a man, a missionary I think, wandering through a green park in which all the picnickers were either insane or dying.'

They sat on for some minutes in the slowly increasing light.

'Columb told me about your wife,' she said at last.

'Oh.'

'I don't want you to think I was sorry for you, or that I'm sorry now, because I long ago gave up the struggle of trying to be sorry about things I found it impossible to be sorry about.'

'It's all right,' he said, 'everything's all right.'

'It sounds smug,' she said, 'but I *have* prayed for her already.'

'Thank you, Anna.'

'What was her name?'

'Mary.'

'Mary Chance,' she said, and got up suddenly. 'What say I make some coffee for us?'

'I'll come and help you.'

'No, you stay there, it's my turn. See if you can work out some kind of plan. After all, this isn't quite Hiroshima, is it? It should be possible to do *something*.'

'That was bad, but I find it difficult to forget it.'

'It's no good. It's what men do, get history-minded. Columb once said the Prophets were the only good historians because they never looked back.'

He smiled. 'I miss MacGrady.'

'Me too. What I meant was that if you're going to figure out some sort of a plan you mustn't start with your passport and the explosion; you must start a couple of hours ahead.'

'I thought we'd start by ringing the Palace and getting them to send somebody round as soon as possible with an official car. At this stage, George won't want to pick a quarrel with the Sultan; and in the meantime we could get Magda to arrange for all your mail, even including my passport, to be sent care of the Palace.'

'I don't agree. I think you ought to take the risk and get out of here with me while you can—always supposing the car comes.'

'One of us must remain here until we're quite certain the passport's not going to arrive. It had better be me for obvious reasons and also because I'm worried about Marcovicz. It's quite possible that if he's guessed my connection with Magda, or got to hear of it in the way ex-convicts do get to hear of such things, he'll be looking for me.'

'Whatever for? I just can't understand your attitude to that little man. You're as bad as Columb where he's concerned.'

'One day MacGrady will probably tell you.'

'Or you will?'

'Yes,' he said. 'Perhaps.'

'Oh maybe maybe *per*-haps! You just love being mysterious, don't you? Why d'you think he's so very dangerous, Chance? Go on, tell me.'

'He's mad,' he said. 'He wasn't originally but he is now. His freedom has proved too much for him; he doesn't know what to do with it. If he'd become a stockbroker or a Rabbi, he'd have been all right. As it is, there's no room for him in the West where they'll almost certainly give him a life sentence if he returns, and none in the East where he'll probably end up with a Berber knife in his back.'

'And what would he do to you?'

'I don't know. I've never quite decided what particular piece of jargon describes his condition. Whether he's a manic-depressive, a paranoid compulsive or a schizophrenic psychopath. But I should imagine that at the moment he'll be in a state of great elation. The threat of the riot, the explosion, everything could combine to make him feel he'd be solving his problem if he killed someone, especially someone he considered personally significant. On the other hand, he might be in his Messianic mood or going through one of his clown phases. One wouldn't know until it was too late.'

She went to the door. 'I think you take him too seriously. You shouldn't let him come into things so much. Now put him where he belongs while I go and make that coffee for us.'

'Are you sure you don't want any help?'

'You keep an eye on the Zone,' she said as she went out to the kitchen.

She was not long, and while she was away he had a shower and put on some clothes: his oldest pair of trousers and a thin cotton shirt. Over his shoulders, with the sleeves tied in the small of his back, he draped a pullover his wife had knitted for him six months before her death.

He was by the window again when she brought in the coffee tray and slid it on to the top of the dressing-table, pushing in front of it bottles of scent, nail varnish, powder bowls and jewellery.

'If you've got yourself dressed we might as well move out of here and have our coffee in the sitting-room.'

'There's a very good view from this window.' He caught her smile. 'We can see everything from here.'

'Yes, the same old everything we can see from the sitting-room window!'

'I didn't realise,' he lied.

'You feel safer here, don't you?'

'Yes.'

She passed him his cup of coffee. 'You know, I've been thinking about this Marcovicz man; what you said about him gunning for you.'

'It was only an idea I had. For all I know he may be running about wanting to save my life. He's not necessarily——'

'He's not necessarily after you, is he? It doesn't have to be you and nobody else?'

'No. If he's in an aggressive mood, anyone would do so

long as he felt they stood in the way of what he imagines to be his destiny or redemption.'

'His redemption?'

'Marcovicz has that feeling which in a lesser degree is common to all of us, I think; the sense of being owed a tremendous compensation by someone for the fact of our existence.'

'You mean gambling? Dice, poker, Lady Luck?'

'Or wills—your father-in-laws,' he said. 'Things are true or false at all levels. It's in our nature to hope for wealth, fame, love, or power; these are what fill the prisons. But a wealthy man never feels wealthy, nor a dictator powerful. As a Catholic, MacGrady must know that hope beyond nature is the only sanity because its fulfilment is impossible here.'

'Of course he knows that very well. It isn't his fault that he doesn't have any hope for himself. He knows what he ought to do, he just can't do it, that's all.'

'Why not?'

'Because something happened to him once. He's never told me what it was, but it's made him humble. He only wants more time and opportunity for grace and that's the only reason he wants to get well and inherit enough to get free of George and the others.' She was a little angry. 'He believes he'll be able to start again then, like you have—full of con-version fervour. He says even St. Peter was converted three times.'

Chance said: 'You call it humility but I think it's damned arrogance. When he was born a Catholic, given everything from the start, why should he be given any more time than Marcovicz who was not even brought up as a good Jew.'

'I don't know. But it's not my business to know and it's not yours either. Don't you see that? There's no comparison between anybody and anybody else.' She broke off. 'Did you hear what I heard?'

Below them in the roadway a car had drawn up and they both went over to the window.

An Arab chauffeur in uniform got out of the Buick and

they watched the Colonel's luggage being loaded on to the roof. In a few moments he himself appeared below them. They saw only his neat foreshortened figure beneath the soft hat, and his gloved peremptory hands as he gave his orders.

Chance called down to him. Beneath the hat-brim his yellow face was raised to look back at them.

'I'm sorry,' he called back thinly. 'I am disastrously late. If there's anything you want you'll have to arrange it with Fraser or with my concierge.'

'Anna,' Chance shouted, '—about Mrs. MacGrady, Colonel —Fraser is refusing to let her leave the flats.'

'Godfrey, you can't do things like this!' Anna joined in. 'You send that woman up with the key to those gates right away or I'll see someone arrests you before ever you get to Cairo.'

He took no notice. He strode round the flat roof of the car giving commands in Arabic about the stowing of his luggage. He looked extremely small and slightly comical.

'Robin knows all about your arms deals,' she cried down to him. 'He's leaving today too; he'll cable the English Press and the *New York Herald Tribune*. Your name——'

'No, Anna,' Chance said. 'Keep him talking. I'll go down and explain.'

But as he reached the door she called him back: 'You're too late, just take a look and see who's there now.'

George Fraser, in a Churchillian siren suit was directly beneath the window; swollen, pale, and morning-friendly.

'Hope you two got yourselves some sleep up there. We need sleep. Everybody needs sleep at a time like this——'

'I want to talk to you,' Chance called. 'Wait for me.'

'—In between bursts of activity of course,' George went on, ignoring his request. 'Things are gettin' under weigh in the Zone. Next few days we're goin' to be news, d'you realise that, Doc? Big news. All the journalists'll be grabbing airplanes and helicopters to take photographs. Old Man Churchill'll be putting in his dentures to mike an historical speech and I-Like-Ike'll be consulting the Treasury. The

Arabs are getting moving.' He put his hands to his mouth and megaphoned.

'There's going to be more explosions,' he bellowed, 'and unidentified people are goin' to get themselves killed: Yanks and Englishmen and Berbers and Riffis and Yids. And by this time next week, d'you know what——?'

'I've got a suggestion to make, Fraser.'

'—It'll all be forgotten—like last night's love. Noub'dy'll be interested. And don't make suggestions at this time of the morning; it's the only time of day I'm not interested in them.' He waved carelessly with one fat hand. 'Maybe later—this evening, for example—you an' I'll get together for a little chat, and the little girl, too, if she isn't in her bed again by that time.'

He turned away, shook the Colonel's hand through the open window and waited for the car to leave the kerb. Without another upward glance he stumped back into the building. They heard the gate clash behind him and there was silence.

Anna said, 'I'm going to get my things packed: two cases, a little one for the Palace and a trunk for England. You'd better pack, too. You won't be here another night; as soon as I can get talking to Yacef Ali I'll get something fixed for you. What time are you going to ring the Palace?'

'I thought we'd better leave it until about nine. I don't know what time people get up in palaces.'

'You surely ought to know, being an Englishman.'

'Oh it's different in England; they get up early there. I think they do breathing exercises and ride before breakfast.'

'Well what say we do our packing and then I'll cook you an egg and some more coffee and afterwards we'll put a call through? I just long to get into communication with the outside world. A few more hours of this flat and George, and I will really begin to think I'm a prisoner.'

'You could try Zoe again. You never know, she might be helpful.'

'That's right. I could ask Robin to come around and pick us both up and take us down to the Sayyid Hotel. After all,

why not? George wouldn't want to pick a quarrel with him—
he knows he's got connections.'

'Try it,' he said.

They went along to the telephone and she dialled the
number.

'Hello, is that you Zoe? . . . What you say . . . ? No, I
wanted Lady Zoe Moore . . . *They're talking Arabic, Chance,
I guess it must be a wrong number.*'

He took the receiver: a distant voice spat and coughed
through the electronic crackles of the earpiece.

'He sounds angry,' he said as he re-dialled the Casbah
number.

'That's just Arabic. They always sound as though you'd
insulted Mahommet.'

The ringing tone ceased and in his ear Lady Zoe's voice,
harassed and a little haughty spoke clearly.

'Hallo! Lady Zoe Moore speaking. Who is that?'

'It's the Doctor—Chance.'

'Oh it's you again. Did you give my message to Anna?'

'Yes, she's here. She wants to speak to you.' He gave Anna
the receiver.

'Hello, Zoe darling. I'm just awfully sorry I never rang you
back last night but . . . What you say? . . . Why that's just
terrible . . . *Chance, she says they've started firing guns in the
Medina* . . . Well, Zoe, what I wanted to ask you was whether
you and Robin'd come and pick us up here to take us down
to one of the big hotels before you leave? I can't explain right
now, but . . . Oh, well look, if Robin's going down to the
British Consulate, do you think he'd ask *them* to come and
collect us? You see, it's George Fraser; he's gone quite addle-
pate . . . Yes, crazy! He's got us locked up in the flat here
and won't let us out. I tried to call taxis several times but they
all seem to have gone out of business . . . Godfrey's gone off
to Cairo . . . What you say? . . . But surely, Zoe, it wouldn't
take long . . .'

Chance took the receiver.

'Lady Zoe?'

'What *is* it?' The voice was taut with vexation.

'Chance here. I think Anna's in some danger . . . No, Mac-Grady is not here; he's in England . . . He's gone to London for a few days. I want you to realise that unless you can help us we may be in a very difficult position over the week-end. We'd be quite willing to share expenses; but we must get out of the flat at once.'

'Folly, my dear! At the moment I can't possibly do anything about it. You neither of you seem to realise that we're just leaving ourselves. There's a nasty man with a machine-gun somewhere on top of the Spanish wall and a *rabble* of armed Arabs surrounding the American Consulate. It would be madness to try to get into the American section at the moment. Robin says the whole thing's quite beyond a joke and that he must get a clear picture of the stresses involved if he's to send a helpful report to Whitehall. He feels it's his duty.'

'What about his duty to his friends?'

'Now, my dear, please don't be pious. You're both perfectly safe where you are. Goodness me, if *we* were sitting in a concrete flat instead of squatting miserably in Heber's perch in the Casbah we'd be prepared to sit the thing out over a whole week-end instead of a mere twenty-four hours. Robin says . . .'

'Blast!'

'What did you say? I'm afraid I really must go; he's getting so agitated. Do try and realise how amusing it all is really; just think what one's friends would give——You do know Nöel, don't you? He'd be so witty about it.'

'If you mean Noël Cuff-Shoot, he's not here, is he?'

'No, my dear, Florida, coining money like mad with his naughty stories. I heard from him yesterday . . . Coming, Darling . . . Robin's looking fierce, he's even got his holster on. I simply must go, but do tell Anna from me not to . . .' The line went dead.

'Well that's that,' he said. 'We'll have to stake everything on Magda and Ali.' He lighted the cigarette she was holding. 'I'm afraid she's not really interested.'

'But, Chance, she was always so nice to meet. Why, we've been bumping into Zoe for the last two years: Madrid, Torremolinos, Rome—and Columb used to know her back in England before the war, she was part of the Claridges set before she married the Earl of Carthage.'

He interrupted her. 'Can *you* hear any firing in the town?'

'No, I didn't hear a thing. You go and have a look while I start the packing.

From the sitting-room window he had an excellent view. Smoke was rising from the Grand Socco; but only from the fires of the fish-fryers. The town was still quiet; there was no audible sound from the distant Medina, no sounds of traffic from the direction of the Avenue Grande. He scanned the far end of the Rue D'Espagnole where it traversed the eastern end of the Bay before rising to the hills to join the coastal road into Tripoli.

With his spectacles on he was just able to make out a thin stream of traffic driving towards the frontier. He guessed that they were large private cars when he caught the glint of chromium reflecting the risen sun as they negotiated the first hair-pin bend on the lower slopes. Higher up, as they disappeared over the nearer crest, he could see the silveriness of their dust-clouds where the tarmac ended and the unmetalled surface began.

'There's quite an exodus,' he called back into the flat. 'Large cars running out over the Tripoli border.'

'That'll be the business people. The big insurance men and the bankers. They're always the first to leave in a riot; they move into their villas in the hills until the dust settles and then then come on in again, one by one, as though nothing had happened.'

'They were all piled up with luggage, like Tyghe's Buick.'

'In that case they'll be moving right out over the Frontier and that means they must be very windy.' She was preoccupied. 'Say, Chance, why don't we try the Palace now? It's getting on for eight o'clock and there might easily be somebody about. As I remember, Yacef did say we'd only got to get a message through for him to send an automobile without any argument at all.'

He went along to the telephone. The receiver was cold and dead in his ear, quite soundless. He shook it, rattled the bridge and, without hope, dialled the absurd Palace number, SUL 1.

'Who are you disturbing now?' came the voice, rough and wickedly weary. 'You don't want to go on worrying everybody at this time of day, Doc. You tried your Countess, and you didn't get any change at all, so why start in on the poor old Sultan? He's a busy man nights, he has to catch up on himself in the daytime. You would too if you had all the women he's got. Why don't you go back to your bed? Take yourself a tranquilliser, there's plenty in MacGrady's drawer. There's nothing to be worried about. You've just got to wait, that's all, like we're all doing. Just hangin' on till it all blows over like it always does. And if it doesn't, for one or two of us, what's it matter? We won't know anything about it. Might even be a relief: "Life's fitful fever" and all that you know! Now be a good boy and hop back into your bed. I've got meself plugged into your line, and every time you get feeling talkative and friendless and wanting to make enquiries about the weather from someone, you disturb *me!* And, in any case, I told you I'd be seeing you later in the day about a little matter of financial security. After all, a citizen's entitled to . . .'

Chance dropped the received back on to its cradle.

'We're cut off, Anna. George has done something beastly to the line; he must have tapped it with his own receiver some hours ago because he's quite obviously been listening to everything we said to Zoe.'

'So that's out, too?'

'Yes, we shall have to think of something else.'

She turned away. 'Help me with this trunk, will you? Let's get it out into the hall right up against that front door.'

'Good idea.'

'Do you feel the same way as I do about that letter-box?'

'It makes one feel draughty.'

'That's what I meant.'

They ate breakfast in the sitting-room: pink melon and Zone sugar, a fried egg for Chance with a slice of toast, jeelie pieces with butter for Anna; coffee and cigarettes.

The sun was well up and the town still quiet. At eleven o'clock as they sat over their cigarettes and coffee they saw through the open french window the aluminium gleam of the London Viscount as it rose from the airfield, drew in its undercarriage and circled the bay before disappearing behind the dome of the Palace.

Anna said, 'I've been thinking what we'd do if there was a fire?'

'I thought of that too. I even decided we'd tie the sheets to one of the pillars of the balcony and slide down one floor at a time to the bottom. But have we got enough sheets?'

'That's the trouble. We've only got three pairs, but with blankets and covers we'd maybe have just enough.'

'Oh they never use those—only sheets.'

'Why not, I'd like to know?'

'Too thick, I suppose. On the other hand, we could start a fire on the balcony. If we made enough smoke someone would almost certainly send out a fire engine.'

In the pause someone began to sing loudly. They heard the voice echoing up from the road in the bright morning air. It was a sailorish song, meaningless, but in its senselessness, meaningful to Chance. It was the raucous song of the prison, of walls and wharves of concrete beyond which men sailed in imagination. He got up.

'Marcovicz!'

Beyond the french window something flashed, curving upwards from below and fell sharply on to the balcony. He saw a tripod of steel hooks fastened to a nylon rope. Before he could reach it, the fibres were drawn tight and two of the hooks engaged in the under surface of the balustrade, biting loudly into the stone.

Twenty feet below him Marcovicz had just kicked himself off from the ledge of the third-floor balcony and was now silent. Chance watched him swarming upwards from one knot to the next in the creamy rope, his concentrated face grinning back at him as the hands and crossed feet worked his body smoothly higher. In his face, one furrow, midway between the brows and the hair-line was as deep as an axe-blow in unseasoned wood; and beneath it, the golden eyes netted with other creases, gazed back as dully as though the climber did indeed experience pain.

He knew that Anna was with him before he heard her gasp. She had looked down once only and then retreated back to the window, her cigarette fallen beside his feet. Without looking to her he called down to the convict:

'Marcovicz! What is the matter?'

But his words were lost in the cripple's laughter.

'Ah ha. I came to warn you, but you caught me. It's nothing to worry about, Doctor Chance, nothing at all. I've only come to explain to you, to tell you all about it.'

'About what?'

His face was level now with the balustrade and he reached out over it to grasp Chance's shoulder. In a moment he had his plastic foot in its unwrinkled sandal on the top, then the other, naked and tendonous, the swelling calf prominent as he crouched there easily then stood upright with all the town behind him.

'The whole story,' he said, and then looking down to the pavement he sighed. 'I haven't done that since I was in Hamburg, but I'm as good now as I was then—twenty years ago.'

He jumped down on to the sunlit concrete and began to haul up his rope ship-fashion, coiling it round between the palm and the elbow of his left arm, jerking the finished circle round the hooks and lashing it fast with the free end.

'I could have come this way for the Yank, couldn't I?' He tossed his bundle through the open window on to the divan.

'At any time, friend! But I didn't. And now it's too late because he's run.'

'What do you want?'

'So you won't talk?' he said in a gangster drawl. 'Doctor Chance is black this morning, he won't speak to the man he saved. But what does it matter when I already know what I do know? That you did for him what you did for me, what you would do for anybody? Saved him, let him wriggle out of the rope when *Justice* was at the other end.' Back went his head to loose the scream of his laughter as he beat Chance on the back with an arm that seemed like a great wing. Chance moved away from him seeing Anna flat as a bas-relief against the wall: her pallor, her stone-frown and the shadows in her mouth.

'I asked you what you wanted, Marcovicz.'

'I heard you. What do *you* want?' He turned round suddenly and his gesture took in the town. 'What do *they* want? You tell me that and I'll listen.'

Chance touched his elbow, on the young wrinkled pouch beneath the short sleeve. He let his hand rest there, cupping the bony point in his palm.

'You'd better come in; or rather, we'd all better go in and then we can talk.'

The German had not seen Anna, he was bounding and physical after his climb; he gave the impression of a man seeing himself in some historical context which temporarily blinded him to nearer things. He walked straight past her, leading the way in through the french window and talking not over his shoulder but into the room itself whose limits threw back his voice.

'I'll tell you what Fraser wants. He wants me to move on back to London, to sling my little hook; though he never knew I had it. Ah ha, you see the joke? But I said "No" to him. "I'll see my doctor first; for why should I go all that way? *You* let MacGrady run," I said, "I gave him to you on a plate and you let him jump, so if anyone's to go and get him it should be you." That's fair, isn't it, Doctor Chance?'

She was standing behind them, waiting and not smiling. The shadow pinned to her feet lay straight across the floor, its head vertical against the white wainscot of the opposite wall. They saw it question their positions, turning in profile first to Marcovicz and then to Chance as he said:

'I don't think you've ever really met Mrs. MacGrady, have you Marcovicz? Anna, this is Jacob Marcovicz.'

He swivelled on his false foot and crossed to her at once, blinking and grimacing in the white sunlight. He bowed over her hand and sighed again. His forehead wrinkled and un-wrinkled as he studied her face closely, standing as still as though his ankles were in stocks.

'Mrs. MacGrady, I never thought—where were you? I never saw you. Were you there all the time?'

'She was on the balcony when you arrived.'

'But you are a beautiful woman, beautiful! Are you married?'

'Well, Mr. Marcovicz——'

'Of course, of course. It's the sun. *Sunstroke,* Doctor Chance! You'll understand, because you know that a man can be blinded not by beauty alone but by dreams as well, and not be able to see until they have gone.'

'Why, that's all right,' Anna said with a pleasant smile. 'I expect climbing up all that way in this heat would make any-one a bit confused for a few minutes. But believe me, Mr. Marcovicz, we're both awfully glad to see you and really we're sorry you couldn't have visited with us in a more normal way; by the lift, I mean.'

'Apologising? To *me*? A lady telling Marcovicz that she is sorry for something! What do you think of that, Doctor Chance?'

'You should forget all those things. They're all over.'

'Prison mentality, is that it? Making high walls out in the open? That's what he means, but it doesn't matter. I'm not old. Twenty years mean nothing to me; another six months and there'll be no walls inside or out.'

He looked at Anna again. 'I've heard you're married to the

American, the man I called a Yank? You'll have to forgive me because it's only a way we have when we get words out of prison. They have to be short and sharp to be whispered quickly. But putting it another way, it was your husband I was talking about, Mrs. MacGrady?'

'Marcovicz, I think you should understand that Mrs. Mac-Grady is not really worried about anything to do with her husband at the moment. You see——'

He swung his arms in embarrassment or delight. 'Well then I can't talk, can I? I can say nothing. If this lady is innocent we can't tell her, Doctor Chance, because she is young.'

Chance: 'I don't think you quite understand. There is no reason we shouldn't discuss anything, provided we're quick.'

Anna: 'Why certainly you can. After all, he is my husband.'

Chance: 'Anna has only been married a very short time, Marcovicz.'

Anna: 'Only three weeks, so you must forgive me if I don't know all about my husband; though, as they say, I'm quite willing to learn.'

The Jew looked from one to the other of them showing himself comical, but suspicious too.

Anna moved into the room. 'That is to say we already had one visitor who made me a little wiser than I was before.' Her blank eyes rested about Chance for a moment, who took his cue:

'I think Mrs. MacGrady means, have you come for money? Does the American owe you anything?'

Anna: 'Well yes, Mr. Marcovicz, that's what I was getting at. You see, since Columb left, quite a number of his friends seem to have been worried about small sums they loaned him. It's strange really because he's only making a short trip an'll be in a much better position to settle things when he gets back.'

'Colonel Tyghe,' Chance was swift, 'came in last night and demanded thousands of dollars rent for the syndicate he represents. He was damnably rude about it, Marcovicz. I'd very much like you to have seen his behaviour.'

'*Verflucht!*'

'Of course, Mr. Marcovicz, we do owe it to him and I did try to explain but Colonel Godfrey——'

Marcovicz was gazing down at his naked foot and they both saw that its toes were squeezing the floor. The deep furrow in the forehead was gone now, smoothed out by the tension of his frown.

Chance: 'There was no excuse for it, Anna.'

'Three weeks!' Marcovicz breathed. 'Oh, Mrs. MacGrady you have taken on all those years of a man's life in three weeks. You have married a man like me, old and busy with half of his doing already done. Not a young man with hair that he can let grow and dreams he can wait for no matter how long they might be; but a man who has had to supply what was missing and beat the pack of his wishes like lost dogs.'

She was turning her wedding ring. 'Why, that's strange. Chance, you never told me he was like this.' Without changing her position she compelled their visitor's attention by a warm approach of personal interest.

'I remember Columb telling me about you ages ago and I really wanted to meet you and if it hadn't been for our honeymoon, maybe I would have done.'

'But not like this, *Gnädige Frau*! When I saw you the once I did not see you because I was not thinking about you and you did not speak to me. That's right, isn't it? You can't know a person you're not thinking about; you can't speak to a man or a woman not in your mind, nor hear what they say?'

'You're just very kind,' she said with freshness. 'I really am sorry that you should have had to visit with us like this.'

'I'd come again a hundred times, I'd throw my rope over the highest wall. If I was that American and you'd so much as put one foot on my sand, I too would have given you not what I was, but all that I ever hoped I might be before my dreams made me bleed.'

'If MacGrady does owe you money, Marcovicz, I think you'd better let us know now,' Chance said.

U

'Oh surely if Columb does owe you money, you only have to tell me just how much it is, Mr. Marcovicz, and if it's not too much, I'll give you a cheque right away.'

'*Too much!* This woman takes on all of a man, living in the world for years before ever she saw her first day, a man on whom crimes have settled like flies on dead meat, and then she says, "If it's not too much, sir."' He rounded on Chance. 'I could weep I tell you, if this were a weeping matter.'

Their embarrassment was very new to them.

Chance: 'It's all very simple, you know.'

Anna: 'And I'm quite serious, Mr. Marcovicz. If Columb's in your debt, though he's not here right now, I know he'd like me to give it to you, especially with all this trouble in the town.'

Marcovicz, sinewy-old, shrunken in his blue denims and washed shirt, took both of her hands in his. There was not enough fat over his muscles for youth, they were the knots of age as he stood there remote from everything but Anna's face, smiling so politely at him.

'Pay me what your husband owes me? How could you pay me everything, all that he has become since he grew rich to find you? Understand me if you can or laugh at me as men have laughed in prisons, but know that I made your husband your debt to me.'

'I think you should be careful about this.' Chance was ignored.

'I was in your future long before you met me or met your husband. I was there waiting for you, Mrs. MacGrady, like freedom or death; and your debt was accumulating, growing great even before you were born. *Pay me what you owe me!* I speak calmly and my word is true: you owe me yourself.' Sensing absurdity he dropped her hands and lost himself in his laughter. 'You see it, don't you, Doctor Chance, what I was saying in Shibam? The facts lie all in the future because that's the only time we recognise them when it's too late. Ah ha, you may not see it but I do. All of it, clearly; and it all fits in.'

In a very well-mannered way Anna said, 'Mr. Marcovicz, would you like a drink after your climb?'

'Not alcohol for me, I never needed it. But if you had some coffee I'd drink coffee with you; I'd like that because I'm like Doctor Chance. Whenever we meet we always have coffee together.'

The way she moved was optimism itself as she passed between them saying, 'Well, I'll get you both some right away.'

'It all fits in with what? asked Chance as the cups clattered in the kitchen.

Marcovicz picked his rope and hooks off the divan and cradled them in one arm: 'With my new plan. Mind you, I admit I wasn't sure at first. I came up here this morning to make up my mind after I'd heard all about it from the baboon in the bottom flat. He told me I was to go to London on a forged passport and threaten to turn over the American to the police if he refused to come on back. The baboon said I'd get off clear, that it was only a bluff which the Yank couldn't jump once I was back in the "Smoke." He even offered to plug me my fare plus five hundred in advance, the rest when I'd got MacGrady back into the Zone.'

'And what did you say?'

'No promises. Never do I make promises if I don't feel like it, because the future belongs to the Most High and I respect it. In any case I saw that it was a trick! I suspected it and I saw the riot coming up, Doctor Chance. I saw the position changing, the past falling flat as a blue joke in a revivalist meeting. Why should I worry? Men running, rich men on their bellies like broken armies with all their business un-finished when they caught the smell of burning. One of them, a blue-nosed Jew, came round to my place last night trem-bling like an uncooked liver. He'd lost his couriers, three of his biggest consignments, and he came blabbering round to me because he knew I was one of the have-nots, a have-not Jew who never wants. He asked me to take something—ah, ah, he was clever.'

'Take what, Marcovicz?'

'These, Doctor Chance.' He shook a little leather pouch in the air and it rattled. 'Two thousand pounds worth of diamonds for Amsterdam.'

'Where did they come from?'

'Liberia, smuggled in there by the negroes from Sierra Leone. And me to get ten per cent. the day he gets the Dutch credit note, the day I bring back one of the rocks.'

'I see.'

'I can't go wrong, can I? What need have I to worry about the past now, about one little alcoholic married to a woman like that? Why, my future's arrived, it's here; for once, I have recognised it?'

There was a prolonged silence; the German moved uneasily and then his jaw tightened as his chin jerked interrogatively towards the Doctor.

Chance returned his glance. 'Do you think you can be sure?'

'Of course.' He slipped his pouch back inside his shirt. 'Have I missed something? Is there something I've not seen?'

'Oh no, I don't suppose so. But if you really believe our present consists in recognising facts and opportunities which were always promised and often missed, why have you come back here? If for once, you're so certain of everything?'

'Aha, that's just it. I *had* to come back to be sure. I had to see you because you're the only man who remembers the future I saw and promised myself when I was as I was, stateless, with so many names that I was nameless: a man unable to return even to his native prison because Germany had ceased to exist. A man, Herr Doktor, paying the penalty for crimes that had themselves been lost, swallowed up, in the tyrannies of a truer destroyer, *Hitler*!'

At the name, saliva gathered in the crevices of the Jew's lips. His eyes enlarged as he gazed beyond Chance and across the town, the yellow irises clearing back to their whites by the drawing of the lids.

'And what a destroyer! A face on which nothing was

written, neither cruelty, ambition nor lust! The visage of Satan himself; a genocide who slew even his dreams for fear they should ever take on the flesh he abominated. The self-slayer whose only kiss was for the muzzle of his revolver in the darkness of a cellar.' He turned to Chance again. 'And then you ask me why I should come to *you*! To whom else should I go when Providence has twice cast us together? Can't you understand that I wanted to look into you as I might look into something reflecting me, light or dark, a mirror that's missed nothing of my life's time. I didn't want to make any mistakes; I knew there was a connection between you and me and I wanted you to say that I was right, that none of *my* dreams and nightmares were wasted. I wanted you to tell me, Doctor Chance, that I've always been justified.'

'You think it's for me to say?'

'Not if you were a friend and not if you were an enemy; but as someone given to me by the Most High to hear all my secrets and know in my worst days what I was after. As a doctor and a believer I wanted you to say my life had made sense.'

'But I wouldn't say that about anyone alive or dead— certainly not about anyone living. I don't think social judgements are of any value.'

'Society! Don't lower me to that; I spit at it. I'm a Jew and as a Jew I appeal to you as a believer.'

'A believer whose beliefs you don't share, Marcovicz.'

'What does that matter? We're men under the sky, aren't we? Doctor and patient, the convicted and the unbetrayed. You know enough and have the words; you can tell me I was always right.'

'You're wrong to expect any man to tell you that.'

'Then who do you trust? The priests I suppose?'

'Certainly.'

'Aha, but whose, yours or the rabbis of my people?'

'Until you've decided that, how can anyone tell you whether you've been right or wrong? What authority do you recognise?'

'None! None but the authority of the great God himself.' He turned. 'You need say no more, I'll leave as I came, as we first met, more even than a Jew—a *man.*'

'Marcovicz, I want to ask you something. I want to ask you if you'll do something for me and for Mrs. MacGrady?'

'What can *I* do for you? You're not frightened of the baboon down below, are you? He's got nothing on you, has he?'

'You know he has.'

'I do? Ah yes, I've had no time to think about that lately; it's gone, I've moved on, I'm free. There is only one other person to see. But what is it you want me to do?'

'As you know, Fraser refuses to let either of us leave the flat. He's got my passport, he's cut off the telephone and it's quite impossible for Mrs. MacGrady to contact her husband in London.'

'Yes, yes, I remember. You're telling me it's my fault, that it was because of my pursuit and my rights that the baboon has this much power over you?'

'I want you to take a message urgently for me to the Palace. There's no time to go over all the ground again; but——'

'Our last argument? You want me to settle that and prove to you that when it is ordained it will be allowed?'

'No, Marcovicz, I don't want you to injure Fraser. All I want you to do is to take a note from Mrs. MacGrady to the Palace—where Magdalena is.'

'Ah, Magda! You think she would see me?'

'I don't know about that, but she would certainly respect you as the bearer of this note.'

Marcovicz was only half listening as Chance explained; there was something within him clamorous as an infant to which he attended beyond his mere senses as a mother listens to hunger or pain.

But Chance elaborated and only remembered the convict's inattention much later.

An old but brightly painted armoured-car arrived from the

Palace at dusk. Long before it drew up they heard it grinding up the President Hoover and watched it come to rest beneath them in the long shadows. From the camp in the vacant lot opposite, children began to swarm up the brown embankment while, lower down the avenue, others ran laughing and shrieking along the pavement. They carried bamboo rattans, stones, fish-heads and rotten fruit from the Soccos and threw these from a safe distance until a thunder-flash was lobbed at them from the open turret.

A door opened and two of the Sultan's Guard carrying sub-machine-guns jumped down into the road. In a few moments they were hammering with the gun butts on the steel grille of the entrance. As George Fraser came out on to the steps they pushed him to one side and entered the building at a run followed by two children from the camp.

Before the lift whined in the foyer, Anna helped Chance to pull the cabin trunk back into the hall.

'Well this is it,' she said as they rested by the bolted door. 'I never thought that crazy man would make it but he evidently did.'

'Providence of God!'

'You'd better make up your mind right away or you'll be tempting it. Which you going to do, come now or come tomorrow?'

'My passport——'

'For Heaven's sake forget that old passport. In two or three days, maybe sooner, we'll have time to talk to Consulates and people. We'll be able to collect it from the Post Office—they'll not be having any deliveries between now and Monday or Tuesday.'

He sat down on the trunk.

'That wretched child,' he began, 'George's little pet with the hat-pin—which ought I to do, Anna?'

She picked up his hand from where it lay in his lap. 'That's pretty swollen. You'll just have to come, that's all. Now go get your bags ready.'

'I've got penicillin somewhere.'

'Get your bags. No, wait, I'll get them.'

The bell rang. 'Let them in,' she called, 'and let them do the manhandling of the trunk.'

He opened the door and the two soldiers thrust into the hall. They wore the familiar khaki with red fez on which the Sultan's arms were embroidered over the Islamic star and crescent.

When Chance pointed to the trunk they ignored him. One stationed himself by the door, the other clicked through in his brown knee-boots to the sitting-room, where he turned about and re-entered the hall just as Anna reappeared with Chance's case in her hand. He saluted her and produced a warrant with the Royal arms on the back.

'For me?' she asked herself as she ripped the envelope. 'I don't make any sense of it.'

Chance moved over and looked at it. 'That's your name in the centre, it must be a safe-conduct.'

'If it is, it'll have to do for two.' She turned to the soldier by the sitting-room door, 'El Señor Doctor, mi amigo——'

But he interrupted her in Arabic and then gave an order to his subordinate who stepped forward and took Chance's case from her free hand.

'No,' she said, pointing to her cabin trunk.

He dropped Chance's case and, left-handed, dragged the trunk out behind him like a carcass, his machine-gun, waist-high, directed out through the open door into the foyer.

'You'd better just bring your own case, Chance, and come with me.'

'At least they can't argue.'

They walked out together in the wake of the cabin trunk with the senior man bringing up to the rear.

They had to wait for the first man to descend with the trunk and then return and they waited in the silence peculiar to departures. Below them they heard the clatter of the gates and the clash of the man's boots on the terrazzo, while from somewhere on the stairway the murmur of children's voices ascended from below. Through the open flat door behind them they could hear the shouts of the other young Riffis down in the street, a bolder ululation now that only the driver was left in the vehicle. Light from the sun poured in across the landing bathing their faces and the swarthiness of their guard with its effulgence.

'Once we get to the Palace we can put your arm in a sling. You can dope yourself up with your penicillin until the riot's over and we can chase a doctor.'

'As long as it's not Friese.'

'Oh that man'll have gone to earth by this time. I'd stake anything he's half-way to Tripoli by now.'

'MacGrady said something about men and doctors, I can't quite remember what it was; but I think it's a terrible thing when professionalism stops half-way, when men become doctors without doctors ever becoming men again. I get a recurrent dream of dying surrounded by very white doctors in a very up-to-date hospital.'

'You're sick, Chance, and I don't blame you. I've got first-night nerves myself; but really, you know, you don't have a thing to worry about now. This is where I take over.'

'I was wondering about Fraser. I can't believe he'll let us both walk out like this without making some sort of an attempt to hold one of us as security. He was talking about it on the telephone this morning.'

She touched the muzzle of the down-pointed machine-gun and the soldier stared back at her blackly.

'George is a very nasty man, he's got a bit of the gangster in him, he must have seen too many movies when he was a boy, but I don't think he'd argue with that.'

Chance was gloomy. 'If only one knew how much Mac-Grady really owes him.'

'You're *really* sick, Chance; it can only be fever that's making you concentrate on the wrong things at the wrong time. All I wish is that man'd hurry up with the lift.'

'He's on his way.'

The gates closed down below and high above their heads the motor began to drone on its perch overlying the shaft. The guard passed between them and took up his position by the grille.

'I meant,' Chance persisted, 'that if he really has an awful lot at stake he's bound to do something when we reach the ground floor. He might shoot one of us in the leg or try a few thousand pesetas on one of these men. Now that Marcovicz has changed sides we're the only hold Fraser has on MacGrady's money.'

She was vague. 'Columb will be through the operation by now, that's all I think about.'

The lift stopped in front of them and the soldier in front reached out and took her case. The other one clapped his heels together and stood to attention, his eyes and gun motioning them into the lift.

Moving ahead of him past the down-thrust gun, she said, 'Where you're concerned, it's different. Chance darling, where you're concerned I just want to get you out of this where you came in.'

'I forget where that was——'

The soldier by the lift had raised his gun horizontally across the entrance so that its grey-black bar seemed to be an integral part of the outer gate. Anna got hold of it with her two hands and jerked it momentarily to one side, but it came back again, sprung powerfully by the khaki-covered arms.

Attempting to dodge beneath it and rejoin Chance she said, 'Just what does he think he's doing?'

Chance jumped forward towards her: the muzzle was jabbed into his stomach between the margins of his ribs and he fell back gasping with his arms doubled across the place of impact. As he straightened he saw the sweep of her thick hair as she caught the soldier full across the face and leapt out past his gun. She pulled Chance slowly upright and with one arm round him, the nails of the ringed hand denting his skin, she thrust her other hand between the buttons of his shirt and rubbed his exposed flesh.

She was leading him back into the flat. 'They can bring the trunk back, we're neither of us leaving tonight.'

'Thug . . .' he managed.

'Don't try to talk. Just get up on the divan while I pour you a drink.'

But she was dragged from him. They had hold of her elbows and pulled her into the lift as easily as though they had been sharing a very light trunk. Chance followed after them as far as the drawn gates of the lift where they permitted him to await the return of his breath.

'Don't worry, Anna. Just let them take you there. They've obviously got orders, or they think they have, to take you——'

Seeing how very pale she was, he did not finish: the bright circles of colour were flushing the high points of the cold cheeks. The great eyes, wide open now, awake, saw as far as the hollowed eyes of marble. They were taking no light or colour at all from the overhead bulb; they were no more than full dark vacancies between her perfect lids.

'Tomorrow, Anna.'

'Yes?'

'Tomorrow it will be different. We shall be able, you can——'

'That's right, Chance,' she whispered as the soldier pressed the button, 'I see now that it will have to be tomorrow.' And, as she sank, 'after all!'

The last two words came from below him, clearly whispered rather than spoken. They hung in his hearing as he moved back into the empty flat, and moved on through the hall into the sitting-room where he found the boy awaiting him, closely watching the movement of MacGrady's clock.

For some moments even after Chance's entry, the front door slammed back behind him, the clock's fascination continued to hold the child crouching before its dome of glass. At the interruption he glanced round only briefly to sight the Doctor's expression and then resumed his greedy invigilation of the twisting pendulum.

Chance sagged down on to the divan, stooping his face low

over his knees as he continued himself to rub the place where the gun muzzle had hit his stomach. The boy heard him groan or swear and took one more interrogative glance at him before returning to his study of the clock. They remained like this for several minutes without either of them moving until at length the boy grew bored or restless. He padded round the walls and examined the pictures, hopped out on to the balcony and came straight back in again, over towards Chance who was still in the same position. He watched him a little and then said:

'I made it.'

No reply.

'My pal got double-quick scared of the guns, but I came right on in.'

Chance put his feet up and lay back with his head on the edge of the roll-shaped Victorian cushion. He closed his eyes and asked the boy what time it was.

'Friday,' he replied as he moved out into the hall.

The sun had gone down now, leaving only a haze of colours behind it to play on the ceiling and the facets of the chandelier suspended above the foot of the divan. Watching them glint Chance heard the sudden hubbub of the children below as the armoured car started up. He sat half-up as the gear-box shrieked and the din of engine and voices mingled and grew. When a thunder-flash exploded, he left the divan and ran across the room to the balcony where he leaned right out and over the balustrade to see the yellow tortoise-shape beneath him drive onwards up the hill to round the right-hand bend and disappear behind the flat-block.

The children eddied backwards like a bird flock against the tarmac: they swung over towards the encampment and then wheeled in upon themselves to sail screaming and calling down the hill, when, as suddenly, they turned back again and reassembled beneath the balcony.

Some of them had their dark faces upturned to him and were shouting something; but others were content merely to be there, playing stick games or arguing, casting only occasional glances upward. He tried hard to catch a meaning from the body of their shouting, from the tone and pitch rather than the words themselves but drew only the impression of a concern as wayward and bird-like as their grouping.

Behind him, Haleb came out on to the balcony and the people-children below fell instantly silent, every narrow face turning upwards in the dusk. Then they shrieked out anew, louder than ever, piercing the air urgently with a confusion of cries and demands.

'What are they saying? What's the matter?'

The boy shrugged. 'You wouldn't know you got it all wrong.'

'*I*'ve got it all wrong?'

'Surething.' He let out a sharp whistle which stilled them at once, told them something brief. They conferred amongst themselves and huddled more closely together. Chance took him by the shoulders and down below they dropped their stones and food-morsels, their canes still, as they strained to see rather than hear what was said.

'What have I got all wrong?'

'Okay okay.'

'Answer me!' His grip tightened on the thin arm.

'You wouldn't know, bud.'

'Are they mad at me?'

'Kinduv. The kids are waiting. They wanna know: I told 'em "Vamoose!" but they don't get it not yet nohow.'

'But what do they want to know?'

'What goes on. They don't catch on to you and the Fraser guy and the other Christians.'

'You mean, it's Fraser they're waiting for?'

'And how. They've been listening in the soccos and they sure fix the Fraser bitch.'

He called down to them, 'Je-heorga-a Frasa-a,' whereat they danced and yelled, brandishing their sticks. 'Catch on?' he asked.

'But why, then, were they getting mad at *me*?'

The boy sagged a little, he seemed to grow smaller as he

had on the night they first met when Chance had thrown the meat to the cats.

'The pale dame fed us,' he said. 'She gave us dough, pesetas, bananas. She was a lolly.'

'Yes?'

'They want to figure why you fire her out after fixing her Americano.'

'Tell them, I didn't. Tell them she's safe and that the Americano was sick and prayed to Allah to be made well and is safe.'

The child's head fell, he moved away sideways with a certain stealth.

'Go on, tell them!' Chance ordered. 'Don't let them be wrong about this. The Señora is good and safe in the Palace with their own Sultan. No harm can come to her. They will see her again.'

'I tell them for you, but don't blame me, kid.'

He cawed down to them shortly, coughing out the dry Arabic words miserably as a betrayal, and when he had finished the effect was immediate: a discord of imprecations and howls. Some of them packed back across the road to the embankment to get a better angle for their stoning, but nothing came up, the missiles fell away clattering into the lower balconies and rebounding from the concrete walls.

'I don't understand it,' Chance said. 'Please tell them to go away.'

'Sure thing you don't.' With another whistle and a wave of both his arms he effectively dismissed them and walked back into the flat through the french windows.

Chance watched them disperse, some in one direction, some in another and then followed him into the sitting-room where he found him gazing into the clock.

'Nice place they got here,' he said politely.

Chance sat down on the divan. 'How long are you thinking of staying?'

'Just waiting about, that's all. Say, you fix that passport yet?'

'No.'

'You not feel so good, Doc?'

'No, I don't. It's my stomach and my arm.'

'Abdul Murjah fix you good with his gun. I watch him. Why you let him take your new dame?'

'I didn't let him take her, you little fool. I've already told you that the soldier guy take the Señora all safe to the Sultan's Palace.'

'Okay okay, don't get mad.'

'I don't know what the devil you think you're doing here, anyway. It's not my flat and it's not yours. Nobody invited you. I think you'd better go because you're annoying me.'

'If you won't talk about her, sure I go.'

'But I *am* talking,' Chance hammered the cushion with his bad hand and then groaned. 'I'm telling you, if you'd only catch on, that the pale dame——'

'You drink whisky and then you get feeling great again,' the boy suggested with equanimity as he went straight over to the table on which the drinks stood. Chance followed his movements inattentively and said nothing.

'Your dame said you get yourself a shot before you do anything else.'

'She is not my dame. My dame is dead. The lady is the wife of the American and she has left me. I have no claim on her and I may never see her again.'

'Guess you're dead right.'

'What did you say?'

'Whisky for you.' He was pouring it out.

'Oh all right. No, not too much,' Chance waved irritably, 'that'll do. Now fill it up with water from the other jug. Thanks.' He took the glass. 'How did you get your friends to go away?'

'My brother tell them I got the run of the place, know the Christians, am your buddy.'

'You run the gang, is that it?'

'Sure, my mob.' He was pleased. 'We pool tips, catch on?'

Chance put his hand into his pocket and brought out a

handful of small change. 'Who blew up the building this morning?'

The child picked the coins out of his hand one by one, scrutinising each before slipping it into his knickerbockers.

'My brothers,' he said.

'Your brothers?'

'And friends incorporated.'

'Why?'

'The Fraser guy sells guns all round is why.'

'All round, you mean to everyone?'

'He sell big time to the Police and Sultan, little stuff to the Riffi. Everybody gets mad and the Colonel runs.'

'And the Riffis get mad with Fraser and Colonel Godfrey?'

'With all dog Christians, not Colonel Godfrey. My brothers figure the Russkies come good. They say sure the Russkies catch on to the dog Bishop racket when they get cracking.'

'What?'

'You don't know a dumb cluck, Doc. Americans jack-hi the desert bomb and Cairo Moslems say the Russkies take over gasolene wells and pay good in guns to fix the Christians all round.'

Chance drank slowly. His head was throbbing and there was a pain in his right armpit which, without investigation, he knew to be due to the spread of infection from his hand.

'Catch on?' asked the boy.

Chance frowned: 'No I don't. Perhaps I should have found out more before I sent her. As it is I shall just have to wait—that's all. Fraser was right; it's all anyone can do.' He thought for a moment. 'Look, you come along into the kitchen and fix some tinned soup—I want to think.'

'Anything you say.'

Chance took him along, lighted the gas and showed him what to do. He was on his way back through the hall when the bell rang once. He stood stock-still and as he waited the flap of the letter-box lifted and a fat envelope slid through on to the blue Persian rug.

It lay there ten feet away from him, but he made no move

to pick it up. He was waiting for the sound of footsteps and the succeeding whine of the lift motor; but he heard nothing. It was only when he remembered George Fraser's rubber feet that he waved the boy out of the kitchen doorway and took the letter through into the sitting-room to read it. The flap of the envelope was still copiously moist and he was able to peel it up without tearing it.

The covering note, signed George D. Fraser, was brief. It said:

'Thought these would interest you. Your passport arrived under separate cover. Sorry about that, Doc, but right now if there's anything in MacGrady's moan about his lifelong loyalty to the sorrowful and the faithful—the answer to a sinner's prayers, then you might be said to be our sole security pro tem. It looks that way from what I've just heard. In any case, until I get him back or know which way he's going to jump I feel you and I have got to stay in the one place. If nothing happens to make me change my mind I'll even send him his passport when the time comes. And by the way, if you are curious, inquisitive or with a nose, as I take you to have, the airmail was picked up G.P.O. this morning. Cable arrived via my telephone about two hours ago. Be seeing you later with or without friend.

Chance read this twice, the punctuation bewildered him and he had the impression that some other voice of Fraser's had found speech in what he wrote. He turned the paper over and saw scrawled in the same hand on the back:

What price Friday sorrowful now. G.D.F.

He went back to the door and shot the bolts and then opened the second enclosure: an airmail letter addressed in MacGrady's hand to *Mrs. Columb MacGrady* and dated *Wednesday*. There were no preliminaries:

'I was in such bad shape I managed to see Dyce down at his office this afternoon, and he has arranged me a priority

W

admission to the London Clinic this evening. He says there is a fairly extensive collapse of the lobe of my left lung which could have been made worse by lousy flight conditions.

I am mailing this and the passport under separate cover before I call my taxi for the Clinic and will surely cable you again tomorrow when I have the verdict. From what this surgeon said today it seems immediate operation will be scheduled if I am to get back anywhere at all. We none of us allowed for this in all the plans we made, though maybe Chance fighting over that extra day had the prophecy on him as usual.

Mostly, as usual too, I am mostly concerned with myself and you'll understand I don't greatly care any longer about the rest of things provided Anna MacGrady is fixed up safely with Yacef Ali before Chance leaves. This much thought I did give you before I go through those curtains, that if necessary you could fly back together and finally call the combined bluff.

Otherwise, though I've never decided whether it is cheaper to pay or to owe, I could get someone to fly over what credit I can raise and buy off the worst of Fraser. I never yet decided what was Caesar's and what God's. This amongst others is a thing which I will not die perplexing if the surgeons are used that way. But you could tell Fraser to take a chance on MacGrady Senior's will—which *could* make no provision for Anna. And by the way you might remind him he cuts to lose if he uses that crackpot Keller and sends what the surgeons leave of me for trial by jury.

In reply to *you*, Chance, I see this now that more than most men I have lived under a dead hand most of my life and that it has taken the prospect of death to lift it from me. You may ask why I never saw this before or why you didn't or the man from the Insurance Company either.

For the operation Friday I have ordered a hundred-guinea Mass at Farm Street which with the doctors will leave my bank account cleaner than a Trappist's cell. They would do it for nothing; but why should they?

For the rest I wish to write that I have not yet made my Confession because I can bluff too and they tell me I cannot make it when I'm dead—if God is interested. And this means I don't go to that table saying, I have wasted God's time and given more, will be the new man; I go saying I have wasted *my* time—that is all.

And here despite your hick instruction from the Maynooth mission you will surmise that if I have been short on the virtues it's because it has always been my freedom or sin to doubt the doctrine of grace where my own soul is concerned—since, unlike the Church Sorrowful, I never wept or suffered for anyone but myself. But it's a sweet dilemma because so long as it is denied me then so long can I continue to deny it. So to end up; as I see it, my survival of what happens tomorrow will make possible at some future time my recognition of grace and all it brings. In the which case I'll no longer have to live by grace as it appears to exist in parts of the Holy Church and her members, which is to say you for example or, most important my wife Anna, whom of course I married primarily for that reason.

Therefore, living, I shall live by the Grace of the Holy Spirit of God alone; and not living I shall die for the lack of it, which they tell me is death in any case.

I pray for you,

Columb MacGrady.'

Chance picked up the last of the enclosures, a typed version of the telephoned cable intercepted by George Fraser and transcribed on his Olivetti:

'Benign chondroma successfully detached from left bronchus. Patient's condition most satisfactory. My full letter follows.

Kind regards,

Dyce.'

'Successfully detached,' Chance repeated. 'As I see it my survival will make possible at some future time my recognition of Grace and all it brings.' *'Patient's condition most satis-*

factory.' 'Therefore living I shall live by the grace of God alone.'

And he meant? What proof of grace was he seeking? Having recognised it elsewhere, to question it in oneself was surely casuistry. For how could the man who was truly blind ever have demanded his eyes if he had never had knowledge of sight?

MacGrady was not blind, he had eyes but would not admit or could not see that he had always seen, and so he had commanded a proof he believed he could appreciate without ever realising the vulgarity of such a prayer.

Chance found the time factor confusing. He recounted to himself the sequence of events in order to be quite sure that once again there had not been some trick of the clock in the presentation of the facts. The letter had been posted in Mayfair at 4 p.m. G.M.T. on Wednesday. It was now 8 p.m. Zonal time on Friday, or 6 p.m. G.M.T. in London where MacGrady recovering consciousness, would shortly be facing knowledge that Chance already possessed: the fact not merely of his survival but the likelihood of his complete recovery. Yet, at the moment, he was unaware of the contents of the cable; for him the result of the operation still lay in the future against which he had preset his will and which he had sought to make a test of the moral course of his life. The letter spoke for the final disposition of MacGrady preparing to die and had been read at the moment of his recovery.

Soon, at any moment by a clock in London, he would know that he had been given more time. Would he expect to feel himself the possessor of grace now that he had made grace a test of his survival? What would he do when he felt himself alive and graceless still, no longer able to live at second-hand on the merits of his faith? What unsweet dilemma would start crushing him more terribly than the dermoid had crushed the access to his lung? What would happen to him now that he must believe he had been given what he wanted? What could be the salvation of the blackmailer if not to be himself blackmailed most subtly?

Somewhere between MacGrady and Marcovicz there was a comparison to be drawn; the pressures under which men moved whether imprisoned or free must somewhere have their counterpart in the world unseen. Momentarily Chance perceived not the image of the dove symbolising the gentle grace which MacGrady had so long questioned; but that of an eagle, high, vigilant and terrible. *And the fourth beast* he remembered, *was like a flying eagle.*

He was interrupted by the jingling of crockery and turned as the boy entered with a tray on which were two plates of soup and a loaf of bread. He put it down on the floor and squatted beside it.

Chance said, 'When you've had your soup I want you to take these letters to the pale dame at the Palace.'

He went over to the bureau and put the papers into a clean envelope. He wrote Anna a brief note several times over, finding that his hand became more illegible with repetition and the lines more crooked. Ultimately he printed it as she had done when she left him George Fraser's roses: her first gift of flowers.

'SO FAR ALL WELL. I'M SENDING THESE WITH HALEB. THE MAN FRASER PUSHED THEM THROUGH THE LETTER-BOX HALF AN HOUR AGO. HE STILL HASN'T SHOWN UP HIMSELF.

IF YOU HAVE ANY NEWS SEND ME BACK A NOTE WITH THE BOY. I SHALL BE ALL RIGHT UNTIL TOMORROW I THINK THOUGH I'M FEELING RATHER DREADFUL. FRASER BY THE WAY HAS GOT MY PASSPORT BUT I HAVE AN IDEA THAT I SHALL GET IT OUT OF HIM THIS EVENING.

LOVE AND WHAT MORE CAN I SAY?

CHANCE.'

He sealed the envelope and handed it to the boy who chucked it down beside him on the floor.

'Don't lose it,' Chance warned him. He wanted suddenly to kick the child, to knock him about, he even visualised himself throwing him out over the balcony. But the boy was watching him with no concern, his mouth moving noisily as he fed it with lumps of bread which he had previously dipped into the steaming soup before him. He passed Chance half of the loaf and Chance went on:

'When you get to the Palace you give in the message and you wait. Give the soldier guard this money and tell him there will be answering words from the Señora MacGrady, which paper you must not leave without.'

'You kidding?'

But Chance was not listening, he was carrying on his imagination of her response, thinking: It won't worry her at all. She'll see nothing but the cable and she'll start dancing. These things never worry women because they accept them in advance as they accept their children. She won't care a damn what MacGrady believes or doesn't believe as long as he's alive. It's all she demanded and she's got it. Perhaps that's why: it may be only her prayer that's been answered, not his at all. But she won't realise that this will be the conclusion he will come to. He will say to himself, 'I still have no grace and I must therefore depend more strongly on her than before because, now I come to think of it, she was the reason I recovered.'

Haleb asked, 'You eat bananas, Doc?'

'No thanks.'

'I go and collect 'em now?'

'Yes, if you want them. I didn't know there were any.'

Grace, he thought, dei gratia. He remembered the young priest with the Belfast accent who had given him his instruction on Thursday afternoons. He had said that grace was one of the most difficult concepts in doctrine, one of the most essential to the understanding of revelation.

Somewhere, Chance recalled, he had noticed a Catholic dictionary in one of the bookshelves. He moved over to them and in a few moments found it. He turned to *Grace* on page 155 and read:

Specifically, grace is a supernatural gift freely given by God to rational creatures to enable them to obtain eternal life. Generally, however, all that one receives as free gifts from God may be termed graces or favours. Grace may be sanctifying or actual; sanctifying grace is permanent in the soul and elevates the soul by its very presence there and is called habitual grace; all infused virtues accompany habitual grace. Actual grace may be either *exciting* or *helping*: that of exciting stimulates the mind to act and that of helping assists in performing the act which already has begun. Each person is granted sufficient grace to enable him to save his soul.

He lobbed the book on to the divan as the boy returned with a bunch of bananas and started to eat his way through them one after the other. Half-watching him, Chance was glad of his presence both because of his headache and of a sense of futility whose origin he found it difficult to discover. Yet the boy was most irritating, he had a monkey-like way with a banana, breaking small pieces off it at great speed and pistoning them into his noisy mouth. In so far as he thought about him with one part of his mind he was thinking about sending him off to the Palace immediately, but deciding elsewhere that he would keep him a little longer, all bananas finished, so that he could talk to himself without being self-conscious about it. He thought he might have a temperature and told the boy suddenly:

'I was going to tell you that when I came here MacGrady was in a fair way to die. He certainly had a growth in his lung which could have been malignant, or become malignant; and in any case, because he could not be sure, his fear of it was malignant.'

'Malignant,' repeated the boy carefully through his banana.

'It gave him an excuse for torpor,' went on Chance. 'A good feeling that now it was too late for him to change anything. He had given up praying about that because it was something by which he could be avenged against himself. If this growth didn't kill him he could say, "There is hope for me; I'm wanted on my own terms." But if it proved fatal he could say,

"This growth was as inevitable as my moral corruption, and my death will be a sufficient answer to them both. It will be edifying." '

The boy nodded. There was only one banana left and he was surrounded by the discarded skins of the four he had eaten. He tucked the last one into the folds of his knickerbockers.

'People are secretly relieved by the prospect of death,' Chance went on, 'but if you take MacGrady at this moment he would be glad, if he were conscious, that he did speak to me that night—because he's cured.' He gestured with the letter he was holding. 'It could have been a carcinoma, but it wasn't. His health will be better than it's ever been. So you can't deny that it's a wonderful thing that I should have come and that we should have met.'

'Sure, sure!'

'I came for a holiday and this is what happened.'

'Holiday!'

'There's no point in my staying any longer at all. If it wasn't for the damned Arabs I could go tonight. That is, once I've got my passport. Anna's safe, MacGrady's cured, even Fraser will probably get some of his money because Anna will now have much more influence on MacGrady and insist on his straightening everything up. They will come into all that money of his father's and might even settle somewhere and have children.'

'Cash is money.'

The boy looked far too comfortable, very full of food, inclined to give himself little scratches and yawns. Noticing him, all of Chance's earlier irritability returned strongly.

'You go take that letter to the Señora at the Palace! Right away now. You can come back later if you can find a way in.'

'No go. I guess the Señora not get visiting with Palace damn likely.'

'Go! Get moving at once. I've given you the money so you get running pronto with the letter.'

The bell rang.

'Mr. Fraser,' said the boy. 'I'd better get hidden.'

'You can go and let him in.'

Leaving the letter on the floor the boy went out and into the hall.

Fraser was carefully shaved: a little cut on his chin had a piece of cotton-wool stuck on to it. He had brushed his black eyebrows and oiled them; his silver hair had been freshly washed and the scalp gleamed between the comb slicks.

He said, 'Howyer, Doc Chance? It's been a long day. I didn't bring my friend along because I thought we ought to palaver alone for a little bit.' Noting the letter he stooped and picked it up. He read the address aloud: 'Tk! tk! Too bad, isn't it? And to think—but who told you?'

'That is mine,' said Chance holding out his hand for the envelope. 'Also I want my passport.'

'Now that's just what I've come to talk to you about. But first I would like to know who was first with the news about not worrying to send your little letter on to the girl friend. Was it the kid here?'

'Haleb was just on his way with it when you came in.'

Fraser handed it to him looking first at the boy out of his very blue eyes and then back at the doctor.

'He was, was he? Well well, he'd better get started. He's got a long journey ahead of him.'

'Take it, Haleb!' Chance ordered.

But the boy still hung back in the doorway, his face closed up and small, his eyes mesmerically following the clock.

'From what I heard she's got what you might call a long start,' said the Australian. 'Mind if I take meself a drink?'

Chance concentrated on the envelope still held in his own left hand, his writing looked efficient and official, scarcely his own. He thought he wrote with more of a flourish than this:

MRS. COLUMB MACGRADY

C/O HIS EXCELLENCY YACEF ALI

THE PALACE

THE INTERNATIONAL ZONE

'You mustn't blime yourself, Doc,' Fraser was saying. 'You did yer best; though knowing what we did I will say I was a little dead duck on your bringing *him* in on the party. After all, he did try it on a couple of times before in Germany; and the leopard, you know, usually does keep his spots once he's past cub stage.'

'Cub stage? What spots?' Chance let the hand and the letter fall to his side. 'A couple of times before? Keller? Is that the leopard?'

There was a pause while the Australian drank half his deep tumberful of whisky and water. 'Let's be kind, Doc. It's one way to break news. Keller, *your* old-timer, your patient. I could be happy holding back on you by telling you he's always saying what a good judge you were, of men. How you once held out against the wigs on the question of his sanity. Why, he said it again a few minerts ago on the telephone so that I nearly put the call through to you and would have done, but then I thought, no this would not be kind; it wouldn't come nicely out of an instrument, it'd leave a man feeling helpless.' He took an unsmiling pace backwards as Chance approached nearer. 'Look, Doc, just get a hold of yourself, a man like you must know that it isn't easy to inform, especially where there've been mistakes. We all mike them, Doc, and cases like Keller are any man's bet; they have to be to give people a living. Why you wouldn't believe the trouble *we* had with him, the money he has cost Xavier Friese to keep him tranquillised on proprietaries from Germany, the States, London and Rome and stop him smothering up the girls that grow so thick in a place like this.'

From where he stood Chance sprang at him. In a single movement he crouched then leaped forward and, unable to stop himself when the other side-stepped, hit the bureau hard, shattering the glass cover of the clock against the wall. The glass rained outwards as he turned to find his adversary, the clock teetering about the vertical with the pendulum swinging fast but still attached.

Fraser had his back to the window; he was six feet away

from the bureau in front of which he had been standing, and scarlet with the suddenness of his movement. At the level of his right hip he was gripping Anna's little revolver with the muzzle aimed at Chance's stomach.

'Just to demonstrate,' he said as the little gun cracked and the clock rebounded from the wall to the floor. 'I know how to use it.'

Chance picked up the shattered clock from beside his feet and flung it at the Australian's head: the great member swayed to one side and the clock went on out of the window over the balcony, low over the balustrade. They heard the tinkle of its fall on the road.

Fraser said: 'You're quite right to be optimistic about yer future, Doc! It 'ud be pointless to hole your navel but I could always put one through your leg.'

'Where is she?'

'Now don't be dumb, Doctor, how do I know where she is? How does anyone? Yew can't trust a nut-case when the moon is high, *yew* ought to know thet.'

Chance had hold of the back of her chair, the one she had sat in by the bureau.

'You're lying. My God! You're telling me a lie.'

George Fraser smiled. 'You wouldn't know, would you? You weren't there and neither was I, but I'd have thought you could put two and two together and make zero when you saw him in the old passion-wagon from the palace, chucking out bangers at the kids.' He crooked a finger at Haleb. '*You* tell him boy. Who was in the big car from the Sultan's place?'

The boy looked across at Chance. 'The lady was took by the bad guy. You sure send her for a ride.'

Chance ran past him to the telephone; he sent the boy reeling across the hall and picked up the receiver.

'Put it through!' he shouted to Fraser. 'Go down and connect it—or tell them to do it.'

With the revolver in his pocket and his arms crossed loosely on his stomach the fat man lounged across to him:

'Friese is down there. I had thought of bringing him up—

he's week-ending with me—but he won't put you through to the palace or the police because he's not interested. If you'd heard what I heard yew wouldn't be interested either.'

The receiver on its snakey cable fell to the floor; for a moment no sound came from it and then like some small animal it began to squeak. The little voice enquired of their feet: 'Fraser, that you? Hello? . . . Hello?'

Fraser picked it up lazily: 'Friese? George here.'

'Yes?'

'I'm telling him now. He's *not* laughing.'

There was a click before he replaced the receiver on the bridge, regarding it absently as his hand dipped back into his pocket for the revolver and levelled it at Chance's head.

'*Yew* killed her. You'd better get it straight, you fool. You did it. Now come on now, get back in there while I put you in the picture. The Doctor'll be here in five minutes to revive you. You're going to need it.'

With his free hand he guided Chance back into the sitting-room, shuffling him easily in the direction of the divan. When they were beside it he gave him a little push and the Englishman toppled backwards on to the cushions. But he brought his feet up cleanly: they caught the big belly hard above the pubis, in the soft part of the paunch, and Fraser grunted.

'Look, Doc, I don't want to have to puncture you, but if yew get brave again I'm going to have to put this little weapon up against part of your anatomy and pull the trigger.'

Chance said nothing, he was sweating heavily and cold as he fumbled into his pocket for a handkerchief. He could not find it so he untied the sleeves of the pullover she had knitted and wiped his face on one of them. While the other was talking he put the pullover on slowly, disappearing inside it, blind, with his arms semaphoring in his search for the sleeve holes. The Australian drew a length of string from his pocket and, taking Chance's thin wrists, tied them together behind his back.

'And interfering,' Fraser was saying; 'mucking up a lot of stakes like a greenhorn in the pool-room who thinks he's got a system. *Yew* sent MacGrady off and there'd have been no headaches there if you hadn't got at the nut man and called his bluff, you ostrich. People got to believe in themselves. Noub'dy minded you making a pass at the girl. "Good luck to him," we said, "he can have her if she likes it that way, poor cow.' Columb didn't mind, he's got a Job-complex anyway, and all we wanted was the money—and *"we" is me.* I lend the money round here. I am Business! Who d'yer think sold the vehicles to the Sultan in the first place? Who financed the bar the black men are smashing up at the moment? Who brings in the lovely lolly? and keeps this stinking place going if it's not for men like me? Go on, lily-face, you tell me all about Society and the place of the bad man whose got to keep it on its rotten feet.'

As Chance's head emerged from the pullover, the Australian caught it with a slow backhander which knocked him back on to the cushions.

'I represent something I tell you,' he went on reasonably. 'I'm rockbottom and I'm needed worse than vice because it can't work without somewhere to work in. Where do the black angels perch? You can have your heaven, but the way we are you've got to stand somewhere to see it, and you've got to stand on something with yer feet on someb'dy's face. If persons are going to stand on me they've got to pay for it: that's the dirty justice of it—*and* I supported them all. We kept it clean: casinos, girls, bureaux, sex, political flutters, a bigger London, Chicago, Berlin. Political flutters, I say, for one and all from Paris to Washington. Somewhere they could unfasten their shirt-tails and then go back home refreshed to a bit more compromise with themselves and their laws.'

Chance said, 'I would kill you.'

'Oh maybe, maybe. They'd all say that, but I don't ever die because I'm essential. You're a Roman and I'll tell you something; I once heard a priest say that if there was one crust of bread left in Europe *he'd* get it because of his vow of poverty. Well, who d'you think would give it to him? Who'd be strong enough to carry it? It'd be me because I'd be the only one with anything left. You'll have to empty the Zoun before you get down to killing me as you've killed off your girl-friend.' He spoke over his shoulder to the boy, 'He's got brains, has the Doctor. He sends his sweetheart off for a ride with the silliest killer in Africa and wonders why she never reaches her destination. Get him a little drink, boy, and one for me too.'

The boy went across to the bottle and filled two tumblers.

'Don't give him the one with lipstick on it,' said Fraser. 'Noub'dy likes the taste of pint from dead lips; it upsets them.'

Chance went for him and was clouted back on to the divan.

'Don't like the thought of her last ride with Jacob Keller, do you? Don't care to think of him talking his way round people and escorting her on a lie? Someone to take the place of his own tart, no doubt, after you'd fixed her up so cleverly she wouldn't look at him. He cursed about that, I can tell you! And I can tell yew what he told me on the telephone when he was beginning to think. It wasn't easy to make him out; but not being a doctor like you or a psychiatrist like Xavier I put it together and it reads like this: she had no brains, she turned him down when he got her to his place. He took that all right, he got swollen up with his sweet ideas and said he'd win her; and what *she* do but start praying? I don't like to think of that, because I know people got to believe in themselves. I don't like to see bluffs called because they're what keeps the big world turning—compromise all the way. And the nut didn't like it either. You're a doctor, you should know what turns the trick in the screw-brain without me trying. As far as anyone could tell from him on the tele-phone, her praying to herself was what did it, he knew she was praying though he could hear nothing. He went right over the edge and he went over to her and he smothered her in the middle of the carpet without even using his hands!' Fraser raised his voice, 'That's what yew did, stupid! That's how it ends, with noub'dy getting anything out of it at all.'

Chance got up and was unmolested: 'You've said enough, don't say anything more.'

'You've got it, have you?'

'Untie my hands and get out. Leave me here. I won't attempt to go.'

'You're dead right, you won't. You're staying right here until we see Columb again. We're going to look after you carefully. *You're* the security on about two hundred thousand dollars owed to the syndicate that's going to be made good before anyone makes any more plans of any kind. And don't think it's not strictly legitimate or in the way of business. Maybe you didn't know that Columb welshed on our post-war enterprise with the ex-army stuff. Those of us who were paid are living nicely on the profits in Florida and the Bahamas; but those who weren't, stayed on, and they've got itching feet.'

Through intense nausea, Chance spoke. 'I'm unwell at the moment, Fraser. I'd be very grateful if you'd leave me alone for a short time.'

'That's too bad! but don't worry, we're going to fix you up with proper treatment. We've another doctor on the premises and you've got to get yourself better quick because if necessary you'll have to come to London with us and explain a few things to Columb. He's got through his first wife's cash and you're responsible for giving him time to get through his father's when he gets it. You could be very persuasive, Chance, and you're going to be.'

Chance walked over to Haleb. He turned his back on the child and thrust his wrists towards him. 'Untie me!'

'Go ahead,' Fraser nodded, 'we've had our talk.'

Obediently the boy began to undo the knots and then paused. Without speaking, he left Chance where he was and ran out on to the balcony with Fraser following.

Gunfire was beginning in the direction of the Avenue Grande: a scatter of single shots without pattern and then, distinctly, the yammer of machine-guns. Fraser came in again and switched off the chandelier a moment before the current of the European section was again cut off at the power station. Over the balcony Chance saw the building blocks and lamp-studded boulevards sink area by area into darkness, the pink and blue glow of neons dowsed at source to lower a sky in which the moon was not yet up. In the darkness he watched the town lose its design and spread formlessly, by guesswork alone, round the Medina and Soccos where a few oil lights still burned. But the towers of churches and mosques remained discernible, thrusting upwards from the reduction of the town into the unseen immensity of the night sky.

Chance called, 'My wrists; please untie them.'

'What's up?' Came the Australian's voice absently from the balcony.

'My wrists!'

'Fix it,' Fraser ordered the boy, 'I've got to get on the phone.'

From the bathroom in total darkness, Chance heard him through his sickness: 'You'd better hold everything and ride up, Xavier. Did Norton and Heber show up yet? . . . Too bad, the stupid bucks. I told them to move in early. You'd better put a call through to the Frogs and ask them what price a few troops now? Get on to Duhamel at the Legation, and tell him to get his General cracking. One tank and three carriers should fix it; tear-gas sooner than grenades. By the way, Friese, it looks as though you're going to be needed for your colleague, he's vomiting his guts in the lavabo.'

From the sitting-room the boy called. 'Say, Doc Chance, guys with guns in the street. Mr Fraser sure better shut all windows.'

'Not on your life. You leave those windows open,' he spoke on the telephone, 'and Xavier, tote up the field-glasses and a dozen crackers. We don't want to kill more than we have to but this block's insured at pre-war value.'

He came into the bathroom. Chance, stooping over the basin, heard him blundering into the doorway and the grunt of his haste.

'Finished?' he asked.

'No.'

'When you have, get back on to the divan if you can find it. The Doctor'll be up in a few minerts and we'll know what's what.'

'Fraser?'

'What do you want? I haven't time for any more chatter. Things are going to be noisy until the Frogs move across the border. Is there a torch in this flat?'

'In the bureau. *Fraser?*'

He was going but he stopped somewhere in the hall. 'What is it, Chance?'

'I want to know about Mrs. MacGrady. Are you sure about it?'

'You can bet she's dead.'

'That's not a lie? I sent her off——'

'What you did was to send her off in a hearse.' He moved away.

Chance turned on the taps and washed whatever it was from the basin. He cleaned his face and hands in the darkness and dried on a towel he could not see. Dizzily he moved back into the sitting-room and lay down on the divan.

'Only a dozen of them so far.' Fraser could just be seen against the sky with the boy beside him. They cut heavy patterns in the stars.

'You! Can you see anything down the road, boy?'

'More men coming slowly. They got lights, Mister Fraser.'

A bullet hit the concrete and shrieked off in a ricochet.

'They got some of our rifles too. We'd better shut up shop until the crackers arrive. Where'd you say that torch was, Chance?'

'She had one in the bureau—she didn't take it.'

'Where she's gone, she don't need it. Where's the desk?'

'Beside you.'

Fraser closed the french windows and the second bullet holed the glass and passed through the chandelier. Crystals tinkled and fell. Chance heard the flap of the bureau flop open and Fraser's fumblings amongst its old bills and letters.

x

He shone the torch against his own stomach so that only a little light was thrown forward: above, it illumined the loose chin and the hanging mouth though the eyes were lost in the shadows of the pink cheeks. He switched it off again when he had seen the shutters, bolting them across and drawing the heavy curtains in front of them.

'If they've got grenades,' he said, 'we've got crackers too, and that'll be just too bad for the Riffis because we've got height as well.' As the lift sighed beyond the door: 'That should be Xavier and Hasan.'

Friese brought a haversack full of grenades with him, two good rifles with loose ammunition and a candelabrum. He wore the field-glasses round his neck with his own dark glasses pushed up on to his forehead now that it was night. Behind him, Fraser's Arab servant carried a basket of provisions and a small gladstone bag.

'What did the Frogs say, Xavier?' Fraser asked.

'Duhamel was indeterminate. Very Gallic. Apparently he was waiting the Sultan's consent. Until they have that, the French government refuse to countenance any intervention, no matter what.'

'They'll give it! They'll get their men across the border within a couple of hours. The Bourse doesn't weigh sultans against diamonds—it weighs them against the franc. No, don't light the candles if you don't mind, we've got to keep them guessing. I was thinking it would be a good idea to light up on the second floor and let them concentrite their fire on an empty room. Hasan! you tike a couple of lights down to number three and mike some shadows on the window. Put 'em in the fireplace and don't open the shutters too wide.'

The servant left the room.

'Chance is sick?' Friese asked.

'Like a dog.'

'I'd better see to him, where have you put him?'

'He's here, on the divan three feet from you.'

Friese laughed. 'I hope you're not the traditionally difficult medical patient?'

'Oah! leave him, we've got to fix the gentry out in the road before we start doctoring casualties.'

'I disagree, Fraser.'

In the darkness, Chance sat up and Fraser turned the beam of the torch on him. 'You stay where you are for a few minerts. We're going to be busy.'

'I must get something to drink in the kitchen, some milk. I haven't eaten.'

'Get back on that bed or you woun't want to.'

'The torch!' Friese requested.

'Now get this, Xavier. I'm giving the orders. We got to fix the opposition before you start dishing out number nines to the Doctor. Your patient's had a shock, that's all. He can wait a little bit. How many Arabs were out there when you came up?'

But Friese was obdurate. The torch changed hands and was directed on Chance again. To avoid its glare he looked down and saw a smear of blood on his left wrist. There were similar thick patches on his trousers and the hem of his pullover.

'Not a shock,' said Friese coldly, 'a haematemesis. You have an ulcer, Chance?'

'Yes.'

'Has this happened before?'

But the shape of the Australian blundered into the light beam:

'Whatever he's had it's got to wait. Pass me the torch and a couple of crackers before the bastards break into my office.'

'I think it would be very short-sighted to allow our friend here to die before he has contacted MacGrady.'

'Die? He won't die for five minerts, and what I'm going to do will take two minerts and then you can get busy on yer first aid.'

'Very well.' Friese had found Chance's pulse. 'Grenades at this stage?'

But Fraser did not reply. His hand was in the haversack

when they heard the explosion. It was near and sharp, coming up through the lift shaft and the open door like something solid.

'They beat me to it. They must have chucked it in through the grille. Why the hell did Hasan leave that door open? We'll have them in the building if we don't disperse them. In just ten seconds they're going to have it.'

The torch went out and the shutters of the french windows opened. Against the sky, lighter now by contrast with the interior darkness the great figure loomed as its arm was twice raised in the action of bowling. Chance stood up, blocking his ears. He waited for seconds and then dropped his hands hearing clatters from the road below, a few voices. The grenades exploded nearly simultaneously; two lemon flashes reflected from no surface and succeeded by intense silence.

'Wait for it,' said Fraser a moment before the cries. His voice, clipped and husky, merged with the sounds from the road, the fall of concrete chips and glass, the delay of agony.

'All round the grille, I'll bet,' he said through the ascending gutturals of pain. 'The silly cows!' He turned and came in again. 'Where's that boy got to, Friese?'

'What boy?'

'Kid of Chance's. He was up here a few minerts ago.'

'I never saw any boy.'

'Of course you didn't, you goat! How the hell can anyone see in the dark? What's the kid's name, Chance?'

Chance was off the divan: 'Haleb.'

'Where you orf to?'

'My room. I must get some tablets.'

'Yew don't get no tablets. You sit on that divan until we're ready.'

'The boy?' asked Friese.

'Must have slipped out. Get some candles lighted and we'll get organised before any more Arabs show up. How many grenades were there in the safe?'

Before the match struck Chance moved through into the kitchen, leaving its door half open behind him. He found his way to the refrigerator and took out an ice-cold bottle of the milk delivered the day before. He removed the top and sipped it slowly, sitting under a table by one of the walls in the darkness. Beyond the doorway he heard them move down to the bedroom, looking for him. As soon as they had gone he took off his shoes and ran through the hall out on to the landing.

He found the stairhead and went down the first flight fast, hearing their conversation as they went searching for him in the empty kitchen. As he reached the second flight, with the lift shaft intervening between himself and the flat, he caught one sight of the candle flames upheld by George Fraser when he stepped out on to the landing above him.

'Take the torch, Friese. He can't be more than half-way. If you chase him out I'll watch for him over the balcony.'

Chance fled down the walled side of the smooth stairs and reached the third landing as Friese called down from above:

'Hasan! The Doctor's on his way down. Stop the Doctor!'

Chance increased his pace. The milk he had drunk collected itself in the pit of his stomach and he returned it on to the stairs as he ran. Behind him he heard the clatter of Friese's heels on the terrazzo and saw the darting whiteness of the torch beam flashing networks of shadow from the lift grilles on to the walls beside him.

'You're wasting your time, Doctor . . . Rest yourself . . . Chance, you have a haemorrhage!'

Friese's voice echoed haphazardly as his torch beam from the sides of the stairway which enclosed them; but Chance ran on. He reached the second-floor landing and on an impulse pushed at the door of the nearest flat. It swung open before him and he entered a hall which he guessed to be identical with the MacGrady's; number three, he remembered, but on the second floor. He had imagined himself to be a floor below that in which the Arab had been instructed to light candles and realised his mistake far too late, for Friese himself now sounded very near.

He saw the crack of light coming from the candles which had already been lighted in the sitting-room; but within moments

of his entry they were all extinguished. Total darkness flowed
back into his eyes, into the hopefulness which had come of his
action. He stood very still behind the open door and heard
Friese hurry past still shouting for the absent servant. The noise
he was making did not recede but was caught up by the tall
shaft and bounced backwards and forwards at close hand so
confusedly that it was impossible to know how far down he
had gone. The seconds were slower than Chance's breathing as
he waited shaking between the door and the wall.

In the hall of the empty flat a draught began to blow. It
reached the sweat on his forehead and cooled his wet lips as he
drank at the air. A torch flicked on and shone out from the
sitting-room to illumine the distemper on the opposite wall.
Chance drew the entrance door closer to his chest and moved
up towards the hinges, his right cheek flat against the wall surface as he watched for the Arab. He was dazzled as the face of
the torch turned towards him searching out the doorway and
the clattering staircase. He heard the creak of soft soles, the
whisper of his breathing as the man came towards him. Within
three inches of his chin a hand felt for the round handle of the
Yale lock and the door was drawn away from him.

The torch face hung for a moment in the darkness, silvery as
a mirror, and then went out. In the conjuration of the night,
shot through with retinal images in the aftermath of the bright
light, the man sighed and was still. Chance moved out towards
him and waited.

'You'll be too late, Doctor Chance, you'd better go back.'

There was a long silence; fruitful; a desert in which many un-
spoken words flowered and withered.

Chance put out a hand and his fingers fell on shoulder
muscles. He searched out the collar bone, the remembered in-
sertion of the sterno-mastoid, its great bulk running up to the
bone behind the ear. He felt the wrinkles in the forehead and
the thick hair curling on the sides of the head.

'Say nothing, Marcovicz!'

'Ah ha, nothing.'

'Wait!' The Doctor closed the door very carefully, with

surgical precision. He twisted the handle of the lock fully round, approximated its mouth to the socket in the jamb and then released the handle fraction by fraction until the steel tongue had clicked home.

'Where's the Arab?'

'What Arab?' The voice was sombre.

'Hasan.'

The ex-convict began to laugh quietly, but choked. He coughed a little, mingling his cough with his unpropitious laughter:

'He was too slow. He didn't know who I was and he tried the knife. I had to truss him.'

'Nothing more?'

'So they've told you? You've heard and you want to be wrong again. You think a man has to do a thing more than once?'

'No, Marcovicz.'

'You've got the prison mentality yourself. You've seen too many of us come back, bright and hopeful because we've returned. That may be so with everything else; but not with death. You're wrong, Doctor Chance, you're wrong. When a man has seen the image of God born into a dead face, dignity, mildness returning, he forswears his ways; he is satisfied, *made.*'

'Please, your voice——'

'I shall shout it! Why should I be quiet? I have learned something, I have sought certainty——'

'For God's sake, Marcovicz!'

'For God's sake,' shouted the other. 'What do you know about God? I'll tell the world my story and they won't believe it any more than they would believe it though one rose from the dead.'

Chance turned from him: 'Very well.' The two words dropped from him colourless as the darkness.

He opened the door and moved out into the hall uncaring of the other. Behind him the torch beam fluttered and swayed probing the vacant lift shaft, the roofing stairs and the steep fall downwards as Marcovicz came up to him and whispered:

'You are giving up, then?'

'Yes I am.'

'You know when to give up?'

'I know when I cannot escape.'

This was considered. From the tail of his eye Chance saw the shape of him beside the open door: the attitude of many thousands of men calculating within the space of their prisons a problem related to the hazards of the past and the promises of the future. Dully, as though this formulation were finding expression of the public darkness, for it would not have been said by day, Marcovicz replied:

'Ah ha, it's still not too late you know; this started a long time ago. You haven't reached the end yet, you've still got minutes to change it all.'

'You're not thinking of yourself, then?'

The question was lost in the renewal of clamour from below. They heard Friese returning. He was coming up from the ground floor at a run.

'Hasan! Have you got him? *Hasan!*'

Marcovicz fumbled: 'Myself? I've done with myself. This is where I begin!'

'Hasan!'

'There's a moment where a man does a thing he's dreamed of for years. *Achievement!* When all the ends of all his thinking, of all he has wanted and desired, become suddenly a fact. Fame or wealth, love or possession. Gone after in his thoughts, a great compulsion driving him on, a conclusion resisted, not much examined, but watched over, refused maybe and wanted over and over again until, at a time, it is realised and is done. He is what he wanted to be: famous, rich for ever, loved by his queen. And then, when he has it, when he has become that man, he finds it is not the end, that it is nothing.'

Friese had reached them. He called up to Fraser and the Australian appeared high above them with his torch in his hand. He got into the lift and came down to them swiftly.

'Just so there's no miscalculation,' he said looking at Marco-vicz, 'I've brought my gun. Get in with them, Friese, and take them up topside.'

'And Hasan?'

'Didn't you find him?'

'He could be in the flat.'

'See any Arabs down there?'

'There were two in a bad way, the others were dead. The grenades made a mess of them.'

'Too bad!' Fraser turned and brooded heavily over the German for a moment.

'What's your game, Keller?'

The prisoner stood very flat on his feet at the back of the lift. He was smiling down at his hands crossed loosely over his groins, but at the question he looked at Chance. Within so many shadows and so much that was not clear, the lack of delineation which is preponderant when brightness is fitful as the expression of chosen thoughts, words selected from the many alternatives of preoccupation, he resumed his address to his friend. He continued as though there had been no incursion.

'Nothing,' he said again. 'When a man reaches that moment by his own actions he is in the position to begin. A man has got to do what he set out to do in order to start. He should fulfil himself the first time, I tell you. He should never wait a lifetime to taste his dreams and spit them out. They should be made flesh for him at the moment of their coming so that he may be rid of them and start as I shall start within the body of my people—dreaming of God, of God, of nothing but God.'

Fraser tapped him in the stomach with the head of his torch: 'I asked you what your game was, Keller?'

'When the girl died, she forgave me. She had enlightenment, she forgave me before she died because she knew what I was going to do. She saw that I was necessary, but I did not see I was necessary until she had gone.' He was very relaxed, leaning back on some silent conclusion.

Friese said: 'I'll get him up to the flat.'

This penetrated: it must have shone, flashed briefly upon those dark apprehensions which had remained unsaid. The German roused himself:

'No injections, none of your drugs or E.C.T. I'll not be mutilated or analysed but keep the dreams which transcend all dreaming. Under questioning or drugs you'll get from me only what I reject, nothing will fall live into your hands——'

'For Christ's sake muffle him, Friese.'

But he would not be stopped; his words rang and echoed from the hard surfaces: 'She was there for me, Doctor Chance. A great truth, the end of all dreaming, the beginning of prayer. I kneeled *myself,* deep down inside myself I kneeled, and I said we must all be forgiven for the torture of our dreams.'

'You screwball,' said Fraser. 'What the hell have you done with my Arab boy?'

Like some great animal fighting for stall room, he shouldered Friese out of the lift and confronted Chance and Marcovicz in the very small space. His short arm came up, torch in hand, and caught the Jew heavily on the temple. The prisoner straightened, his hand locking immediately upon the fat neck.

'Don't you forget it!' he shouted. 'You see a man who has torn the temple veil and shouted the forbidden Name in the place of desolation. And you too, you ape! I could send you where I sent her if there'd been but one prayer in your life; but you're not ready for it, you're not ready for release.'

The revolver, unseen until this moment, produced with dexterity in the climax of embarrassment, was fired three times near to the centre of the chest whose ribs were pressing against Chance's own; and over the face of Marcovicz spread a great dusk. He smiled foolishly, his lips parting right back over his ageing teeth and then struggling, as though autonomously live, into the beginning of an enunciation which was itself lost in the rising of his cough. His body faltered against the veering of his mind, falling away from the panoply of channels and fibres which held the two together; at the end of his veined arms the thumbs reappeared slowly from the folds of his victim's flesh. As his knees gave way he slid cleanly to his haunches on the floor of the lift, his lips first dewed then cataracting blood and oxygen on to his feet.

Fraser backed out and slammed the gates behind Friese.

'Take him up!'

With a jerk which rolled the dying man's head on its thick neck, the lift ascended to the MacGradys' flat.

Saturday

CHANCE came through the night and the morning suddenly as the sun which lay all about him in the room. There were heavy plaques of it on his bed weighing down the coverlet, and more on the wall bright and white as the beams thrown through the motes and particles curling in the air before lakes of looking-glass in the wardrobe doors.

When Friese came in at some time, the sun took him as it had taken the edge of the coverlet, the mirrors and the snowiness of the pillow to show them for what fiery things they were, held together in the heat of a moment; for Friese, walking unknowingly through this light, was illumined in every particular: each hair reflected it like high pine-needles, his face round the green caverns of his spectacles blushing whiter than live coals as he leaned over Chance to examine his pupils. When his hand pulled Chance's wrist out on to the sheet and felt for the radial pulse, the fingers of both shone and Friese's nails were as clear onyx.

'You'll need blood,' he said. 'I tried to get it from the Misericordia this morning; but they're conserving supplies . . . Do you hear what I'm saying?'

Chance questioned this without speaking. He saw the wonder of the door reopening into the sunlight, its paint icy and blinding with George Fraser emerging from behind it.

'How is he?'

'Happy. It's the injection. Fortunately, I was able to check his haemoglobin this morning; it was just forty-five per cent. I've been telling him that he's got to have some blood—and quickly.'

'Is he still bleeding?'

'Probably, but not disastrously.'

The Australian hummed a bar or two of some ballad, abandoning it suddenly:

'What'd he say?'

There was again a considerable pause which was allowed to progress without interruption, not even with a whistled or intoned sound; so that the speakers in their abstraction, reporting so little of their preoccupation, might have dissolved in such light. For the volume of the silence as of the light was so abundant that it dwarfed the temporal, and rolling over into short pauses like waves into pools made them one with the ocean which contained them.

The gentle voice of Friese replied: 'He's not with us yet. I very much doubt if we shall get any sense out of him at all until he's had a transfusion—at the least some glucose-saline. D'you think there's any possibility of contacting the hospital again?'

'Depends on the Frogs.'

'Are they making any progress?'

'You bet! They've mopped up the Avenue Grande and the best part of the European section; but they're having trouble with the churches and round about the mosques. Noub'dy wants to take responsibility for any religious fracas at a time like this. Duhamel rang through to say they're counting on having the Soccos and the Casbah sorted out within twenty-four hours.'

Chance opened his eyes as the fat man sat into the sunlight on his bed. He saw it fall back on him to search out his pallid skin, his ruby nostrils and the broken veins of his cheeks; his white hair burned smokelessly in the transfiguration.

Again he sang fragmentarily, affixing the exhortation to the middle of a bar:

'You've got to pull him through, Xavier. I don't want him fading out like so many of the jacks I've seen.'

And now they over-spoke in the expansions of a latitude they could not measure; Friese remonstrating:

'I'd rather you took that chair, if you don't mind . . .'

'Religious jacks die easy when they think they're meeting up with what they never had . . .'

'The least disturbance may renew his haemorrhage.'

'MacGrady, for instance, was what you might call reluctant to live or die; but once it was offered on a plate would be the sort of jack who'd curl his toes in a London hospital.'

'Would you mind moving off the bed?'

'Couldn't you fix him up with something like they would Outback when there's only a vinegar bottle and a bowl of goat's milk?'

'At this stage, only intravenously.'

Fraser's eyes were sapphires under the black brows as they encountered those of Chance.

'He don't see anything,' he protested remotely. 'I'm looking at him but he sees no more than a dead fish. Why don't you get one of those Frog doctors to come across in an ambulance from the Misericordia?'

His eyes were not much older than a child's; it was strange to see them beneath the virility of the writhing brows, so much blueness and light over creases. Even the white crescents of ageing in the lower half of the irises shining like new sickles.

His face was withdrawn and then his black shoulders as he went thumping back into the dazzle of the window. A gun was firing regularly out there, its noise like more gobs of light; and behind it, bullet sparks tracing sound patterns in the hugeness of the outside world.

'MacGrady's lost out on it all round. When he hears how this cow got his wife garrotted for him, he'll become a proposition, because, bar the pleasures of forgiving him, he won't have anything to come in for any more. MacGrady could be a strong man again.'

Friese rolled back the stormy sheet and laid hands on Chance's stomach.

'I talk and think in a simple way,' said Fraser lighting a small cigar.

'I said nothing.'

'You said a lot with your upper lip. I know this claptrap of yours by heart and I don't like it. I'm too old for it. What I'm trying to tell you, Friese, is that if you let the Doc die too, the Yank'll get another attack of monastery-fever, that is to say Columb MacGrady will drowse about in London and go to the priests. We'll all be left owed our money.'

'I understand you very well—if you don't mind I'd rather you didn't smoke in here, Fraser. I can't take the risk of having him coughing.' His hands were quite evidently doing something on the remote surface of Chance's body; a whisper of activity.

'I respect your forthrightness,' he continued, 'but you must believe me when I tell you that our definitions have very precise and practical meanings. When I define MacGrady as a psychopath whose inadequacies are partially compensated by his religious conditioning, I'm anticipating his future behaviour with more than intuition.'

'Men are men, you'll never explain them by dog-talk. Look, Friese, you ought to get yourself a job in a kennels. I don't criticise what you do with your hands but when you get down on your hands and knees in the straw to explain what goes on in a man's head, you know less than a nut like Keller who started high and not low.'

Friese ignored this, his hands continuing their examination, he said:

'There's a good deal of guarding but I'm pretty sure he hasn't perforated.'

'I want MacGrady back here, and if Chance dies on us there won't be anything to bring him back.'

'My dear Fraser, quite apart from the challenge of a haematemesis in these circumstances and the psychiatric consideration, my own interest in what I'm owed ensures my bona fides.'

'Whose is this?' Chance heard the rattle of the rosary as one of them picked it up.

'Columb's, isn't it?'

'I imagine so.'

'Down under in the winter I used to catch myself looking into the fire, watching the flames and the hot coal and the colour changes until I forgot it was a fire for a few minerts. And when I came back to myself they used to say, "George's been praying."'

'Dogs are great fire-watchers too, Fraser.'

'A dog doesn't know what a fire is. Well then, how the hell could a dog know what a fire isn't?'

'We'll see. I don't need to tell you that in his present state our friend on the bed is more of an animal than a man. Such an animal should respond to his bone.'

It hung on its strong links with its crucifix swinging in the light. A thing of wood and metal no less wondrous than the door but as nothing to the hands which held it between incandescent fingertips. When it fell on to his chest, Chance felt as little as though it had fallen through him into some deep cavity.

'No visible response.'

'And what does that prove?'

'There are many possibilities.'

'I said before and I say it again, I don't like possibilities. They didn't have them when I was young. People were either for or against and I'll tell you what, Xavier; you'll never make a good grafter until you go for certainties like the police.'

'What is the time, please?'

'It's late, that's all. How long are you going to go on mucking about in here? We've got a lot to do down in the flat?'

'I should leave all that to Hasan.' Friese was filling a syringe with light. 'Have they got the fires under control?'

'There's nothing to them so far, so long as they don't start in on the churches.'

'They may well do just that. You remember the Peron riots in Buenos Aires some years ago?'

'Paper talk!'

'The tabernacles are a very powerful draw in group disturbances.'

Y

'—— groups!' The Australian's voice was weary again. 'I'm going to have meself a shower.'

The door shone for a moment and then closed softly as the Doctor swabbed Chance's right arm with something cold. The needle slipped into him, the plunger was depressed and the syringe withdrawn.

Friese was amused, whispering or even laughing a little to himself:

'I would like to save your life, Chance, because I do value my hands, whatever may be his opinion of my head.'

He must have accepted the silence as an interrogative; for, as he went away, he added, 'Quite apart from that, it is long time since I was involved in anything so simple.'

Chance lay hearing the same gun firing in the town hollow down by the sea. Rifle-fire, very small and bright, was more frequent now and machine-guns called from different distances like birds in a wood. All the woods he had ever known, at noon at dusk at nightfall, were remembered without joy: people moving through them, their gone voices and glimpses, the expectations and presentiments they had roused.

One wood in particular was distinct for him where they had often gone before her death and which he had continued to visit occasionally in winter when the traffic beyond its boundaries was slack. The moon rising and owls: forests of dead bracken bowed between the pines: black horizons.

Friese had returned. He chattered a little, not sure of the extent of his solitude in the still room with its still man:

'It might interest you to know that I spent the night in here. As a child I was subject to asthma and when my mother stayed in my nursery throughout the night I indulged in certain fantasies . . .'

In the light Friese was most beautiful, cut sharp about the head, his nose clearly aligned to his brow and chin. He had taken off his spectacles and the rays swarmed about his eyebrows scintillating like the cut edges of crystal wherever his flesh began.

In many gatherings people had turned against the light and contributed to it substantially. A thousand occasions or more and many more thousands of people moving through different lucencies all his life; light from the sea, stars, electricity and lightning flashes; from the flames of candles, foreign climate and the lights of blackout.

'But do not think that as a professional man I've ever had much respect for death. That was before our time, Chance.'

This reached Chance, returning all those living who in association had become the horror of death and the dying. He walked the hospitals, the mortuaries and the cells. He remembered the darkness of Dublin and the brash 'residence' as a student: death between tea and supper, consultations in corridors, the words thrown back over the busy shoulder:

'Oh six days at the outside,' and, 'Doctor, we'd better put that leg in the deep freeze, it might be needed.'

'What we like are plenty of burnings at two guineas a time.'

Mr. Blunt had once instructed: 'She is eighty and she is disturbing my thyroids, give her another three grains, Doctor Chance.'

Then much later at that first prison: 'He left a hundred and twenty thousand, most of it to the boy who shopped him.' But Sims on his first house job had said, 'She's dying; let's see what's happened to her reflexes.'

Friese reminisced, 'I played Rugby for Bart's in 1925, Chance. That was the beginning of my career; but strangely enough I made my money by specialising in machines, as a clinical integrator, an interpreter. It was only in 1935 that I took up psychiatry in Wimpole Street.'

The little girl drowned in the Liffey had sand in her groins and hair.

'But don't think that I am sufficiently old-fashioned to consider death merely a clinical disaster. A study of it might be very rewarding. In fact I'll admit I'm surprised that no one apart from the Nazis has so far troubled to investigate what I might call "Terminal Phenomena." Taste does not enter into these things, so I suppose it need not be left to the Russians.

After all, my dear Chance, we owe much of our knowledge of embryology to the indiscretions of the aristocracy. Which reminds me that I believe I heard your own wife was dead? You live in reduced circumstances, I should say. I personally could not imagine a further reduction for the asthenic type. Though I once made the mistake of believing Medicine was a gentleman's occupation, I don't think I'd ever have entered the Prison Service. But turning to larger issues, I'm not suggesting that your conversion was due only to a somewhat drab existence. I have read my William James! I'll go so far as to say that the moment it might even be more helpful than the very small quantities of morphine I may give you. I say "might be" advisedly, because it would be rash to ignore the effects of such conditioning when cerebral anaemia's as severe as it must be in this case. In fact, it's quite likely you may be wishing most fervently for those eternal rewards in which you've come to believe. On the other hand, for all a mere rationalist can know, you may be profoundly afraid . . .'

He was gone. All of the sunlight was gone: the bright room and fold of sheet, even the remote sensation of his own weight on the mattress.

The isolation was complete; as complete, he saw, as that conferred at birth; but more terrible. Dying, he knew he was about to be identified for ever, reborn full of time as no baby is, into a life without shadows; and resentment was so much the resentment of terror that, enabled, he would have shrieked his way out, as a baby wails itself into survival. But the approaching outrage held him initially paralysed and voiceless, unable to formulate any word.

He seemed to be disintegrating from the centre, the distrusted but essential identity splintering against something, fragmenting into separate terrors, faceless and idiotic: a madness of fear rather than a fear of madness.

By will alone he reached some remembrance of words; a gibberish of prayer as ugly as cowardice. Behind the words he spoke he sensed laughter, his own and greater . . . Holy Mary, Mother of God . . . of God . . . of God . . . Mother now and

in the hour of our death. MacGrady demanding and confusing: mad Marcovicz . . .

Our Father . . . Pater Noster qui es in caelis . . . in caelis
. . . in heaven . . . Our Father, if you were ever there . . . Holy
Mary, Mother of God . . . And to end in what had seemed a
beginning . . . A vexation welling up in him. Tyghe and Sax
sneering at nothing because they had perfected their knowledge of it . . . and Anna never knowing with what flame she
had played . . .

Now and in the hour of our death, he repeated. Now and in
the hour of our death . . . In the hour. Given life, one more
instant, he would speak his contempt. Not his, but more than
his, towering. Contempt depersonalised, original, satanic . . .

Hallowed be Thy Name, he managed, Holy . . . The forbidden Name. Love causing such hatred, such wrath. Fraser
middle-aged, the dying youth, the deformed child, corrupting:
his beauty an insult. MacGrady stooping beneath Marcovicz,
trying to divide the kingdom . . . Oh Father . . . Abba! For-
saker!

Wet with the death wetness and breathless in his flight, his
lips dried by it, he returned sick to the iniquity of the sunlight
in the empty room.

Some time later, perhaps in the early evening, Friese returned as a star returns to its accustomed place when a curtain
is withdrawn; high, stable, performing some slow evolution,
some revolution to be measured only by the world's turning,
there against the night sky and not to be glimpsed by day, but
created and existent in the artefact of the temporal. He
pressed Chance back into the pillow and being an immaculate
man, wiped the wetness from his hand as it left his forehead.

'I'd be grateful, Chance, if you'd continue to keep still while
I enter a vein.'

'Confession!'

'You must try and help me. I've managed to make up some
glucose-saline which I'll give you in your left arm.'

'Friese, I must be rid of certain things.'

'But you have to keep still.'

'Hear them.'

'I understand only too well.' He was working away some-where to the left of him. 'You experienced a fugue of some sort, a depressive transference. I'm afraid your haemorrhage—if we don't get some saline into you, Chance, I'm afraid you've a very short time to live.'

'Hear me!'

'In a few minutes I'll be entirely at your service. One must be practical and put first things first!' Then, as though he had accused himself of exasperation:

'Of course, if it relieves you to recount your anxieties, I will, if you like, be an ear.'

Panting, Chance lay as between one accident and the next.

'You should realise,' Friese added, 'that it will be unnecessary for you to unburden yourself to anyone if I fail to refresh your plasma. It must be done cautiously; we do not want to trigger off another haemorrhage. But we may still secure either blood or packed cells before morning, and in that event no time would be lost in the setting up of the apparatus.'

In his mind he was a staked man looking left at the trifle of the sunlight, right at the dwarfed doctor whose little skull was a definition against the door. Chance saw his ingenuity, contrivance, engineering. An inverted milk-bottle corked and affixed to a lamp standard, a red rubber tube fitted into the cork with a pen filler and a hypodermic needle attached to its end. Beside it there was a dressing-case with a bowl of pledgets and a bottle of acriflavine. Feeling his arm held and swabbed he tried to enter his protagonist's activity but found it impossible to relate such chemistry to reality. He thought: I must be very careful and explain my need intelligibly.

'Whether fugue or not, Friese, it was there. I saw the desert I never entered. Something coming out of it that was there from the first. I've realised that I've been starving. There was darkness from the edge extending all the way into the centre and, if you can understand me, at the centre of the centre there was a sharp light. Please listen to me, Friese.'

'I'm listening most attentively.'

'I may never get so far as the centre of the centre because I may not want to. That is my terror; there seemed always to be so much time that I've not been in the habit of wanting to. Well now that I can say it please let me say that I do want to, that I despair of the uses I made of time when it was so exact. You must hear me.'

'All this will pass, Chance. What you are experiencing is no more than a profound psychic disassociation. If you do your best to co-operate we shall soon banish it by transfusing you.'

'It wasn't particular acts, Friese. Please don't imagine I'm worried by my sins. It's too late for that, it's what I learned from them. I feel as cheated as Marcovicz and haven't his excuses. Nothing ever came true for me and I developed a habit of the most subtle hatred from the getting of my pleasures. Friese, my desires were so thin they'll no longer hide my loss. MacGrady had faith but I had hope as well and I knew what I was doing. They were right to trust me but they can't help me now. For God's sake absolve me from my hatred. Give me absolution.'

'It's quite impossible to get a priest for you at the moment, Chance.'

'In an emergency, it mightn't matter. Anyone might do so long as they had the intention.'

Friese sighed. 'In that case, if it's of any help to you, you're absolved.' He gripped Chance's hand. 'Perhaps you will try to recall your own practice. Let us seek safety in the rational. Don't think that I am sneering at you, it is simply that our viewpoints differ. Please recollect the facts one by one; a haemorrhage, anoxaemia, considerable vaso-vagal tension. Under the circumstances we've no choice but to pursue the medical as opposed to the surgical remedy: rest, replacement of fluid, sedation, reassurance, and rest again. These facts, Chance, since they are experiential, are what you should think about. They will keep you sane. If you recount them to yourself one at a time you will be considerably helped.'

'Time,' Chance repeated. With more coherence he began the Angelic Salutation again.

'Precisely. A little more time and we'll get you into a hospital, but you must have the will to survive and if you regress into the nightmares of your childhood you'll lose that will.'

Fraser came in. Chance saw him in his bathing-robe of rose-coloured towelling.

'How's it go, Xavier?'

'We've just made our confession in somewhat general terms.' Friese did not laugh. 'I believe I gave him absolution.'

'Absolution? MacGrady's moan?'

'These things help. He was remarkably coherent, very tense.'

'You're not worried, then?'

'Not unduly. Initially I found his intelligibility disquieting as it can be a bad sign. However, I've established one point in our favour. He does not now wish to die.' He added courteously, 'Do you, Chance?'

But Chance was trying to complete the act of contrition; hearing the direction of their conversation as though it had been the muttered Latin of the prayer of absolution.

'Don't you believe it!'

'Nevertheless——'

'What's a religious jack like him to come back for now you've kidded him up with forgiveness? Would you want to come back to MacGrady after what's happened? No wife, no money, lousy health, a job in a prison? For Christ's sake, Xavier, why didn't you tell him he'd have to hang on for a priest?'

'Apparently there's an escape clause of some sort and quite apart from that, the phrase, "to be frightened to death," is still occasionally a clinical reality.'

'——clinical! Is he still bleeding?'

'A little, I imagine. The important thing at the moment is to get a few pints of fluid into him.'

'Well, I hope you know what you're doing. I've managed to get a cable off to MacGrady in Chance's name telling him he'll have to hang on for news of Anna.'

'You're withholding the news of her death?'

'Only for the present. If we decide to hang on for a bit, he'll get it through the press in a few days' time, or we could tip off the American Consulate. It's a nice point, it's got to be played carefully.'

'Carefully! My dear Fraser, news of that kind after a major operation——'

'I told you before, I'm watching points. With a man like MacGrady it might be the one thing that'd pull him through and back to the Zone. He'd want to know all about it. He'd chase up Chance here to jaw with him. They'd spend the rest of their lives working it out and forgiving themselves.'

Chance wanted to speak but could not. The last paragraph of MacGrady's letter was in his mind, the words clear and unequivocal: '. . . my wife, Anna, whom of course I married primarily for that reason. Therefore, living I shall live in the grace of God alone, and dying, I shall die for the lack of it, which they tell me is death in any case.'

Friese insisted: 'It's a question of timing, both from our point of view and MacGrady's.'

'Who's to know? You don't, Xavier, and I don't; and when I'm in doubt I hold the floor and wait for something to give.'

They should be told that it was unimportant, that the fact of her death was enough. The eagle had stooped. MacGrady had bargained for the taste of grace, for its proof within himself, for time to know that he was capable of heaven. The austere answer awaited him.

Fraser said, 'If you let Chance snuff out on us, Mac-Grady'll never get the real truth now that I've had to plug Keller.'

'Ah yes, Keller. It occurred to me it might be a good idea to run his body down to the Casbah after dark. If it were made unidentifiable, a corpse more or less would pass unnoticed when the International Force gets in and starts to clean the place up. It would be as well where MacGrady is concerned for his death to be unconfirmed for the present.'

Chance was able to speak: 'He won't care.'

He sensed their astonishment; but it was a small thing, an interruption to them in what they were saying, and for him an interruption in what he had to say. He experienced a simplicity of knowing which took for its expression so many images and words that the one syllable he would have said became an elaborate approximation.

'The desert is a good death. He is freed.'

Receding once again he heard their discussion.

'What's that. What's he say?'

'He is brooding about Keller.'

'No, he means MacGrady.'

'. . . curious transference of identity.'

'. . . religious jacks . . .'

'. . . desire to unify concepts and experience . . . Terminally they are usually more afraid of the deic than the anti-deic.'

'Poor buck!'

His anger was returning but it was his own mingled with sorrow. He felt it strongly, a surge in which he lay without fear.

Time passed and when he next became conscious, Friese was saying:

'The will to live has been laughed out of court; but it is still a factor.'

Chance heard this very distinctly and without astonishment. He lay within his body, dearly familiar, and awaited the Australian's reply. Fraser was yawning, yawning, his hands and face, his whole warm bulk pausing in the weight of its fatigue.

'It's gone two and it looks like a dud graft. I think you'd better get yourself some sleep,' said Fraser. 'It's going to add up to a whole lot of complications having him croak here with you attending him. Pity you ever took it on.'

'I don't think so.'

'You should've called in one of the Frenchmen before he got too bad.'

'On the contrary, his pulse has improved considerably in

the last half-hour and fortunately he has a sound heart—always a vital factor in severe haemorrhage.'

There was a second silence like a yawn, as though the whole world had lifted its hand and swayed from momentary stupor into steadiness, recollecting itself.

Friese said, 'The ambulance will almost certainly be late. Perhaps it would be a good idea to give them another ring in the morning.'

Chance opened his eyes and intervened abruptly. 'Where are you sending me?'

They were men unaccustomed to surprise, they had not the habit of astonishment and were in any event so much at personal odds that like so many incompatible men they welcomed whatever might be comical.

'My dear Chance,' said Friese at last, 'a short time ago you were very nearly dead. Would you bear this in mind, please?'

Chance caught Fraser's eyes. 'I'd like to know where you're sending me.'

'Tell him, Friese.'

'Into the Catholic hospital.' Friese smirked a little after the manner of Colonel Tyghe. 'I was fortunate enough to secure a bed, my dear Chance, through one of the nursing sisters. I did not tell her you were a Catholic as they tend to be more interested in Mohammedans there.'

Chance asked Fraser: 'Is the riot over?'

But the Australian did not reply, being still apparently heavy over the earlier exchanges.

Friese said precisely, 'There are a number of fires but they're mainly under control.'

'I can't hear anything.'

'And you won't,' said Fraser. 'They've got French troops in the town. The place is packed with journalists. If you hear anything it'll be the sound of booze and brothels.'

'About MacGrady,' Chance persisted. 'I heard you talking I think. Did you decide to cable him about the death of Anna, or not?'

Fraser: 'No.'

Friese: 'Not advisable.'

'Why not?'

'Because,' said Fraser, 'we've only the word of a nut case for it. Ten minutes ago some Arab got on the telephone to Hasan. It's not likely, I'll bet, but it seems there could've been some mistake.'

Chance tried to move himself, but succeeded only in raising his head from the pillow: 'A mistake? You mean she may not be dead at all?'

'We don't know.'

'When I was last conscious you were sure of it. What do you believe now?'

The question was ignored. The big man was pale, he was sweating under the light round which many night-flying insects fluttered and burned. His anger and impatience surfaced.

'We don't go through all that again. You're more than sick, Chance, you may be dying. What's it matter to you what we believe?'

'It's MacGrady,' Chance said, 'if she's alive he'll never know that she was dead. He'll believe he's won.'

Friese came nearer to him. 'I'm afraid you're a little confused. If Mrs MacGrady is alive she cannot have died.'

'But Fraser told me she was dead.'

'We should have kept our mouths shut,' Fraser said, 'Chance, noub'dy's saying anything because they don't know.'

Chance, ignoring this, did not intend an accusation. He was only incredulous of his inability to abandon his arraignment of circumstance.

'*I* believed it. For me she was dead. We all believed it.'

'As Fraser has explained, we are still unsure,' put in Friese.

'But we'll find out in the morning all right,' Fraser concluded.

'That will be too late for MacGrady. Don't you see that he'll have nothing left?'

'He'll have himself, you silly cow.'

'For MacGrady that's not enough,' Chance replied. 'If he recovers he'll imagine that he's bargained successfully, and that's impossible for a man who believes in God, as he does.'

Fraser pushed his hands into the pink pockets of the towelling. Pushing them down hard, pushing his whole body deeper on to the floor.

'Oh for Christ's sake! What have you done to him, Friese? Can't you give him something to get us all a night's rest?'

'Just a moment. What are you trying to tell us, Chance?'

'It's MacGrady. He staked his life on a bargain which it's difficult even for a Christian to understand. When he recovers he'll expect to feel and be different; but he won't. His reason will be endangered. We should let him know that we believe her to be dead because then he will be forced to believe in his own grace as well as in the Church's.'

Fraser began to laugh, turning his response away from Chance and directing it at Friese. 'That's good! We'll put his name to the cable as from one friend to another: "Your wife murdered. God bless you, Chance." That'll encourage him on his bed of sickness.' He shouted suddenly, his face bursting with blood in the swollen veinules. 'That's a pretty joke!'

Chance lay still, his anger mounting.

Friese said: 'It's subtle, but there are psychiatric parallels.'

'——parallels!'

'I think that in the Catholic position the Jungians might perhaps allow the argument a certain force.'

'I'm not interested in Jungians,' said Fraser. 'If you think he might be talking sense, ask him which is most likely to get us our money: Anna dead or Anna alive?'

'If she's dead or he ever believed her dead,' Chance said, 'I should imagine you'll get everything you're owed. But if she's alive and he hears of her death only as a story over a glass of whisky, I don't think you'll ever get a cent.'

'Back that up, but don't give us any jargon!'

Friese: 'You really make things very difficult for one, Fraser.'

Chance said, 'All I can say is that if MacGrady gets away

with this he'll have even less reason for faith, and therefore for morality.'

Fraser was loud. 'That's good! Don't you know he's been sidestepping the lot ever since he lost his first wife?'

Friese was watching Chance, but he said nothing.

'If he believed he'd lost his second wife through his own presumption, he might be reconverted,' said Chance. 'He'd never forget; he'd be driven back into knowing himself a child of God, and for a Christian that is the only sanity.'

Fraser was flat down on his heels, his head bent so that his chin rested on his breast.

'Kids!' he said heavily.

Friese made some small movement: he cleared his throat as though he were about to speak, but before he could do so Fraser said:

'By your ideas I'm a very wicked man, Chance, because I go for kids?'

Friese: 'Really, Fraser, I don't think this is the moment to indulge in recrimination.'

Fraser: 'You shut up, Xavier, I've heard all your cock before, I want to hear Chance's.'

Chance said, 'What does it matter what anyone thinks?'

'I'm asking you!' Fraser began to laugh. 'You might convert me from your deathbed. Go on, you tell me just how wicked I am, wanting kids the way I do.'

'Your inclinations,' Chance said, 'are one thing, your actions are another. In prison the only people who'd have any time for you would be the psychiatrists and padres——'

'I'm not in prison.'

'—and they,' Chance concluded, 'would treat you as though you were a diseased child yourself; because, essentially, you are.'

Friese tittered, 'You've got your answer, Fraser.'

The Australian ignored him: 'You'd say I was a child of God too? Me and MacGrady?'

'Yes.'

'All the Arabs, the lot?'

'Yes.'

'What a family!'

Unwisely Friese put in: 'It's a Christian projection of the archetypal father-figure.'

'——archetypal!' Fraser brooded over Chance for a moment and then turned to Friese. 'Forgetting all that, what d'you think about this cable, Xavier?'

'I think he has something. We must remember that they share the group reactions of their religion and have the advantage when it comes to predicting each other's behaviour.'

'Oh to hell with that!' Fraser broke away as above him a large moth circling the light-source broke and fell twitching to the counterpane. 'What do we put in the cable, Chance?'

'Are you going to send it?'

'What do we put in it?'

'Say, "Anna missing, believed killed in the rioting last night. Writing from hospital where I am detained."'

'And you want us to put your name?'

'Of course.'

Fraser moved over towards the door. 'We've been in two minds all along. I'm going to send it.' He looked once more at Chance as he said from the encirclement of his secret pre-occupation. 'After all, what've we got to lose?'

There was a brief silence after the door had closed behind him, and then Friese turned with relief to his dressing-case to select a syringe as Chance drew up one of his sleeves.

Sunday

A BELL was striking. There was that clatter which is the aftermath of disturbance in individuals, in families, towns, or nations. He remembered many men on many mornings in the prison hospital; their resumed good faces, soaped ears from the first shaving: the delicacy of their skins cleansed from the toxins of violence or despair as they said, 'All right today'; and stood there like the man whose name had been legion.

Under the continuing bell, the town was looking to itself. By elbowing up on the pillows he could see the topmost shags of fire-smoke from the buildings and churches which had burned: smoke without flame dispersing over the harbour and sea, hanging high over the Miramar and the Villa Hutton. Although he could not sit high he could guess at the reflections of whiteness from the Casbah, the returning shuffle in the soccos, the haphazard mingling of populations, troops, donkeys, Bren carriers, police and veiled women: the different motions of very many tongues contriving the sounds of their languages as the bell went on above them and the muezzins prepared for the noon summons.

Somewhere picks rang, shovels grated in rubble as the walls of gutted buildings were brought down. Ambulance sirens diminished into distances or approached hesitantly like bird-calls in some forest of stone, to cease suddenly, mysteriously silenced at the last. Greedily, he awaited events within the frame of the window: the advent of aeroplanes to pick up or deposit more journalists, the announcements of shipping, even the grapple of argument from the road below. But save for the drifting smoke, the square of sky beyond the win-

z   369

dow remained void: such aeroplanes as he heard never
appearing.

Without impatience he cast wider than the window, guessing at the desert on the far side of the snow-covered moun-
tains, his mind moving over the South beyond the increasing
aridities to the true sand whose waves moved heavily against
the walls of foundering settlements. He thought of Pearl
returning to her mother: a journey through many tribes that
might take her so long she might find both her parents
dead on her arrival. He thought uneasily of London and
MacGrady; briefly of Colonel Tyghe *en route* for Cairo,
of the Moores, perhaps already returning to the Zone,
amused.

But beyond it all he came back to the prison, to small
details: the fish which had to be fed in the tank in the big
ward, the men themselves who watched them so observantly,
preventing cannibalism, infanticide, anticipating many other
destructions within the cleansed water. He remembered many
prisoners individually and the dead good cheer of all officers at
all times, his own sense of relief when the outer gate, the inner
gate, the hospital gate and the office door had all closed upon
him and the men started to file in to the corridor.

From these thoughts his attention returned to his surroundings again when he noticed the wireless-noise from the bottom
flat. It was playing loudly: Arab music, the susurration of
stroked vellum, wires and little bells sounding beneath the
giant bell of the tolling church. There were frequent interrup-
tions from the Algerian announcer in French, bulletins of the
riot in the Zone:

*'Les troubles dans la Zone Internationale sont presque
apaisés. Le Général Pléssis a annoncé que les morts et les
blessés sont minimes . . . Le franc restera stable.'*

Then more music: a woman singing in Arabic, her voice
scaling higher than the smoke, long-drawn, extending thinly
into some chromatic stratosphere.

On his return to the prison, he thought, there would be a
resumption of the interviews at his desk in the hospital office:

the medical orderly waiting outside, the prisoner mustering his tongue to find the words, the credible lies, the ghost of truth, as the government clock clicked from minute to half-minute and on to minute again. And of these searchings, long discoveries, chatters, confessionals, living autopsies, all Jacob Marcovicz had said in retrospect was: 'Take the doctor from behind his desk, I say, and show me a man.'

Ah, but not yet, he thought. The desk, the doors, regulations, a constituted order, speech: all manner of doing, fumbling, alternations of light:

'The nights do pass,' he remembered, 'and rise again the days.'

He demanded many days, months, years. Time for amendment of life.

Friese had said the ambulance would arrive at noon and it was noon now. The bell for Mass at the church which he could not identify had stumbled against silence and fallen. But another arose, deeper, a little ominous; a tenor bell striking twelve now as it had struck for him eight days earlier when he was sitting outside the bus station waiting for Marcovicz to bring back the tickets.

He counted its chimes carefully. ONE for sorrow. TWO for— blessed be sorrow and joy. 'I am a man, Chance,' he remembered, 'privileged to Heaven and Hell.' For MacGrady at this moment it would be striking ten across the river at Westminster, or nine? He could not remember which. THREE. 'At the third stroke it will be—precisely.'

MacGrady between his sheets physically helpless as the result of disease in one lung, as he himself lay most weak in consequence of some minute gastric imperfection. And at this moment, suspended between the two Times, the cable widowing, FOUR at the eleventh hour.

Well, it was done; and not impulsively. It had seemed, for some reason he nearly knew, to be right at the time; essential and of great consequence, not just in view of MacGrady's letter, nor because of the simplicity of Death, but for some

other combination of factors which he could not quite recall
. . . A little uneasily, with the beginnings of self-criticism, his
mind moved on . . .

The Arab was right to cross the sands for his dead camel,
to do what he believed to be good. There might even be justification for Marcovicz: an honest man driven to madness by
untruth. But MacGrady sported with Truth. FIVE 'I know
what's right——' 'He knows what's right——' 'I just don't do
it, that's all.' They had both said it.

At the time I insisted on the cable, I did not remember
that. SIX What did I remember then? What were my motives?
Dead or alive I wanted nothing from her at that time, nothing
that either of them could give me for myself, not even justification. But my God, SEVEN I did want him to have more
time. For what do we know but our promises of Love?

He had asked her that before she was supposed dead as his
own wife was dead, as so many of his loves EIGHT were dead
of his attempt to honour such promises. Dead to him because
he had not known that love is no more than a perpetual
promise NINE like the sound of a bell ringing out of the void,
out of the fullness of Heaven: a ringing whose waves hit
shore and broke—breaking down remorselessly by foam
wilder than dreams.

'Ah, les chiens dévorants!' Parents and children: the young
patricide he had attended in the condemned cell stubbing out
his cigarettes on the bedside paint, TEN a row of scorched
circles measuring the hours . . .

One man only he had known who had broken free: a
mystic: seeming to stand those whom he loved away from
him, standing himself well back in the habit of his Order and
praising dispassionately by such interest, such affection that
they grew most beautiful in an illumination not their own nor
his. ELEVEN . . .

'Why, Chance!'

He had not heard her coming in nor coming along the hall
sharply on hard heels, straight in through the door in black,
wearing a pearl brooch. No warning. Only those words.

And so blanched in so much sun. The light rolling off her face, dripping like water from the planes of her hair, lodging in the pearl cross and sinking in deep into the deep black of the coat and skirt. Her eyes so amazed beneath the uncreased forehead; concern in the dark mouth with the lips so darkened that they might themselves have been in mourning.

She moved quickly round his bed, curving round it, dragging vortices of light behind her blackness and pallor. Quite scentless. Grave. Risen, it momentarily seemed, from some tomb unplaced and hollowed out he could not say by whom. But risen into such a very great waste of light that she had the reality of an hallucination.

'They didn't warn you?'

He was looking from his fixed position, not able yet to move even his head without great effort; seeing her devoid of association and therefore as bewildering as first love.

'They never warned you I was on my way? I never thought to ask them. I just naturally assumed they would. Why, you must have been terrified to see me coming in like a ghost. Hurrying. I hurried all the way ever since first thing this morning. I just can't understand them not telling you because I spoke to George much earlier. Do you mean to say they didn't tell you a thing?'

'They told me the ambulance was coming.'

'But it must have been a *shock*! Your face when you—I mean, when I came in. You thought I was dead?'

'I wasn't sure. Yes, I believe I did.' One of her eyes was a little pink, he saw. Dust? or she had rubbed it on her way across from the Palace. A few minutes ago probably, perhaps even while he was counting. He had reached eleven; never even heard the twelfth stroke; and at the realisation was so troubled that he admitted:

'I forgot.'

'You forgot? What did you forget?'

'I was counting the clock striking twelve, waiting for the ambulance. I must have missed one. I got as far as eleven and then you came in.'

She looked at him measuring something, her eyes suddenly gauzed again with calculation before she laughed aloud: 'Oh, Chance, I disturbed you! You were all set for the ambulance man and it was me?'

He smiled back at her remembering his *fou-rire* with Mac-Grady on the second day. But that particular laughter was very dead; nothing would ever be quite so solemn again.

He said, 'Tell me yourself——'

'Oh I will.'

'——exactly what did happen.'

'Well it was Magda. She wanted to see you very badly; unfinished business maybe, or to nurse you, I just don't know. But you must have made an impression there. I felt so niggard leaving you that if I'd been in a stronger position, we might have fought about it: my duty, *her* affection. I really did feel so very mean that to try to stop her would only have made me look meaner—I *did* care how I looked. And then that crazy Keller, he was in the car they sent, he butted in and he said he'd bring Magda back here; that he'd forgiven her for leaving him and all that; one of his long speeches about money—no, diamonds—and freedom. So nobody raised any objection, and with him as escort she was less frightened even than before, just laughed at the idea of armour-plating and automobiles. And we let them go.'

'*We?*'

'Yacef Ali and me and the Sultan. He seemed so sensible, so polite, so balanced—Keller, I mean—that it just never occurred to any of us that he'd do her the least harm.'

He made no interruption of any kind, not the smallest movement; but she seemed to find protest somewhere, for she went on:

'But don't ask me about it. Please don't question me at all, because I know very little. I don't know just where he did it or when or why. I don't want to think about it any more. I've been to Mass for her this morning already and that's the only way I ever want to remember her or anything that's happened since.'

'Since?'

'Since I don't know when: since you came, since I got married, since I met Columb. Since everything.'

He was silent. Her eyes most aware of him, she questioned him by a sudden mark of her physical attention, a redirection of her head and shoulders. But he was thinking only of her words, 'Since everything.' It was the eighth day since he had arrived in the Zone. His fortieth year. A line of poetry leaped and passed: *'It was my thirtieth year to Heaven.'* He flinched; and by her movement was made aware of her again when she asked:

'Are you in pain?'

'No, only tired.' His mind had returned to the cable. Wearily. Trying to find a certainty which delicately eluded him; and while she talked and he replied, he sought for this most honest reason.

'You had a very bad time, didn't you?' she was saying. 'That Friese was telling me before I came up that you lost an awful lot of blood in the night. The trouble was that with George cutting off the telephone I couldn't ring you or anything. But I did get Ali to promise he'd bring you across to the Palace the very first thing today. Then, earlier on, George rang through to ask after *me*. He didn't expect them to know anything about me and told Ali that Keller had almost certainly slaughtered me down at his room somewhere in the French Section.'

His obsession with the cable, he was thinking, was concerned with its timing. All that morning he had been attentive to minutes and hours, possessed by the striking of midday, of the seconds a bell took to tell the hour.

'George took so much convincing that I was still breathing, he finally insisted I spoke to him myself; and when I did, he told me about Keller ringing up to say he'd killed someone—a girl—and that later on he'd got knifed himself.'

MacGrady had wanted time: even Marcovicz had realised that. There was something which he had once said about him which he, Chance, must remember.

'You're not listening to me, are you?' she accused him. 'I know I shouldn't be tiring you like this, but you said you wanted to know everything.'

'You were saying that George told you Marcovicz had been knifed. Did you believe him?'

'I certainly believe that he was dead; and even if I hadn't just then, I'd have believed it later because that little boy of yours who was watching the flats came around and caught me on my way to Mass. Apparently he'd been in the flats all night and seen just about everything. A very important witness. He saw George shoot Keller in the lift and it was he who told me how very sick you were after George had beaten you up. He followed me all the way to the Notre Dame chattering all of the time and trying to make some sort of a bargain.'

'You weren't afraid to come round here alone?'

'Not after George's call. He was very conciliatory; he read me the cable from Columb's surgeon and said we'd have to talk everything over calmly. He made out that with Keller dead he'd changed all his plans. When I finally got around here he had me into his office and gave me Columb's letter and your note.' She moved a little nearer to the bed. 'He also told me you'd insisted on them cabling Columb that I was probably dead.'

Ah, this was it. This was the moment when he must give an account of himself to her and he was no longer so sure of his motives or his reasons.

He admitted: 'Yes, I remember that.'

He could not see her face against the stare from the window, only the shape of it and the holding of the light in her smooth hair. Her face was a contained shadow within these limits, ending abruptly where her chin countered the silveriness of her neck like the capital of a pale column rising from the black shoulders.

'Why did you do that, Chance?'

'It was what we were made to believe.'

But he knew the inadequacy of such a reply. He had interfered in the timing of events, in MacGrady's future, without any apparent right. She would believe this for ever. Yet he knew that at the time of his action his own belief had been most simple.

'But not Columb,' she insisted. 'It was not what Columb was made to believe. He wasn't here even to know about it.'

No, he thought; but he was there once before, with Marcovicz at the death of his first wife, waiting as he thought for the grace of decision. And suddenly, without the sense of vindication he had expected, he remembered the incident he had sought: the convict's phrase outside the café, 'the American had reached that moment where a man may do one thing or another, where there's no time because there's no decision.'

She was waiting, reiterant: 'Then why, Chance?'

'Because it seemed to be true that you were dead for a time.'

'For you?'

'For all of us.'

'Chance, this is very important to me. When you say, "for a time," d'you mean that when you had George send that cable you weren't sure?'

'Yes, I do mean that.'

'And yet you made him send it?'

'Yes.'

'Why?'

'I can hardly tell you,' he said, 'it was such a long time ago.'

'It was yesterday.'

'I don't mean that, I mean that my reasons are old.'

'Your reasons, Chance?'

'Yes,' he said, trying to remember, and not wanting to.

There was a long silence. She did not move, did not repeat her question, but was there as so many people had been there in her stead from as far back as he could remember, wanting him to explain what could not easily be explained. He thought: I shall not answer. In a few seconds, minutes, she will go. My answer will be useless anyway to her, it is between myself and God. Surely she will go.

But she did not go and he could hear nothing. It was as if

she'd blocked out the light, the whole town and its sounds, the past and the future, with her waiting.

Suddenly he said, 'In a way, I hated him.'

She said nothing and he began to forget her. She had absorbed the empty window, the town, all that lay beyond it; and he was speaking not to her but to the sum of his eight days, to his life and what must be his work.

He said: 'You can't hate prisoners. If you hated prisoners you would go mad. But I hated MacGrady, and he got hold of my hatred and gave me something to hold for the first time.'

Again, her silence. He was recalling his first day in the Zone.

'I met Marcovicz almost as soon as I got here,' he said. 'I couldn't get free of him, but because I could pity him I didn't care. He was nothing. He was my old self, moving about, floundering. In a way I could love him as we do love our prisoners for doing it for us.'

'You mean doing the sentence?' he heard her say.

'And the crime,' he said, 'the crime and the sentence. You wouldn't know what it's like in a prison—that it's possible to know a man for months without ever bothering to find out what he's charged with. You see him, his good eyes, his small personal ways of doing his hair, approaching you or talking about something. You become casually intimate with him despite your position. You think: I know that man, we have much in common; with little said, we respect one another. And then one day you see the police report and the charge. You don't believe it. At first you don't believe it. But eventually you do, and then you never cease to believe it. It tinges your conversation, the quality of your observations, and you are diminished. Every prisoner that you love diminishes you because he's alive. A little of you gets washed away every month until you have to adopt an attitude for your own safety, to preserve yourself. But conversion liberates you: it seems to, and it does.'

She made some small movement. He did not see what it

was but he heard it: some whisper of fabric or a breath. He
heard her say, 'MacGrady.'

'He had no right,' he said. 'MacGrady had no right to
surrender himself to evil like Marcovicz.'

'Because he was a Catholic?'

'*Is*,' he said. 'Is a Catholic.'

'You hoped he would be like you—like your new self? I
think I know.'

'You don't, you couldn't know. You haven't worked for
prisoners. You don't know what a temptation it is to do something to their lives afterwards, follow them up; to say, I know
what's best for you . . . I'll teach you the lesson of love by
wrecking your marriage so that you'll never do that thing
again . . . I'll hammer you with God until you see that it's
not worth it . . . And then when you've dropped all that
because you've come into the Church you meet MacGrady
and he blackmails your charity, your hope and your faith;
he hands you his bride and his despair and there's nothing
left but the supernatural.'

'And it failed you?'

But he did not answer. He was remembering the restful
anger he had felt before he decided to send the cable.

'At that moment,' he said, 'I thought I could do no wrong
because, until I saw what death was like—the first part of it—
I'd been prepared to die for him. Then, when *I* wanted more
time, when I, like MacGrady, wanted more time and was
given it, I thought I was in a state of grace and I saw what
I could do. When I realised that MacGrady might escape this
knowledge of your death—because, Anna, you *were* dead to
me—I saw him with his prayer answered: and then with
some great distortion that came from somewhere, I said: that
is the wrong answer. God meant him to be saved and punished
now before it's too late. I hated him then with an original
hatred; but I believed that because I hadn't failed him once
despite all he'd done to me, my hatred was as loving as the
anger of God. I had, you see, found my occasion of sin.'

In the pause, sound crept in through the window: the far

siren of an ambulance, fading as it negotiated distant turnings, then momentarily regaining strength before merging into the other sounds of the active town.

'You could have been muzzy with the drugs and the haemorrhage,' she suggested.

'No, I was perfectly clear. I think it's like that at moments of the greatest sins, you do sense your clarity.'

In the flat below, the wireless was switched on again: a blare of singing.

'For that reason,' he added, 'it can never really be explained, it is not justifiable. But there is one thing I remind myself of.'

'Yes?'

'That like everything else that has happened since I came here it was in the providence of God. The cable must have been allowed for, the wickedness of it coming from so far back in my life.'

She smiled then; he happened to catch it as she said, 'Mine too.'

There was a further pause until she said, 'Did you hear what I said?'

'What did you say?'

'I said that my cable too was in the providence of God.'

'Your cable? When did you send one?'

'From what George has just told me, I think it must have gone just half an hour after yours. I was worried in case Columb had heard alarming rumours of the riots here, so I sent: "Safely ensconced in the Palace stop all love from Chance me and the Zone." ' She was opening her bag with quick fingers. 'I have the reply here, it came through on the Sultan's private line an hour ago. It says, "Recovering fast ask for masses and tell Chance to get confessed before he gets any worse will arrange everything for you both now that I am the new man." '

The relayed singing ended abruptly and the siren cut into the silence, louder and louder until it faded out immediately beneath him as, somewhere, a High Mass began beneath a distant microphone: *'In nomine patris, et filii, et spiritus sancti . . . Introibo ad altare Dei . . . Ad Deum qui laetificat juventutem meam . . .'*

'So you see?' she said.

He was straining to hear the ambulance siren.

'And you still hate MacGrady?' she asked.

'More or less,' he said.

She looked at him. 'I'll go with you to that old hospital,' she said. 'Between us we'll see you lack for nothing.'

Chance managed to sit up a little way: and it was then that their eyes met in amazement, in some silent unconsidered laughter.